THE
GIRLS
ON
CHALK
HILL

THE
GIRLS
ON
CHALK
HILL

ALISON BELSHAM

bookouture

Published by Bookouture in 2023

An imprint of Storyfire Ltd.
Carmelite House
50 Victoria Embankment
London EC4Y 0DZ

www.bookouture.com

ISBN: 978-1-80314-663-8
eBook ISBN: 978-1-80314-662-1

ONE

MONDAY, 9 JANUARY

She ran as if her life depended on it, until she couldn't, couldn't, couldn't go any faster. Her heart was bursting, muscles stretched to breaking point, but she was determined not to slow down despite the fatigue that weighed against every stride. Creeping undergrowth crowded the path and bare branches formed a dense canopy overhead. Brambles scratched her naked arms and legs, their spiny thorns ripping her skin, drawing blood. The narrow track was uneven and stony, criss-crossed by tree roots – it would be easy to stumble, easy to fall. Although she could see the emerging dawn diluting the dark sky between the tree trunks ahead, there was no light down here. She was running blind.

The woman sprinted uphill, adding to the pressure in her lungs and legs. Her breath was a harsh rasp deep in her throat. Or was that the sound of someone else coming up behind her? There was frost on the ground and her trainers crunched and skidded. Was it just her own footfalls she could hear, or was somebody following her? She glanced over her shoulder. There was no one there. Just the silent forest. Still as death, quiet as the grave.

But she had to keep up the pace. She couldn't stop. She was compelled to keep going, driving through the pain barrier, running through the fire.

The track took a sharp turn to the right. The slope became steeper and the path narrower. As her pace slowed, she felt a surge of anger. She had to push herself harder. She had to be stronger than this. Each breath ripped her lungs from her chest. Every fibre of every muscle was burning.

One. Foot. In. Front. Of. The. Other.

She was almost there, almost there, almost at the top...

Light-headed, vision blurred, she burst out of the treeline at the brow of the hill. After vaulting the stile that divided the woods from the pasture, she collapsed onto the ground, feeling the prickle of the frosty grass through the thin fabric of her running kit. The sky above her was the colour of wet slate, but over the crest of the hill, beyond where she lay in the shadows, the horizon was now washed pale lilac.

Her chest rose and fell to replace depleted oxygen, frantic for the first few seconds as the cold air ripped down her throat. Her stomach cramped and her leg muscles tightened. It would be a few minutes before she'd be able to get back on her feet. A minute passed, then she tapped the Fitbit on her wrist to check her stats. Not a personal best, but certainly not too shoddy for a frosty January morning before sunrise. She watched the digits change as her heart rate gradually returned to normal.

As her breathing calmed, the sun rose over the top of the hill behind her and lit up the Weald, which stretched out below her in a patchwork of fields, villages, roads and rivers, like a living map. This spectacular view was her reward for heaving herself out of bed before dawn.

But then she noticed something that didn't make sense.

She sat up and clambered unsteadily to her feet.

Down the hill was a huge chalk carving – the Wye Memorial Crown. Covering an area about the size of a tennis court, the land had been cut away to expose the pale limestone of the North Downs in celebration of the coronation of Edward VII. But this morning, she could see two dark outlines on the white chalk, and black stains spreading from them. Bags of rubbish? Who would dump their litter up here?

As she stepped closer, her eyes widened with dawning horror.

The stains weren't black.

They were red. Blood red.

And the lumps weren't rubbish sacks.

They were bodies.

She ran down the slope towards them, unable to compre-hend what she was seeing. Her heart rate rocketed again – pounding harder and faster than it had when she'd reached the top of the hill. What the hell had happened?

Two young women – teenagers, she thought – lay on the wide cross at the top of the crown, their heads pointing down the hill. Their throats had been slashed and the white chalk was drenched with their blood.

They were wearing frothy white gowns of gauze. Layers of tulle fluttered around them in the breeze. The necklines of the dresses were bloody, the red bleeding to pink as it spread through the fabric. Below the bodices, the free-flowing material of the skirts was twisted around pale legs and bare feet. Both of them had delicate, glittering tiaras – one was still in place amid the girl's long hair, while the other had come askew and was lying next to its owner, still tangled in her blonde hair on the bloodied chalk. The girls were holding hands, slack fingers entwined, and in their other hands each of them clutched a dark and velvety red, red rose.

Frost glistened on their eyebrows and on the lashes of their wide blue eyes. Their lips were tinged blue, and there was no flush of life in their bloodless cheeks.

The two grimacing faces were identical.

And the woman suddenly realised she was looking at sisters. Twins.

She stumbled, her legs weak. Her head spun as blind, cold terror swept through her. She fought down panic, the urge to run, to hide, to pretend she hadn't seen what was lying in front of her. She wanted to look away but, taking a deep breath, she forced herself to take in every last detail of the two dead girls. Nothing could be overlooked, nothing forgotten, no matter how painful it was for her to see.

Concentrate. Don't give in.

She thought about these girls... so young, maybe sixteen, seventeen. So much living in front of them and she could see they had been beautiful when they were alive. But with one quick, sharp cut, their futures had been stolen, and their family would never be the same again. Their parents, still blissfully ignorant, would soon hear the news that every parent dreads. And then they'd forever wish they could have paused life on the day before this one. They would wish they'd done something, anything, differently to have changed the course of events that led to this. She knew how they would feel and she understood only too well what they were about to experience. Someone had taken everything they held precious. She'd been the bearer of news like this too many times before. She felt her heart breaking all over again.

She pulled her phone from the pocket in the back of her running shorts and started taking photos.

Behind her, footsteps crunching up the track made her jump. She heard a gasp.

'Hey, what do you think you're doing?' It was a man's voice, speaking louder than he needed to.

Taking a steadying breath, she turned back to the path. A middle-aged man in a Barbour jacket was coming towards her. At his side, a sinewy boxer was straining on its lead at the scent of blood. As he registered the two bodies, he stopped in his tracks, dropping the dog's lead.

'You're taking pictures of a crime scene?' he said. His voice trembled. 'You're sick. You need to wait for the police to arrive. Don't you know anything?'

The dog ran towards the corpses.

'Call your dog off,' snapped the woman, moving to block its path.

Coming to his senses, he called the dog and lunged forward to grab its lead.

She walked over to them and took a photo of the man as he squatted to calm the dog. His hands were shaking. The dog, sensing his master's distress, growled.

The woman pulled something from a pocket on the back of her phone case. She held it up and stepped closer to the man so he could see what it was. He glared at it, reaching out to steady her hand so he could read the words on the plastic ID.

'I am the police,' she said. 'DI Lexi Bennett. Now, get yourself and your dog off my crime scene. Don't *you* know anything?'

TWO

Detective Inspector Lexi Bennett snapped into work mode. She drew the dog walker away from the bodies and took his contact details. Still staring back in horror at the two dead girls, he looked as if he was about to throw up and the last thing she needed was a crime scene contaminated by vomit. She didn't have time to deal with him now, so she sent him away down the hill. She'd task an officer to interview him later in case he'd seen anything useful on his way up.

Then, checking her Fitbit for the time, she called Canterbury police station. She suspected it was too early for any of her team to be in yet, but the desk sergeant could call their mobiles and reroute them here. Perhaps not the ideal way to meet your new colleagues on your first day in a new job, but this was where she needed them.

When the desk sergeant answered, she quickly explained who she was, and that she was now in charge of Canterbury's new Major Investigation Team.

'Can you call DS Olsen, DC Kulkarni and DC Flynn, and ask them to come directly to me – I'm at a murder scene at the Wye Memorial Crown. I'll also need a team of uniforms straight away to secure the site, and then ongoing to canvas the neighbourhood,' she said.

'Yes, ma'am,' said the desk sergeant. 'Shall I call CSI?'

'Good man – a full team with a crime scene manager, and whichever pathologist is on duty. Let them know we've got two bodies, and an outdoor location.' She looked at the sky. Dark clouds were rolling in across the Stour valley. 'We need weather protection over the site as a matter of urgency. And send me the contact details of the CSM as soon as one's been assigned.'

'On it.'

Lexi shivered. Her high-tech running kit was designed to draw sweat away from her body and cool her down – not exactly a desirable outcome as she waited on the frosty hillside for the arrival of her team. And tousle-headed, wearing minimal clothing, wasn't quite the way she'd pictured introducing herself to them either.

Pacing up and down to keep warm, she ran through tasks in her mind so she'd be ready as soon as help arrived. Securing the crime scene was the priority for the first contingent of uniforms. As soon as the CSM arrived, he or she could take charge of erecting tents and screens to protect the girls from the weather and prying eyes. The Memorial Crown was visible from the road below and the last thing she wanted was a load of rubber-neckers taking photos and sharing them on Twitter.

Standing beside the low, round Millennium Stone directly above the chalk carving, Lexi looked over the site. This field was fenced off from the others on the hillside. The North Downs Way ran along above it, accessed by a stile at one corner, where she'd come in, and a wicket gate at the other corner. It would be easy to have these points taped up and manned by a couple of PCs to turn walkers and runners away. There was also a five-bar gate into the field at the top of the hill, and there appeared to be a track coming up through the woods from Coldharbour Lane at the bottom.

They needed to work out how the killer had brought his two victims here. And why he'd staged the scene the way he had – the dresses, the tiaras, the roses. The reason he'd placed them on the Memorial Crown. It had to mean something, to the killer at least. If they could work out what it meant, the answer might lead them to whoever had done this.

The desk sergeant answered her second call with a sigh. He seemed to think she was taking up rather a lot of his bandwidth this morning. She wasn't sympathetic.

'Can you alert everyone that there's currently no vehicular access to the site? We're going to need stepping plates to protect the ground until we can work out the route used by the unsub to enter the site.'

'Unsub?'

'Unknown subject.' Four years working in America with the FBI and she'd come back speaking a foreign language to her UK colleagues.

In return he gave her the name and number of the CSM – Emily Jordan, who was currently en route with her team.

Now Lexi could see blue lights flashing through the trees at the bottom of the hill. She started walking down towards them.

'Hello, DI Bennett?' called a man's voice from the woods.

'Up here,' she said. 'Stay where you are.'

'I'm DS Olsen. Tom.'

She met him at the treeline, almost at the bottom of the hill. Tom Olsen was short and dark-haired, with an expertly trimmed beard that was almost just stubble. His tanned face would have been handsome, but for a slightly wonky nose that suggested a history of rugby playing or boxing. The suit he wore fitted him perfectly – possibly a little too snugly – and definitely hadn't come from M&S.

She didn't bother with hellos – they had to get straight into it. 'Until we've worked out how the killer accessed the site and brought the victims in, I want minimum disturbance to the ground. That means entry only for those that absolutely need to come in, and stepping plates all the way up to the bodies.'

'Bodies?' said Olsen. 'In the plural?'

'Two, female, possibly minors. Both with slit throats, and I'd guess they were killed here by the amount of blood on the ground. But that will be for the pathologist to confirm.'

'Who found them?'

'I did. I was out running.' She glanced down, as if to explain the kit.

Olsen took off his jacket.

'Here, ma'am, take this. You look bloody frozen.'

'Thank you.' She shrugged into his suit jacket and felt immediately warmer. The sleeves came down to the tips of her fingers. There was a faint, but pleasant, smell of his aftershave. 'And it's Lexi.' She stuck out a hand. 'Pleased to meet you.' He shook it and Lexi glanced down. His grasp was firm, his hand warm and not remotely clammy. Nails short and clean. A man's hands could tell you a lot about him, she always found.

'Not quite the induction the Chief Super had in mind, but you've hit the ground running.' He grinned. 'No pun intended.'

An hour later, despite Lexi's efforts to limit the number of people coming onto the site, the side of the hill around the Crown looked like a small village had sprung up. A pair of white tents had been erected to fully cover the area surrounding the bodies – and only just in time before a fine drizzle washed in from the northeast. In the damp air, the smell of death invaded every breath.

Tom Olsen had quickly introduced her to the rest of her team – DC Ridhi Kulkarni and DC Colin Flynn. Flynn had looked her up and down in a way that made her take an instant dislike to him. He was late twenties, skinny, with curly blond hair, and his skin had the grey pallor of a habitual smoker. Lexi glanced down. There were telltale nicotine stains on the nails of his left hand.

'I know this wasn't what you were expecting for your new boss, DC Flynn,' she said, nodding down at her running kit, 'but believe me, this wasn't what I was expecting for my first morning either.'

Colin Flynn gave a small shrug of one shoulder as his gaze wandered to the view beyond. He wasn't impressed.

Ridhi Kulkarni was Flynn's polar opposite. Friendly, smiley, and more than a little nervous, which was probably down to the fact that she'd only just joined the team, and this was her first job out of uniform. She fluffed her hello, rolled her eyes, and gave it a second shot. Lexi liked the way she'd plaited her black hair into a braid around her head and the way she was eagerly taking in all that was going on around her. Lexi could remember being that hungry to learn when she'd first started in the job.

'I need someone to give me a lift home so I can change into something more suitable,' Lexi had said. 'Ridhi?'

'Me?'

'Yes, you.'

'Yes, of course.'

Lexi gave her a reassuring smile. She could sympathise with first-day nerves.

It was a scant two miles from the Memorial Crown to Lexi's rented cottage on the far side of Wye, but she couldn't spare the time to jog there and back. Ridhi could drop her at home, and she would return in her own car.

'Tom tells me you're new to the team,' she said, as she buckled into the passenger seat. 'First murder scene?'

Ridhi nodded, gripping the wheel tightly. Lexi noticed that her fingernails were bitten down to the quick. The constable grimaced as she pulled out from the lay-by where she and the rest of the police vehicles had parked. 'Made me feel quite sick and upset, to see those poor girls, but I suppose I'll get used to it.'

Lexi glanced across at her sharply. 'Don't you dare get used to it. You need to be shocked by every single murder scene you ever work. Shocked – and outraged. Angry on behalf of the victims and on behalf of the families.'

Ridhi looked momentarily surprised by Lexi's outburst, then nodded.

'We're advocates for the dead,' Lexi continued, 'and you'll need all your rage to carry you through the investigation.'

'Yes, ma'am,' said Ridhi, slowing down as they came into the village.

'Lexi will do fine.'

'Yes, ma— I mean Lexi.' Ridhi rolled her eyes once more. 'What about "boss"? Is that okay?'

Lexi grinned. 'Of course.'

Within half an hour, Lexi was back at the crime scene, more suitably dressed in a black trouser suit and a pair of sturdy black ankle boots. She had a feeling she'd have to climb up and down the hill many more times before the day was out.

Tom came down the slope to meet her. He was accompanied by a dark-haired woman in her mid-forties, wearing a white crime scene suit.

'I'm Emily Jordan,' she said, as soon as Tom had introduced Lexi. 'I'm your crime scene manager. The CSIs report to me, and I'll be running all the forensics for the site, as well as being your first point of contact for test results, etc., etc. I'm sure you know the score.'

Her manner was brusque and efficient, both fine by Lexi.

'Let me know as soon as you have any idea how the girls were brought up here,' said Lexi. 'There must have been a vehicle involved and finding it will be one of our top priorities.'

'My team's working on it,' said Emily. She turned to go back up the hill.

'What else?' said Lexi, looking back to Tom.

'Pathologist's here,' he said. 'Want a word with him?'

Nodding, Lexi pulled a pair of blue shoe protectors over her boots, then followed Tom up towards the main hub of activity.

When they reached the top of the Crown, Lexi paused and looked out over the sodden landscape below. Police vehicles crowded Coldharbour Lane at the foot of the hill, but thankfully there was no sign yet of a press presence or even local rubberneckers.

So why, as hairs stood up on the back of her neck, did she get the sudden feeling she was being watched?

THREE

I raise the binoculars to my eyes, pushing my glasses further up my forehead. Everything's a blur until I turn the focusing wheel. Then the landscape becomes pin-sharp, and I'm looking up at the sweeping slopes, shades of grey in the predawn gloom. I turn my head slowly, traversing the landscape until I locate the Crown, a pale cutmark on the dark hill.

And there they are – two black smudges at the top of the chalk.

My two princesses. Beautiful sisters, devoted to one another.

Still lying quietly where I positioned them. They looked so beautiful in the moonlight when I left them, serene and peaceful. Now the moon's set and it's the darkest hour, just before dawn. They could be sleeping. The sleep of the innocent, untroubled by dreams. Or nightmares.

I lower the binoculars. It will be a while before anyone comes up the hill, so they're still all mine for a little longer. I close my eyes, remembering them as they were a few hours ago. So vibrant and full of life. Brimming over with fear, clutching each other. They begged for their lives, they really did, but their pretty tears fell on stony ground. And then their blood. Eden first, Lucy afterwards.

It's cold in the car. It's been a long night, in fact a long few days. I wrap my arms around my chest and rub them with my hands. The friction creates a little heat, but it's not enough to stop me shivering. But I've got to stay here until I'm sure the girls are in safe hands.

I crack my knuckles to pass the time. Nothing to see here. Just a man waiting for someone to discover his crime.

I hope it's her.

It's no coincidence that I left those girls in that particular spot. There's a plan, and now that she's back I can put it into action. I'll play my part and she'll play hers. Our circle will finally be squared.

Here she is, right on time. But she hasn't seen them yet. She's lying on the grass not fifteen feet from my beautiful girls. I can almost see the rise and fall of her chest as she sucks in cold air. The three of them lying there together, one of them alive, two of them dead. The way it was meant to be, all those years ago.

The memory of what went wrong tastes sour in my mouth.

She stands up. She sees them and staggers. I continue to watch as she instructs the first responders. I watch her leave and come back, changed out of her running kit into her workaday clothes. She's in charge of the site, there's no doubt about that. My girls are in safe hands.

And then she looks in my direction. Straight through me and beyond.

Lexi, Lexi, Lexi Bennett. It's so good to see you again.

I've been watching and waiting. Because I knew you'd come back here one day.

Now I'm ready for you.

Ready to finish what I... what we started.

FOUR

Lexi shook off the feeling of discomfort and looked around. Ridhi Kulkarni and Colin Flynn were peering in at the entrance of the tent sheltering the two girls.

'Colin, Ridhi,' she said loud enough so they would hear her over the flapping of the plastic sides of the tent in the wind.

The two DCs turned in unison and quickly came the few feet up the slope to where she and Tom were standing. Ridhi looked paler than before.

'Why are they dressed like that?' she said, her feelings betrayed by a slight quaver in her voice.

Lexi shook her head. She didn't have an answer. 'Look, things are under control, so there's not much for you to do here,' she said. 'Get back to the office and you, Colin, start by checking where we've got any traffic cam coverage round here – it's not going to be much down these country lanes, but maybe where the main road joins the motorway.'

'Yes, ma'am.'

'And me?' said Ridhi.

'Look up the latest missing person reports – our girls

shouldn't be hard to find. I don't imagine that many sets of twins go missing.'

'On it, boss.'

'If they've even been reported missing yet,' said Flynn. Right, a smartarse. Lexi was getting his measure pretty quickly.

'I'll see you back in the office when I've spoken to the pathologist,' she said, ignoring the remark. 'Get the incident room set up. I'll ask the CSM to send over images ASAP – get them printed out as soon as they arrive.'

As Ridhi and Colin disappeared down the hill, Lexi followed Tom into the shelter. Inside, under the glare of a couple of portable fluorescent lamps, a man in a white crime scene suit was bent over one of the bodies. He was taking the temperature of the corpse and dictating his findings into his mobile. It was only when he stood up, and she saw his grizzled grey hair as he pushed back the white hood of the suit, that Lexi recognised him – it was Mortimer Barley, probably the most experienced pathologist in the county. She'd worked with him on several cases before she'd gone to America. Good. He was a safe pair of hands.

'Lexi – you're back,' he said.

'Missed you too, Mort,' she said.

But Mort had never been one for small talk. It was one of the things she liked about him.

'Of course, it's too early to have pinpointed the exact time of death for either of them,' he said. 'However, I can tell you one thing. Girl A—' he pointed at one of the bodies— 'died at least an hour, maybe two or three hours, before Girl B.'

It was the sort of detail that made Lexi's stomach churn. Not because she was squeamish, but because information like this would help her to picture in her mind how these girls had died and what they'd experienced in their final few hours.

This was the first piece of the jigsaw puzzle, and she knew

she wouldn't rest until she had the last piece in place. And that meant putting whoever did this behind bars.

Tom looked puzzled. 'Is that what you'd expect in a double murder of this kind?'

Mort Barley glared at him. 'I don't *expect* anything. I look at the evidence and report what I find. It's up to you lot to work out what happened.'

'Anything else jumping out at this point?' said Lexi.

Mort gave a small shrug of one shoulder. 'I'm pretty certain your killer's right-handed, but so's ninety per cent of the population – not much help to you.'

'No,' said Lexi, pursing her lips. 'Any signs of sexual assault? On either of them?'

The pathologist gave her a pained look. 'You're getting ahead of yourself. Internal examination will have to wait until I've got them back in the suite.' He was talking about the autopsy suite in the city morgue.

'I get it. But any really obvious external injuries or bleeding that would suggest sexual assault? Because this sure as hell isn't a mugging.'

'Nothing "obvious" so far.'

The mood inside the tent was becoming fractious, but Lexi had to push for information fast.

'Listen, it's a double homicide, and I'm already seeing the signs of a ritual killing. I need whatever you can give me on this signature as quickly as possible.'

'Then let me get on with my job.'

'Seen anything like it before?'

'Lexi, you'll get my report when you get my report. I'm not speculating now.'

Mort bent back down to the body he'd identified as Girl A and carried on with his work. Lexi frowned. She watched as the pathologist put clear plastic evidence bags over the girl's hands, securing them in place with elastic bands. One of the crime scene team nudged past them into the tent and started taking photographs. Mort stood up to get out of the way.

'You almost done here?' said Lexi.

'A couple more minutes,' he said. 'Then we can get them into body bags and shifted.'

'No ID on them?'

'No handbags or purses, no phones, nothing like that,' said Mort. 'Girl B is wearing a pendant.' He pointed and Lexi looked down. Around the butchered neck, encrusted with her blood, was a fine chain. A gold letter 'P' hung from it, slick and red.

'Thanks,' said Lexi. She turned to Tom. 'Can you phone that detail through to Ridhi?'

Tom already had his mobile in his hand.

'Come on, let's get to the office.'

Tom followed her out of the tent, relaying the information to Ridhi as they walked down the hill.

The team, including Ridhi and Colin, were assembled in the large, open-plan office that had been allocated to Lexi's unit. One wall was made up of a series of whiteboards so it could be used as an incident board, and when Lexi and Tom walked in, Ridhi was already taping up photos of the two victims. There were two more DCs and a handful of civilian support staff, but the introductions could wait until later.

'Morning everybody,' Lexi said, going across to stand by the whiteboard.

Ridhi scurried back to her desk and sat down.

'I'm DI Bennett. You can address me as Lexi or you can call me boss—' she glanced in Ridhi's direction to be rewarded with a grin '—but I won't answer to "ma'am". Okay?'

Most of the team nodded. Colin was scrolling on his phone.

'Something to share with the team, Colin?'

The DC hurriedly tucked his mobile into the inside pocket of his jacket. 'No. Sorry, boss.' So at least he'd been listening.

Lexi turned to the whiteboard and pointed at the photographs – a larger image showing both girls together, as well as individual pictures and close-ups of the wounds on their necks.

'We've got two victims, clearly sisters, both with their throats slit. The bodies were discovered this morning at dawn, by me, on the Wye Memorial Crown, just outside Wye on Coldharbour Lane. The CSIs are currently working there, and the bodies should be brought back to the morgue soon. Any questions at this point?'

Tom half raised an arm. 'You mentioned you'd spotted a signature when you were talking to Mort up on the Crown. Can you clarify for the team what that is, and what it means?'

'The signature of this crime scene is that it's been posed, and that in itself tells us a lot about the killer. Do you all know the difference between posing and staging when it comes to murder scenes?'

Ridhi shook her head and some of the support staff looked puzzled.

Fair enough. A big part of her role in setting up the new Major Investigation Team was to share what she'd learned at Quantico – she'd spent four years at the cutting edge of criminal behavioural science. Now it was time to spread the gospel.

'Staging is when a killer rearranges the crime scene to try and mislead the police. For example, making a murder look like a botched burglary or an accident. Posing is when he positions the body to send a specific message – using the body like a prop, put on display. That's clearly what we have here with the roses and the tiaras, and the positioning of the bodies at the top of the Crown, holding hands. The roses are real – long-stemmed, must have come from a florist within the last day or two. That's one thing to get working on. The tiaras, on the other hand, are anything but real. Plastic and rhinestones. Fancy dress or hen nights – so something else to be digging into. Were the girls dressed like that when they were taken or is it part of the killer's signature? But even bigger questions remain. Why did he choose twins? What does the posing of the scene signify? The dresses, the tiaras, the roses? And why did he place them on the Memorial Crown?'

Tom nodded. 'This is all part of his signature, right, as opposed to his MO.'

'Right. The modus operandi is the practical element – slitting their throats. The signature illustrates the underlying compulsion, and we have to work out what that is, sexual or otherwise.' She ran a hand through her wind-tangled hair. She hated the arrogance of the men who committed these crimes and thought they could get away with it. 'But, at the end of the day, it doesn't matter what his twisted little fantasy is. Our first and only job is catching him and putting him away. So never get caught up in his game, Tom – or any of you. The killer wants us to play it, but that's something we don't do. Ever.'

It was something she'd learned the hard way in the backwoods of Virginia.

FIVE

Lexi sank into her new chair, behind her new desk, in her new office, which was a small room next door to the incident room. She took in her surroundings, but little had changed since she'd spent her first year in the police in this very station. Same naff 1960s architecture outside, same tired and stressed furniture inside. Not that it mattered to her. She wasn't on the career ladder for a corner office with a view of Canterbury cathedral.

Her first day in the new job had been derailed by the discovery of the bodies on the Crown – at this minute she should have been doing a meet and greet with the new team. Instead, their first encounter had been her barking orders at them. The relief she felt at having avoided the get-to-know-you chit-chat was tinged with a little guilt, but she'd long come to terms with the fact that, when it came to work, she was something of a loner. She just wanted to get her head down and get on. She was here to do the job – to put killers behind bars and reunite victims with their families. Preferably while they were still breathing, though sadly it didn't often turn out that way.

After assigning various tasks to members of the team, she'd needed coffee as a matter of urgency, and the civilian support,

Michelle, who'd offered to go and fetch her a cup had made a stupendously good first impression.

Ridhi appeared in the doorway, looking anxious.

'What've you got?' Lexi asked.

Ridhi held up a printout of a missing persons appeal. 'I found them.'

Lexi took the piece of paper from her and looked at it. Most of the page was taken up by a large colour photo, slightly grainy, pitched at an angle. It showed three girls, squashed together on a banquette – it must have been taken in a pub or a restaurant – smiling and laughing, holding up glasses to whoever took the picture. The girls were identical, and they looked very like the two bodies she had discovered on the Crown.

'Triplets?' Her heart leapt to her throat and her head spun. She was thrown back to events that she'd spent more than a decade burying as deep as possible.

Her mouth felt dry as cardboard. She needed water.

It had to be a coincidence.

'Are you okay, boss?' Ridhi's eyes widened with concern.

Lexi nodded, swallowed and took a deep breath as she scanned the rest of the page.

MISSING
EDEN, LUCY AND PAIGE CARTER
TRIPLETS, AGE 17
LAST SEEN: FRIDAY, 6 JANUARY 2023
ALL THREE DISAPPEARED IN OR AROUND CANTERBURY AT DIFFERENT POINTS DURING THE DAY. THE GIRLS ARE IDENTICAL TRIPLETS – 5'5" TALL, WITH SLIM BUILDS AND LONG BLONDE HAIR. EDEN WAS WEARING A PALE PINK SWEATER, BLUE JEANS AND BLACK TRAINERS...

Lexi skipped over the descriptions of the girls' clothing – it was enough to tell her that they hadn't been dressed as princesses when they'd been taken. There was more information about where each of the girls had last been seen, plus the usual contact details at the bottom, with a request for witnesses.

Lexi swallowed again. She needed to hold it together.

'So there are three girls missing and we've found two bodies. Where's the third sister?' She swept out of her office into the incident room, where the team were already working hard on the tasks she'd given them. Ridhi trailed behind her.

'Heads up,' she said, sharply enough to make them stop what they were doing. 'It looks likely that our bodies are two of the Carter triplets.' She held up the flyer. 'We don't know which two they are, but more importantly it means the third sister is still missing – and we have to assume that the killer still has her. There's no way of knowing whether she's alive or dead, so we work on the assumption she's alive and make finding her the main focus of our operation.'

A shockwave rippled through the room – gasps, whispered expletives and horrified faces, all looking towards Lexi with unasked questions.

Lexi ignored it.

'Basically, this turns everything on its head.' That was something of an understatement. With the double murder, they would have been working against the clock to find the killer before he struck again. They might have had days, weeks or even months. But with this new development, the time available to them had been cut to hours. The third sister, whichever one of the triplets she was, had now been missing for three days and with every minute that passed, she was more likely to turn up dead.

'What do you need us to do, boss?' said Tom.

Lexi's mind was racing. She needed to calm down and think straight.

'Colin, where are we with traffic cams?'

'There are no cameras on Coldharbour Lane, a couple in

Wye and, of course, down at the motorway intersection. I've requested footage and ANPR records from them for the last forty-eight hours.'

'Okay. We know now where each of the girls went missing. Cross-check all of the ANPR records in the vicinity of these locations with the cameras round Wye. My hunch is we'll be looking for a van, but that's by no means a certainty.'

'On it,' said Colin. He looked anything but happy about the development. It would be hours of work and anything it gave them might be too late anyway.

'And can you also organise a fingertip search fanning out from the crime scene in case we missed a third body? Put every uniform who can be spared onto it.'

'Will do.'

'Ridhi, track down whoever took that missing person report and see what extra details they can add. Tom, find out which FLO has been assigned to the Carter parents and get their address – we'll go there now.'

Death notifications were always agonising, but this was going to be beyond that. Lexi was going to have to tell the Carters that two of their daughters were dead, and that their third daughter was still missing. Then, as they reeled with shock and their world collapsed around them, she was going to have to pump them for information that might just save the girl.

But at this point, she didn't even know what she needed to ask.

SIX

The Carters lived in a quiet suburb to the north of Canterbury.

'It's a cul de sac, Brockenhurst Close,' said Lexi, directing Tom as he drove. 'You get to it via Salisbury Road.'

The house was easy enough to find, despite being one of hundreds of identical 1980s-built semis. Tom pulled up to the kerb outside and Lexi studied the house. It looked small for a family of five, with an integral garage taking up space on the ground floor, but the front garden had a neatly mowed lawn and the bins stood in an orderly line on the edge of the drive, leaving just enough room for a dark green Skoda estate.

As they got out of Tom's Jeep, a woman got out of a hatchback parked on the opposite side of the road and approached them.

'DI Bennett?' she said.

Lexi nodded.

'I'm PC Reid, Family Liaison. Philippa.'

'Lexi. And this is DS Tom Olsen.'

They briefly shook hands.

'It's going to be tough,' said Lexi. 'Two daughters dead and one missing. And the worst thing is, we don't know which two we've got in the morgue and which one is still out there.'

'Damn,' said Philippa Reid under her breath.

'I'm going to need you in there as my eyes and ears once they start to come round from the initial shock.'

'I understand,' said the FLO, but the colour had drained from her face. She clearly knew how gruelling the next few hours was going to be for the Carter family. 'I spent time with them yesterday, after the girls were reported missing – they're good people and they're beside themselves with worry.'

They walked in single file past the Skoda, and Lexi rang the doorbell.

Inside, she could hear a dog barking. Then footsteps coming towards the door.

'I've got it, love,' called a muffled voice from the other side.

The door opened and Lexi saw straight away that the man who faced them had already suffered an enormous toll. His three daughters had been missing for more than forty-eight hours. But his eyes looked at them with a flash of hope, which quickly turned to despair when he read no sign of good news in their faces. A woman in a quilted dressing gown appeared at his shoulder, immediately picking up on what was happening.

'Oh my God, no.' Her knees buckled and she slumped against her husband, who fumbled to stop her falling.

Philippa Reid stepped swiftly past Lexi and put her arms around the woman, supporting her and comforting her at once.

'Come on, Joanne,' she said. 'You need to sit down.'

They shuffled down the hall and into a small lounge, Mr Carter, Tom and Lexi following slowly. Philippa guided the now-sobbing Mrs Carter to the sofa. Her husband stood in the middle of the room, too confused to know what to do. A wavy-haired spaniel loped in through a doorway from the kitchen. It sniffed the newcomers, then went to its master, looking for attention. Mr Carter ignored it.

'Why don't you sit down as well?' said Lexi gently, pointing to a vacant armchair opposite the sofa. 'I'm afraid we have some bad news for you.'

Joanne Carter gave a howl of anguish.

'I'm so sorry,' said Lexi, as her cry ended. 'This morning, two bodies were found on the Downs outside Wye. We have reason to believe that they're your daughters.'

Mr Carter shook his head. 'No, no. We've got three daughters, not two. It can't be them.'

'I'm afraid it is, Mr Carter,' said Tom. 'I'm so very sorry.'

Joanne looked from one to the other of them with wide, fearful eyes. 'Which two? Paige or Eden or Lucy?'

Feeling as if someone was ripping her heart out, Lexi answered. 'At this point we're not sure. One of the girls was wearing a pendant with the letter "P" on it, so...'

'Paige... not Paige?' Joanne started to wail again.

Her husband just stared at the floor in silence, looking as if he was about to be sick. Then he turned to Lexi. 'Where's my other daughter? You said two – where's the other?' He staggered to the sofa and sank down next to his wife. They clung to each other, both crying now.

Philippa came across to Lexi to speak quietly in her ear.

'Don't you have photos, so they can at least know which two have been found?'

Lexi drew the FLO over to the window and cupped a hand in front of her mouth. 'We can't show them pictures – the girl's throats were cut. Once the autopsies are done, they can come to the morgue to identify the bodies. The wounds will be covered up.'

Philippa nodded, then went back to the sofa to try and comfort the distraught couple.

Lexi stared out at the Carters' back garden. There was a rabbit hutch on the grass, though no sign of a rabbit, and washing on the line, despite the rain.

She turned back to face the room.

Tom was standing by the fireplace, looking stiff and uncomfortable. Philippa glanced up at him. 'Maybe Mr Carter – Andrew – would like some water,' she said.

Tom jolted to life. 'Of course.' He went out in the direction of the kitchen, bending down to briefly scratch the spaniel between the ears as he passed it.

Lexi went to the sofa and squatted down in front of Joanne Carter. She took one of the distraught woman's hands in her own. It was wet with tears, even though Philippa had given her a tissue. Family liaison was a job she didn't envy – comforting the bereaved while gently pumping them for useful information.

'Tell me about your daughters,' she said. 'Which is the oldest?'

Joanne looked at her with wide, watery eyes. 'Lucy,' she said, hiccupping slightly as she fought another upsurge of tears. 'Lucy was born first, then Eden, and Paige came along a good twenty minutes after the other two.'

Tom came back into the room with glasses of water on a tray.

'But Paige is the boss, right?' said Lexi. 'The ringleader when they get up to anything?'

Joanne's eyebrows shot up. 'How...?'

Lexi smiled. 'I'm a triplet myself – the youngest, and the bossiest.' Of course, this didn't hold true for all sets of triplets, but it had been a gambit to get Joanne to talk about her daughters. Lexi needed to learn as much as she could about them as quickly as possible.

Joanne almost smiled, but then her face crumpled again. 'Paige... She's the leader of the gang, isn't she, Andy?' She was still using the present tense. It would take a long time before talking about her daughters in the past tense became natural.

Her husband's eyes momentarily went to her, but he remained silent.

'She looks out for the other two,' said Joanne. 'What happened to them? Where's...' Her voice faltered. Not knowing which of her daughters was still missing was too much, and she slumped against Philippa, unable to talk.

The silence stretched out for several minutes, punctuated only by regular sniffs and gasps from Joanne. Lexi chewed on her bottom lip. It was excruciating to see their pain up close.

She stood up. 'Philippa, a word outside – in a moment, when you can.'

Philippa nodded.

Lexi and Tom slipped from the room, and a moment later, Philippa joined them on the drive.

'I'll need to make a few calls, check up on the team,' said Lexi. 'In the meantime, you get a brew on and give them something to eat – cake, biscuits, something sweet for the shock. I need them ready to answer questions.'

'It's too soon,' said Philippa, frowning. 'They don't even know which two are dead and which one is missing.'

'That's the point,' said Lexi, sharper than she meant to. 'There's a chance that the third sister is still alive, so I need to keep going. Get them ready for me to question in ten minutes.'

Philippa nodded and went back indoors.

The house looked the same as it had when Lexi and Tom had arrived, but inside was a completely new landscape of pain.

SEVEN

Lexi shivered. It seemed colder out here after the over-heated environment inside the Carters' house. She dug out her phone to check in with the incident room. Tom stood next to her, listening to the call, his expression bleak.

Lexi lowered the phone – no one had picked up yet. 'Tom, can you check in about how they're doing at the site?'

He nodded and stepped away.

A tinny voice emitted from her phone and she placed it back to her ear.

'Ridhi, is that you?'

'Yes, boss.'

'Can you get me Colin?'

The line went dead as Ridhi transferred the call, but it seemed an age before Colin picked up.

'Yes?' He was a little out of breath, and Lexi wondered where he'd been.

'Have you got a team working on the traffic cameras?'

'Yes. They're putting together a list of any vehicles that were picked up at more than one of the locations where the girls were last seen, or anywhere along the route from Canterbury to Wye between Friday and this morning.'

'Good.'

'It'll take a while, but I'll let you know as soon as we have anything.'

'Sure. Meantime, can you get down here to the Carters' house? Bring Ridhi. I want the two of you to search the girls' bedrooms while I'm questioning the parents.' Normally, Lexi would have wanted to do this herself, but there wasn't time for that. Everything needed to move as fast as possible.

'What are we looking for?'

'At this point, anything. Diaries, phones, iPads, laptops. Evidence of friendships, relationships, places they went to often, or not so often...'

'I get it.'

Lexi wondered why he'd asked.

Tom finished his own call and turned to face her.

'Anything?' said Lexi.

'They're doing a fingertip search. Picking up litter, which is probably unrelated, and working out how they'll lift the blood-stained chalk once the bodies have been removed.'

It would be some time until they got any meaningful results from the forensics.

As they went back towards the Carters' house, Lexi briefed Tom.

'I'll ask the questions, and you write down the answers – verbatim if possible, paying close attention to any names, locations, you know the drill.'

'Why not simply record the interviews?'

Lexi gave a one-sided shrug. 'We'd have to ask their permission to do that, and when people know they're being recorded, they clam up. I'm hoping to capture as much information about the girls as we can. We can take a more formal, recorded statement later on, when they're more composed.'

Tom nodded his understanding as he knocked on the door, and Philippa let them back in. Lexi told her that Colin and Ridhi would be arriving shortly.

The Carters were still sitting on the sofa, but now there was a tea tray on the table in front of them. Two slices of fruitcake sat untouched on delicate floral plates, but at least they'd drunk some tea. Andrew Carter put a reassuring arm around his wife's shoulders as the two police officers sat down in the armchairs opposite.

'Joanne – is it okay if I call you that?' Joanne Carter nodded. 'Joanne, I need to ask you some questions about each of your daughters in turn so we can start to build up a picture of what might have happened to them.'

Although she was in a hurry, Lexi made a point of addressing Joanne Carter gently and slowly. She leaned forward in her chair, to be sure of hearing everything the girls' mother might say.

As it was, Joanne Carter simply nodded again. Then she took a sip of her tea, readying herself to speak.

'First off, can you tell me a little bit about Lucy? Who her friends are, what she enjoys doing, that kind of thing?' Lexi was careful to keep it in the present tense. After all, one of the girls might still be alive.

'Lucy,' said Joanne, with a long sigh and a glance at her husband. 'She's the oldest. Quietest, too. Not that she's specially quiet – they're all outgoing, friendly, aren't they, Andrew?' Her husband nodded. 'But... I suppose you could say she's more thoughtful, more considered in what she does.'

'Eden's the impulsive one,' added Andrew. 'Always Eden that gets into trouble, or leads the other two astray.'

Lexi smiled. Siblings, the world over. 'What sort of trouble?' She could hear Tom's pen scratching across the paper of his notebook.

'Nothing that bad,' said Andrew, with a father's indulgence.

Joanne frowned slightly. 'She's had a couple of warnings for playing truant. Or being absent from class, as her form teacher puts it.'

Tom's head jerked up. 'Would you be able to give us the exact dates when it happened?' he asked.

'We had a letter each time,' said Joanne. She turned to Andrew. 'They'll be in the file, won't they, with the school reports.'

'I'll fetch them,' said Andrew Carter, rising from the sofa.

At the same time the doorbell rang.

'Let me get it,' said Philippa, following Andrew out of the room.

'But her playing truant won't have anything to do with this, will it?' said Joanne, suddenly distraught again.

'Did she tell you what she was doing when she cut school?' said Lexi.

'There was a row, of course there was.' Joanne looked at the door through which her husband had disappeared. 'Andrew grounded her...' She dropped her voice to a whisper. 'It didn't do any good. I knew she used to nip out sometimes at night. I think she met up with friends – I heard them giggling on the street outside once or twice.'

'Just Eden, or did Lucy and Paige also sneak out?'

Joanne shrugged.

Philippa came back, and Lexi could see Colin and Ridhi lurking behind her in the doorway.

'You two were quick,' said Tom.

'We blue-lighted it,' said Ridhi, suppressing a grin.

Lexi frowned at Colin. Sure, she wanted them here fast, but it hardly qualified for lights and sirens.

'Philippa, can you show them which rooms to search?' she said.

Philippa nodded at Colin and Ridhi with a grim expression, and left the living room as Andrew Carter returned.

Joanne had looked as if she was about to say something, but Andrew's return rendered her silent. It made Lexi wonder about the dynamics of their relationship, and of Andrew's relationships with his daughters. She made a mental note to follow up this line with Joanne – they would take formal statements separately from each of them down at the station.

'Here,' said Andrew, thrusting a couple of sheets of paper at her.

She scanned the letters. They were on Weald Academy headed paper, and detailed two separate incidents when Eden had been missing from school. Both were signed by someone called Susan Edgehill.

'Susan Edgehill is her form teacher?'

'Yes,' said Joanne.

Lexi folded the letters and put them in her bag. 'You'll get them back,' she said. 'I'd just like to make copies of them. Are all three girls in the same class?' They would need to talk to all the teachers that taught them, as well as to their friends.

'No.' Joanne shook her head. 'We asked the school to separate them. We wanted to give them the chance to find their own identities and their own friends. It seems important.'

'My parents were the same,' said Lexi, 'and it was definitely the right thing to do.'

'You were three girls as well?' said Joanne.

Lexi nodded. They had been, until... 'Tell me about Paige.'

'Tomboy. Plain to see, as soon as she was old enough to run around. Stubborn. Bossy with her sisters.'

'She loves sport,' said Andrew. 'Captain of the netball, hockey, swimming – a total all-rounder.' His chest swelled with pride. 'She plays netball for the county, in fact.'

Sports coaches, teammates... three victims would mean three times as many people to talk to. 'Would you mind writing a list for me for each of the girls, detailing their closest friends,

what sports they played, hobbies, after-school activities...
anything like that?'

Both Carters nodded their assent, and Philippa tore pages
out of a notebook and gave them each a pen.

'Swimming.' 'Hockey.' 'Art club, don't forget that.' 'Eden
still friends with that Davis girl? You know, Pam and Tony's
girl?' There were shrugs and nods and momentary disagree-
ments. 'Remember, Lucy does volunteer reading in the kids'
library.'

'So Lucy's the bookish one?' said Lexi, gathering the lists
from them.

'She gets her homework in on time, if that's what you mean,'
said Andrew.

Joanne burst into tears. 'They're all bookish. They love to
read – we all do.'

'What about boys? Do any of them have a boyfriend?'

Andrew Carter practically bristled. 'For the love of God,
they're schoolgirls, only just seventeen. Bit young for serious
boyfriends.'

'But maybe not so serious? Friends who happen to be boys?'

'They're sociable girls,' said Joanne, 'with a big circle of
friends. Of course some of them are boys.'

'But none of them have anyone special?'

Both parents shook their heads, but Lexi had to wonder.
Andrew Carter's attitude would hardly encourage confidences
from his daughters. Perhaps their schoolfriends would know
more.

'And they get on all right, the three of them?'

'Of course,' said Joanne, a little too quickly. 'They're sisters.'

Lexi knew all about sisters getting on and not getting on.
The bonds between triplets or twins were especially close, but
that didn't mean they couldn't be broken.

Andrew pitched in. 'They had their moments, just like
other siblings. But most of the time they were thick as thieves.'

Philippa, hovering behind the sofa, pointed at her watch. She was right – Joanne had certainly had enough, and probably Andrew too, though he didn't show it. But they'd made a start, learned a little about the girls, laid the foundation to move forward. Being able to show empathy with a victim's family early on was important for securing their co-operation over the long months ahead.

'Mr and Mrs Carter, thank you for answering my questions,' she said. 'I'm so sorry for your loss. Philippa will stay with you now, and a bit later, whenever you're ready, perhaps you, Mr Carter, would come down to the morgue to formally identify your daughters' bodies.' It was only then that they would know which two girls they had on the slabs. 'Please believe me when I say I will do everything in my power to find whichever of your girls is still missing and to identify and bring to justice whoever did this to them.'

The shell-shocked man and woman hardly took in her words. It was no surprise – this was probably the darkest day of their lives so far, and every day from now on would be just as dark. And Lexi hated herself for the part she'd played in it.

Tom followed her out, and they spoke with Philippa outside for a few minutes.

'Let me know when they feel ready to visit the morgue and I'll meet you there,' said Lexi. 'And text me details of anything else you find out about the girls that might be useful.' She turned to Tom. 'Come on, let's get going.'

As they stood on either side of the Jeep, Tom fixed her with a stare.

'Inside,' he said, 'you mentioned you were one of triplets.'

'Yes.'

'The Bennett triplets? That horrendous case... you and your sisters were abducted, weren't you? And only two of you came back?'

Lexi nodded, tight-lipped.

'I'm sorry, I hadn't realised.'

'Why would you?' said Lexi, heart pounding. 'It was a long time ago. Seventeen years.' She needed to shut this conversation down fast – talking about what had happened to her family was strictly out of bounds, especially with someone she hardly knew.

'Wow. Sorry.'

She pulled open the door and started getting into the car. 'Come on, back to the office. There's a lot to do.'

Tom didn't say anything, but once he was in the driver's seat, the look he gave her was different. One she'd seen too many times before.

Sympathy. Laced with pity.

EIGHT

They drove back to the office in silence, Tom looking contrite and keeping his eyes on the road ahead, and Lexi making a mental list of the most pressing tasks. Time was slipping by too quickly and they couldn't afford to waste a minute. If Girl C – which was how she had to be thought of until the identities of her dead sisters were confirmed – was still alive, it would only be a matter of time until she wasn't. Unless she'd somehow managed to escape... Disturbing memories bubbled up, a jumble of mental images that Lexi couldn't afford to dwell on. She dragged her mind back to the present.

They would need to set up a press conference with an appeal for information from the girls' parents. Three girls going missing on one day – someone must have seen something. Philippa would need to judge when the Carters would be ready to do this, but it had to be sooner rather than later. And she needed to check in again with Emily Jordan, the crime scene manager, to see if anything else had been discovered at the site.

Tom parked up in the station car park and they walked towards the rear entrance.

'Sorry about before, Lexi,' he said. 'I shouldn't have mentioned it, should I? Foot-mouth.'

'No worries, I'm used to it. Much as I might want to, the past can't be totally expunged or forgotten. After all, what happened to me and my sisters is one of the reasons I joined the police.'

'Well, if I ever say the wrong thing, get too close to the knuckle, let me know, yeah?'

Tom Olsen seemed like a decent bloke, and she had a feeling they could forge a good working relationship.

As they came into the incident room, one of the civilian research staff got up from their desk and intercepted Lexi.

'Boss, the Chief Super's downstairs. Said she'd like a word with you when you got back. She's in Room 1G.'

'Thanks.'

Chief Superintendent Maggie Dawson was Lexi's direct superior and had been instrumental in her appointment as head of the Major Investigation Team. But she was more than that. Ever since Lexi had joined Kent Police more than a decade ago, Maggie had been her mentor, spotting her talents early on and guiding her through the ranks – even to the point where it had been Maggie's idea that she should try for the FBI's course in applied behavioural science. Of course, it hadn't been the plan that she should stay away for four years, but no one had been as enthusiastic and supportive as Maggie when Lexi had been invited to join the Bureau's Investigative Support Unit on the back of her performance.

As Chief Superintendent in charge of serious crime, Maggie Dawson was based at the Kent Police HQ in Maidstone. Her usual duties wouldn't bring her down to Canterbury nick, so Lexi wondered what she was doing here. She went down to the first floor and was quickly shown into the empty office that the CS had commandeered.

'Lexi!' Maggie Dawson was on her feet as soon as she saw

Lexi in the doorway, and rushed round the desk to give her a hug.

'Maggie, so great to see you.'

They embraced each other tightly. Then Maggie held Lexi at arms' length for a moment, studying her features as if for signs of change – it had been some months since they'd seen each other face to face. 'You look well,' she said.

They sat down and for the first few minutes, they caught up on personal news. Maggie had a son at university and a daughter in her final year at school. 'Though, God knows, the pandemic has probably torpedoed her exam results.'

Lexi was sympathetic. 'Ellie's a bright girl, and they're all in the same boat. I'm sure she'll be fine. How's Pete?'

Maggie shrugged and pulled a face. 'Why would you expect his mother to know? He never calls, but we believe he's having a ball!'

A PC came into the office with two cups of coffee.

'Thanks, Paul,' said Maggie. 'Originally, I'd thought maybe we could get a quick lunch together, it being your first day and all, but I hear you're already stuck into a case.'

'We – I, in fact – found two female bodies up on the Memorial Crown outside Wye at first light this morning. Throats cut – I'm fairly certain that's the cause of death, though we'll have to wait for Mort's report to be one hundred per cent sure. We ID'd them pretty quickly as they were identical. Twins, we thought at first, but as it turns out, they're two of a set of triplets, reported missing three days ago.'

Maggie's expression clouded. 'I gathered that.' News travelled fast in a busy police station. 'Look, you know what I'm going to say.'

Lexi nodded. Of course she did, but it didn't mean she was going to agree with it.

'Forgive me, but are you really sure that you're the right person to handle this case?'

Lexi took a breath and let two or three seconds pass in silence. When she was ready she spoke. 'But this is exactly the sort of case that you brought me in to investigate.' She looked down at her hands, folded in her lap. She knew she was being obtuse.

Maggie answered quietly but determinedly. 'There's really very little chance that the two cases aren't linked. You have to agree, Lexi.'

'There's no evidence to indicate that.'

'It's triplets. All three taken at once. To my mind that means your abductor is back at work, or we've got a copycat on our hands.'

'Of course, it's possible. But I think it's unlikely to be him after all these years. This type of offender follows a progression – the crimes don't just stop and then restart decades later. We'd have seen something in between. But copycat? Maybe.' Lexi clenched her jaw. She refused to consider the possibility that the man who abducted her and her sisters could be back – these girls were murdered. It wasn't the same as what happened to her. But she felt cold sweat on the back of her neck.

Maggie's eyebrows climbed towards her hairline. 'Does anything seem familiar to you? The dresses, the tiaras, the fact that they were placed on the Memorial Crown? Would a copycat have known about things like that?'

Lexi shook her head. 'None of that's familiar – or at least I can't remember anything like that. I've been racking my brains but, honestly, I can't see a link. Our abduction was different.'

'There's a reason you don't remember the details,' said Maggie. 'Your mind's protecting you. A case that's so similar to your own... I'm not sure it's fair on you. I could easily pass it to DI Rogers. He's a good man, quite capable of handling it.'

'Seriously? He doesn't have the experience for a case like this.' Lexi fought to keep an edge of anger out of her voice. 'And why? Just because they happen to be triplets? You think I can't handle it?'

'I'm not suggesting you can't handle it. I'm thinking of the pain it might cause. The memories it might bring up. How much do you actually remember?'

'Fragments. It's all quite sketchy – at least until the point Amber and I were running out of the forest. Snippets pop into my mind... It's like a patchwork. The dark interior of a van. A window with a pane of glass missing – and it's cold, so cold. My sisters crying somewhere out of sight.' Rose, lying broken and abandoned on the forest floor. 'Perhaps one day I'll be able to join the dots.' Lexi sighed, annoyed at herself for volunteering so much information. Annoyed at Maggie's sympathetic expression. This wasn't how she wanted her boss to see her. 'But you know why I do this job. To assuage the pain, to make good on what happened to Rose and to Amber.'

'And to you. Don't forget how much you've suffered.'

Lexi could feel colour rising in her cheeks. Maggie was implying she was damaged goods and it infuriated her. 'The fact that I'm a triplet and I lost one of my sisters is exactly why I'm the right person to take on this case. I understand the dynamics, and I understand exactly what the Carters are going through.'

Maggie's face wore a pained expression. 'So the Feds didn't knock that streak of stubbornness out of you, then?'

The tension in the room dissipated, but inside Lexi was still angry. She hated it when people gave her the kid-glove treatment. She'd been through what she'd been through, and she'd survived it. She felt suddenly exhausted. It seemed like it had been a long day and it was only just lunchtime.

Maggie watched her closely.

'Just promise me one thing, Lexi. If it gets too much for you, there would be no shame in stepping back. And also, talk to me. I'll be at the end of the line any time, day or night.'

'That's two things. But of course I'll keep you informed how the case is doing.'

'How *you're* doing,' said Maggie. She didn't look convinced. 'Have you even seen your sister yet?'

For the next quarter of an hour, Lexi avoided personal questions and filled her boss in on what she had the team doing so far and what actions she would take next. Hopefully this would set Maggie's mind at rest, convince her that Lexi was the right person for the job.

Once they'd parted company, Lexi didn't return to the incident room. She needed a breath of fresh air, so she headed out into the car park.

She was kidding herself. It wasn't fresh air that she needed, but a moment of solitude. She unlocked her car, slipped into the passenger seat and closed her eyes with a sigh. Maggie's concern had hardly taken her by surprise. Learning that the dead girls were part of a set of triplets had blindsided her, even if it was a coincidence. Snippets of memories from seventeen years before were seeping back into her consciousness. And with them came a host of questions. Was she the right person to lead this investigation? Had she done the right thing by coming back to Canterbury when she could have applied to any force in the country?

Canterbury was her home, it was where she'd grown up and gone to school. But it was also where the terrible events of 2006 had unspooled. Her sister, Rose, was gone for good and nearly every corner of the city held a shared childhood memory. It was painful, but she couldn't run from her past forever. Maybe this case would give her a way of confronting what had happened.

Maybe that was what Maggie Dawson was afraid of.

Questions left unanswered, Lexi made her way back to the incident room. There was a girl still missing, a girl who might just still be alive.

NINE

Lexi worked for a couple of hours in her office, munching on a cardboard sandwich as she thrashed her way through an inbox that was already overflowing with emails. Colin and Ridhi arrived back from the Carters with a carton of bagged up items. Lexi found Ridhi logging it onto the system to maintain the chain of evidence.

'Where's Colin?' she said.

'Gone for his lunchbreak.'

'What about you?'

'I asked him to bring me back something.'

'Right, what've you got?'

'No mobiles, but that makes sense as they would have had their phones on them. There was an iPad in Lucy's room...' She pulled a clear plastic evidence bag from the box and Lexi could see a tablet inside. Ridhi studied what was written on the white square on the outside of the bag. 'No, sorry, this was from Paige's room.'

'You're sure? We can't afford to muddle things up.'

'I'm sure,' said Ridhi. 'This is my writing.' She showed the label to Lexi. It stated, as required, where the evidence had been found and the time and date. It was from Paige's room.

'I suppose it's locked?'

'Yes, facial recognition or a password required.'

'Okay, send it over to the tech guys, see what they can get.'

'That's probably the most interesting thing we came across,' said Ridhi. 'No smoking gun – just a couple of diaries that look ancient, membership cards for the library and the sports centre, schoolbooks and folders, birthday cards, notes from friends, lists...'

'That's good work, Ridhi. Can you spend the next hour or so going through it all – they went missing on Friday, so take particular note of what they might normally be doing on a Friday, and put together a list of friends and contacts for us to question.'

'Will do.'

'And call me immediately if anything sticks out.'

Her phone buzzed with a text message – it was from Philippa Reid, saying that the Carters were now ready to view their daughters' bodies. She made the arrangements with Mort so this could take place. He'd moaned – he wasn't ready for it – but he agreed to make the girls look presentable. He understood how critical this moment would be for their grieving process – and from a policing point of view, it would also tell them which two girls they had found and which one was still missing.

Lexi drove up to the mortuary in Maidstone and met Philippa and the Carters outside the viewing suite. They were dressed as if for church – Andrew Carter in a navy suit, with a white shirt and a dark tie, and Joanne wearing a plain, dark green dress. Her face was puffy from crying, and although she'd put on some make-up, the mascara was already smudged down one cheek.

An assistant went to fetch Mort, and five minutes later he led them through to the counselling room adjacent to the viewing suite. There was a window in one wall, with a curtain drawn across it.

'When you're ready to see them, I'll pull this curtain back,' he explained, 'and you'll be able to look through the window.'

'Aren't we allowed to go into the room?' said Andrew Carter.

'I'm sorry,' said Mort, 'there isn't actually space for that. We don't usually have two bodies being viewed together.'

Andrew Carter's face fell, but he didn't seem to have the strength to push.

Lexi threw Mort a frown. He replied with a tiny shrug.

'Are you both ready?' said Philippa gently, placing a supportive arm around Joanne's shoulders.

'We'll never be ready, but it's got to be done, hasn't it?' said Andrew.

Mort drew the curtain to one side, and the Carters stepped towards the glass. Andrew took his wife's hand and gave it a squeeze.

From behind them, Lexi could see the two bodies lying side by side on a pair of hospital trollies. Both were covered with white sheets that had been drawn up tight under their chins to prevent their parents from seeing the frightful wounds in their necks. Their hair had been brushed and their faces cleaned of blood and the flecks of dirt and grass that Lexi had seen on them up at the Crown.

Joanne Carter almost pressed her face against the glass, then gasped. 'But... where's Paige? You said Paige would be here.'

Lexi stepped up to the window next to Andrew Carter. 'What do you mean? Isn't one of them Paige?'

Andrew Carter turned to her. 'No. That's Lucy,' he said, pointing to the nearer of the two bodies, 'and that's Eden.'

Lexi's head spun for a second. Of course, the two girls looked the same to her. But to their parents, all three were distinct individuals. She knew this from having been a triplet herself – while other people would muddle up which of them was which, their parents never did.

Unfortunately, Mort chose this moment to wade in. 'Sometimes loved ones' appearances can change a bit after passing,' he said. He pointed through the window. 'She was wearing the pendant with the letter "P" on it. Are you sure that isn't Paige?'

Joanne turned on him with a furious expression, placing a hand on his chest in a half-hearted push. 'That's Lucy. I know my own children, even if they are dead. It's Lucy and Eden…' She started to cry again, noisily, and batted her husband away as he tried to comfort her.

'Damn you all,' she gasped between sobs.

She opened the door to the viewing suite and went to her daughters. Andrew followed her in, and they each bent to embrace one of their daughters.

Mort started after them, but Lexi placed a hand on his arm.

'Let them be.'

The room used at Canterbury police station for press conferences wasn't really big enough, especially when word had already leaked out about the murder of two young women. The local and national press representatives were vying for position in the front rows of chairs and there was a palpable buzz of excitement. Lexi could understand the press pack's hunger for a juicy story, but she found it distasteful that the reporters could behave like this, chatting and laughing, knowing that the dead girls' parents were hovering just outside the room.

When she got the go-ahead from the camera operator, she went out of the room to where Philippa and the Carters were waiting. Lexi had spent half an hour with them beforehand going over the format for the presser, and the two of them were as ready as they ever would be for what would be a gruelling ordeal.

'Okay?'

They nodded at her, with tired, sad expressions and she led them into the meeting room. It fell immediately silent as all eyes turned towards them. A barrage of flashes fired off and continued as the four of them took their seats at the raised table. Behind them, a hastily erected screen featured the Kent Police logo, and a telephone number and email address for members of the public who had information.

'Good afternoon, everyone,' said Lexi, leaning closer to the microphone. 'We're here to appeal for information that might save a girl's life. Seventeen-year-old Paige Carter has been missing since Friday afternoon, and this morning the bodies of her two sisters, Lucy and Eden Carter, also seventeen, were found on the Memorial Cross outside the village of Wye. If you're watching this at home...'

TEN

I am watching this at home, and I'm very much enjoying it. TV Lexi is asking us all to come forward if we have any information relating to the disappearance of Paige Carter, seventeen. She looks the part – her dark trouser suit is well cut, sober. Plain white shirt underneath. She's authoritative, calm under pressure, measured with her choice of words. In fact, just the sort of person you'd want to put in charge of an investigation like this.

I remember how smart she was back then. Far cleverer than either of her sisters. They looked identical, but their minds certainly weren't the same. It was something I noticed long before I took them. I would watch them together and when it was just the three of them, none of their other friends around, they would fall into familiar roles. Amber was the goody-goody, always uptight about getting into trouble – not because she was inherently good, but because she cared too much about what people thought. Lexi was clever and bossy and fun. She was the noisiest of the three, and it was always her voice I could hear. And Rose, sweet Rose, was the peacekeeper between her two fractious sisters. Not as quick-witted as the other two, not as self-aware, but always kind.

But Lexi was the most interesting. And it was Lexi who caught my attention. I think I loved her from the moment I saw her. Funny to think that the young girl I knew and adored – whose heart I tried to capture in return – is now this important woman on my television screen. Appealing directly to me, as well.

Yes, I have information on the disappearance of Paige Carter, plenty of it, all in the most amazing detail. And naturally I have knowledge of her current whereabouts. I would love to share it, to sit down across a table from Lexi and have a long chat, maybe reminisce about the good old days. She and I go back a long, long way.

Paige is the bait. She's how I'm going to reel Lexi in, because Lexi is the one I really want. Lexi and her sister, Amber, so I can finish what I started. But I'll have my fun with Paige as well, while I've got her. In some ways they're the same, Lexi and Paige. The feisty ones. Paige is a challenge and I always relish a challenge.

Now Lexi's showing off Paige Carter's poor, sad parents, like a pair of prize pigs at an auction. Which reporter will bid the highest for their daughters' life stories? Ma Carter is pleading for information about who took her daughters. Pa Carter stares directly at the camera and begs Paige to come home. Oh, she would if she could, believe me.

I can't sit in front of the television all day. I need to go and feed and water the little princess. I switch off the box and pull on my cagoule. It's still raining – I'm getting a bit fed up with it. January should be crisp and frosty, with a bright sun low on the horizon. Not just these flat, grey skies and endless drizzle, the light starting to fade almost as soon as you've finished lunch.

I grab the car keys and set out. It'll be dark by the time I get there, which means I can creep up on her and give her the fright of her life. I take my fun where I can get it these days. I couldn't get away with playing tricks like this on the people I work with.

En route, I stop at a petrol station and pick up a couple of chocolate bars and a bottle of water. The roads are quiet, and it doesn't take me long to get there. I park some distance away so I can maintain the element of surprise. I walk up to the place and open the gate carefully, so it doesn't grate or squeak. I tiptoe up to the window and gently tap-tap-tap on it.

From inside, I hear her gasp. I've given her a shock. Then I hear scuffling sounds. She's probably trying to get herself untied or move nearer to the window. She doesn't know if it's me out here or someone else. Should she scream for help? I tippy-tap on the window again.

'Is someone there? Please help me...'

Her voice is remarkably strong and steady for a girl who must be scared half to death. I wait in silence, leaning back against the wall.

'Is anybody there?'

This time, she sounds more nervous.

I eat one of the chocolate bars while she waits to be rescued. But I'm not a cruel person, so eventually I unlock and open the door.

'Good evening, Paige.'

She's slumped against the far wall. When I switch on the camping light – left well out of her reach by the door – I see that her cheeks are shiny with tears. She's shaking and it's hard to know if it's with fear or because of the cold. The air does feel quite icy in here.

'What? No "hello" for me?'

She stares up at me defiantly. She won't speak. Not yet. But I know how to make her talk.

I walk towards her, and my feet crunch on something. Those bloody bones that litter the floor in here. I can see her eyeing the remaining chocolate bar and the bottle of water I'm holding, but I haven't decided yet whether to give them to her.

'Talk to me, Paige. There are things I want to know about you and your life.'

She turns her face away from me as far as she's able.

I slap her. Not hard, but enough to jar her teeth and to make her cry.

'Tell me what it was like to be a little girl, growing up as a triplet. If you tell me things your sisters haven't already told me, I might just keep them alive a little longer.' In my mind's eye, I see the two girls lying dead on the Crown. 'And if they tell me things that you haven't told me, I might keep you alive for a little longer. It's a sort of game, you see?'

She stares up at me, horrified.

'Come on, you want to play, don't you?'

She relents. These girls have the best manners. 'Yes, I want to play. What do you want to know about?'

Her voice betrays her fear, and it's like a shot of adrenalin to my chest.

ELEVEN

As soon as the presser was finished, Lexi hurried back up to the incident room. She called Emily Jordan as she took the stairs two at a time.

'Anything new?'

'It's probably nothing,' said Emily. 'A small sliver of bone, almost certainly avian. It's unlikely to be connected to the crime, but I'll add it to the evidence.'

'Will you finish with the site tonight?'

'I don't think so. It's a large area for a fingertip search – and we can't do that after dark. Also, I want to lift all the blood-stained chalk and take it back with me to the lab. We'll probably be here most of tomorrow.'

'Okay, I'll arrange for some uniforms to stand guard overnight. We don't need a bunch of true crime podcasters stamping all over. What about access – how did he get the girls up to the Crown?'

'We've taken a cast of some tyre prints from beyond the five-bar gate. They go around the edge of the ploughed field on the other side of the hill. I think he brought them up through the field in a van – we'll get a better idea of the vehicle size once the tyre prints have been matched. Whatever it was, he drove it up here, stopped by the gate, then reversed until he reached a suitable place to turn back around.'

'And the gate? You've checked it for prints?'

'Of course. But it's part of a public bridleway. We found a multitude of partials, though I think you'll be looking at a killer smart enough to have been wearing gloves. No matter, we'll check them all for matches.'

Lexi hung up with a sigh. The donkey work of forensics – checking thousands of tiny pieces of evidence that were unlikely to yield any useful information.

In the incident room, someone had already had the foresight to put up a large map of the area surrounding the Crown on the wall. Lexi pointed out the field via which Emily thought the killer had accessed the site.

'Colin, we've got tyre tracks coming up along the edge of this field, which could be the vehicle he used. Emily Jordan thinks it's likely to be a van of some sort.'

Colin came over to the map. It didn't show exactly where the gate was situated at the bottom of the field, but wherever it was, it would open onto a narrow lane along its northern edge. He traced its path with his finger.

'Look, it's a dead end if you turn to the east,' he said. 'It just leads up to a couple of farms. He must have come from the other direction.'

Lexi followed the route with her eyes. The single-track lane meandered through an area of dense woodland, before reaching a T-junction with another equally narrow lane that ran north-south. Turning south would bring him back down to Coldharbour Lane, while going north would take him in the direction of the tiny villages of Crundale and Godmersham.

'I assume there are no cameras around for miles?' said Lexi.

'You're right. It's a desert as far as ANPR is concerned.'

Lexi sighed. They needed to catch a break somewhere,

somehow – just a pointer that would maybe send them in the right direction. But so far nothing was standing out. She checked her watch. It was almost six, but they couldn't afford to knock off.

'Colin, can you get out there and door knock those two farms at the end of the lane? See if they noticed any suspicious vehicles in the area. After all, there can't be much traffic around there.'

'Now, or in the morning?'

'Now, of course.' It came out more sharply than she intended, and Colin scowled at her. 'If you had plans for the evening, change 'em. This is more important. We're on a ticking clock. You should know that.'

'Yes, boss.' His voice and his demeanour were sullen, but that wasn't Lexi's problem.

'Ridhi, I want the time and place where each girl was last seen pinned onto the map. Then help Colin to correlate the ANPR reports between them.' The more responsibility she could give Ridhi, the more her confidence would grow, and the more useful she'd become to the team.

There was a large-scale map of the city pinned up on the other side of the whiteboard and Ridhi filled her in on the details as she completed the task.

'All three girls went missing on Friday. It was a school day, and they were all in class at various points.' She pointed a finger at the Weald Academy. It lay to the west of the city, sandwiched between the railway track and the A2050, about a mile from where the girls lived. Lexi knew it well – her own school had played hockey and netball matches against the Academy with boring regularity. 'Lucy seems to have gone missing first. She never reappeared in class after the lunchbreak.'

'What did they do about it?'

'According to the initial report, the teacher made a note and thought no more of it. Not exactly unusual for kids to cut class on a Friday afternoon, is it?'

Lexi frowned. Sure, truancy was an everyday occurrence, but it was one of those cinch points in a case when, if somebody had acted differently, there might have been a different outcome.

'No one can remember seeing her for the rest of the afternoon.'

'What about the other two?'

'Paige left school at the usual time and went with some friends to the McDonald's branch on St George's Street.' Ridhi stuck a pin with a red plastic head into the map. 'After eating, they went their separate ways, but she never arrived home.'

'So what time was that?'

'There's some CCTV footage that shows her leaving at ten past five.'

'And Eden?'

'She was supposed to be going home with Paige, but apparently the two sisters had a falling out as they walked into town, and she went off somewhere on her own.'

'When was the alarm raised?'

'Mr Carter phoned the police station at eight twenty-five. They'd expected all three girls to be home for their tea at six. They waited a while, then phoned a few of their friends to see if they knew anything. Then they started to get worried.'

'Okay, well done, Ridhi.' She turned to address the whole room. 'I know the missing persons team will have gathered any available ANPR reports and CCTV footage, but we need to put fresh eyes on it. Emily Jordan suspects the abductor used a van, so that's what you're looking for, possibly cruising around the vicinity of the school or following the girls as they walked into town.'

'Overtime?' said one of the civilian staff.

'Yes, overtime,' said Lexi. 'No one clocks off, no one sleeps till we get a lead on where Paige Carter is being held.'

Her phone pinged with a text.

It was from Emily Jordan:

You might want to get up here – unofficial vigil for the two girls gathering. Need to keep them off the crime scene.

It was almost dark, but Lexi's ancient Chrysler Crossfire ate up the eleven miles between Canterbury and Wye in next to no time. Steering with one hand, she pushed a petrol station cheese and onion sandwich into her mouth with the other. It was uninspiring in terms of flavour and the texture was limp, but she was hungry enough for it to hit the spot.

Tom was following in his own car, and they parked up behind the CSI van on Coldharbour Lane. There were more cars stretching in either direction, and as they made their way towards the small copse at the bottom of the hill, she could see torchlight and hear the murmur of voices. A small crowd had gathered.

Close up, it seemed to be mainly teenagers – schoolfriends of the dead girls, Lexi guessed. There were about twenty of them, some with torches, others holding up flaming lighters. They were all facing up the hill, and Lexi could sense the pressure they felt to move forward. A uniformed sergeant was blocking the path up to the Crown, with both hands held up before him, palms outward, trying to move the crowd back.

'Come on, guys,' he called, 'this is a crime scene. I need you all to disperse and go home.'

A couple of girls at the front of the group were crying loudly, clutching bunches of limp flowers. A boy stepped forward.

'No way. These are our friends you're talking about. We need to see where it happened.'

Another joined him, shoulder to shoulder. 'Shouldn't you be trying to find whoever did this?'

It seemed a bit unnecessary, but emotions were running high.

A man with a professional-looking camera stepped out in front of them, his flash going off as he photographed the youngsters. Bloody press – they'd probably be all over it from now on.

Behind them, Lexi heard car doors slamming and turned round. Andrew Carter was putting an arm around his wife as they neared the copse. Philippa Reid hurried behind them and, when she saw Lexi, she shrugged. Someone must have alerted the Carters that the vigil was happening, and who could blame them for wanting to be there?

'How d'you want to play it, boss?' said Tom.

They needed a strategy before things got out of hand.

A camera flash went off close to the bereaved parents. The press photographer – he'd probably told them about the vigil so he could get some shots.

'Leave it to me,' said Lexi.

She walked over to Andrew and Joanne Carter.

'Hello, Mr and Mrs Carter,' she said, loud enough for the teenagers to hear. She shook Andrew's hand and pulled Joanne into an embrace.

The Carters nodded at her, both looking shell-shocked at being the centre of attention.

Lexi turned to the crowd. 'Listen up – as my sergeant has just told you, this is a crime scene. We need to keep it clear until the forensic team has finished. If you trample all over it, you'll make our job harder, and that won't help us to find Paige. And it won't be fair on Eden or Lucy, or the rest of the family.' She looked around at them, purposefully catching the eyes of the two boys that had spoken out. 'Please bear with us. Tomorrow, once my team have given us the all-clear, you can hold a vigil. Okay? Is that fair?'

The first boy to speak spoke again. 'All right. We'll come back tomorrow.' He gestured for the others to follow, and started down towards the Carters. When he reached them he stopped. 'I'm sorry,' he said simply.

Joanne Carter dissolved into tears. Andrew Carter shook the boy's hand.

The girl he'd been with also expressed her condolences, and a line formed behind her as each of the teenagers offered what comfort they could.

Lexi stood her ground next to the Carters, nodding as each one said their piece. She scanned their faces and listened. Killers notoriously returned to the scene of the crime, but she didn't think these murders had been committed by a teenager. Even so, she knew her job. Out of the corner of her eye, she saw Tom videoing the scene from a distance. Good man. And up at the top of the hill, in the shadow of the trees, Emily Jorden gave her a wave, relieved that her crime scene had been preserved.

As the last of the teenagers filed past, Lexi spoke again.

'I know how horrifying this is for each and every one of you,' she said. 'So please believe me when I tell you I am making it my mission to find Paige and bring her home. And we'll do everything in our power to arrest whoever did this.'

The press photographer's flash went off in her eyes.

'If any of you know anything, or have any thoughts about what has happened, please get in touch with me, DI Bennett, at Canterbury Police Station.'

The crowd broke up into little knots and went back to the cars they'd arrived in.

Philippa Reid led Andrew and Joanne Carter back to her car.

Tom arrived at Lexi's side.

'Do you think he was here?' he said quietly.

Lexi turned to look at him. 'The killer? Without a doubt. Let's hope you've caught him on film.'

But if he had, did that mean Lexi was about to encounter a figure from her own past?

Only time would tell. For almost seventeen years, Lexi had dreamed of being able to confront him, but now that there was a chance she might be able to, she wasn't so sure. Anxiety knotted her stomach. An imagined monster was so much easier to deal with than the prospect of a real one.

TWELVE

TUESDAY, 10 JANUARY

Sleep took a back seat. Lexi's mind was buzzing, and as she lay in the dark with her eyes shut, it was only her body getting any downtime. The day had been long and difficult, and the focus had been on information gathering, mainly about the three Carter girls and where they'd last been seen. The Major Investigation Team had formally taken over the case – it was already a double murder investigation and Lexi's major concern was how they could prevent it from becoming a triple killing.

After the attempted vigil, she and Tom had returned to the office and studied the footage he'd shot several times. But all they had was a gaggle of youngsters, some in tears, some almost zombified with shock, but no one who looked like they might have been capable of a double homicide. This had been an accomplished kill by an experienced killer.

The killer. Her thoughts turned in the night to the man who'd done this. There were a number of things she could say with certainty. It was, to her mind, undoubtedly a man. What she'd seen so far were the classic hallmarks of a narcissistic serial killer and ninety-nine per cent of them were male, came from dysfunctional family backgrounds and had suffered abusive childhoods. But anyone who watched serial killer dramas on TV or listened to true crime podcasts could surmise that much. She needed to dig much deeper into how the killer's mind worked, and to do this she needed information. Mort would be doing the autopsies in the morning and Lexi had to hope the bodies would reveal something about what had happened – the sort of details that would enable Lexi to worm her way into the killer's psyche.

Something stirred at the back of her mind, like a beast waking from a long sleep, and she didn't like it. Shadows were taking form in the darkness. But you can't fight shadows. Perhaps it was time to confront the reality of the situation.

Unable to sleep, she got up and went for a three-mile run – though not in the direction of the Crown this time. Her mind churned through the facts they had so far for the hundredth time and she got back feeling as frustrated as when she'd set out.

After a quick shower followed by a double espresso, she was on her way to Maidstone to join Mort for the autopsies on Eden and Lucy's bodies. She felt she had to be there in person – anything he found might be a critical clue as to where the unsub was holding the third girl. Paige. The youngest of the three. Lexi's heart jumped erratically as she pulled out onto the M2. This was all hitting too close to home.

She arrived in the car park of Maidstone Hospital in a dark mood. Tom was waiting for her by the entrance to the mortuary, but she simply gave him a cursory nod and pushed through the heavy double doors.

'We've had a good response to the information appeal,' he said, catching up with her in the small, clinical reception area.

'Anything of any use?'

'I've asked Ridhi and Colin to follow up on a couple of leads.'

'But nothing concrete?'

'Not as yet...'

'Damn!' She ran a hand through her damp hair. 'I'm sorry, Tom. But time's running out.'

Mort Barley appeared in the doorway and led the way deeper into his realm of death. He was wearing a white coat. To a stranger, he looked just like any other doctor they might see in the hospital corridors – no one would guess that every one of his patients was dead before they reached him.

'Lexi, Tom.' He gave them each a nod, and they followed him through to the autopsy room.

Two gurneys. Two bodies, each covered with a white rubber sheet. Eden and Lucy Carter.

Mort pointed to a row of hooks next to the door. Tom took off his jacket, and Lexi hung her bag along with her coat. They knew the drill, and pulled on pale blue disposable lab gowns. Lexi put on a surgical mask and fetched latex gloves for herself and Tom from a box on one of the room's stainless-steel counters.

'Ready?' said Mort. He'd also put on gloves and a mask, and was wearing a Perspex visor to protect his eyes.

'Sure,' said Lexi.

Mort went round to stand at the head end of the two trolleys. He pointed to the body on the left. 'This is Lucy Carter, as identified by her father, and this—' he indicated the other one '—is Eden, also identified by her father.' He walked to the other end and flicked back the rubber sheets to expose four bare feet, two of which had plastic tags attached to the big toe. 'Should you forget which is which, they're labelled.'

'Which one was wearing the "P" pendant?' said Lexi.

'Lucy,' said Mort.

'Why would she be wearing her sister's pendant?' said Tom. 'Could it be some kind of message?'

'Where's the pendant now?' said Lexi.

'Everything removed from the bodies has been passed

across to Emily Jordan for forensics,' said Mort. 'The pendant, the tiaras, the dresses.'

'Underwear?' said Lexi.

'None,' said Mort, 'and no footwear. Photographs were taken as they were removed, and they'll be included in my report. Right, let's get started – Lucy first.'

With a small mic clipped onto the lapel of his lab coat, Mort dictated his notes as he went along, recording details of her height, ethnicity, hair and eye colour. He started with an external examination of every inch of Lucy's skin, using a fine pair of tweezers to remove particles or fibres, which he placed into individual, numbered evidence bags, carefully recording exactly where each piece of evidence was found.

'No tattoos, birthmarks or notable scars. Ears pierced, navel pierced.'

The details of a life, reduced to physical attributes. Lexi tried to imagine a much younger Lucy nervously waiting to have her ears pierced and feeling so grown-up once it was done. And then at a later date, feigning boredom, covering her excitement, at the prospect of a pierced navel.

Mort took further photographs of the wound on the girl's neck. Lexi had to look away.

'Other than the single lateral cut across the throat, the body doesn't have any obvious external injuries,' he intoned into his mic, 'apart from a couple of minor scratches on her left foot and a faded bruise on the right leg, just below the knee.'

'Do you have a time of death for us yet?' said Lexi, as he paused in his recording to remove the plastic bag that had been secured around Lucy's right hand. She knew he would have taken the body temperature at the murder site and would have assessed the progression of rigor and lividity as a matter of urgency the previous day.

'Early thoughts,' he said. 'As I surmised at the scene, Eden, who we originally tagged as Girl A, died first, sometime between one a.m. and three a.m. on Monday morning, and Lucy, our Girl B, died later. I'd say between four and five. I'll probably be able to narrow that down once I've examined the stomach contents.'

He selected a small scalpel and scraped under Lucy's fingernails, again catching the matter in an evidence bag. 'It doesn't look like there's any blood under her nails, so I don't think she fought back.'

He did the other hand, and Lexi noticed Tom averting his eyes. She got it. It was horrible to have to watch the indignities piled onto a murder victim.

'Blocking my light, love,' said Mort, as she leaned further in to see what he was doing.

'Sorry.'

Once he'd finished with the fingernails, he repeated the exercise with her toenails. 'It's not something we routinely do,' he said. 'But they appear to have arrived at the site barefoot and there might be some dirt or plant matter that could later be matched to the Crown area or elsewhere.'

When that was done, he went to a steel cabinet at the end of the room and fetched an ultraviolet light, which he passed over the body from head to toe, stopping momentarily to secure other minute scraps of evidence. Then, putting the light to one side, he gently lifted Lucy's legs apart so he would be able to give her an internal examination. This was one of the most important parts of the autopsy – it could tell them if she'd been subjected to sexual assault or trauma. Lexi glanced across at Tom. He looked distressed.

'We don't need to watch this,' said Lexi. 'We'll wait outside.' Lucy deserved some dignity in death.

After a few minutes, Mort called them back.

'Well?' said Lexi.

Mort shrugged. 'Well, nothing. No sign of trauma, no cuts or abrasions.'

'Nothing at all to suggest sexual assault?'

'No. I've taken a swab to check for the presence of sper-matozoa.'

But it puzzled her. It was unusual for a ritualistic killing not to include sexual assault of some type, either pre- or post-mortem.

Standing at the counter that ran along one wall of the autopsy room, Mort made up a couple of microscope slides from the swabs he'd taken. He put the first of them under a large microscope and beckoned the two detectives over.

'If there's any sperm, we'll be able to see it on these slides.' He put his eye to the eyepiece and twisted the focus knobs until he could see clearly. Then he let out a low whistle of breath. 'You little beauties! Yup, sperm present.'

'Can you tell how long before she died she had sex?' said Tom.

'Not by eye,' said Mort, 'but I'll come back to you on that.'

'But no sign that it was assault?'

'Nothing suggesting assault, for sure. But she could have been scared into compliance or she could have been drugged. You'll need to wait for the tox screen results.'

'We need to know if she had a boyfriend or not – maybe she had sex with someone shortly before she was abducted,' said Lexi. 'And we can't discount that if she had a boyfriend, he might be the killer.'

Mort placed the slides into evidence bags and stood up. 'I'm going inside the abdomen now – you sticking around for that?'

Lexi was bitterly disappointed. She'd been expecting at least one evidential gold nugget – a piece of information that would help her get a handle on the crime and tell her something about the killer. But there was literally nothing. Perhaps the blood toxicology or the analysis of the fibres and particles recovered from the girls' bodies would yield results. Only time would tell.

'No thanks, Mort. We'll head back to Canterbury. But give me a shout straight away if you find anything useful on Eden.'

'Of course.'

'Because we're going nowhere fast, and it doesn't make sense.'

Mort shrugged and picked up a scalpel. He didn't care – solving the crime wasn't his problem.

Lexi followed Tom towards the door and heard the soft rasp of a blade cutting through flesh behind her as she left.

THIRTEEN

As Lexi pulled into the car park of Canterbury police station, it was nearing midday. She ran up to the incident room, and was relieved to find that it was a hive of activity. Tom followed her in – they'd been discussing next moves on the phone as they drove back from Maidstone in convoy, and now it was time to act.

'What progress?' she said as Ridhi looked up at her from the computer screen.

'I've arranged with Weald Academy for you and Tom to go over and speak to the girls' friends and teachers.'

'Great.' She looked at Tom. 'Just let me grab a coffee and check my emails, then we'll go.'

Tom nodded, dropping into his chair and firing up his own computer.

'Colin, is the crime scene finished with?'

'Not last time I checked.' He glanced at his watch. 'That was about an hour ago. Maybe now...'

'Find out and let me know. Then we can tell the Academy they can organise a vigil for those students who want one. Anything else cropped up this morning?'

'Nothing conclusive from the ANPR reports, in that there's no one vehicle that turns up in all the locations and on the road out to Wye – the system's not foolproof. But we're looking at any that crop up more than once.'

Lexi went to her office, wishing that the team had had more to report. But like always, the first twenty-four hours were information gathering. That information had to be analysed to build an accurate picture of what happened. Only then could she hope to find something that would break the case. But the situation with Paige meant she needed it to happen super-fast. She scanned her inbox and drank a scalding black coffee in one quick draught.

'Let's go,' she called to Tom, heading towards the stairs.

As Tom drove them across town to the school, they discussed how to approach questioning the students. Lexi leaned back in the passenger seat. Tom's Jeep smelled of pine – one of those scented cardboard air fresheners hung from the dashboard – and the interior looked freshly cleaned. Nothing like her own car that was always in need of a wash.

'All three girls are – were – in Year 12, studying for their A levels,' she said, consulting the notes Tom had typed up since they spoke to the Carters. 'The headmaster is called William Doig, only took up the position last year, so probably still feeling his way. He's being co-operative, but according to Ridhi, he reminded her that all the pupils in the same year as the Carters were interviewed a few days ago by the missing persons team.'

'His point being?'

'I suspect he's worried about police heavy-handedness with the kids.' Lexi shrugged. 'One of them might just know something that will lead us to Paige, so we'll ask what we have to ask.'

The Weald Academy was a mixed school with more than thirteen hundred students. It was a sprawl of modern buildings and sports facilities, with a large staff car park at the front. They followed signs to the Visitors' Reception, where the headmaster's secretary met them with all the bustle of a professional busybody.

'Follow me,' she said, 'Mr Doig is waiting for you.' She marched ahead of them down a long corridor. There was a faint locker room smell about the place, but no sign of any kids. Presumably they were all in the classrooms.

Lexi and Tom exchanged glances. You could tell a lot about people's attitude to the police by the way in which they greeted you. Some were over-effusive, to cover nerves, while others wore a permanent expression of guilt on their faces, whether they were suspects or not. A few feigned disinterest – which generally meant they were bursting with curiosity. Mrs Donovan, according to her name badge, didn't bother to hide her interest, and Lexi suspected she would be listening closely at the keyhole of Doig's study while they spoke.

'In there,' said the secretary, pointing at a closed door with a brass plate screwed to it: *Headmaster's Office*. She didn't bother showing them in, but lingered shamelessly in the corridor as Lexi knocked on the door.

'Come,' said a voice from inside.

They went in and Lexi looked around. It wasn't quite how she remembered the headmaster's office from her old school. That had been vast and cavernous with dark wood panelling. This in contrast seemed bland and corporate, with office furniture straight out of a catalogue and no evidence of a personal touch beyond a clutch of degree certificates on the wall. The man standing up to greet them matched his surroundings – grey hair, grey suit and expressionless features.

'You're in charge of the case, are you?' he said. He shook his head. 'Such a mindless tragedy. All three of them showed enormous potential, and now we'll never know...'

'Mr Doig, we're doing all in our power to locate Paige Carter. We still have hopes of finding her alive.'

William Doig's expression showed that he wasn't convinced, and Lexi despised him for it. She explained to him why it was necessary for them to interview the children again, as well as any of the teachers who'd taught the Carter sisters. Tom produced the list of friends that the girls' parents had provided and asked if they could see the kids named on the list first.

Doig listened to all they had to say with pursed lips, shaking his head from time to time, but Lexi wasn't sure whether this was to indicate how broken up he was or out of pique at their demands.

Finally, he picked up the phone and asked his secretary to pull the first few students on the list out of class.

'The teachers all have full teaching timetables – you'll need to see them either first thing in the morning or at the end of the day.'

'I understand you've warned the students not to walk home on their own,' said Lexi.

'Naturally. And to report anything suspicious that they see.'

'Some of your students turned up at the Memorial Crown last night. They wanted to hold a vigil, but the area is still being treated as a crime scene. We had to turn them away.'

'I'm sorry. I can ask them to keep clear, if you like.'

Lexi shook her head. 'Not at all, Mr Doig. I totally understand the need to grieve as a community. As soon as my team has finished up there, I'll let you know. Then perhaps you can organise a more formal vigil for the students.'

Doig nodded. A sorrowful smile crossed his lips. 'Thank you, Inspector Bennett.'

'We'd better get on now,' said Lexi, always mindful of time, and of minutes wasted that could cost Paige Carter dearly.

William Doig found an empty classroom for them to use,

and moments later a small blonde girl appeared and sat down opposite them. Lexi led the questioning.

'You're Melanie Roper, right?'

The girl nodded and stared at her feet.

'Melanie, I understand you're a close friend of Paige Carter's.'

Melanie looked up, wide-eyed but silent.

Lexi gave her a smile of encouragement. 'It's all right, you're not in any trouble. We're just trying to learn a bit about all three girls.'

'We're not really friends,' the girl said. 'We were in junior school, but that was years ago.'

'Oh. What happened?'

'When we got here, she went off with the cool kids. She just didn't want to be friends with me anymore.'

Lexi remembered exactly how cruel pre-pubescent girls could be to each other.

'Okay,' said Tom, glancing at the list. 'Who would you say she was close friends with now?'

Melanie reeled off half a dozen names of both sexes. Lexi looked across at the piece of paper on the desk. None of the names Melanie mentioned matched the ones that the Carters had given them.

They let her go back to her classes.

Tom stashed the Carters' list back into his notebook. 'So much for their parents knowing anything about their lives. It's going to be a long afternoon.'

Lexi wasn't surprised. How many teenagers kept their parents even half up to date with the ebb and flow of adolescent friendships? She certainly hadn't.

There followed a succession of kids who, though no doubt voluble when hanging out with their mates, were entirely mono-syllabic. No information was volunteered – it had to be prised out of them, and what they did get featured multiple contradictions.

'God, it's like pulling teeth,' said Tom at one point. 'Sure, they're traumatised by what's happened, but don't they realise that details matter?' He was right. Somewhere in the minutiae of the three girls' lives lay the lead that they needed to crack the case.

'Lucy wasn't going out with anyone.'

'Eden was two-timing with Reggie and a boy in her history group.'

'Paige was gay. No, bi.'

'Eden worked in a bar at weekends.'

A friend of Lucy's told them that she often bunked off school on Friday afternoons. 'Sometimes a few of us would go and hang out in Whitefriars – you know, try things on in H&M, get some gear from Primark. But sometimes she just wanted to go off on her own. I think she was dating some guy who doesn't go here.'

They questioned her further on this, but the girl couldn't remember his name.

'Paige was into shoplifting.'

'I did modern dance with Eden – she was a legend.'

'Lucy was a slag.' This from a boy with acne and a mouthful of braces who Lexi guessed had been knocked back by her at some point.

'Give any credence to any of it?' she said, as Tom showed another kid the door.

He shrugged. 'The shoplifting?'

Lexi gave a wry laugh, but none of the kids had said anything that set alarm bells ringing in terms of the triplets' abduction. Apart from additional details of various sports clubs and a few mentions of cafés where the girls had hung out – drinking bubble tea, whatever the hell that was – it was mainly just playground gossip. They asked about boyfriends – whether any of the three was seeing anyone, and particularly Lucy, given the autopsy evidence. A couple of the boys had been out with one or other of them at points in the recent or not so recent past. Paige and Eden didn't appear to have current boyfriends. But Lucy's closest friends seemed to clam up at the question. No one admitted to knowing anything, but Lexi couldn't help but feel some of them were holding back.

She phoned Ridhi. 'I'm going to text you the names of a couple of cafés and a tennis club that Paige was a member of. I want you to visit them, show them a picture of the girls, and see if they can remember seeing anything unusual in the last week or so. Particularly if any of them came in with someone that might have been a boyfriend.'

'On it, boss.'

They had one more girl to see, apparently Eden's BFF.

A tall, lanky girl called Lisa came in, chewing gum and smelling strongly of cigarettes. They put the same questions to her. Eden wasn't seeing anyone, and she didn't know about Paige.

'What about Lucy?' said Lexi.

'Yeah, Lucy's been going out with Josh for almost a year.'

At last.

'Josh who?'

'Josh Pendleton. He's all right. Bit of an arrogant git, though. Quite a bit older than her – works at a garage on the Wincheap estate. She pretty much kept it a secret from everyone, though Eden told me.'

'Why so secretive about it?' As far as Lexi could remember, when any of her friends got boyfriends at that age they would never shut up about them. But it explained why none of the others had mentioned him by name.

Lisa shrugged. 'The age difference mostly – he's in his mid-twenties, and he's a bit rough. I think some of her mates had been a bit snobby about him in the past. A garage mechanic – and them all planning to go off to uni.'

'Finally, some sort of lead,' said Tom, once Lisa had gone.

Lexi wasn't so sure. Not one of Lucy's friends had even mentioned the possibility of his existence, though she'd impressed upon them the importance of even the smallest detail about boyfriends or any other men showing an interest in the girls. Maybe Lisa was the sort of girl who would embellish a story to get some attention. But if Lucy was seeing this somewhat older man, how did he fit with the profile that was starting to build in her head? And the suspicions that had swirled just out of sight as she'd lain awake in the darkness the previous night?

She took a deep breath. It was the main lead they had, so they needed to take it seriously.

'Right, time to track down Josh Pendleton.'

FOURTEEN

A quick call to Ridhi back in the incident room established that there was only one garage listed on the Wincheap industrial estate. At the same time, she tasked her to arrange interviews with the girls' teachers outside school hours.

Ten minutes later, Lexi pulled onto the forecourt of Slade Motors and got out of the car.

A middle-aged man with a paunch straining against his navy overalls looked up from the open bonnet of a pale green Honda Jazz.

Lexi walked over to him. 'Are you the manager?'

'You got a bookin'? We're full today, love.'

Lexi simply flashed her police ID in response.

'Right,' he said, wiping his hands on an oily rag hanging from one of his pockets. 'Yes, I'm the manager. What's your problem?'

'We're looking for Josh Pendleton,' said Lexi.

The manager looked at her, then glanced at Tom, who was leaning against the driver's door of the Jeep. Tom gave him a cheery salute that somehow managed to look menacing at the same time.

'He in trouble?'

'We'd just like to speak to him,' said Lexi, keeping her tone light.

'I sacked him on Saturday.'

'What for?'

'Basically, for being crap. He didn't show up for work on Friday, and it was one time too many.'

'But you saw him on Saturday?'

The man shook his head. 'No, he didn't come in Saturday morning either, so I called and left a message telling him not to bother coming back. Though I expect he will be back – I still owe him for a couple of days.'

'And you've got no idea why he didn't show up for work?'

'No, not this time. He'd done it before. Hung-over from clubbing all night was the usual excuse. But like I said, I didn't talk to him.'

'Have you got his home address?' said Tom.

'Yeah, in the office. Give me a mo.'

He went into a small office cubicle at the side of his work-shop. They could just see him through a grimy window, as he sat down at the desk and opened a clunky-looking laptop.

'Missed work on Friday,' said Tom. 'The day the girls went missing.'

The manager came back and handed Lexi a slip of paper with an address scrawled on it.

'Thanks.' She gave him a card. 'D'you know if he has a girlfriend?'

'He doesn't exactly confide in me. But I hear the lads' banter while they work. I'd say Josh is a player – always seems like there are plenty of girls interested in him.'

'But no one steady?'

'They come and go. A lot of drama. I don't think he treats them very well.'

'Will you let us know if you hear from him?'

He nodded, though somehow Lexi doubted he would.

Josh Pendleton apparently lived on Brymore Road.

'Know it?' said Lexi, passing the scrap of paper to Tom as they buckled their seat belts.

'Yeah, it's off Sturry Road. A couple of miles' drive from here.' Sturry Road was the main trunk out of town in the direction of Margate.

Ten minutes later they were ringing the door buzzer for a second-floor flat in a small 1970s block on Brymore Road. Hopefully they'd lay hands on the elusive Josh.

But there was no answer.

Lexi rang all the other bells in turn, until a woman's voice came over the intercom.

'Hello?'

'Kent Police here,' said Tom. 'We need access to check out one of the other flats. Can you let us in?'

There was a loud electrical buzz. Lexi leaned on the wire glass window of the door and it swung open.

'Thanks,' said Tom into the intercom, but the woman had already gone.

They made their way up two flights of stairs – no lift – and found the front door of Josh Pendleton's flat.

'Police. Open the door,' shouted Tom, banging on it with his fist.

No answer.

'What now?' he said. 'Paige Carter could be in there.'

'You think he's keeping her captive in a small flat?'

'Well...'

'I doubt it too,' said Lexi. 'But we need to check the place out. Do you think you can kick the door in, or shall I go down to the car and fetch the Enforcer?' The Enforcer was a small red battering ram designed to crash through locked doors in emergency situations.

'What about a warrant?' said Tom.

'We won't need one. If we have reason enough to believe that Paige Carter could be being held in this flat, then we're okay to enter without a search warrant.'

Tom went down to the car to fetch the Enforcer and a minute later they were inside the flat. It smelled of beer and cigarette smoke, and the carpet crunched underfoot. Like every bachelor pad anywhere, there were empty pizza cartons on the coffee table, half-full coffee cups on the kitchen counter, dirty plates in the sink and sour milk in the fridge. There was no sign of Josh Pendleton, or of any flatmates.

'Three bedrooms,' said Lexi after making a quick recce. 'The far one is Josh's.' She'd worked this out from a gym membership card on the bedside table. 'We'll search that one first. Can you call Emily Jordan? I want to know if there's any sign of any of the three Carter girls having been here – fingerprints, hair, DNA. Then call Flynn and put him onto finding the flatmates – they might know what's been going on with Pendleton.'

Tom went outside to get a signal.

Lexi spun round in the centre of Josh Pendleton's room. A book lying on the floor, half-obscured by a pair of gym shorts, caught her eye: *Helter Skelter*. She knew it well. It was the story of the Manson family murders, written by the lead prosecutor on the case. Flicking through it, she noticed various passages underlined in green ink. She paused and read a couple of them, descriptions of how the girls in the Manson family had murdered Sharon Tate and her friends in 1969, and then how they'd gone on to paint crude words on the walls with their victims' blood. Naturally, Lexi was familiar with the case, but the choice of the passages underlined made her blood run cold.

Multiple killings, posing... She dropped the book into an evidence bag.

She checked Josh's chest of drawers quickly – nothing but T-shirts, jeans, socks and pants – then opened the wardrobe. A few shirts and a leather jacket. A pair of black ankle boots with scuffed toes and worn-away heels. Hanging on the inside of the wardrobe door there was a calendar. Someone, presumably Josh, had been crossing off each of the days with a black marker pen. Up until the previous Thursday. None crossed off since Friday.

'Where are you, Josh? And where the hell is Paige?'

The room had no answer for her.

FIFTEEN

When you first come across a set of identical triplets, they all look exactly the same. Yes, that is stating the obvious – three human beings cleft from a single egg. But when you see more of them, you start to spot the tiny differences that mark them out as individuals.

Amber was the prettiest of the Bennett girls. She always was, even when Rose was still alive. Lexi was sporty even back then and now she has a hint of coarseness to her – all that running and cycling and swimming in dirty ponds. She's got muscles. Amber's more elegant. But Lexi's infinitely more interesting.

She was the first of the three Bennett girls I saw, and even on her own she fascinated me. But then I realised there were three of them – it literally blew my mind. I would watch them, captivated. After coming across them by chance, I began to seek them out. Sisters. Identical and intriguing. I could almost see the bond that flexed between them. Stretching away from one another but always drawn back.

This was a sibling bond I'd seen before. I had twin sisters and they were similarly close. Caught up in their own secret world. A secret language of in jokes and references only they could understand. I was excluded. They wouldn't let me join their special club, even though I begged and begged. They teased me. They whispered behind their hands and giggled. They ran away from me. They hid. But eventually they paid for it.

When I came across the Bennetts, all those feelings were stirred up again. I became addicted. I wanted them for myself. I wanted to be in the space in the middle, between those three bonds, even though I knew I never could be.

But most of all, I wanted Lexi. She was the glue that bound them so tightly together. And she was the wedge I was going to use to prise them apart. It was my pet project back then, watching triplets, watching twins. I was trying to work out how far you can stretch those bonds before they break. My sisters, the Bennetts, the Carters... all guinea pigs for me to play with.

Now I'm sitting by the window in the Bishop's Finger on St Dunstan's Street, slowly sipping a Coke. It's directly opposite Amber Bennett's office – she works for a small firm of accountants that occupy a swanky Georgian red-brick townhouse. I don't know what she does for them but I like to watch her work through the window. On winter afternoons, when the light's on in the first-floor office she shares with another woman, I can see her sitting at her desk. She types furiously, drinks coffee, speaks on the phone and eats the occasional biscuit, with a guilty grin at her colleague.

She seems to have grown up well, become a responsible member of society. I'm sure that she has lasting scars from what I did, but they don't manifest themselves in her outward appearance.

I've kept track of her all these years as well as Lexi. I feel a sort of responsibility towards them. The bond between the three of us will never be undone, so I like to keep an eye on them both.

My two princesses. I always knew I'd come for them again. For Lexi. And that time is close.

The light in Amber's office goes off and I look at my watch. Five thirty. I finish my cola and emerge from the pub at the same time Amber leaves. She turns to the right without looking around, and I cross the road and fall into step a few feet behind her on the narrow pavement. I can smell her perfume. She's heading towards the centre of town. That's not where her car is parked, but this evening she'll go and listen to her son singing in the cathedral choir before picking up her daughter and driving home.

I've made a study of her life. I know her daily and weekly habits. Hers, and her children's. Being in the choir means that her son, Sam, lives in the cathedral grounds in Choir House and goes to St Edmund's School. He's twelve, and away from home most of the time, which is something that puzzles me – is Amber happy to be separated from her boy that much? When Amber goes to listen to choir practice, I quite often sneak in and sit at the back, a few rows behind her, and listen too. The boys' voices are truly uplifting.

I will admit that some of the things I do are audacious. Following her through town, just a few steps behind. Watching her watch choir practice or sports matches – the boy plays football and the girl hockey and netball. Browse the books that she's just browsed as I stalk her through the library.

But there's no chance she'll recognise me. She never saw my face back then. And there's no chance she'll recognise me now because I've got one of those eminently forgettable faces. People never recognise me from a previous encounter. I know that from work.

She passes through the Westgate and hurries along the High Street, heels clacking. Although it's dark now, most of the shops are still open. There are bright lights and enough people around for her not to realise she's being followed. We turn left down

Mercery Lane, past the souvenir and sweet shops, to cut through to Christchurch Gate into the cathedral precinct. They charge tourists a fortune to come in here, but when we show our Precinct Passes, they let us in free, recognising us both as locals. It might technically qualify as a city, but Canterbury is like a large village at times.

We sit, just a few feet away from each other, for nearly an hour, before the rehearsal finishes and she spends a few minutes with her boy before he goes back to his boarding house. I watch Amber with her children, and it makes me feel sad. I wonder what it's like to have such a blessed childhood. A mother that cares as much as she does. Maybe I'm jealous.

I follow her back towards her office, to where her car is parked.

I'll burst their bubble soon enough.

SIXTEEN

Two girls dead. Two people missing. And so far, virtually no evidence.

Lexi called the incident room as she and Tom left Josh Pendleton's flat. Colin Flynn answered. He sounded sleepy, but Lexi wasn't surprised. Running checks on ANPR records was about as dull as it got, and she reminded herself to find him and Ridhi something more active soon to keep them on their toes.

'Colin, put out an APB on Josh Pendleton. He was Lucy's boyfriend, and no one seems to have seen him since Friday. Didn't turn up for work, no sign of him at home. Do a Holmes check on him in case he's got priors and find out if he has a car, and check it against all your ANPR files.'

More deskwork, in other words.

Colin grunted and Lexi could tell he wasn't thrilled by the assignment.

She and Tom got back into the car.

'Eden worked at a pub at weekends. Did you get the name of it from the Carters?'

Tom got out his notebook and thumbed through the pages. 'The Brewer's Arms.'

'I know it.' Lexi remembered it from her own youth. 'Spit and sawdust. A pretty seventeen-year-old working behind that bar is sure to have attracted the wrong sort of attention.'

It only took them ten minutes to drive from Josh Pendleton's flat to the Brewer's Arms.

'Okay, let's go,' she said.

Inside, there was little notable about the place – low beamed ceilings, a few horse brasses on the walls, a small fireplace and the smell of stale beer wafting up from a red-patterned carpet. Lexi had spent her late teenage years sneaking in and out of pubs like this. She knew she'd been here, drinking alcopops with her mates, though she couldn't remember anything specific. Now, however, early afternoon on a weekday, the clientele was notably older and all male.

A scrawny young woman, though not as young as Eden, was emptying a glasswasher behind the bar. She held up a pint glass to the light and, seeing it was cracked, tossed it into a black plastic bin behind her. The smash of glass made a couple of the punters look up from their pints, but only held their attention for a second or two.

'What can I get you?' she said, as Tom and Lexi approached the bar. She was chewing gum and sported a nose piercing.

Lexi held out her ID card. 'I'd like to speak to your boss.'

The girl immediately looked worried, and Lexi wondered why. Had the pub broken some minor licensing regulation? She couldn't care less.

'Dom?' she called through a doorway behind the bar. 'Can you come out here?'

'No, I'm in the middle of changing a barrel.' There was an echoey quality to the reply – the voice's owner was clearly down in the cellar. He sounded grumpy.

'We'll wait,' said Lexi. She looked around, taking good note of the pub's half dozen or so customers – probably regulars, which meant they'd likely been served by Eden. Could one of them have developed an obsession for her? None of them looked particularly shifty, even though they had probably already guessed that she and Tom were cops.

Tom tapped a cardboard beer mat impatiently on the bar. Impatient. Driven to make forward progress with the case. Lexi liked that about him.

The manager seemed to be taking his time, but eventually a large man appeared in the doorway at the back of the bar. He had a beer gut that hung over the top of his jeans, but his arms were well-muscled enough to handle any drunken trouble. His short black hair morphed into heavy black stubble on his chin, and his eyebrows were dark and luxuriant. A middle-aged Heathcliff, Lexi thought to herself.

'DI Bennett,' she said, flashing her ID again. 'I assume you know why we're here.'

The landlord looked bemused and shook his head. 'Um, no. Enlighten me.'

Beside her, Tom drew himself up to his full height.

'You know, don't you, that one of your barmaids has been murdered, and her sister is still missing?' said Tom.

'What? Who exactly?'

'Eden Carter,' said Lexi.

Dom nodded. 'I know the name – those three girls that have been in the news. But none of them worked here.'

It was Lexi's turn to be puzzled. 'Eden Carter didn't work here?' She looked at Tom.

'Brewer's Arms, that's what her parents told us,' said Tom.

'She's never worked here? You're sure about that?' Lexi pressed.

Dom wasn't impressed. 'It's my gaff. I know who works for me.'

Lexi realised she could demand his employee records or his payroll, but she had no reason to disbelieve him. If he was lying to them, it would be too easy to disprove. There was no point.

'Thank you,' she said. 'Our mistake.'

Out in the car park, she wasn't quite so calm. 'What the hell?'

'Either she lied to her parents, or her parents lied to us. Which do you think more likely?'

'Oh, I know exactly who was lying. She even told her friends she had a bar job. But then what was she doing, and where, when she claimed she was working at the pub?'

Back at the station, Lexi went straight to her office and switched on her laptop. There was an email from Maggie wanting an update, and several messages from journalists wanting an interview or a statement on the case. They would have to wait. She put in a quick call to the PR department in Maidstone to demand they keep the press off her back. Her stomach rumbled and she checked her watch. It was mid-afternoon and she hadn't eaten since breakfast. A canteen sandwich was hardly appealing but it would have to do.

As she returned to her office with a triangular cardboard package purporting to be an egg sandwich, she found Ridhi waiting in the doorway.

'Come in. What are you working on at the moment?'

'Following up the response to the presser.'

'Anything?'

'One good lead out of dozens of useless ones. A woman claims to have seen one of the triplets – she couldn't say which, not surprisingly – walking along Orchard Street with a man. They seemed to be arguing.'

'About what?'

'She wasn't close enough to hear.'

'What time did she see them?'

'Early afternoon. Friday.'

'Have you interviewed her yet?'

'We spoke on the phone, and I'm going to go round to see her shortly.'

'Excellent work, Ridhi. It could be Lucy and her boyfriend, Josh Pendleton. See if you can get a photo of Pendleton from social media and show it to the witness.'

'We've checked Lucy's social media, and there are no pictures of her with a boyfriend at all.'

'I suppose that makes sense, given she seemed to be keeping her relationship with Josh secret. Get onto Pendleton's Facebook account, okay?'

'Will do.'

If a row with the boyfriend had resulted in a violent altercation, it could have kicked off a series of events that culminated in Lucy and Eden's murders. But why would Pendleton still be holding Paige? And despite the underlining she'd seen in Josh's copy of *Helter Skelter*, if he had killed the girls, why would he have left them up on the Crown dressed as princesses? Nothing about this case was making sense.

'And any luck on suspect vehicles?'

Ridhi shook her head. 'Do you know how many vans there are driving around Canterbury on the average day?'

'No.'

'Nor do I, but every single one of them was spotted by someone.'

'You're collating the sightings with where each of the girls was last seen?'

'Yes.' She said it with an air of finality that suggested nothing had come of it.

It was tedious work, and Lexi wanted Ridhi to get more hands-on experience. 'Okay, leave that for now. I've asked to see one of Eden's school friends again – Lisa Atkinson, who first told us that Lucy was seeing Josh. Why don't you come with me?'

Ridhi's face immediately brightened. 'Of course. That

would work well – I've got an appointment to see Lucy's class teacher, Mrs George, in an hour's time.'

They drove to the Academy and Lisa was brought to the same room they'd been given earlier.

Lexi introduced Ridhi and then asked if it was okay to go over a couple more questions.

'Anything to get out of double maths,' said Lisa.

Ridhi smiled conspiratorially at the girl. 'With you on that – always hated maths lessons.'

Lexi liked the way she was building rapport with the interview subject. Ridhi had the potential to be a skilled detective with time.

'What did you want to ask me about?' She sounded nervous, and it made Lexi wonder if she'd held something back last time they spoke.

'A member of the public has reported to us that they saw Lucy arguing with a man on the street, early on Friday afternoon. We think that man is likely to have been Josh Pendleton. Can you tell us any more about their relationship?'

Lisa bit down on her lower lip. 'I only know what Eden told me. I didn't really know Lucy well, and I've never met Josh.'

'That's okay,' said Lexi. 'Just tell us what Eden said.'

'She said they fought a lot. Josh was always putting pressure on Lucy to do things that would have got her into trouble with her parents.'

'Like skipping school?'

'Yes, and going to the pub. He was a bit of an alky, apparently. Eden thought they sometimes took drugs.'

'What sort of drugs?' said Ridhi.

Lisa shrugged. 'I don't know.'

'Do you know if he was ever violent towards her?'

Lisa breathed out and looked around. It was as if she was weighing up in her mind whether to say something or not.

Ridhi put a hand onto Lisa's knee. 'You're not telling tales, and this isn't a courtroom. What you say to us here won't go any further.' That wasn't quite true, but Lexi didn't comment.

'Lucy came into school once with a black eye, and her cheek was all bruised. She said she'd walked into a door and of course no one believed that. I know some people thought Josh had done it.'

'What did Eden say?'

'That she didn't believe Lucy, and that Lucy had lied to her and their parents about what had happened.'

It wouldn't sound good for Josh Pendleton if this story came out, but did it tag him as a murderer? Maybe it was one brick in the case they would need to build.

'One other thing, Lisa,' said Lexi. 'Eden's job – do you know the name of the pub she worked in on Friday and Saturday evenings?'

Lisa's kohl-rimmed eyes widened for a second, then she shook her head. 'Can't remember.'

'She never mentioned it?'

'Not really. She didn't want us all piling in when she was working, so she kept quiet about it.'

Lexi could tell she was lying. There was more to it than that, she felt sure. 'You'll let me know if you remember?'

Lisa nodded, unconvincingly. She didn't have anything else to add, so they reluctantly let her return to class.

They had ten minutes before Ridhi was due to speak to Mrs George.

'I'll get back to the station now. You okay to get the bus back?'

'No problem.'

'Walk me to my car,' said Lexi. 'Make sure you ask her about her impressions of Lucy's life outside school – some teachers can have a pretty good read on what's going on in their pupils' lives.'

Ridhi nodded, then caught Lexi's eye. 'Boss, can I ask you

about something?' They were standing on the path along the edge of the teachers' car park.

'Shoot,' said Lexi.

'Colin said you were one of triplets and...' She paused.

Lexi knew why. What could she say? '...*and one of your sisters was murdered*'? Both Ridhi and Colin were probably too young to remember the news at the time, but the station rumour-mill would have gone into overdrive with the Carter girls' abduction and murder.

'You want to know what happened?'

Ridhi gave an embarrassed nod, as if she'd been caught with her fingers in the cookie jar. 'If it's okay. Triplets is a coincidence. Your story might shine a light on the current case.'

'Fair enough. My sisters, Rose and Amber, and I were abducted and held for several days by a man who threatened to kill us.' Lexi took a deep breath. She hated telling their story to strangers, but she had to remain detached. She always kept it to the bare bones minimum. 'Amber and I got away. Rose didn't. She was never seen again, and the man was never apprehended.'

'My God!' Ridhi's hand went to her mouth. 'What do you think happened to her?'

People always asked the least appropriate questions when they were shocked, but Lexi had constructed a tough shell around her feelings to deflect them. 'I don't like to think about that, Ridhi.'

'Oh God, no – I'm sorry. I can't imagine what it must be like to lose a sister. I don't know where I'd be without my sister.'

'Older or younger?' said Lexi, shifting the conversation onto safer ground.

'Younger. Meera. She wants to join the police too. I'm sorry for prying.'

'It's fine. It was a long time ago.' *As if that made a difference.* 'Obviously, there are some parallels between what happened to me and my sisters and what's happened to the Carter sisters. That doesn't mean that I think it's the same perp, but it could be a copycat.'

Ridhi nodded in agreement.

'We need to keep an open mind and track down every lead.'

Her mobile rang. It was Maggie – too impatient to wait for an answer to her email. She waved Ridhi back to the school building and took the call.

'Finally,' said Maggie.

'Sorry. I was talking to a witness.'

'Fair enough. Sorry to hound you, but I need to know what's going on. And, more importantly, how you're coping.'

'We're following up the girls' friends to try and get leads on Josh Pendleton, Lucy's boyfriend. He's been missing since the day they were taken.'

'You think he's involved?'

'It's possible.'

'And how are you feeling?'

'I'm in the car with Ridhi.' It was a blatant lie, but it would excuse her from answering the question. 'It's all good, and I'll update you as soon as there's anything more to report.' She hung up despite Maggie's protestations.

She got into the car and pulled out of the car park. It was great having someone like Maggie to watch her back, but at times her concern could be a little stifling – as if she didn't trust her to stay detached and follow where the evidence led. It made Lexi even more determined to dot every *i* and cross every *t* to make sure she didn't miss anything important.

Back at the station, she went straight to the incident room.

'Listen up, team. I want Josh Pendleton logged as a person of interest – possibly a suspect in the Carter murders. He was seeing Lucy Carter, but we've had reports that he was something of a player, and also suggestions that he might have been abusive to Lucy. He didn't show up at work last Friday, the same day that the girls went missing. Finding out when his flat-mates last saw him is now a top priority.' There was a flurry of movement as people took notes.

'You think he did it, boss?' said Colin.

'He's our best lead at the moment,' said Tom. 'His disap-pearance is too much of coincidence not to put him in the frame.'

'We drew a blank on Eden's job at the Brewer's Arms,' said Lexi, 'so we need to find out how she was spending the time when she told her parents she was at work. Tom, you come with me. We'd better talk to the Carters again, press them a little harder.'

'Sure, boss,' said Tom. His glum face told Lexi he didn't relish the prospect.

'Paige Carter has been missing for too long now. Time's just about running out.'

SEVENTEEN

The Carters were sitting on two armchairs, opposite each other in their living room. Tom and Lexi sat perpendicular to them on a plush, dark green sofa that still smelled new. The house smelled of recent cooking – it was nearly seven o'clock, so they'd probably just finished their supper. Philippa, the FLO, was in the kitchen making everyone the requisite cup of tea.

How many of those had she made in the line of duty, Lexi wondered.

Tom cleared his throat. They'd agreed that he should kick off the questions.

'Mr Carter, Mrs Carter, are you completely certain that Eden worked at the Brewer's Arms? You couldn't have mixed it up for another pub, like, say, the Draper's Arms?'

Both of them shook their heads. Andrew Carter spoke. 'No, I'm certain it was the Brewer's – she'd been there a few months.'

'Right,' said Tom. 'You see, when we checked at the Brewer's Arms, they had no record of her working there.'

'But that can't be right,' said Joanne Carter.

'I'm afraid we think that your daughter lied to you about the job.'

It was hard to say which one of them looked more shocked, but Andrew Carter expressed his indignation out loud.

'That's absolute nonsense. Why would Eden lie about where she worked?'

Philippa came in and placed a tea tray on the coffee table, but sensing the mood in the room, stepped back in silence.

'Eden wasn't the sort of girl who lied,' said Joanne.

The best liars never are, thought Lexi. She stretched forward to place a comforting hand on the distraught woman's arm. 'Can you think of anything she ever said or did that suggested she might have been hiding something?'

'No,' said Andrew Carter. It was clear that he was shutting down the conversation.

Philippa stepped forward and raised the teapot. 'Tea?'

'Thank you,' said Lexi. 'Just one other thing.'

Joanne nodded.

'One of the girls' friends said Lucy came into school with a black eye a little while ago. Can you tell us what happened?'

'If you're trying to imply...' Andrew Carter's hackles were rising.

'I'm not implying anything,' said Lexi firmly. 'I just need to verify certain facts. There's been the suggestion that she was seeing someone, an older guy called Josh Pendleton. Do you know anything about this?'

Joanne Carter shook her head and looked confused.

'Never heard of him,' said Andrew. 'I remember when she got the black eye. Someone hit her in the face with a basketball, close up.'

Joanne nodded. 'That's right. That's how it happened.'

Lexi nodded too. She didn't want to tarnish their daughter's memory more than was necessary. 'Would you mind if we took a quick look around Eden's room?'

'A couple of your colleagues have already looked at all three girls' rooms,' said Andrew, resentfully.

'Yes, I understand that. But they might have missed something important. I think it would help if DS Olsen and I took another look. We want to leave no stone unturned.'

They extricated themselves and went upstairs, following Philippa's directions.

'Those were the days, eh?' said Tom. 'Lying to your parents about where you were and what you were doing. And who with.'

'You did a lot of that?' said Lexi.

'Just my fair share. Every teenager does.'

'To a certain extent. But it looks to me like Eden and Lucy were both running rings round them.'

They went into a bedroom that looked like virtually any other seventeen-year-old girl's bedroom – nearly everything was pink, there were stuffed toys on the bed and posters of pop stars Lexi didn't recognise on the walls. She went to the bedside table and opened the drawer. She didn't know what she was hoping to find – just something that might lead them to something else. Or someone... But it yielded nothing of interest. There were some pots of face cream and tubes of acne gel, a comb with a couple of broken prongs, hair elastics, tweezers, a torch with a flat battery. No diary, no condoms, no notes from boyfriends.

'Anything?' she said to Tom, who was rifling through the wardrobe.

'Nothing here.' He pulled down a shoe box from the top shelf and put it on the bed before opening it.

Lexi watched over his shoulder, hoping it would be a trove of photos or love letters.

'Just trainers,' said Tom. He tipped them out on the bed. A silver, star-shaped keyring fell out with them.

Lexi snatched it up. 'No keys.'

'Wait,' said Tom. 'Give it to me.'

Lexi handed it to him.

'I thought so. It's from the Pole Star.'

'You're kidding!'

The Pole Star was Canterbury's most notorious pole dancing club.

'What do you make of it?' said Tom, as soon as they were back in Lexi's Crossfire.

'It might mean nothing,' said Lexi. 'She could have found it in the street. Or perhaps Andrew Carter brought it into the house and she took it.'

'But you don't believe that, do you?'

'I'm not going to jump to any conclusions at this point, but, if...'

'If that was where she was working rather than the Brewer's Arms? It would certainly explain why she lied to her parents.'

'If that's the case – and it's a massive if at this point – if she was working there, or had some other connection to the club, then it's hugely significant. Strippers and sex workers are targeted for sexual assault. And if Colin Flynn had done his bloody job properly, we might have found this sooner...'

She left the implication hanging in the air, but it was clear what she meant.

Tom looked out of the window, then back at her. 'That's not really fair, boss,' he said quietly. 'When he and Ridhi searched Eden's room, they didn't even know she claimed to have the job in the pub.'

Lexi gunned the engine furiously. 'It doesn't matter what they *knew* at the time. The point of the search was to discover more, and this might be pretty damn critical. Colin was the more experienced officer and he should have checked it out.'

She turned off the ring road onto Wincheap, heading out towards the industrial estate. Like a lot of so-called 'gentlemen's clubs', the Pole Star was located in the commercial area on the edge of town.

Neither of them spoke as she wound her way between the warehouses and factory units.

'If Eden was dancing at the club, there's a high possibility that it was what brought them into the killer's range,' she said eventually.

'Why do you say that?'

'Because serial killers target sex workers. It fits with their Madonna-whore world view. If he latched onto Eden and started stalking her, it wouldn't take him long to realise she had two sisters. Three for the price of one.'

'But Lucy and Eden didn't show any evidence of sexual assault.'

'You're right – they didn't. But their murders had all the hallmarks of an escalating serial killer. It's not about sexual gratification, it's about domination and fear.'

She stopped talking. Her heart was racing. This was the break they needed and with any luck, the Pole Star would point the investigation in a new direction.

'So does that let Josh Pendleton off the hook?'

'No, not at all. No one's off the hook until we know for sure that they had an alibi. Having multiple leads isn't a bad thing. In fact, it makes it more likely that we'll find out what happened and find Paige.'

Five minutes later, she pulled up outside an anonymous-looking single-storey building, the walls of which were entirely black glass. There was a double door at the front and above it a spangled silver sign read *Pole Star*. The black glass doors were decorated with constellations of silver stars which, Lexi realised as they got closer, were in the form of dancing girls with big breasts.

'Nice,' she said, pulling a face.

Tom grinned. 'Didn't have it pegged as your type of place.'

'And hopefully yours neither.'

'Uh, no way. Maybe if the dancers were guys, but still probably not.'

Lexi had wondered but had been too polite to ask. So Tom was gay – not that it made any difference.

She pulled open the door and they were enveloped into darkness. The lighting was low, presumably to protect anonymity, and Lexi had to wait for her eyes to adjust before she could see that they were in a narrow reception area. All the walls were hung with black velvet curtains, making it difficult to work out how to get further into the club – until a slit of light appeared and a young woman slipped through and went to stand by the counter.

Before she could speak, Tom thrust his ID card at her.

'I'm DS Olsen and this is DI Bennett, Kent Police,' he said. 'Can we talk to your boss?'

The girl scowled. 'I'll go and check.'

She disappeared between the curtains. As far as Lexi was concerned there was no question as to whether the boss would talk to them, so she followed the girl through the gap.

They emerged onto the main floor of the club which, apart from the stage area, was just as dark. She could just make out a ring of tables close to the stage, while booths lined the walls. There were figures at several of the tables, men, mostly sitting on their own, faces raised towards the stage where two topless girls in tiny silver thongs were twisting sinuously around gleaming chrome poles. The men's eyes shone in the reflected light and Lexi could see the undisguised lust in their expressions.

Could one of them be the man that had taken the Carter girls?

The receptionist changed direction and went towards the bar that ran down one wall of the club. She said something to the barman – Lexi couldn't hear what over the throbbing music – and he went to a door behind the bar.

The girl looked round and realised Lexi and Tom had followed her. She didn't look pleased, but she wasn't about to start an argument. That would be above her pay grade.

Lexi was taken aback when a middle-aged woman in a sequinned dress appeared.

'I am the manager here. I understand you are from the police?' She had an Eastern European accent that Lexi couldn't place.

'That's right,' said Lexi. 'Can I take your name?'

'Nikki Kovalenko. Now, what is this concerning?' She moved a bit further up the bar to ensure they were out of earshot of a man who'd come to order a drink.

'We have reason to believe that you employed a girl called Eden Carter. Is that so?'

A muscle tightened in Kovalenko's jaw. She swallowed, then nodded. 'Yes, she worked here.'

Lexi noticed that she used the past tense. 'You've heard what happened?'

'I saw it on the news... I saw you talking about it. She's dead now, yes?'

'She is. You realise that she was a minor?'

'No, I did not know that. I wouldn't have employed her if I had known she was under eighteen.'

The woman's response was so casual that Lexi was finding it hard to bite back her anger. 'And when one your employees turned up murdered, you didn't think to get in touch with us?'

At least now she had the decency to look sheepish. 'I don't know anything about what happened to her, so what would you expect me to tell you?'

'Anything you did know about her. How long had she worked for you?'

'Two, three months,' said Kovalenko with a shrug.

'And you didn't ask her to provide ID when you employed her?' said Tom. His words were clipped.

Kovalenko rolled her eyes. 'All the kids have fake IDs these days.'

She hadn't answered the question.

'What did Eden do here?' Lexi prayed that she had simply worked behind the bar, or even better, just collecting or washing glasses.

'She was a dancer. She had a real talent.'

Lexi glanced sideways towards the stage. The suggestive movements of the women draped around the poles were not something a seventeen-year-old should have been aping. The men's eyes lapped up every thrust and gyration. She fully accepted an adult woman's right to be a sex worker, but the exploitation of underage girls was a completely different matter.

She turned back to Kovalenko on a wave of fury.

'Turn the music off.'

'What?'

'You heard me. Turn off the music. I'm closing you down.' She glanced at Tom, who gave her an approving nod. 'Get the rest of the team out here. I want all the dancers interviewed, then all the punters. If it turns out that a single one of them showed a glimmer of interest in Eden Carter, take them back to the station for further questioning.'

Kovalenko took hold of Lexi's wrist.

'Please, you can't do this to me. My boss...'

Lexi twisted her arm out of Kovalenko's clasp. 'I just did,' she said.

EIGHTEEN

I knew it wouldn't take Lexi long to discover Eden Carter's dirty little secret. She was such a peach of a girl and she knew how to use her body. Those sad inadequate creatures that frequented the Pole Star didn't stand a chance. I used to watch her dance and I'd watch the men watching her. Wide-eyed and slack-mouthed. Deep breathing and squirming in their chairs.

I felt like I should save her from herself, before she became too soiled by the environment she was working in. But I liked her dancing too much.

Today, of course, I'm not watching Eden bumping and grinding on the pole. When Lexi and her hapless sidekick left the Carters, I followed them. I had a bit of time before I was due at work, and if they were heading back to the police station, we would be going in the same direction. But then, when they took the turn out towards Wincheap, I couldn't resist seeing what they were up to. What might Andrew and Joanne have divulged that would send them out here?

Pulling up across the road from the club, I watch them go inside. I presume Eden's parents had no idea she worked here, but something has given it away. A few minutes later, I follow them in.

The manager comes out to talk to them. She's an absolute dragon when she needs to be – if one of the johns is bothering one of her girls – but with Lexi, she's showing a whole different attitude. Lexi's the dragon.

I slide up to the bar and, keeping my body turned away, I order a Coke. I should be at work by now. I'll certainly be late, but at least my breath won't stink of alcohol.

I still can't hear their words, but the temperature's rising. Lexi turns and watches the girls on the poles for a couple of seconds, face as dark as thunder.

I know what's coming, so I slip away, leaving my drink on a table, heading straight for the exit. As I escape through the slit in the velvet curtain, the music stops abruptly. I jog across to my car. No one in the club knows my name. I've always paid cash and I won't be going back. I don't think they'll come looking for me.

Not yet, anyway.

NINETEEN

Lexi leaned back in her chair, raised her arms above her head and stretched her spine. The wall clock read ten p.m. Her body was both tired and in need of exercise, while her brain was fizzing, jumping from one thought to the next as she tried to make sense of the case so far.

Coffee. Perhaps that would bring clarity.

She went through to the incident room to fetch one. Colin Flynn was standing by his desk, putting things in his briefcase. Knocking off for the evening, while everyone else was still working. Lexi bristled.

'You know, Colin, if you'd done your job properly when you searched Eden's room, we might have been a bit further along with this case than we are now.'

Colin, and everyone else in the room, stared at her. 'What?'

'That keyring from the Pole Star. You missed it.'

His eyes widened and he gave her a defiant shrug. 'Saw it – but it's just a keyring, no keys on it. How was I to know it was from a strip club, or that she might have been working there?'

'It's our job to question everything we see.' She knew she

was being unreasonable, but she felt so frustrated at their lack of progress.

Tom was still hunched at his desk, but now he looked up at her. 'Coffee break, Lexi?'

She nodded. Everyone was tired and tempers were frayed, but that didn't make it all right to take it out on the team. Tom was right to intervene. They'd all spent the last hour writing up the reports on the interviews with the dancers and customers from the Pole Star that they'd rounded up earlier in the evening, and it was fair enough for Colin to be calling it a night if he'd finished his work.

She glanced back at Colin. 'Sorry. That was a little unfair of me.' Then she spoke up to address the whole room. 'Get home now, everybody, and get a good night's sleep. I need you back here first thing in the morning ready to go.'

There were a few murmurs of 'Goodnight, boss,' and the team filed out.

'Anything from your batch?' said Lexi, as she and Tom stood waiting by the coffee machine. The ones she'd spoken to hadn't given her any information of value.

'Eden was well-liked among the dancers – they seemed to view her as something of a mascot,' said Tom. 'One of them told me she was doing it to save up for drama school, because her parents wouldn't pay for it.'

'What about the johns?'

'Half the punters I spoke to pretended they didn't know one dancer from another, while the other half thought she was too young and claimed to be more interested in the older women who worked there – by which I mean the ones in their early twenties.'

'It's the first of those groups that will bear further scrutiny,' said Lexi.

'Also, Eden didn't dance during the daytime, just on Friday and Saturday evenings – which means mostly office dos and stag parties, though there were some regulars we still need to interview.'

'Who told you that?'

'One of the dancers.'

Lexi had interviewed the manager, Nikki Kovalenko. 'The queen bee wasn't so forthcoming about which punters favoured which dancers.'

Tom frowned. 'If I have anything to do with it, she'll never open those doors again.'

Lexi raised an eyebrow. She hadn't realised Tom would feel so strongly about it.

'I've got a daughter,' he said. 'Billie, nine years old, and if I thought anyone was exploiting her in that way, I'd...' He pressed his lips together, but Lexi knew exactly what he'd want to do. She got it.

'Put together whatever we need to charge her for employing a minor and pass it on to the CPS.'

'Try and stop me,' muttered Tom.

Lexi picked up her coffee and headed back to her office. It appeared that someone else was burning the midnight oil – there was an email in her inbox from Greg Chambers. He was the cyber forensics analyst tasked with examining the iPad that had been retrieved from Paige's bedroom. There was a link in the email that would allow Lexi to examine the contents.

Seconds later she was scanning the list of apps the iPad contained. All the usual – camera, photos, weather, clock, Gmail, calendar, iTunes, games, TikTok, Twitter, WhatsApp, contacts, Instagram, mobile banking – and plenty more she didn't immediately recognise. A window into Paige's life. Where to start...

She opened Paige's Gmail inbox and scrolled through it. A few emails from school – assignment instructions from teachers, details of sports fixtures and the like. Plenty of junk mail, hundreds of beauty product offers and cheap clothing sales mostly expired or out of date but never deleted. Lexi flipped over to check the sent emails. Hardly any. It appeared that Paige didn't see email as a primary communication tool.

She clicked on the WhatsApp icon and a split screen opened – a list of conversations on the left-hand side and the current conversation on the right-hand side. The current chat was a group made up of Paige, a girl called Ellen they'd interviewed at the Academy and another girl called Saz. Lexi wondered if this was a shortening of Suzanne – there had been a Suzanne among the girls they'd spoken to. She made a note to get Ridhi to check that in the morning.

The chat between the three girls was long-running, dating from some point on Friday morning before Paige had gone missing to a point a few months before when one of them had set up the little group of three. Lexi read the most recent entries, trying to work out their own private slang and making a note of the names of anyone else they referred to. Saz seemed to constantly moan about a boy or man called Otis who she appeared to be dating on and off. There was a lot of talk of breakups and makeups and endless crying emojis. There were plenty of derogatory comments about other girls from all three of them, including Paige bitching about Lucy and Eden, and lots of arrangements to meet up at McDonald's or other fast-food joints around town. It made for tedious reading and if it hadn't been for the much-needed injection of caffeine, Lexi might have dozed off. She jotted down the names of a couple of boys Paige referred to, but they seemed to be just in passing. But on several of her posts she mentioned a mysterious 'He' or 'Him', always capitalised, who Lexi couldn't identify.

She switched over to a chat group between Paige and her two sisters. Arrangements to meet. Moans about their parents. Minor spats. Criticism of their friends – Paige seemed as happy to run down Ellen and Saz to her sisters as she had been to run down her sisters to Ellen and Saz. Eden mentioned the PS a few times – presumably the Pole Star. Lucy chronicled her relationship with Josh Pendleton, which seemed as bumpy as the one between Saz and Otis. She noticed that Paige made no mention of the mystery man to her sisters. Curious.

She scanned the other chats near the top of the list. Other friend groups plus individual chats with some of them, netball and hockey teams, occasional messages from her mother or father, usually checking in where she was or whether she'd be home for a particular meal. Just as she was close to calling it a night, Lexi opened a final chat with someone identified as 'MM'.

The posts were infrequent, but definitely flirtatious. MM was male, and each snippet of conversation seemed to be initiated by him sending her a compliment or asking her something.

MM: You looked sexy today

Paige: No way. I looked a mess

MM: New lipstick?

Paige: Strawberry crush

MM: It made your lips look kissable

Paige: But not for you

Lexi read on. Low-level flirtation that had been going on for weeks. No one had reported that Paige had a boyfriend, and there was nothing in this exchange relating to dates or meeting up. Paige always responded, but reading between the lines, it seemed as if she sometimes felt uncomfortable with the attention.

'Tom!' Lexi ran to the door of the incident room. 'I might be onto something.'

Tom was in the act of pulling on his coat. His briefcase stood on his desk, ready for departure. He turned quickly. 'What?'

'Paige was WhatsApping with an unidentified male. Come and look.'

They went back to Lexi's office and Tom bent over the desk to study her screen.

'Look,' he said, 'a reference to how she looked in class. This was going on in school.'

'Yes, and further up here—' Lexi scrolled through the exchange '—she mentions biology prep. So maybe someone in her biology group. Have you got a list of all the classes the girls attended?'

'On my desk – I'll get it.'

He was back within a minute. Lexi took the paper from his hand and scanned the class lists until she found Paige's biology group. There were fourteen of them in the class, studying for A level biology. Nine boys and five girls. She checked the boys' names.

'None of them have the initials MM,' she said.

'Maybe it's a nickname?' said Tom.

They'd hit a dead end.

'Right, we'll have to get in touch with the phone company. But also I'll call the biology teacher first thing to see if they can shed any light on it,' said Lexi. She checked the page for the teacher's name.

And it all became obvious.

'Shit.' The messages took on a completely different complexion.

'What?'

'The teacher. He's called Mike Madison. He's the MM we're looking for.'

TWENTY

Tom reached out a finger and pressed the doorbell. Lexi heard a set of chimes going off somewhere beyond. At close to midnight, it came as no surprise that there was no answer. Tom pressed again, keeping his finger on the bell for longer this time.

Glass panels on either side of the front door showed a light going on somewhere inside. The Madisons were home. A few seconds later the front door swung open.

'Yes?' It was a small boy, maybe six years old, in his pyjamas, sticky eyes and tousled hair suggesting he'd been asleep.

Lexi bent down to talk to him. 'Hello there, is your dad at home?'

She heard the sound of footsteps thudding down the stairs.

A woman's voice cut across her question. 'Oli, what are you doing? Go back to bed. I've told you so many times. Don't open the door – wait for me or Daddy, okay?'

Oli looked back over his shoulder as his mother approached.

'I'm sorry,' said the woman, shoeing the boy back from the doorway. She pulled a towelling dressing gown tighter round her body. 'Who are you and what do you want?' She seemed perplexed that someone would ring her bell at this time of night.

Oli stumbled a few feet down the hall and stopped to slump against the wall, looking curiously at the strangers.

'I'm DI Lexi Bennett, this is DS Tom Olsen. Is your husband at home?'

'What's wrong? Has something happened to Mike's parents?' She sounded panicky.

'No, nothing like that. We'd just like to have a word with Mr Madison, if that's okay?'

'At this time of night?' Still bemused, the woman turned away and raised her voice. 'Mike? Can you come down?'

'What is it?' A man's voice came from somewhere above.

'Give him a minute,' said the woman.

There was a thump on the ceiling and sound of a door opening. Footsteps on the stairs.

'Mike, there are some people here for you.'

'What people?' His voice sounded closer, then a man appeared in the hall. He was tall and slim, with the sort of bland good looks that send teenage girls wild. He was wearing striped pyjama trousers and a plain navy T-shirt that showed off a well-muscled chest and shoulders. Lexi guessed that half his pupils probably had a crush on him.

'They're from the police,' said his wife, much more quietly. She obviously didn't want the little boy to hear. Lexi wondered if there was a note of accusation in her tone or whether it was just grumpiness at being woken.

Mike Madison took his wife's place in the doorway, while she hovered at his shoulder.

'How can I help you?' His tone was clipped and impatient, as if he resented their intrusion.

'Could we have a word in private?' said Lexi. She was careful not to look at his wife as she spoke.

'What's it about?' said Madison.

Lexi took a deep breath. 'We're investigating the murders of Lucy and Eden Carter.' She was surprised that this hadn't been his first thought. He must have known that two of the pupils at his school had been murdered, and one was still missing.

He turned back to his wife. 'School stuff – why don't you get Oli back to bed?'

Mrs Madison obviously didn't care for the way she was dismissed but put a hand on Oli's shoulder and whispered something in his ear. Lexi waited until they'd disappeared up the stairs.

'We have been given information that you were close to the missing girl, Paige Carter. Is this true?' she said.

'Close? What d'you mean by that?' Madison's temper exploded. He stepped out onto the doorstep, pulling the front door shut behind him. 'That's crap.'

'But you did know her?' said Tom.

'Yes, I taught her biology,' said Madison, guardedly. 'Her and at least a hundred other students at the Academy. Look, officer, I don't know where you're getting your information from, but it's utter nonsense. This came from a disgruntled student, didn't it? Something to do with the complaint.'

'What complaint would that be?' said Lexi.

A look of regret flashed across Madison's face as he realised his mistake. 'I was fully exonerated. Nothing happened.'

'Who made a complaint against you?'

'Like I said, it was nothing.'

'Then you won't mind telling us all about it down at the station, will you? And one other thing.' Lexi took a scrap of paper out of her pocket and handed it to Madison. It had a mobile phone number written on it. 'Is that your number?'

'Yes.'

'That's how we know about you and Paige. Messages from this number on her iPad.'

Madison's face went bright red. He glared at Lexi without speaking.

They gave him five minutes to get dressed, then he came

down the stairs still scowling. Tom looked triumphant as they escorted him out to the Jeep, and even Lexi wondered if perhaps they had their man.

However, as Lexi expected, he refused to answer any more questions without his solicitor present. While they waited for a representative from a local law firm to arrive, Lexi went up to her office and quickly emailed an update to Maggie. Then she called William Doig's mobile.

The headmaster's voice was groggy with sleep as he announced himself.

'This is DI Bennett of Kent Police. I'm sorry to rouse you in the middle of the night but I have an urgent question for you.'

'Yes?'

'It's about one of your staff members, Mike Madison. There was a complaint made against him recently. Can you tell me what it was about?'

'Um... that was several months ago. How can it be urgent now?'

'I'd rather not say at this point. Please just tell me what happened.'

Doig sighed. 'A complaint was lodged by one of his students, but it came to nothing.'

'A complaint of what nature?'

'One of the girls in his sixth form group, Alicia Reece, alleged inappropriate behaviour. She said he'd tried to kiss her in the lab technicians' room. When we investigated further, she withdrew her complaint.'

'Mr Madison told me he'd been fully exonerated.'

'Well, the girl didn't want to take it any further.'

'So he was off the hook?'

'There's not a lot we could have done. She admitted she'd been lying.'

'Is this student still at the Academy?'

'No, she changed schools shortly after it happened.'

'And have there been other complaints against him – in the past, or since then?'

'No.' Doig cleared his throat. 'I'd appreciate it if you could take me into your confidence, Inspector. Is there something I need to know to safeguard my students?'

'At this moment, I don't know. But rest assured, if there's something I need to share with you, I'll call you straight away.'

'Thank you.'

She wondered if it was true that there hadn't been any other complaints, but she had to believe that the headmaster wouldn't lie to her.

Tom appeared in the doorway to her office. 'No solicitor available until the morning.'

'Just hold him in the cells then. We'll talk to him first thing.'

'Do you think it's him?' said Tom. There was excitement in his voice.

Lexi shrugged. 'Sexual aggression against one of his pupils makes him a villain, but it doesn't necessarily make him a killer. Let's just keep all our options open for now.'

Could Mike Madison have cut Lucy and Eden's throats? Was he even now holding Paige somewhere, still possibly alive? Or was it one of the punters from the Pole Star? And what about Josh Pendleton? Still missing but definitely connected to the dead girls.

Hopefully, tomorrow would see some of these questions answered.

TWENTY-ONE

WEDNESDAY, 11 JANUARY

The alarm clock roused Lexi from a dream that was nothing more than all her anxieties churned into a malevolent presence in the darkest corner of her bedroom. She hardly felt rested and the short run she attempted could only be deemed a failure as she was significantly behind her usual time.

Skipping breakfast, she headed into work early to wait for Mike Madison's solicitor to show up. An hour later, she took a call from the desk sergeant.

'Ma'am, there's a lady here to see you. Says it's important.'

'The solicitor, right?'

'No. Something personal, I think.'

What the hell could that be?

'I doubt it. Did you take a name?'

'She just said you'd know her.'

Lexi frowned. 'What's it to do with? Does she have information on the missing girl?'

The desk sergeant grunted. 'She won't talk to me. Insists on seeing you.'

For a moment Lexi felt inclined to instruct the desk sergeant to show this self-important mystery woman the door, but if it was a genuine tip, she couldn't afford to miss it. More likely the woman was attention-seeking. There were always people who wanted to associate themselves with the supposed 'glamour' of a police investigation. But at least a trip downstairs would give her the opportunity to fetch more coffee.

She opened the door into the station's reception area, then stopped dead in her tracks when she saw the woman drumming her fingers impatiently on the desk sergeant's counter.

It was like looking in a mirror.

Well, not quite. Amber had had her hair cut into a short, sleek bob since Lexi had last seen her. But then that had been five years ago, at their parents' funeral, just before she went to America. Her sister looked thinner and the expensive navy shift dress she was wearing flattered her figure.

Amber looked up on hearing the door open and held Lexi's eyes with a steady gaze.

Neither of them moved towards the other.

'What are you doing here?' said Lexi.

Finally, Amber took a step forward. 'What am I doing here? I bloody live here, Lex. I've always lived here. You were the one who disappeared. What are *you* doing here?'

'I meant here in the station.'

Amber rolled her eyes. 'Were you going to bother to get in touch? Let me know that you were back? Because it seems beyond weird that the way I found out was through seeing you on television talking about the abduction of a set of triplets.' There was an undercurrent of anger in her voice that was all too familiar.

Lexi realised she needed to dial things back quickly. She got why Amber was upset. 'Of course I was going to get in touch – I... I suppose I was waiting for the right moment.'

'And when would that have been?' Amber's eyes were flint hard.

'Look, I'm waiting for a solicitor to arrive so I can interview a suspect, but I've got time for a quick coffee.'

Amber's expression softened. 'Those poor girls? You've arrested someone?'

Lexi shook her head. 'Not exactly. I should have said a person of interest.' She hoped the desk sergeant wasn't listening in. 'Let's get out of here. There's a place over the road.'

Amber didn't make an immediate move. She seemed pensive. But it was she who had come here. Surely she wasn't just going to walk away again.

'Honestly, I'm sorry,' said Lexi.

Amber took a deep breath. 'Okay.'

The sergeant watched them leave with a bemused look. He would no doubt feed the station gossip mill, but that was the least of Lexi's worries.

It seemed like a partial truce had been declared. They walked in silence, using the subway to cross the ring road, passing through the arch in the medieval city walls to come onto Watling Street. There was a small independent café about fifty metres up on the left, and Lexi pushed open the door. She hadn't been there before. She hadn't been to any local cafés yet – it was only her third day on the job. The interior was sparse and utilitarian, with cheap pine tables and chairs. The cakes lined up under glass domes on the counter looked home-made – and not in a good way.

'This is a little weird,' said Amber, sitting down gingerly.

'Yeah, it is. Sorry.' Lexi wasn't sure if she meant the café or the fact they were meeting at all. What was it about Amber that made her keep apologising? She went up to the counter and bought a couple of coffees, not holding out much hope for the quality.

Amber took a sip and pulled a face. She pushed the cup away across the table.

'So...' said Lexi, wondering what her sister expected of her, why she'd come. She tasted the coffee and had to agree with Amber. Neither cup was going to be drunk.

'So what the hell are you doing on this case?'

The question surprised Lexi. 'Seriously? It's my job. I'm in charge of the Major Investigation Team here. Two girls have been murdered...'

'But surely they don't let you investigate something when there's so clearly a conflict of interest.'

'Seriously?'

'They're triplets. Come on, Lexi – how can it not be connected?'

'To what happened to us?' This was the last thing Lexi needed. 'I doubt it's got anything to do with us and Rose. That was seventeen years ago. Killers like that don't wait seventeen years before they strike again. And is that really what you came to talk about? My suitability for the case?'

Amber's mouth opened as if to speak, but no words came out. She shook her head. 'I don't know. I saw you on the television. I saw a report about triplets going missing.'

'You thought there might be a link, and it might lead us to Rose?'

She shook her head vehemently. 'Not that. I know Rose is gone.' She paused. 'Actually, it was because I wanted to see you. It's been too long.'

'You were the one who shut me out, remember?'

'I know, and I'm sorry for it. But you reminded me of what happened. I couldn't stand the memories.'

Lexi felt a moment of sympathy for her sister. After all, she had the same memories. 'And did it work? Did banishing me banish the past?'

Amber chewed on her bottom lip. 'It did for a while. Until now.'

'What do you remember?'

Anger flashed across her face. 'I won't go there, Lexi. I've spent too long building walls around those memories. I'm not letting them back out.' She played nervously with her teaspoon. 'But do you think it could be him? Repeating history in some way by killing these girls?'

'We got away, remember? It's not the same. These girls had their throats slit.'

Amber gasped, and Lexi looked around the café sharply. 'Do you think that's what he did to Rose?'

'We'll never know what happened to Rose.'

None of the details had been released to the media and she shouldn't be discussing it in a public place. But the café was virtually empty, and the only other punter was an elderly man reading the paper with his hearing aid on the table beside his cup of tea.

Amber looked pale. 'I don't know how you can bring yourself to do your job.' She was an accountant, and her working life was a world of numbers and screens. 'After what happened... Isn't every day a horrible reminder?'

A reminder of the terror? The years of anxiety attacks and bad dreams? Maybe. But she'd blanked out so much of what had happened to them. It frustrated her beyond belief, but she knew it was her mind protecting her. She stared down at the cold cup of coffee in front of her. She couldn't meet Amber's gaze. She didn't want Amber to see how close to tears she was.

'How could I do any other job?' she said. 'I let Rose down – I made a mistake – but at least I might be able to help some other girl in a similar position.'

'So this is really all about you exonerating yourself? It's not about those poor girls at all.' Amber shifted in her seat, about to stand. 'You always were self-centred, Lexi. Putting your work in front of your family. Some things never change. Honestly, I don't know why I came.' She stood up and turned to leave but Lexi beat her to it.

She slammed out of the café and marched as fast as she could back down Watling Street towards the station. Going for coffee with Amber had been a mistake. A bitter reminder of how much she'd let down Rose. She couldn't afford to fail Paige in the same way.

TWENTY-TWO

Back in her office, there was no time for Lexi to ponder on her encounter with Amber – the moment she sat down, the desk sergeant called to let her know that Mike Madison's solicitor had arrived.

She went downstairs with Tom, and the solicitor introduced himself, apologising for not having been able to come out when they'd first taken the teacher into custody.

'Don't apologise to me, Mr Hess,' she said, as they shook hands. 'I'm quite happy to keep an interviewee waiting. Tends to make them more talkative.' She gave him a quick smile to show that she wasn't being entirely serious.

Hess didn't return her smile. 'I'll be advising my client to give a no-comment interview. I'm sure you understand.'

This would mean speaking to Madison would be a waste of their time. 'I see,' said Lexi, not bothering to hide her irritation.

'And a few WhatsApp messages and a previously dismissed complaint don't give you grounds to hold him any longer. You've certainly got nothing to charge him with, so you might as well release him now.'

A no-comment interview would be a doddle for Madison.

He'd get a tougher interrogation from his wife when he got home than he'd get here. But Lexi wasn't going to be deterred.

'We'll still go ahead,' she said.

Tom raised his eyebrows but didn't say anything, while Hess grimaced. He clearly didn't see the point.

'So, Mr Madison,' said Lexi, ten minutes later when they were seated opposite each other in the interview room, 'tell us about your work at the Academy. What subject do you teach?'

'No comment.'

'Come on, that's hardly a controversial question.'

Madison stared across at her defiantly.

'You taught all three of the Carter girls, didn't you?'

'No comment.' He sounded firm and confident. Easy enough when you intended to say the same two words throughout.

And so it went on. When she asked about the previous complaint, about its outcome, about his relationship with Paige – all of her questions got the same answer. He sounded like a broken record.

'Did she have a schoolgirl crush on you, or was it something more?'

'No comment.' Madison's leg jiggled under the table.

Press home. 'Did you reciprocate her feelings, Mr Madison?'

'No comment.' Each time he said it, Lexi could hear his voice getting tighter and sharper.

'Were you in fact...' Lexi paused for effect. 'Having an illicit affair with a seventeen-year-old schoolgirl?' Out of the corner of her eye, she saw Hess practically wincing.

'No... comment.' His anger made him falter.

'You know it's against the law for teachers to have relationships with their students, don't you? If we find the evidence, you'll be charged faster than you can blink.'

'No comment.'

'That wasn't a question.'

Madison glared at her. He was riled up now, and if she kept needling him, perhaps he would break. She'd seen it happen before.

Hess finally decided it was time to earn whatever fee he would be charging Madison.

'Look, Inspector Bennett, this interview clearly isn't serving your purposes, and it's applying unnecessary pressure on my client, who has done nothing wrong. Please terminate it.'

'I haven't finished yet,' said Lexi. 'And as for unnecessary pressure, I'll be the judge of that. If I find out your client has been screwing around with one of his own pupils, this doesn't begin to match the pressure I'll put him under.'

The solicitor gave Madison a worried look.

'Was it just Paige, or have you had some sort of involvement with other children you teach?' She used the word 'children' on purpose. She knew it would wind him up.

'For Christ's sake, she's seventeen. Not a child.' Madison slammed a fist on the table and pushed his chair back as if to stand.

Lexi had found the needle and the balloon had burst.

'In the eyes of the law, she counts as a minor as far as you're concerned. Sleeping with a student is exploitative.'

'It wasn't like that.' Mike Madison was furious. His face had turned scarlet, and a bead of spittle landed on the centre of the table. Hess placed a hand on his forearm to calm him down, but he snatched it away, almost snarling.

'Then tell me what it was like. True love? A beautiful romance? Are you forgetting that you're a married man, twice her age?'

Madison glared at her with undisguised hatred. 'Nothing happened. No comment.'

Lexi slid her foot sideways to nudge Tom's shoe. It was a signal.

'Mr Madison, could you give us an account of your whereabouts last Friday afternoon and evening?' her partner asked.

'No.'

'Are you inferring that my client had something to do with the disappearance of the Carter sisters?' said Hess.

'If he has an alibi for that afternoon and evening, he'll be in the clear,' said Tom.

'You have to understand,' said Lexi, 'that we need to consider every man that might have been in a relationship with any one of those three girls.'

'I wasn't in a relationship with her.'

'The private WhatsApp messages between the two of you look pretty damning.' Lexi spoke in exactly the same tone as she had for all the previous questions, determined not to give away how she felt. But inside, her heart was pounding.

Madison said nothing, but the nervous movement of his leg under the table became more pronounced, betrayed by the shimmering surface of the water in the cups that stood on the table.

'It's time to come clean, Mike. Were you in a relationship with Paige?'

'No comment.'

'Or with one of her sisters?'

'No comment.'

'Did you in fact abduct all three of them? And then murder Lucy and Eden?'

Madison shifted sideways in his chair to face Hess. 'Make her stop, dammit.'

'Just say if you need a comfort break,' said Lexi sweetly.

Hess frowned. 'I'd like five minutes with my client, if you don't mind.'

'Of course.'

Lexi and Tom stood up from the table and filed out of the room.

Great.

'Right,' said Lexi, once they were out in the corridor. 'Organise a two-man team to go to Madison's house to pick up his phone and his laptop.'

'But you'll need a magistrate to grant a warrant.' He looked at his watch. 'That'll take a couple of hours.'

'Then get on it.'

'Have we got enough cause for that?'

'Come on, Tom – he's been sexually harassing one of his pupils via WhatsApp. Yes, that's enough to justify an examination of his gear. And if we don't find anything, we can let him out under investigation.'

But there wasn't a doubt in her mind that they'd find something incriminating on Mike Madison's phone or computer.

TWENTY-THREE

When they returned to the interview room, Lexi said the questioning would be suspended pending further investigation. As she handed Madison over to the custody sergeant, Hess protested but it was feeble at best. He seemed to realise that his client was skating on thin ice. Tom headed away to apply for the warrant, while Lexi put in an application to the station superintendent to extend the number of hours they could hold him without charge from the usual twenty-four to thirty-six. If they needed longer than that, she would have to reapply to a magistrate, but she'd cross that bridge when she came to it.

While she waited for the warrant to come through, she gathered the rest of the team.

'Colin, updates on anything?'

Colin went across to the whiteboard and pointed at a photo of Josh Pendleton. 'Turns out Pendleton's DNA is already on our database – he was done for joyriding a few years ago. And that's come up as a match to the sperm found inside Lucy's body. Mort's guess is they must have had sex shortly before she was abducted.'

'That doesn't necessarily rule him out from being the killer, but if he's not, then it would appear the killer didn't have sex with either girl before killing them. Good work. Anything else?'

'We followed up on Pendleton's flatmates,' he said. Lexi could hear a note of pride in his voice, so she hoped he'd come up with something worthwhile. 'They stumbled in drunk last night to find us taking their flat apart. Ridhi and I brought them in for questioning – they were fully co-operative. Confirmed that the last time they saw him was Friday, breakfast time.'

'That's it?' said Lexi. 'Did they know he was seeing Lucy Carter?'

'Yes,' said Colin.

'But they didn't put two and two together with all the publicity about Lucy's murder?'

'Not the sharpest knives in the box,' he said. 'Seems they were waiting to hear from him. Didn't want to tell the police he was missing in case they got him into trouble. To be fair, they were pretty drunk when we spoke to them. But if nothing else, we now know what he was wearing when last seen – a dark grey hooded windcheater, white T-shirt, jeans, trainers.'

That could literally describe half the young men in Canterbury.

'Right then – follow up with them now they're sober. Get a list of Pendleton's other friends, anyone they can think of that he might have gone away to visit, anything he might have said recently about a holiday or a trip. Also, whether he recently argued with Lucy.' She raised one shoulder. 'You know, the routine stuff.'

'Yes, boss.'

'Anyone got anything else?'

One of the civilian researchers stuck up a hand. 'Emily Jordan left a message saying it would be at least twenty-four hours before she'll have any information for us from Pendleton's flat.'

'Fair enough.' And really, would it be news if they found

traces of Lucy in her boyfriend's flat? Even her sisters might have been there legitimately. It would tell them nothing.

Tom slipped back into the room and gave her a nod. The warrant application had gone in. Ridhi followed him in.

Now the whole team was present, it was her turn to update them.

'We've now got good reason to take a closer look at Mike Madison, Paige's biology teacher. Thirty-six years old, married, father of one.' She taped a picture of Madison, downloaded from the school website, to the whiteboard, and underneath it a printout of some of the more damning WhatsApp messages he'd sent to Paige. 'We're holding him downstairs, and I've applied for a warrant to search his electronic devices.'

'Do you think he's responsible for the abduction?' said Colin.

'His age fits the standard profile. He seems to have been grooming Paige. He's said nothing to rule himself out at this point.' Lexi counted off the points she was making on her fingers. 'If we charge him, I'll need to put one of you on checking out any alibis he comes up with. Ridhi, find out what car he drives and check the ANPR reports for the day of the abductions.'

'Yes, boss.'

'Anything useful from Mrs George?'

Ridhi shook her head ruefully. 'Nothing. She was able to tell me the grade of every piece of homework Lucy had ever done but knew damn all about her as a person. I'm still trying to pin down Eden and Paige's teachers for interviews.'

Lexi could hear the frustration in her voice, and shared it. Progress was too slow.

'Thanks. Keep up the good work.' She turned back to the whiteboard. 'Madison's not the only man in the picture. Colin, bring us up to speed on the Pole Star punters. Any of them looking likely?'

Colin took her place at the whiteboard and Lexi perched herself on the edge of Ridhi's desk. He clearly still felt a need to redeem himself after missing the Pole Star clue during the first search of Eden's room, and Lexi noted a fresh enthusiasm as he filled them in.

'We're focusing our attention on the Friday and Saturday night regulars from the Pole Star – that's when Eden worked, so those men are the best leads.' He pointed at a row of photos on the whiteboard. 'Three men have been brought in for interview, having been flagged up by the other dancers as taking a particular interest in Eden.'

'Great,' said Lexi. 'I'll start questioning them now while we wait for the data extraction on Madison's devices. We need to push hard on where they were when the girls went missing and whether they fit the profile for our killer.'

Ridhi raised a hand. 'What is the profile?'

In Lexi's head she had a clear image of the unsub, but she hadn't committed it to paper yet. She had to be careful not to plant bias in the team's minds – they needed to be open to anything, and without the extensive training and experience she'd had at Quantico, trying to fit a suspect to a half-formed profile was a dangerous game. But Ridhi, and the rest of the team, deserved an answer to her question.

'It's early days, but the broad picture will be that we're looking for a white male, late twenties to late forties, escalating history of sexual predation...'

Colin stuck up his hand. 'But there was nothing to suggest rape, was there?'

Lexi nodded her head in acknowledgement to his point. 'That doesn't rule out a sexual predator. He posed the scene – he dressed the girls up before killing them. Indications of fetishist behaviour.' She didn't have time to give the team a lecture on profiling. She was aware that they were all staring at her. The news must have spread throughout the station – she was one the famous Bennett triplets. She knew what they would be wondering. She felt her cheeks blaze. 'Listen, like I said, it's early days. Let's just focus on the suspects we have so far, see if we can rule any of them out, see if we can press one of them into letting something slip or making an error. Meantime, keep checking out any tips from the public – we need to locate Josh Pendleton as fast as possible. Paige might just still be alive, so let's not waste another minute.' A whip of anger flashed through her. Every minute that passed would seem like a hundred years to Paige.

She went back to her office, calling Colin to come with her.

'Tell me about the Pole Star punters you brought in.'

Skipping lunch, Lexi went down to the ground floor with Tom, where the three Pole Star regulars were waiting in separate interview rooms.

'Have you been keeping an eye on them?' she said to the desk sergeant, a thickset career PC called Roberts. She walked along the corridor, peering in through the small wire glass windows in the rooms' doors.

Roberts followed on her shoulder. 'This is Peter Fraser,' he said, outside the first room. 'He's been in here about an hour. Quite calm, asked if he was here as a suspect or a witness. I said witness. But I think he's getting impatient, so you might want to talk to him first before he tries to leave.'

Lexi saw a dark-haired man in a suit, about forty years old. He was spinning an empty disposable coffee cup around the table, and he looked bored rather than nervous. She didn't think he was a good fit to the profile of the killer – he didn't look like a man who'd had a moment of self-doubt or sense of inadequacy in his privileged, entitled life – so she moved on to the next one.

'Stefan Nowak,' said Roberts. 'He was brought in first. Been very agitated, apparently refused to accompany the officer until he was threatened with arrest. They picked him up at his home in Sturry, and his wife was there – I think it caused an issue.'

Issue was one way of putting it, when your husband is hauled in for questioning by the police. Nowak was dressed in jeans and a baggy fleece, with work boots on his feet. The details they had about him said he worked as a foreman on a construction site.

He spotted Lexi looking in and marched up to the door.

'You can't keep me here.' He was loud and angry, and banged on the back of the door with his palm.

Lexi opened the door. 'Mr Nowak, please be patient. We'll talk to you shortly.' She closed the door again without bothering to listen to his muttered answer, though she did catch the word 'bitch'. He'd just earned himself a longer wait.

'This is Toby Yates. Very quiet, looks devastated.'

Lexi looked through the cloudy glass and could just make out a tall, skinny man with tousled hair. He was standing with his back to her, leaning against the wall, looking to all the world as if he was willing himself to disappear.

'We'll talk to him first,' she said, turning back to Tom. 'What do we know about him?'

Tom consulted the notes Ridhi had typed up after talking to the dancers.

'Seems like he had quite a crush on Eden. Tipped generously whenever he saw her, and apparently waited outside to talk to her a couple of times after her shift. She wouldn't have anything to do with him. According to the girl who gave Ridhi this stuff, Eden wouldn't talk to any of the punters outside the club.'

'What do we know about Yates?'

'Thirty-nine years old. Out of work currently.'

'So where's he getting the money to spend in girly bars?'

Tom shrugged. 'Casual work, maybe?'

'What did he do when he did have a job?'

Tom held up his hands. 'The information from the Pole Star doesn't run to that.'

Lexi opened the door of the interview room.

'Mr Yates, we have a few questions for you. Please sit down.' She led the way towards the table on one side of the room, bolted to the floor so it would remain in the best line of view for the window in the door. Canterbury nick didn't run to the two-way mirrored walls that every TV cop shop seemed to have. 'Do you need anything? Tea? Coffee?'

Yates turned to look at her with a shake of his head, and she saw his face for the first time. She caught her breath, conscious of not showing a reaction to what she saw – the entire left-hand side of Toby Yates's face was one vast scar. It looked like a burn. Most of the damaged tissue was white, but there were patches that were still red and livid, and all of it was criss-crossed by a web-like pattern of calcified scarring. His left ear was partially gone, the rest of it a protrusion of leathery scars, and there was no hair on that side of his head.

'That's it,' he said, 'take a good look.' His voice was a low rasp, but rather than challenging, the tone was weary, as if he'd tired of people's stares and having to explain himself.

Tom wasn't so adept at hiding his shock. He'd let out a short gasp, then momentarily closed his eyes. 'Sorry,' he said quickly.

As they sat down, Lexi asked the desk sergeant to bring them some water.

'Would it be okay if we recorded this interview, Mr Yates?' said Tom.

'Would it be okay if I said no?'

'It's in your interest to have it recorded,' said Lexi. 'That way, we can't twist your words.'

'Which is something you'd do?' But he gave a slight incline of his head, and Tom switched on the recorder. After the long beep to mark the start of the interview, Lexi stated the time and date and the names of everyone in the room.

'Mr Yates, I understand you were a regular customer at the Pole Star in Wincheap, Canterbury?'

'Define regular.'

'It's our understanding that you would go there a couple of times a week. Would you say that's a fair assessment?'

The small nod again.

'Please answer the question, yes or no, so we have a record of your answer.'

'Yes.'

'Did you know one of the dancers there, a girl called Eden Carter?'

'Are you accusing me of her murder?' He'd clearly heard about the crime in the news.

'No, I'm not,' said Lexi, getting the feeling that this interview was going to be an uphill struggle. 'I'm asking if you knew her.'

'I don't know if I knew her. I don't know the names of the dancers.'

Lexi opened the file she'd brought with her. She found a picture of Eden and put it face up on the table in front of Yates. It was a school photograph, and she was wearing uniform, her hair scraped back into a high ponytail and no makeup. Lexi guessed she must have looked very different when she'd been dancing.

While Yates studied the picture, she studied him. Was he a fit for the profile in the back of her mind? Certainly, with his facial disfigurement, he would have found it difficult to date women. She needed to find out when and how it had happened.

Eventually Yates shrugged. 'I don't recognise her.'

He was lying.

'Mr Yates, can I ask what happened to your face?'

'You can ask. I might not answer.'

'Is it a burn?'

Yates scowled. 'I don't see what my injury has to do with

any of this.'

No matter. There would be other ways of finding out. If it had been a work-related incident, it might explain why he was no longer working. And if he'd received compensation, that might be what gave him the money he spent at the club.

Lexi glanced at Tom – signalling for him to take over.

Tom ran through a list of questions covering Yates's whereabouts when the girls had last been seen. He answered 'I don't remember' to each one.

It was frustrating, but to be expected. If they spoke to him again under caution, he'd no doubt insist on a lawyer. Any sympathy Lexi had felt for him was evaporating fast.

Taking advantage of a pause in the questions, Toby Yates pushed back his chair and rose to his feet. 'I'm leaving. Try and stop me.'

Lexi snatched up the photo and put it back into the folder. 'Thank you. You've been a great help, Mr Yates.'

He ignored her and left the room.

They sat in silence for a few moments, listening to his steps receding down the corridor.

'Do you want him stopped?' said Tom.

Lexi shook her head. 'We can't hold him. We need to build some sort of case before we risk arresting him.'

'What do you make of him?'

'He fits the profile. He's uncooperative. I think we need to take this seriously and dig deeper.'

'He'll be able to manufacture alibis, now we've revealed the days and times we're interested in.'

'Sure,' said Lexi. 'And if they're false, we'll tear them down. Put together a surveillance team – I want to know where he is from now on. Every minute of the day. And apply for an emergency warrant to have his house searched.'

'You seriously believe he's our man?'

'At this point, we can't rule him out.'

TWENTY-FOUR

After Yates's abrupt departure, Lexi took a moment to call her contact in the tech department, Greg Chambers, to make sure Madison's phone and laptop would be their number one priority as soon as they got them. The warrant for Madison's devices had been granted while she and Tom were talking to Yates.

'How quickly will you be able to get back to me?' she said. 'I'm interested in sent and received text messages and email from the past couple of months, and a list of websites visited.'

'It shouldn't take long,' said Greg. 'If you've got a warrant, we can use data extraction technology to download everything on it in a matter of minutes.'

'The warrant's just been granted. My guys are picking up the devices right now.'

Greg promised to get back to her as soon as he had anything.

The warrant Tom had applied for covered not only Madison's electronic devices, but would also allow them to search his house and his office at the Academy. Tom was quickly briefing a team to do just that.

'So does this latest development mean you're letting the Pole Star punters off the hook?' asked Maggie, when Lexi called her to update her on the latest progress.

'Not a chance.'

'So you'll investigate them at the same time as Madison?'

'Absolutely – I have to follow up on every single suspect until we work out who it is. And I'll be going after Madison for being a paedophile.'

'Based on a few text messages on Paige's phone?'

'It's given us enough to dig further. Whether or not he has anything to do with the abduction and murder of the Carter girls, I have reason to suspect that he's been preying on at least one of his pupils – and I'll take him down for that.'

'And what have you got on Yates so far?'

'An unhealthy interest in Eden Carter. I'm putting him under surveillance.'

'So even less to tie him to the case than Madison? And what about the other men from the Pole Star you brought in?'

'I'm about to speak to them now.'

Maggie sighed. 'You're all over the place, aren't you? Multiple weak suspects, no strong leads and a girl still missing. We need progress on this case right away – the press pack is baying for blood, and I'm getting it in the neck from higher up. Don't spread yourself too thin.'

'I agree – I'm stretched to breaking point. But I've got to follow every single lead and work with what I've got. Madison doesn't quite fit the profile – he's in a settled relationship, he's got a good job that commands respect. It's just not what you see in serial killers. Yates is closer. I still need to see what the other two look like.'

Maggie gave a snort of derision. 'The profile? What about evidence? That's what you're going to need when it comes to trial.'

'I thought you understood profiling.'

'I do – it's a useful tool. But don't let it steer you away from the facts.'

'Which is why I'm following up on all the suspects, Maggie. None of them are in the clear until we're one hundred per cent convinced... by the evidence... that one of them is the guilty party.'

'You need some help. This is running away from you.'

She wasn't wrong.

'Okay. Let me talk to Harry Garcia and get a recommenda-tion for a forensic psychologist over here.' Harry Garcia had been Lexi's boss in the FBI for four years. He'd practically invented criminal profiling and he knew everyone working in the field. It wasn't a call she'd enjoy, but she knew it made sense.

'Good. Get someone in. Show them whatever you find on Madison's computer.'

Lexi hung up with a sigh of relief. It wasn't like Maggie to micromanage in this way, but Paige Carter was slipping away from them, and both she and Maggie needed a win on the new team's first case.

She thought about Paige and her chest tightened. So scared, and so alone. Lexi knew what it was like. A living hell. All the time, almost wishing you were dead... anything to make it end. But she wasn't going to let that happen. She would find her and bring her home safely, and no one was going to stand in her way.

Tom appeared in the doorway. 'Shall we go down and talk to the other two?'

'Let's.'

Lexi and Tom interviewed the other two men from the Pole Star who had shown what might be termed an unhealthy interest in Eden. Peter Fraser, the businessman, had an alibi – he'd been up in Glasgow for a conference until Sunday. Of course, they would check that the details stood up, but Lexi was prepared to believe him. It was less clear cut with Stefan Nowak. He seemed to have an alibi for when two of the Carter sisters went missing, but only his wife's word for where he was when Paige disappeared. Lexi designated him as a person of interest, and tasked Colin with looking into his alibis in more depth, but she didn't feel strongly that he was involved. It was more a case of ruling him out.

Lexi felt drained. It seemed whatever she did, whichever way she turned, she wasn't coming any closer to finding out what had happened to Paige Carter or who had murdered Lucy and Eden. Sure, they might have a suspect in Toby Yates, but the reports coming back said that he'd left the station and gone home. He hadn't emerged in the couple of hours since – no doubt he'd spotted the silver Ford Fiesta parked outside his house with a couple of plain clothes policemen in it. If he was the killer, they'd just given themselves away to him.

After the interviews, she called Maggie back about getting a search warrant for his property and putting a tap on his phone. They would have to apply to a judge, giving compelling reasons why he was being treated as a suspect, and apart from generously tipping Eden at the Pole Star, they didn't have anything more substantial to tie him to the case. Maggie agreed that they should go ahead with the application, but neither of them were hopeful.

Now she was sitting in her office, staring out of the window at a bruised sky. As rain clouds rolled over the city, she wondered about Paige Carter's fate. Was she alive somewhere out there, captive plaything of the psychopath who'd murdered her sisters, or was she already dead?

Pull yourself together and do something that will make a difference.

But she'd tasked the team with everything she could think of, and chasing them up hardly seemed like a big step forward.

Where the hell was Greg with the data from Mike Madison's phone? There was no point calling Harry Garcia until she'd seen what Madison's mobile phone threw up – which meant she needed it now. As she started to dial Greg's number, an email popped into her inbox.

Greg answered the phone at the same moment. 'Chambers.'

'Greg, is this email what I think it is?' she said, quickly adjusting the tone of voice she had been going to use.

'Certainly is. Just click on the link and it'll let you download the contents of Madison's phone and laptop.'

'That was quick. I owe you one. Big time.'

She called Tom into her office and together they impatiently watched the download bar inching across her computer screen.

'What are you hoping to find?' said Tom.

'Incriminating texts or images to show that he had an inappropriate relationship with Paige Carter would be gold. Evidence that he's been accessing child pornography will be enough to charge him and hold him for longer. Either of those would probably give us enough to get a warrant to search his car.'

There was a small ping as the download completed, and Lexi double clicked on the folder icon to open it up.

'Jesus!' said Tom.

Lexi agreed as she scrolled down a never-ending roster of files, images and videos. There was a separate folder of emails, and more folders from various messaging apps that Madison had been using.

'Where to start?' She clicked on a random image file. A picture of Mike Madison and his son, Oliver, playing football filled the screen. She clicked another – a family Christmas. And another – a car in a showroom. There were hundreds.

'What about text messages?' said Tom. 'Try the ones with attachments, in case he was exchanging pictures with someone.'

Lexi went to the folder of text messages and opened it. There was an enormous list, each one identified by the number it went to or came from.

'What's Paige's mobile number?'

'I'll go and find it. It'll be in the file.'

While Tom went to the incident room, Lexi explored more of the content from Madison's phone. She decided to try videos next, though no doubt they would mostly be of his son or his wife. The first couple were – Oli learning to ride a very new-looking bike, his wife diving into a sapphire swimming pool somewhere that clearly wasn't the UK. People thought investigating murder was a glamorous job, but going through other people's private lives was anything but. Boring and mundane was how Lexi would put it.

Until it wasn't.

The video she pulled up next seemed to be in black and white. It was grainy and indistinct, like a surveillance camera, and it took Lexi a few seconds to work out what she was looking at.

'Tom,' she called from her doorway, towards the incident room.

He came hurrying out. 'I've got Paige's number.'

'Wait a moment. Take a look at this.' She led him back to the desk, and they stood side by side, backs slightly bowed as they studied the laptop screen.

'Is this what I think it is?' she said.

The smudgy image showed a large room with no windows. Down one wall there was a row of what looked like lockers, and there was another line of free-standing lockers in the centre of the floor. Between the two rows, there was a long wooden bench, seemingly strewn with clothes.

'A changing room,' said Tom. 'In a sports club?'

'Or a school?'

Lexi heard Tom's sharp intake of breath.

'Oh no,' said Lexi, her heart sinking. 'He was watching them get changed. And none of them realised.'

There was no sound on the footage, and Lexi felt like she was watching a silent movie as a gaggle of animated girls piled into the small space and started tugging off their sports kit. Their mouths moved, they smiled, they laughed. Some of them disappeared out of shot with towels – presumably to a shower area, while others changed straight back into their uniforms. The video carried on running. Some of the girls left, while others took their time, drying themselves and getting dressed.

Lexi counted ten girls changing, and a few others flitted backwards and forwards going to other parts of the changing room.

Eventually, there were only two girls left.

'Is that one of the Carter sisters?' said Lexi. One of the girls was still wrapped in a towel.

Tom leaned closer. 'I think so, but I couldn't say which.'

Neither could Lexi. The film was too blurry.

Then, as the other girl turned away and pulled a blouse on, the girl in the towel finished drying herself. For a fleeting couple of seconds she was standing naked in front of her locker. Then she pulled on some underwear and turned to her friend, chattering away as they both finished dressing.

Lexi slammed down the lid of the laptop. 'School is supposed to be a safe place, the one place parents don't need to worry about. I swear, Tom, we'll take Madison down whether or not he's involved in the abduction.'

TWENTY-FIVE

It came as no surprise to find more videos of the girls' changing room at the Academy. Lexi and Tom concluded that while the focus of his attention had definitely been Paige, she wasn't always present. Madison, or whoever was responsible for the filming, seemed happy to watch any teenage girl getting changed.

Lexi's first impulse was to storm down to the cell where the teacher was being held and punch him, but that wouldn't get him where she needed him – in prison, for a long stretch. Instead, she smashed her fist hard against her office wall. Pain shot up to her elbow.

She stepped back and took a deep breath. It was this anger – born out of her experience and all the cases she'd investigated since – that drove her on, day after day, in a job that most people would find way too harrowing. But she had to keep it under control. If she let it get the better of her, she'd be as bad as the men she put away.

She went round to the incident room, rubbing her knuckles.

'Colin!' Flynn was leaning back in his chair, his feet up on the desk, with a packet of Wotsits in one hand. Lexi could hear him crunching them from the other side of the room. They smelled revolting.

Hearing his name, he quickly swung his feet to the floor and sat up.

'Yes, boss.'

'Get down to the Academy. Madison has been filming in the girls' changing room. Take it to pieces until you find the camera, then get it over to Emily for fingerprinting. I'll send you a copy of some footage so you can work out its location. You'll have to inform the headmaster but instruct him not to mention it to anyone else until we've found out whether other staff members were involved.'

'Got it.'

'Tom, you and Ridhi work your way through the rest of the material from Madison's phone, and log anything that relates in the slightest way to the Carter sisters, as well as anything else you find that suggests inappropriate interests or activity.' She paused before thinking of something else. 'Oh, and chase up those warrants we need to search his house and his car – we've definitely got grounds now.'

'What will you do?' said Tom.

'I'm going downstairs to bait the bear.'

Naturally, Madison called for his lawyer again when Lexi had him brought to the interview room. This case was going to turn into a nice little earner for Mr Hess after all.

While they waited for him to arrive, Lexi set up her laptop and played several of the videos they'd found on Madison's phone. As soon as he realised what she was doing, he turned his head away.

'These were on your phone, Mr Madison. Was it you who set up a camera there or someone else?'

He didn't answer.

Cold fury swept through her, making her clench her fists where they rested on her thighs. 'You disgust me,' she said, 'and I'm going to see that you get what's coming to you.'

Madison ignored her, but she saw, as he took a sip of water, that his hand was shaking. He knew exactly what sort of trouble he was in. It would spell the end of his career, and more than likely the end of his marriage. He'd serve time in prison where, as a convicted child sex abuser, his life would be hell, and when he got out he'd spend the rest of his days on the sex offenders' register.

Hess arrived, looking more than a little disturbed. As Lexi played more clips from the phone, Madison turned pale and gripped the edge of the table.

'Surely they can't take things from my phone without my permission?' he hissed.

'I'm afraid they can in this instance,' said Hess. 'They're investigating a serious crime.'

Lexi snapped the laptop shut to get their attention.

'You're right. This is incredibly serious. My officers are preparing a case against you as I speak and we'll be passing it to the CPS imminently. In the meantime, we've applied to extend the number of hours we can hold you, and I have no doubt our request will be granted. Mr Madison, if you were to provide information on the whereabouts of Paige Carter, the court would be sure to look favourably on it.'

As she spoke, Madison's eyes had grown wide with fear. Sweat was beading along his top lip. His tongue flicked out to lick it away. 'You think I did that? You think I killed those girls?' His voice rose in a crescendo of panicked anger and he stood up, leaning forward. 'I had nothing to do with her sisters' deaths and I have no idea where Paige is.'

His panic was real, and Lexi believed him, but it wasn't something she was going to admit. However, he didn't fit the profile for someone who could cold-bloodedly slit two girls' throats, one after the other. He was a pathetic piece of shit, and she'd seen enough of him.

'I'll be back when the charges are ready,' she said, picking up her laptop and walking to the door. 'The custody sergeant will return you to your cell.'

As she pulled the door shut behind her, she heard Mike Madison crying like a little boy.

TWENTY-SIX

It's time to go and see my darling.

I'm humming to myself as I drive. Disposing of Lucy and Eden Carter was the right thing to do. It's far less stressful, just having one little princess to deal with, and it was always going to be Paige. It became clear very, very early on that she was the strongest of the three. And that meant she was going to be the most responsive to my challenges. She'll do anything I ask to protect her sisters. Sisters she hasn't seen now for nearly a week. But I'm keeping them alive and well – at least that's what I tell her.

This is my chance to rewrite history. The mistake I made with Lexi, Amber and Rose was keeping all three of them in the same building, all alive and quite close to each other. I underestimated Lexi.

Sibling dynamics fascinate me, but they puzzle me, too. The experiences I had in my own family showed that not all siblings are created equal. Not all siblings like each other. It's not the way it looks on TV, but that's what it's like in real life.

What I saw with the Bennetts, and what I'm now seeing

with the Carters, is similar to the dynamics of my own twin sisters. That tight bond is entirely familiar. They shut the rest of the world out. I was never part of my sisters' world, and they weren't part of mine. I felt alone, even in the midst of family.

My mother was no help to me. I only ever saw her take her sustenance from a bottle. She resented being a mother. She couldn't be bothered. Meals were sporadic, the house was filthy. She left us to fend for ourselves, and in turn the twins left me to fend for myself. I looked up to them, they looked down on me.

I got by on school lunches and, when I was a bit older, by stealing chocolate bars from the newsagents around town. I got caught more than once, but most times, looking at the state of me, the proprietors would just send me packing without bothering the police.

Funny that the apple of my eye is now a policewoman, isn't it?

I park the car and walk in through the woods. I could park closer, but this way is less likely to attract attention – and it doesn't give Paige warning of my arrival.

The weather's taken a turn for the worse and the sun has been blotted out by the clouds. I smell rain in the air, and then I see the first few drops pitting the dark surface of a puddle. Poor Paige must be freezing, but at least she's out of the wind and sheltered from the wet.

I hear her shrieking in the distance. She's calling out her sisters' names, I suppose because she thinks they're being held somewhere close by. But no matter how much she strains her ears, she won't hear them answer.

I'll have to put a stop to that in case someone hears her.

When I reach the shed, I peer in through one of the narrow, grimy windows that run along the top of the wall to allow in daylight. She's stopped her yelling for the time being, and I see her crouched on the floor with her head on her knees and her arms wrapped protectively around her torso. I can tell from the way her shoulders are shaking that she's crying. I watch for a while, and she keeps on crying. Such sadness in one so young. It's quite upsetting.

Actually, not.

I enjoy the spectacle for a couple of minutes more, then I scratch gently on the pane of glass with my nails. She doesn't hear me at first, so I scratch a little harder.

Her head flies up and she looks around frantically. When she sees me, I grin and she seems to shrink inside herself. Now she's shaking with fear. It's interesting how strong emotions play the body like a finely tuned instrument.

I undo the padlock that keeps her captive and go inside.

'No, don't stand up – it's only me.'

She wasn't trying to stand up. She scuttles backwards across the floor like a spider, taking refuge in the corner. Though nothing will protect her from me.

On a rainy afternoon like this, it's virtually dark inside the shed. The place stinks of her excrement. It's overpowered the faint smell of chicken shit that suffused the place when we first arrived. And it's freezing cold in here. Not a nice place for such a pretty girl to be spending time – I'm sure she longs for her small, safe home and her dull parents and pretty sisters. No matter. I'm here in their stead. It's like something out of a fairy tale.

'I heard you shouting as I was coming along the path,' I say. 'For that, I'm going to punish one of your sisters. Shall I hurt Eden or shall I hurt Lucy?'

She lets out a sob. 'Please... no, please don't hurt them.'

'It's up to you. If you misbehave, they get your punishment.'

'I'm sorry.' Her words trip over a sob. 'I won't do it again.'

I love the sound of panic in her voice. She's suffering for those poor girls, who suffer no more.

'Promise?'

'I promise.'

I put down the carrier bag that contains the food and water. Maybe I'm spoiling her, but today I've brought her a sandwich and a small KitKat. I don't know if I'll let her have the chocolate yet.

Now, it's time to get down to business.

'Paige, let's play a little game. If you tell me something that I want to hear, then I might be able to go easy on Lucy and Eden.'

She sniffs and nods. She'll tell me anything to save her sisters.

'Remember, I'll know if you're lying.'

She believes this, of course, even though it's not remotely true.

'I asked Lucy and Eden a question, and now I'll ask you the same question. If your answer matches theirs, you'll get something to eat and drink. But if it doesn't, one of you will be punished.'

She whimpers at the word 'punished'.

'Here's the question. Which of you is your mother's favourite?'

She stares at the floor, wringing her hands in her lap. I notice how filthy they are, with black arcs of grime under her nails. I glance around, wondering if she'd been trying to dig her way out, but there's no sign of it.

'Come on. You know the answer.'

'I don't.' She shakes her head vehemently.

'Lucy and Eden knew the answer straight away. If you can't tell me, I'll have to punish them both.'

I thrust my hand into my jacket pocket and withdraw a pair of poultry shears. She gives a little shriek as she realises what they are. I snap them open and shut to prompt her answer.

'Lucy? Did they say Lucy?'

I laugh. 'No, that wasn't their answer.' Of course it wasn't. They're dead.

She starts to cry again.

Still laughing, I pick up the bag with the food and water and leave.

And I laugh all the way home.

TWENTY-SEVEN

Lexi sat staring at her phone. She'd promised Maggie she'd get some expert input on profiling the killer, but Harry Garcia was the last person on earth she wanted to talk to. Harry would have an opinion but he wouldn't have time – he was already too much in demand in his own country. However, he'd steer her to someone here she'd be able to rely on.

So why couldn't she make the call?

She thought about the last time she'd seen him. A few weeks after they broke up, just before she got the flight back to England. A few weeks after they'd brought in the Diamond River Killer. The case that bust them wide apart. Everything inside her seemed to lurch as if the ground had suddenly fallen away under her feet. She gripped the side of her desk and took a deep breath.

Count to ten. One, two, three...

Another deep breath. And another. Slowly, things rebalanced.

Maybe there was someone else she could talk to. Not about profiling. But someone who would understand why this case was proving so tough for her. She clicked away from Harry's details and scrolled up the list to C.

Despite the number being out of date, it didn't take her long to find out what had happened to DI Len Clayton in the seventeen years since she'd last seen him. He'd seemed old to her then, when she was seventeen, so it came as no surprise that he was now living in a nursing home, somewhere on the edge of Herne Bay. She hoped his room had a sea view and that the food was good – he'd been a decent copper, kind, and hadn't treated her and Amber like children, which was more than she could say for most of the other professionals they'd come into contact with after their ordeal.

He would be able to give her some perspective on the case. Perhaps it was an act of desperation. But Amber's suggestion that the Carter sisters' murder was somehow linked to their own abduction seventeen years before had chimed with her own suspicions, and now she needed to face the possibility – just to rule it out. She understood how the men who preyed on young girls worked, and how they behaved. And they didn't act on their fantasies once, forget all about it for nearly two decades, only to then give it a second shot.

The fact that there had been no similar crime in all the subsequent years meant something. The man who had snatched her and her sisters couldn't have risen from the dead to strike again, could he? Because Lexi had believed that he was dead. It wasn't something she was ready to discuss with the team yet, but Len Clayton knew the case better than anyone, and she was sure he'd have an opinion.

The woman who opened the door of the ugly Victorian mansion looked her up and down with surprise. 'It's not visiting time – we're in the middle of having supper.'

Lexi assumed the 'we' actually referred to the residents, rather than the staff. She said her name and held out her ID. 'I need to talk to Leonard Clayton on an urgent matter.'

'Suit yourself,' the woman said, stepping back to let Lexi in, 'but you'll get short shrift from him for interrupting his tea.'

The entrance hall smelled of cabbage and furniture polish, and was as glum and unwelcoming as anywhere Lexi could imagine. She supposed a police pension didn't run to somewhere nicer. Poor old Len.

The woman, middle-aged, dressed for comfort rather than style, led her deep into the bowels of the building. The original large house had been extended at the back with the addition of a blocky, unsympathetic extension. Passing into the modern section, the woman showed her into a dining room that was reminiscent of a school refectory or a works canteen. There was nothing homely or welcoming about the plain, white-topped tables and straight-backed pine chairs. The flimsy false curtains failed to absorb the noise of cutlery on china and the shrill chatter of the female residents. The men seemed quieter, more interested in clearing their plates.

Lexi looked around and spotted Len at a table by the window, sitting on his own. He'd changed since she'd last seen him. Of course he had. So had she. After all, she'd been a teenager when he'd been assigned to the abduction of her and her sisters. His hair was sparse and faded, and his face had the grey pallor of a long-term smoker. He was sitting in a wheelchair and there were plastic tubes hooked round the back of his ears, delivering oxygen.

'DI Clayton,' she said as she got closer to his table.

He looked up from his meal with a frown. 'Who wants to know?'

'I'm Lexi Bennett,' she said. 'I don't know if you remember...'

His expression softened momentarily. 'Of course I remember. You don't forget a case like that.'

No, you don't, thought Lexi to herself. There were cases she'd worked on that had seared themselves into her psyche. She knew how it felt.

She took a seat at the table, uninvited. 'You were a good cop. Unsolved cases have a way of working themselves into your DNA. They're like an itch on your back that you can't quite reach, and it keeps itching, keeps driving you mad.'

Clayton's eyes said he agreed with her, even though he didn't speak.

She took a breath. 'All these years, you've been looking out for him, right? Digging into headlines, going down rabbit holes, just in case, because maybe...'

He gave a dismissive shrug and speared a piece of potato with his fork.

'Is he dead, the man who took me and my sisters? Is he? I need to know what you think.'

'He might be dead, he might be in prison, he might have moved far away, he might have changed his MO...'

'Len, you're parroting theories. I didn't drive over so you can tell me things I can work out for myself.' She'd learned all of this at Quantico, the place where those theories had been born.

'So what do you want?' He met her eyes with a steady gaze.

'I want to know what you really think. What you believe. If you ever saw anything over the years that convinced you he was dead and gone. Something concrete.'

'I knew you'd come knocking when I saw you on the television. As soon as I heard the girls were triplets.' So he'd known who she was the moment she'd walked into the room.

'Then you know what I'm up against.'

'I dream about you and about Amber. Even about Rose. More nights than I don't. And these days, I don't know whether they're dreams or memories.' Len pushed his plate to one side and leaned forward. 'I can tell you what you want to hear, or I can be honest with you.'

'What do you think I want to hear?'

'You want me to be certain that he's dead and gone. That's what I would want if I was you.'

She gave a slight nod.

'You know I can't tell you that. There's no certainty until we know who he was and his body turns up. That's not going to happen. We don't live in a world that ties things off with neat little bows.'

'What's your gut feeling?'

Clayton gestured to the woman, who came towards them. 'I'd like some ice cream, please, Janet. Vanilla.' Giving himself time to think.

The woman nodded and took away his abandoned plate.

Clayton looked up at Lexi. 'Do I think he's dead?' He asked the question slowly, sounding out every consonant. 'No, I don't. But what I believe doesn't matter. It's not my case.'

Lexi's heart rate went up a notch.

He remained silent as Janet reappeared and placed a small green bowl containing two scoops of ice cream in front of him.

Janet went away. He ate the ice cream in silence and Lexi waited, her gut churning.

What's your gut feeling?

When he finished, he pushed the bowl away. 'Push me out to the garden, would you? I need a smoke.'

What difference could a cigarette make? He looked close to death as it was. She got up and went round to his side of the table. Janet glared at her as she wheeled him out of the dining room. He directed her to a glass veranda door and they went outside. A wall light illuminated the terrace with an amber glow, but the lawn stretching down the slope disappeared into the inky shadows of a row of tall trees.

Len unhooked the oxygen tubes and drew a packet of cigarettes from the pocket of his cardigan.

'Want one?'

'No, thanks.'

He lit up and inhaled deeply, his chest rattling until a cough erupted.

'Now,' he said as he got it under control, 'tell me what you believe. That's really why you're here – you can't know what you think until you've said it out loud. I'll listen.'

Lexi walked a few paces away from him. In the dark garden, everything was still and quiet, with not even the rustle of a breeze in the trees. The rain had stopped, though the cement path was still wet underfoot.

What do you believe?

It was time to give voice to the doubt that any of the suspects they'd identified so far were the man they were looking for.

She walked back to where Len sat waiting, the smouldering butt of his cigarette lying on the path near to his wheelchair. Lexi stubbed it out with her heel. Len lit another one.

'I was the one that found the bodies of Eden and Lucy Carter.' She spoke tentatively at first. 'They were up on the Memorial Crown outside Wye, just a mile from where I live.'

Len coughed violently, but she could see from his eyes that he was engaged.

'I was out for a run at the time – my usual run. Every morning, early, since I moved into the house, I've run up the hill and watched the sun rise over the Crown.' She swallowed, her mouth suddenly dry. 'And then on Monday morning, there they were. Two dead girls.' She looked Len in the eye. She was saying things she'd hardly dared to articulate as thoughts. 'He left them there for me to find. Holding roses. Roses, Len.'

It was no coincidence.

This was no cheap copycat killing.

The man who'd lived rent free in the darkest recesses of her mind for seventeen years had just stepped back out into the light. And she'd been trying to ignore the fact because it made her scared. More scared than she'd ever been in her life.

TWENTY-EIGHT

After they spoke, Len Clayton had directed her to take him back to his room.

'Up there, on top of the wardrobe, see that box?'

Lexi had craned her neck.

'It's copies of the case files and all my notes.' He'd coughed, guttural and phlegmy. 'It's the only case I bothered to copy. I always believed that somehow I'd be able to solve it, but I never could. I'm passing the baton on to you – take the box.'

Lexi had to climb onto a chair to reach the battered box file, and when she'd pulled it over the edge of the wardrobe, the weight of it had nearly toppled her over. She'd dropped it clumsily onto Len's bed, where it slumped onto its side with a thud.

Now it was in the boot of her car and as she drove back to Canterbury, she was having a reckoning with what was going on. If the roses were a message to her from the killer, referring to Rose, why hadn't she seen it earlier? Maggie's voice sounded in her ear, asking her if she felt strong enough to take the case, and then Amber, posing the same question. She heard her own voice, confidently batting them away, when all along, deep in her soul, she'd felt the darkness rising.

She'd been in denial.

And the chances were that Paige would have to pay the ultimate price because of it.

She slammed the heel of her hand against the steering wheel and let out a roar of anger. Because of her own pig-headedness. Because of the precious time she'd wasted.

Of course, she should have accessed the case files sooner on the Holmes computer, but fear of the darkness inside her had held her back. The memories had been suppressed for years and she'd been scared to wake the sleeping bear. Now she had no choice. If the man who had Paige Carter was the same man who'd taken her, Amber and Rose, it raised far more questions than it answered. And this box of files might have the answer. She could no longer turn away.

She'd never seen the man's face, and she couldn't replay his voice in her head. He haunted her nightmares, but she knew nothing at all about him. He kept to the shadows, in life and in her imagination, and now all she wanted to do was shine a light right in his eyes, bright enough to blind him. Len's files might just be the torch she was looking for.

She went into the station through the back door and staggered across the corridor towards the stairs, hefting the cardboard box in front of her.

'Let me take that,' said Tom, as she almost knocked him over on the bottom step. 'What is it?'

Lexi had been hoping to sneak it into her office unobserved.

'Just some old case files.'

'What case?'

'They're Len Clayton's files from seventeen years ago.'

Tom took a few steps before he realised what she was saying. 'From your case? Your abduction.' He turned sideways to study her face. 'Are you okay, Lexi?'

She shrugged. She knew her make-up was a mess. She felt exhausted and bruised.

'Talk to me.'

She walked ahead of him into her office without bothering to answer, but he followed her in, dropped the box on the floor and sat down opposite her.

Finally, she allowed her eyes to meet his. 'It's complicated, Tom.'

'But there has to be a connection between the two cases, no?'

'I don't know, given the time span. But I can't ignore the possibility.'

'So how does that tie-in with our current suspects?'

'That's what we have to uncover. Where are we with Madison?'

'The charges against him for accessing and possessing child pornography are with the CPS for approval, but I can't see any problem there.'

'Good. I suppose he'll apply for bail and I'm sure we'll oppose it. What about Yates?'

'We're keeping eyes on him, but he knows we're interested, so he's not going to do anything incriminating.'

'And still no sign of Pendleton?'

Lexi's mobile rang as Tom shook his head.

'DI Bennett?' It was the desk sergeant downstairs. 'There's someone on the line for you – your sister, I think.'

Lexi realised that her phone had been set to silent since her meeting with Len. She'd probably missed dozens of calls. 'Put her through, thanks.' There was a hum, then the line came clear. 'This is Lexi.'

'Lexi? Thank God – I've been trying to get you for almost an hour.' Amber's voice sounded panicky.

'What's up?'

'There was a face, a man's face, staring in at the window.'

'Where are you?'

'Home.'

'Is he still there?'

'I can't see him. I'm looking out into the garden, but it's totally dark. I screamed when I saw him, and he just seemed to fade backwards.'

'Sit tight – I'll come to you.'

Driving over to Summer Hill, where her sister lived, Lexi didn't feel quite so clever about what had happened that morning. It was all very well to climb on her high horse about doing everything she could to discover who'd taken Paige and murdered her sisters, but she knew Amber had a point. Her parting remark, about Lexi trying to exonerate herself, had stung. It reminded Lexi how sharp Amber could be and why they had been estranged for more than fifteen years. Amber's kids were growing up fast and Lexi had never even met them.

When she'd returned to Canterbury from America, it had been in the back of her mind to search out her sister and try for a reconciliation. She'd been putting it off, and this morning, when Amber had reached out, she'd almost blown it. Perhaps because, when she saw Amber face to face for the first time in years, she realised she wasn't ready for it yet. But if she wasn't ready to make peace now, would she ever be?

Amber and her husband, Grant, had moved a few years back, and Lexi had never been to their house. Summer Hill was one of the smartest parts of Canterbury, on the western edge of the city. The Victorian houses were large and detached, set back from the road with mature gardens and drives that had space to park three or four cars. Grant Riley was a councillor and local businessman, though Lexi had never been able to work out exactly what he did. Anyway, it clearly netted them enough to afford an expensive piece of property.

She found the house easily and parked directly outside. The light above the front door was bright enough to illuminate the entire front garden. There was one car on the circular carriage drive – a sporty-looking Saab, which she assumed belonged to her sister.

Lexi walked up to the drive, her boots crunching on gravel. The door opened and Amber stepped out into the pool of light. She looked frightened.

'Thank God you're here.'

'Are you alone?' said Lexi, as she followed her sister into a wood-panelled entrance hall.

'Grant's away on a business trip in Italy, but Tash is here.'

A slight, pale-faced girl came down the hall towards them. 'Mummy?'

Tasha. Her eleven-year-old niece she'd never met. But Lexi would have recognised her anywhere – it was like seeing a carbon copy of Rose at that age. She even wore her hair in the same scruffy ponytail.

Amber put an arm around the girl's shoulders and pulled her close. 'Tasha, this your Aunt Lexi.'

'Your sister?'

'That's right,' said Amber.

Lexi stepped forward. 'Hi, Tasha – it's good to meet you at long last.' She wasn't sure whether to stretch out a hand or open her arms for a hug.

Tasha stepped forward, possibly with a gentle nudge from Amber, and Lexi bent down so she could embrace her.

'You look just like my mum,' Tasha said as they disengaged.

'I know. We looked even more alike when we were your age. We were identical triplets.'

There was an awkward silence. No one wanted to start a conversation about what had happened to Rose.

'Listen, Tash, I've got to talk to Aunt Lexi about something. Why don't you go upstairs and get started on your homework?'

The little girl pulled a face but didn't argue, and Lexi watched as she reluctantly plodded up the stairs.

'She's amazing,' said Lexi. 'Is Sam around?'

'No, he's at school. He has to board as he sings in the cathedral choir. I hate it, but it's what he wanted – and he really does have the voice of an angel.'

Lexi felt a pang of regret at all she must have missed out on. She wondered if she and Amber could overcome their differences so she could get to know her niece and nephew.

'Tell me exactly what happened,' said Lexi.

Amber led the way through to a large kitchen-diner and pointed at a bay window that overlooked the back garden. Below it was a curved window seat. Its blue striped cushions were scattered with documents, some of which had fallen onto the floor.

'I was sitting over there, reading some work stuff.' She went across and started to nervously gather up the papers. Lexi went to help her. 'I looked up to see a man's face staring in at me.'

'Did you recognise him?'

She shook her head. 'No, I'm certain I didn't. But then he was gone so quickly. I ran to the back door and flipped on the garden lights, but there was no one there.'

Lexi peered out into the back garden. The lights were still on, and she could see it was well-maintained. There was no one there, but there were plenty of long dark shadows to melt away into. She went to the back door.

'I'll take a look outside.'

'Are you sure?'

'I'll be fine. I'm the police, remember?'

Amber picked up a set of keys from a dresser and came across to unlock the door. Lexi watched, pleased to see that the door was secured with two separate mortice deadlocks. The cold hit her as she stepped outside.

'Do you want a torch?' said Amber.

'No worries, I'm pretty sure he'll be gone by now.' She walked down the centre of the lawn, looking carefully from side to side. Smart houses like these had a habit of attracting attention from the wrong sorts. Maybe it was someone looking for an empty house to break into.

Maybe it wasn't. If the killer knew that she lived in Wye, he could also have found out where Amber lived. She shivered at the thought.

She went right up to the far end of the garden. The lights didn't quite reach this far, and the small orchard of apple trees at the back wall was pitch black. Lexi stood quietly and listened. There was the soft rattling of the wind through the branches above her, but other than that, she could hear nothing. She wanted to look over the wall, but it was too high. Not too high, though, for someone athletic to scale.

The sound of a branch snapping on the other side of the wall took her by surprise. Hairs stood up on the back of her neck. Was someone there? She listened a while longer but heard nothing more, so returned to the house.

'What's beyond the back wall?' said Lexi.

'A field – usually a couple of horses in it, and beyond that a patch of woods before you reach the road.'

'Are the horses there now?'

'No, just during the day. They're stabled at night.'

'It wouldn't be too difficult to scale the wall, so the chances are the guy came over from the back, rather than risk being seen out front – but it's hard to say.' She didn't mention the sound she'd heard. She thought about calling it in, to have some uniformed officers sent out to search the field and the woods behind the house. But if there was someone there, they'd have scarpered long before anyone else would arrive.

'Has it happened before?'

'No. I've always felt perfectly safe here, even when Grant's away.'

'Is that a lot of the time?'

Amber shrugged. 'He usually has a couple of trips a month, but just for a day or two.'

'You might consider putting a security light with a movement sensor at the back of the house.'

'We had one for a while, but it kept getting set off by foxes, so Grant took it down.'

'Time to put it back,' said Lexi. 'I know it's annoying, but it works as a deterrent to people thinking about breaking in.'

Amber sighed. She seemed calmer now, but things had a way of becoming less frightening once you weren't on your own.

'Thanks for coming, Lexi. Glass of wine?' The offer sounded tentative, and Lexi supposed being together was as strange for Amber as it was for her.

'I've still got work to do,' said Lexi. 'But a coffee would be good.'

Amber set up her coffee machine in silence, and poured herself a glass of white wine from an open bottle in the fridge. 'Milk, sugar?'

'Neither, thanks,' said Lexi, shaking her head. Imagine, sisters – they'd grown up together – and now Amber had to politely ask her how she took her coffee. Again, Lexi felt a pang of regret for what had passed between them.

After a moment's thought, Lexi knew she had to say something. 'Listen, Amber, I don't want to scare you, but I am concerned. There's a slim chance that the man who took the Carter sisters is the same man who took us. If he's in the area, it's only natural that he might want to...'

'What?' said Amber, her eyes wide with fear.

'See what we're doing. Spook us.'

'You think he'll come after us again? The Triplet Killer?' It was the name the press had given their abductor at the time, even though two of them had escaped him, and Rose's body had never been found.

'Don't call him that.' Lexi hated it.

'But do you think…'

'That he's back?' Lexi shrugged. 'I have to consider it's a possibility.' She still hadn't got her head around it yet, and she certainly wasn't ready to go into the details with her sister.

'Great. What about Tash? What if he goes after her?' said Amber, chucking back her wine and going to the fridge for a top-up.

'Be extra careful about locking all your doors, draw the curtains and get that light put back. You've got an alarm, I take it?'

Amber nodded.

'Then set it at night, especially when Grant's away.'

'I do.' Amber glanced around the kitchen nervously. 'Look, would you mind staying tonight? I just feel a bit spooked.'

'You want me to stay here?'

'I know it's a lot to ask, especially as things have been a bit…' She struggled for the right word.

'A bit shit between us?' said Lexi. She spotted the glimmer of a smile on Amber's face.

'Tasha would love to get to know you better.'

It was too tempting, but with things the way they were, she couldn't afford to take time away from the case. 'I'm sorry, Amber, really I am, but I was on my way back into the office when you called.'

Her sister's face fell. 'I get it, I understand. Work first.'

Lexi felt bad. For everyone else, it was family first. She'd lost Rose forever. She'd lost Amber for years. But now, here was the chance to reconnect with her only surviving sister – and to get to know the next generation of their family.

'No, that's not fair of me. I'll stay – for as long as you need me.'

'Just a couple of days. Grant will be back on Friday.'

'Okay, let me just go home and grab some stuff, then over to the station to pick up some files I need to read through.' Amber didn't need to know they were the police files on their very own case.

Amber smiled with relief. 'Have you eaten yet this evening?'

'No.' She'd hardly had a thing all day.

'I'll make something for when you get back.'

'Great.'

As she went out to the car, Lexi wondered what sort of cook Amber was – she'd never tasted a single thing cooked by either of her sisters. But the thought quickly turned sour. The man Amber called the Triplet Killer had stolen such simple pleasures away from her. He had poisoned her life.

And now she couldn't help but think that he was back.

TWENTY-NINE

It's a heart-warming sight – to see my two princesses back together again.

I knew I could effect a reunion between the two of them if I tried hard enough.

Friends at last. That bond reinstated. It never really went away, it was just stretched almost to breaking point before springing back. I could see genuine warmth in their interaction this evening.

Do you suppose they're twins now, rather than triplets, given that one of them is dead? I never really thought of it before, but seeing them standing together in Amber's kitchen reminds me of a pair of twins I used to know...

They're dead to me now.

They're dead to everybody for that matter.

So sad.

THIRTY

Amber's cooking turned out to be good. She was, after all, the consummate wife and mother, in contrast to Lexi's fridge-grazing single existence. While they ate pasta primavera, accompanied by garlic bread and a fresh green salad, Lexi listened entranced as Tasha told them about school and drama club and the birthday present she wanted to buy for one of her classmates.

'She's wonderful,' said Lexi, when Tasha had gone upstairs to get ready for bed. 'A real credit to you, Amber.'

The sisters were still sitting at the dining room table, finishing their glasses of wine. Amber fetched a bar of dark chocolate from a cupboard in the Welsh dresser nearby and snapped it into squares on the open wrapper. She offered them to Lexi.

'I shouldn't,' said Lexi. 'I'm in training for a triathlon.'

Amber's eyebrows went up. There was so much they didn't know about each other. 'Go on,' she said. 'Isn't dark chocolate supposed to be good for you?'

Lexi relented and took a square, and as they finished the wine, they exchanged stories of how life had treated them over the past few years. It all seemed so normal, and Lexi wondered if they could truly put the past behind them or whether this would turn out to be an uneasy sort of truce because the recent killings had frightened them both.

When she helped Amber clear the plates and glasses back to the kitchen, she caught sight of Len Clayton's box file sitting on the kitchen table where she'd dumped it earlier.

'I'd better get on with some work now,' she said, as Amber loaded the dishwasher.

'Sure, go ahead. I could do with an early night anyway after all the excitement. Have you got everything you need? More wine?'

'No thanks – I can't afford to be fuzzy-headed in the morning.'

'Fair enough. There's tea and coffee.' Amber pointed to a couple of cupboards and the coffee machine. 'Or help yourself to soft drinks from the fridge.'

'I'm great. Sleep well.'

Once Amber had gone, Lexi made herself a coffee and took the box of papers through to the living room. She tipped it up on the floor and a stack of manilla folders slid across the carpet, dust making her sneeze.

Where to start?

She picked up the folder closest to hand with a feeling of trepidation. The police investigation into what had happened to her and her sisters, and the subsequent search for Rose, had gone on for months and generated thousands of newspaper articles. Lexi and Amber had been regularly ambushed by journalists as they made their tentative return to school, creating a distrust of the press that Lexi still suffered from. Naturally, she'd wanted the whole thing to go away, and if they couldn't find Rose, she didn't want to hear about what might have happened.

The folder in her hand didn't have a title, just a number on the cover in what she had to assume was Len's handwriting. It was quite irregular – even wrong – for him to have copied all the police files and taken them home, but his insights might just give her a handle on what was happening today, so she needed to read them.

She opened the file.

Inside, there was a stack of witness statements. Lexi flicked through them, recognising the names – school friends, teachers, her parents...

She sat back, leaning against the side of the sofa, and read the statement their mother had given the police when her parents had reported the three of them missing.

> *Mrs Bennett: I last saw all three of my daughters when they left for school on Thursday morning. I was expecting them home for supper, Lexi maybe a little later than the other two, as she had hockey practice. When none of them had appeared by seven, I started to feel a little concerned. I tried to call them on their mobile phones, but none of them answered. My husband got home from work, and I asked him to drive up to the school to see if he could find them there. I was starting to get really worried...*

Tears blurred Lexi's vision and she stopped reading. Of course, she knew her parents had been devastated by what had happened, but they'd been hugely relieved to get her and Amber back, and somehow managed to hide their fear and grief over Rose. Lexi had never thought about what the first few days had been like for her mother and father, when all three of them were missing. It made her think about what the Carters were going through now. Two of their daughters were dead, and they would never get over that, but she might still have a chance to retrieve Paige for them.

She shut the folder of witness statements. She didn't think

they'd contain what she was looking for, whatever that might be. She flicked her way quickly through the other folders, stopping occasionally to read things. The details of the police investigation seemed sketchy compared to the way things would be recorded now. There were suspect interviews, but most of the men the police pulled in for questioning were able to provide alibis, and there was no evidence that linked them to the place where the sisters had been held before she and Amber escaped. She spent three hours in the silent house reading through a multitude of documents, but nothing jumped out at her.

She stood up and stretched. Walking across to the window overlooking the back garden, she had to wonder if he was out there now – watching her from the shadows or watching Paige suffering in solitude. There was no doubt in her mind that the man was a watcher. One of the few things she remembered from her time in captivity – not a memory, more of a feeling that lingered long after she was home – was the skin-crawling conviction that she was being watched. Eyes on her every move, watching her all the time, whether she was awake or asleep.

She turned back to the mess of papers on the floor. It was time.

Time to confront what had happened to her all those years ago.

She knew somewhere in the pile would be her and Amber's interviews with the police after they'd escaped. She knew that there was likely to be information in those interviews that had long since disappeared down the sinkhole of her memory – that black hole inside her mind that ate up the worst of everything to protect her from the horror.

It was time to drag some of those memories back out into the light.

She picked up one of the last unopened folders, wondering if it was the one. It was. Inside, there were the transcripts of two interview: hers and Amber's. She looked at the one marked as hers. It was time-stamped seven a.m. She remembered the cold, hard interview room, and realised it was the same one in which she'd interviewed Toby Yates earlier.

She'd had no sleep – there had been too much adrenalin coursing through her body for that – and she'd felt dog-tired. She remembered the plastic cup with sweet, weak tea in it, that felt like the best thing she'd ever tasted. But maybe that was because she was sitting between her father and a WPC, and she was no longer at the mercy of the man in the mask.

Her eyes hovered over the document, not reading the words that had the potential to put her fragmented memories into some sort of order, and to maybe fill in the gaps that had been missing for all these years.

There were two decanters on a small side table next to the fire, cut glass tumblers on a shelf below them. She poured herself a generous measure, fetched her notebook and a pen from her bag, and settled down on the sofa. The whisky burned a heat trail down the back of her throat, bolstering her for the ordeal.

She started to read, pausing over each answer as the past swam back into view. It hurt, reliving what that so much younger version of herself had lived through, joining the dots with each question answered. Too many times, she had to stop reading to wipe away tears before she could focus on the page again. But as she read, she made notes. The information was valuable. She could use it to build an accurate profile of the man who took her, and if it was the same man who was now holding Paige it might just lead them to her.

Her younger self had told the police about how the man had grabbed her from behind and shoved her into the back of a van. She couldn't remember the outside of the van. She could only say that the inside was painted black and virtually empty. She'd been alone, walking home from school after hockey. It had been dark. She was on her usual route. She walked part of the way with her friend Cathy, and after reaching Cathy's house, she'd continued the rest of the way alone.

On the page, in black and white, the information appeared very matter-of-fact, but Lexi could remember how much it had cost to describe what had happened, and she felt the same anxiety now as she read through her long-distant answers.

She scanned every detail and tried to remember more than just the words on the page. What were the similarities with the current case? What was different? Could it be the same man, all these years later?

He called me princess. He knew my name – I never told him. But he always called me princess.

And now she heard his voice in her ears again. Softly spoken with the slightest lisp.

Princess.

No copycat killer could know that.

He'd left two dead girls, dressed as princesses, where she would find them.

He'd come back for her. And he wanted her to know it.

Lexi shivered and finished the tumbler of whisky. There was enough in here, and in Amber's interview, to construct an accurate profile. She would ring Harry Garcia first thing in the morning and talk to him.

But as she stacked up the files and put them back into the box, she remembered the time difference. When it was breakfast time here, Harry Garcia would be fast asleep. She looked at her watch. Midnight. So it was seven p.m. in Virginia currently. She could call him now. Inside, she squirmed. She didn't relish the prospect of talking to Harry again, but this had been an evening of returning to the past.

Finally, with reluctant fingers, she pressed a speed dial number that she'd thought she'd never use again.

'Garcia speaking. Who's this?'

Ouch – that hurt. He'd removed her from his contacts?

'Harry? It's me.' Harry Garcia had been first her tutor, then her direct superior during her time with the FBI. But he'd been far more than that.

'Lexi! Sorry, I'm driving, so I didn't see the name come up.'

'No worries.' At least he had recognised her voice. There was an awkward silence until she remembered that she'd called him, and needed to tell him why. 'Listen, is this a good time to talk?'

'It's fine – I'm on the ninety-five, about fifteen miles from the office and the traffic's terrible.' He was referring to the I-95 that ran south from Washington to Quantico – as deputy head of the FBI's Investigative Support Unit, he made the journey backwards and forwards at least a couple of times a week.

'Still too cheap to pay the toll for the express lane?'

Harry Garcia laughed, but he didn't deny it, and the sound of his laughter carried her back to another time. Pain and regret flared. Then anger, for what he'd done to her.

'How's it feel to be back home?'

'Good.' She didn't elaborate.

'You know, you should have stayed. You'll never get a case as challenging as Diamond River – you Brits just don't kill people the way we do.'

'I know. That's exactly why I'm pleased to back here.' The Diamond River Killer had been the most gruelling case she'd ever worked on – seven bodies piling up in seven days – and it had practically broken her. Even Harry had aged five years over the course of the few weeks they'd spent tracking the sadistic killer responsible. And then that terrible betrayal that had left her vulnerable.

'So what can I do for you?' he said, correctly reading that she didn't want to talk about it.

'I've got a profile I need to do, and I can't find my way into it.'

'Shoot.'

'Two victims, teenage girls...' She filled him in on the details of the bodies and the crime scene, how it had been posed and what the girls were wearing. Harry punctuated her monologue with an 'uh-huh' every now and again, but he held fire on questions until she'd finished.

'I couldn't get a handle on his signature,' said Lexi. 'What was his compulsion? No torture, no sexual assault or battery. There's only evidence of sexual activity in one of the girls, and no sign that it was rape.'

There was silence at the other end. 'Harry, are you there?'

'Sure, I'm here. Just thinking.'

She walked over to the window and looked out over the dark garden again.

She hadn't told Harry the two girls had another sister, still missing. She wanted to see how he read the scene first.

'So we both know he gets off on seeing his victims suffer. How have they suffered? What's he done to them that we can't see?'

There were ways of inflicting pain on people that didn't leave a mark. Was that it?

'He's terrorised them,' she said, thinking out loud. 'Not physical pain, but something mental.'

'Look for patterns. Climb inside his mind and curl up in there. Wait for the patterns to repeat. Wait – you said you had a problem with his motivation. But you don't now? What do you know?'

'There's a third girl, still missing. Triplets.'

'What the—? You didn't tell me that.'

'I'm telling you now.'

'That changes everything. You know what it means.'

'That he's back, and I've got to get a handle on him fast to save the third sister. Can you help me?'

'I can't, Lexi. I'm swamped. You want someone close by, who can give you a hundred per cent.'

'Who?'

'I'll send you contact details. Gotta go – incoming call from the Commander-in-Chief. Working on something for him.'

'Seriously?' *The president?*

The call disconnected abruptly, and Lexi was left no better off than when she'd dialled him. Worse off, in fact. Because now she wanted to hear his voice again, and not just for the wisdom of his words.

She needed to sleep. As she climbed the stairs up to the spare room Amber had shown her earlier, a text came in. It was from Harry.

Talk to Ed Harlow, forensic psy prof at Kent Uni. Tell him I sent you.

Contact details followed.

Lexi knew the name – of course she did. Dr Edward Harlow was the UK's most celebrated criminal profiler, constantly in demand from forces up and down the country. Like her, he'd spent time at the Investigative Support Unit at Quantico, but that didn't make him Harry Garcia, and it was Harry's opinion that she still valued, despite all that had happened between them.

She dialled his number from Amber's kitchen as soon as she'd downed her first cup of steaming coffee. She wasn't too proud to take help if she could get it, and brainstorming with a more experienced profiler could make all the difference.

Not surprisingly, Dr Harlow didn't pick up a call from an unknown number. She left a message explaining who she was, how she'd got his number, and asked him to call her back to discuss a case she was working on. It was only seven a.m., so the chances were that he wasn't up yet.

After a quick breakfast, and having reassured Tasha she'd be back that evening, she drove from Amber's house to the station – hardly any distance compared to her usual journey from Wye. She kicked herself for not having picked up her running gear when she'd gone home the evening before and determined to fetch it later in the day if she got the chance.

As if that was likely, in the middle of murder investigation...

Her phone rang just as she was manoeuvring through the gate into the station car park. She didn't recognise the number.

'Lexi Bennett speaking.'

'DI Bennett, this is Ed Harlow.'

'Great. Thanks for calling back. I wonder if I could talk to you about a case I'm working on – a double murder—'

'Whoa!'

'What?'

'I've been up twenty-four hours straight working on a profile in the field. I was just calling to acknowledge your call and let you know that I'll get back to you when I'm back in my office – whenever that will be.'

'I'm sorry, that was rude of me. But I've got a third girl, still missing, possibly alive. I can't wait for a couple of days.'

Harlow sighed. 'I've literally just got home from the other end of the country. I'd like to help you but...'

'Where are you?'

'Just outside Sandwich, but—'

'I'll come to you. Please, just spare me half an hour or so – if not for me then for Paige Carter, whose life is hanging in the balance.'

'Fine – half an hour,' he said begrudgingly. 'When will you get here?'

Lexi was already reversing her car out of the car park entrance. 'Less than half an hour. I'm leaving Canterbury right now.'

He gave her an address as she negotiated the ring road. She was thankfully still ahead of the main rush hour and once she was on the A257 she was able to cruise along at just above the speed limit. As she drove, she called Tom and left a message to let him know what she was up to.

. . .

Being a professor of forensic psychology clearly paid the bills. The house her satnav directed her to was a newly converted barn, one wall replaced with glass and a red-brick oast kiln at the far end. The scrunching of her tyres on the gravel drive seemed to have alerted its occupant, as a door opened and a man walked out towards her.

Lexi got out of the Crossfire and walked towards him. 'Ed Harlow?'

The man nodded. He was in his early forties, tall and well-muscled, but the most striking thing about him were his piercing blue eyes. They drilled right through her, his brows lowered, giving her the impression that he wasn't entirely pleased to see her. He didn't dress quite how she imagined a professor would dress either – a plaid cowboy-style shirt with pearlized studs instead of buttons, dark indigo jeans and, she saw as he came closer, well-worn Timberland boots. His hair, black with the slightest sprinkling of grey, was combed straight back from a high forehead.

'DI Bennett?'

'Call me Lexi. I'm so sorry if I'm keeping you up after a long night.' Not that she'd managed much sleep herself after the previous evening's bedtime reading.

He looked her up and down. His look was cold. He didn't smile or tell her not to worry. He simply glanced at his watch and then beckoned for her to follow him inside.

'You've got twenty minutes, DI Bennett.'

'Sorry,' she said again, instantly regretting the repetition, 'I thought you said you'd give me half an hour.'

'I did, but you've already missed the first ten minutes by arriving later than you said.'

Wow. Nice guy. Duly noted.

He showed her into a sleek modern kitchen that was all

blond wood and vitreous tiles. It overlooked a long lawn beyond which, across the fields, she could see the tiled rooftops of Sandwich. An idyllic spot to live.

They sat down on opposite sides of the kitchen table, but he didn't offer her coffee.

'Okay, let's get to it then,' he said.

She pulled the hurriedly copied case notes out of her bag and pushed them across to him. As he scanned them, she recapped the main points of the case out loud.

'My problem is,' she said, as he finally put the pile of papers to one side, 'that although the crime was elaborately staged, suggesting this wasn't a first kill, I'm not seeing, from the results of the post-mortems, what his compulsion is, why he's killing – and without that, I'm struggling to put together a sufficiently detailed profile to help the investigation.' She wasn't ready to disclose her suspicions about the Triplet Killer to him yet – she wanted to see what he made of the case first.

'It's an interesting problem, I'll grant you that,' he said, placing his hand palm down on the pile of papers. 'But hardly worth driving over here in such hurry. You could have emailed me this stuff.'

He was beginning to irritate her, but she bit back the sarcastic reply that sprung to mind. 'I find that brainstorming with another profiler always helps.'

One eyebrow raised. He didn't necessarily agree with her. Message received loud and clear.

'If this crime scene isn't telling you enough, you need to fill in the gaps. It's not his first kill, so go back in time. I assume you're positing a link between this unsub and the man who took you and your sisters?'

Garcia was right – the man was good.

'You've done your homework.'

'I teach the Triplet Killer on my course.'

'I see.' Of course he would have recognised her name, and the Carter girls' murder had been splashed all over the press.

Harlow was watching her closely.

'I'd rather you didn't refer to him as the Triplet Killer,' Lexi said at last. 'After all, two of us survived and my sister Rose's body has never been recovered.'

'You're hoping she's still alive somewhere?'

'We digress.'

Why were they sparring when they were supposed to be on the same team? The guy was a jerk.

'Yes. The clock's always ticking.' His phone lay face up on the table. He was watching the time.

'I need to find Paige Carter before he kills her too.' Lexi wondered if she was going to get anything worthwhile from the man. 'And you're right. I do believe that this is the same man who snatched me and my sisters. Some of the posing suggests things that only the killer would know.'

Harlow's head jerked up. Now she had his interest.

'This case must be triggering memories for you?'

She raised one shoulder. She wasn't here to discuss the personal. 'The issue I'm struggling with is his motivation to repeat the crime. Domination and control – the classic reasons why an inadequate individual becomes a serial killer. But why triplets again, and why now? It's been seventeen years since he took us.'

'It's unusual, I grant you. But there could be any number of reasons why there was a gap.'

Harlow picked up the sheaf of papers again and flicked through them.

'You've missed something. How did he treat you and your sisters in captivity?'

'I remember being attacked and shoved into his van, and I have chequered memories of being held, sometimes with my sisters, sometimes on my own. Amber has spent the last seventeen years repressing everything that happened – and I understand that – but it's not much help.'

'But something's telling you this is the same man?'

'I visited the senior officer on the case at the time, Len Clayton, and now I'm working my way through the old case files. There are transcripts of mine and Amber's police interviews, which are helping me rebuild what happened.'

Harlow's eyes seemed to pierce her very soul. 'When you remember how he operated with you and your sisters, you'll be able to see if there really are parallels between the cases or if you're on a wild goose chase. And if you're not, come and talk to me again.'

In a burning rush, more of the memories that had been lost for seventeen long years came flooding back. Cable ties cutting into her wrists. The stench of going for days without washing. Thirst turning her throat to sandpaper. Random images flashing before her eyes. Things that had lain coiled and dormant in her psyche, now as sharp as if they'd happened yesterday.

Suppressing the panic, fear and horror that was washing through her, she abruptly pushed her chair back from the table.

'You might teach my case on your bloody course, but I didn't come here to be a study subject for you.'

And, as she stumbled out of the kitchen and back to her car, she was blinded by the vision of her sister, Rose, in their last moments together, as Rose's fingertips had slipped from her grasp.

THIRTY-TWO

Lexi pulled into the car park of Canterbury police station with no recall of the drive back from Sandwich. She knew she'd broken the speed limit, but she didn't care. Paige Carter's life hung in the balance, and if the terrifying memories that Harlow's words had precipitated could give her any sort of fix on who the Triplet Killer might be, she would embrace them.

The incident room was already busy when she walked in. Good. It meant they knew what needed to be done and they were getting on with it. But she knew she needed to level with them about her suspicions. It wouldn't necessarily change the direction of the investigation – it could still be one of the suspects they'd identified, Madison or Yates. But not Josh Pendleton – he was much too young to have been the man responsible for her sister's disappearance.

However, she needed a moment first. She still felt too shaken by the barrage of memories that had surfaced over the last twelve hours to be able to talk about her ordeal with the team. She gave them a brief nod, then went along the corridor to her office. Tom followed her inside, closing the door quietly.

She dropped into her chair and rubbed her eyes, which were dry and gritty from the cumulative lack of sleep.

'You look like you had a bad night,' he said.

She looked up.

'I've been trying to reach you. Why didn't you answer your phone?' He loomed over her.

She'd been aware of the phone ringing on the drive back, but she'd been in no state to take calls. Even so, this reaction seemed out of line.

'Sorry. Didn't you get my message? There are some things we need to talk about.'

'Go ahead.'

'The details I found in Clayton's files and my subsequent discussion with Harlow have made me reassess how we're approaching the case.'

'How so?'

Lexi took a deep breath. 'It might sound strange, but I think we've got to consider the possibility that the man who has Paige could be the same man that abducted me and my sisters.'

Tom's eyebrows shot up. 'But that was seventeen years ago. Why do you think this?'

'A lot of it's gut feeling... but also, the roses in the bodies' hands and the fact that he placed the bodies so close to where I live...'

'You think those things were directed at you?' Tom's voice struck a note of disbelief.

'We can't discount it.'

'So what does it mean for the investigation?'

'I'm still working that out. Obviously, we keep pursuing the leads and the suspects we've got – Yates in particular. But we also need to explore the earlier case for any additional clues.'

Tom was about to say something when there was a knock on the door. Ridhi came in.

'You need to see this.'

She held out her phone. Lexi took it and studied the screen. It was an email.

'It came in to the tips email address that we gave out during the press conference,' she added, as Lexi read it.

To: Kent Police

Subject: Attn DI Bennett – The body's in the woods

Princess,

I've left a surprise for you in Chequer's Wood – why don't you scurry on up there and find out what it is?

xx

Lexi's heart stopped.

They were too late. Paige was dead – that much was evident from the subject line. And the sender had addressed her as 'Princess'. Only one person in the world had ever called her that. The man who'd abducted her.

'It's probably a hoax,' said Ridhi, taking her phone back. 'But I've sent a couple of uniforms up there to check it out.'

'It's not a hoax,' said Lexi. 'It's Paige. Chequer's Wood is huge.'

'I know it well,' said Tom. 'We walk the dogs up there most weekends.'

'Dogs?' What was he talking about?

'A pair of Dalmatians. Mad beasts.'

But Lexi wasn't listening. Her head was spinning, and her heart was pounding.

Tom raised his phone to his ear. 'Get as many people as you can spare up to Chequer's Wood now. There's been a report of a cadaver, we don't know exactly where... Right, thanks.'

She had to get a grip. The email confirmed it. He was back – and she was going to get him.

'Come on.' Lexi grabbed her bag and ran past Tom for the door. 'Have the whole area cordoned off as a crime scene until we've located the body,' she said as Tom followed her down the stairs.

They took Tom's Jeep, and Lexi called Emily Jordan and asked her to get some CSIs out to the location.

Chequer's Wood was a vast open area that covered two-hundred-and-fifty acres of forest and scrubland on Canterbury's eastern edge. It had originally been owned by the Ministry of Defence and used for army training, and there were still some areas that were fenced off from public access. But for the most part it was used by joggers and walkers, criss-crossed by a network of paths, and bordered along one side by a busy golf course.

By the time they arrived, ten minutes later, in the narrow lane that gave access to the wood, there were already several marked police cars at the scene, blue lights flashing as various uniformed PCs unspooled crime scene tape in every direction.

Tom parked up and Lexi saw a WPC running towards them from the edge of the trees – Chequer's Wood was made up of mostly oak and birch, well-established, with plenty of undergrowth. Narrow paths led away through banks of fern and brambles, while a wider gravel track led directly into the centre.

'Ma'am, I've found the body.' Up close, the young woman's face was pale with a greenish tinge. She pressed the back of her hand to her mouth.

'Are you okay?' said Lexi.

The girl took her hand away and nodded. 'I am now. But I was sick a minute ago.'

Tom had opened the back of the Jeep. He pulled out two crime scene suits.

'Let's get these on,' he said to Lexi. Then he turned to the

WPC. 'There are some bottles of water on the back seat. Help yourself.'

A minute later WPC Acaster – as she informed them once she'd recovered her composure – was leading them along a small path through the trees. Ahead of them, Lexi could see another PC reeling out more blue and white crime scene tape and twisting it around a stand of pine to the left of the path.

'Look out for footprints or tyre prints, and if you see any, expand the crime scene cordon to include them,' she said to the man as they came level with him.

'Yes, ma'am.'

Acaster pointed in the direction of a large fallen tree. 'It's behind there.'

Lexi ducked under the tape and approached the tree. It was a tall birch with a thick trunk.

'Where were you sick?' she said to Acaster, who was hanging back. She clearly didn't want to see the body again.

The WPC pointed away into the woods. 'I tried to get as far away from him as possible,' she said. 'I knew it would be a crime scene.'

'Him?' said Lexi. 'Don't you mean her?' What sort of a state could the body be in that Acaster couldn't tell its sex?

Lexi skirted around the huge bolus of roots. It must have taken some storm to fell this monster, but it looked like it had been down for a considerable time – a well-established bramble bush was entwined in the tangle of bare roots. As soon as she rounded the end, she saw a pair of trainer-clad feet, attached to two legs in dark indigo denim.

Nothing prepared her for what she saw next. The man – because it was most definitely a man – was lying on his back. That much was clear from the fact that his feet were pointing upwards. But less clear from a first glance at his head. Where his face should have been was nothing but a bloody pulp. Lexi's eyes recognised the shape of a torn, bruised ear before she had to turn her head away and take several deep breaths.

But it wasn't Paige.

'No wonder you were sick,' she said to Acaster, who'd remained on the other side of the tree.

'Sorry, ma'am. I'd never seen anything like it.'

Lexi had, but her mouth still filled with saliva and her stomach muscles were contracting hard. She gritted her teeth and swallowed. She was determined not to throw up.

Just breathe.

She steeled herself to take another look at the body.

Thank God, it wasn't Paige. But it meant that someone else had been brutally murdered on her patch, which was just as serious. And she had no doubt that it was linked to the abduction of the Carter girls. The email told her that.

She could guess who it was. Missing from the day the girls had disappeared, Lexi would put money on it that this was Josh Pendleton's body. The clothes certainly seemed to match the description of what he'd been wearing.

It was sickening to see, but she needed to make a professional assessment as quickly as possible. The man was wearing a hooded anorak and the remains of his head were cradled in the hood which, along with his T-shirt, was soaked with blood. She looked closely at the ground in the vicinity of the body, and then cast her eyes across the whole crime scene.

'Lexi, hello? Where are you?'

She straightened up to see Mort Barley and Emily Jordan approaching, both suited up with blue shoe protectors on their feet. The rest of Emily's team were behind them and started to fan out around the crime scene, the photographer already snapping away to make sure that nothing was missed before the scene was further disturbed.

'Round here,' said Lexi. 'Steel yourselves – one of the nastiest I've seen in a long time.'

'Thanks,' said Emily. Of course, Emily and Mort dealt with cadavers all day, every day, so were more used to seeing death than she was. But the sheer ferocity of this attack was so shocking that even they would be repulsed.

They came round the end of the tree and gasped in unison. However, they didn't hesitate before coming closer.

'He's dead,' said Mort, 'and you can take that as my professional opinion.'

'Thanks,' said Lexi. 'I wasn't entirely sure.'

It wasn't unusual for Mort's sense of humour to rear its head at the most unlikely moments and a bit of levity had the effect of quelling everyone's nerves.

Emily felt the exposed skin on the man's hands. 'He's cold – probably been out here for several hours.'

Mort opened the bag he had slung over one shoulder and pulled out a thermometer. Emily checked the pockets of the man's jeans and jacket. She pulled out a set of keys and dropped them into an evidence bag. There was no wallet, just some loose change, and nothing else to give a clue as to the man's identity. Meanwhile the photographer had come round to view the body and swiftly turned away.

Lexi waved at Tom, who was sensibly staying well back. 'Can we get some stepping plates out here, ASAP?'

He nodded and went away to sort it out.

Lexi turned back to Mort and Emily. 'I've got a theory for you to consider.'

'A bit early, don't you think?' said Mort.

Lexi ignored the comment. 'Look, there's no sign of a murder weapon, and there's no blood spatter or tissue debris on the ground around his head. That makes me think that this isn't where he died. He was killed somewhere else and then dumped.'

Emily and Mort both looked at the ground.

'I agree,' said Emily. 'But that doesn't mean he wasn't killed somewhere out here, and the body just moved a bit to get it out of sight of the path. I'll widen the crime scene area – if the body was moved, there should be signs of it.'

Lexi considered what Emily said. 'But if the killer didn't want the body found, why not bury it?' The killer's email suggested that he did want it to be found. At a time to suit him. It made Lexi feel manipulated and that made her angry.

'Time constraint?' said Mort. 'Lack of equipment?'

'No shovel,' said Emily, 'but he obviously had something heavy to use as a weapon – a sledgehammer or mallet, maybe?'

'There are a lot of things he could have used,' said Mort. He would never commit to an opinion before he had to, apart from confirming the body was dead.

'Or maybe,' said Lexi, 'he was moved here because the killer actually wanted him to be found? We received an email alerting us that there was a body in the woods.'

'You think the email was from the killer, rather than just from someone who saw the body but didn't want to get involved?' said Mort.

'I know it was – and the savagery of this murder tells us plenty. Whoever did this, it wasn't just about killing. He went on pulverising the head long after the moment of death. A message to the dead man? A bit pointless. So, maybe a message to someone else – a threat, perhaps...'

Mort and Emily got on with their work in silence. They dealt in facts, and facts alone. It was Lexi's job to interpret those facts.

And she didn't like what she was seeing.

THIRTY-THREE

It was almost lunchtime by the time they left Chequer's Wood. The CSIs were still busy processing the site, and Emily Jordan was preparing for the removal of the body to the morgue. Mort had done all he could out and would conduct a post-mortem once the body arrived in Maidstone.

Lexi felt dejected as she, Tom and the pathologist walked back to where they'd left their cars.

'Another murder on our plate,' said Lexi. 'All we need. I suspect it could be Lucy Carter's boyfriend, Josh Pendleton, but we'll need to find something to link the two murders.'

'It was a frenzied attack,' said Mort. 'Suggests a lack of control, and people like that make mistakes. There'll be something for you to work with.'

Lexi didn't doubt him, but whatever they found would have to hold up in court.

'You're not going to get enough for a dental ID, are you?'

'Unlikely – the jaw and all the teeth are probably too smashed up to make a match.' He unlocked his car. 'I'll send DNA for testing against Pendleton's. But if it's not him, we really don't have much to go on.'

As Tom drove them back to the station, Lexi tried not to think about anything. She let her mind drift, listening to Radio Three without really paying much attention. They needed to confirm who the victim was and they needed to track down whoever sent the email. The killer. He was taunting her – addressing her as 'princess' – that much was evident. Arrogant. Overconfident. Those qualities were fully in line with the standard serial killer profile. But there was something else going on here. The choice of victim, a man, and the way he'd been bludgeoned in the face, was unlike anything in either of the cases they were trying to link it to.

And why lead them to the body with an email?

What was he saying?

Perhaps once the identity of the victim became clear it would tell them more about his motive.

She realised she was hungry and they made a quick detour to the nearest Tesco to pick up a couple of packs of sandwiches.

Before she ate, though, she needed to fill in the rest of the team.

Standing in front of the whiteboard, she used a red pen to mark out a clear area, then pinned up a hastily printed out photo of the body as it had been found in the shadow of the fallen tree.

'We've got no formal ID so far. Male. However, the clothes possibly match what Josh Pendleton was wearing when he went missing. Early thoughts are that he was killed somewhere else and dumped. I've asked Mort to check the victim's DNA against the sample we hold for Pendleton, but it'll take some time to get the results. Meanwhile, when we get height and shoe size, Ridhi, can you cross match them against Pendleton and – if they don't match his details – check them against the latest misper list?'

'Sure.'

She'd asked Mort to get that information over to them as soon as he had possession of the body. 'It should be in any minute – if it's not, chase Mort.'

Ridhi nodded.

'The rest of you, stay on the Carter case.' Paige Carter needed to take precedence – she'd been missing nearly a week. That was longer than Lexi had been held for, and she was scared. The abductor would only wait so long before turning the case into a triple murder. 'We've got an overtime budget, so press on where you can. I want you lot all over Yates – dig up more on his background. There are some very good reasons to think that whoever has Paige was the same man who abducted me and my sisters...' A ripple of shock went through the incident room as she revealed this, but she ignored it. 'This means we need to track down where Yates was and what he was doing at that time, as well as what he's been getting up to since, given that Madison was in custody when the email was sent.'

'Boss?' Ridhi raised a hand.

'What is it?'

'I did a search for any unsolved murders of other sets of triplets. There were none on record. But when I expanded it to twins, there were quite a number, including several in Kent.'

'Good work, Ridhi. Take a deeper look at the ones in Kent and see if any of them share features with the Carter case. Get back to me as soon as.'

'What should I be looking for?'

'Similar patterns of abduction followed by murder a few days later. Posing of the murder scene, particularly using similar dresses and accessories.'

Lexi went back to her office. Her coffee was cold and the sandwiches that lay next to her laptop looked distinctly less appetising than they had under the bright lights of the supermarket. She needed to call Maggie to get approval for the overtime she'd just authorised.

Thankfully, Maggie agreed that it was needed – the pressure to make progress in the Carter case was increasing all the time. Lexi filled her in on the new murder and Maggie's heavy sigh at the other end of the line reflected her own feelings. The weight of the two cases was making itself felt.

She tore open one of the packs of sandwiches, eating because she knew she had to, not because she had an appetite. She'd barely finished when there was a knock on her open door. She looked up.

'Dr Harlow, what can I do for you?'

Ed Harlow stepped, uninvited, into her office.

'It's what I can do for you,' he said, advancing towards her desk. 'I feel I didn't give you a fair crack of the whip this morning.'

Lexi wasn't sure how she was expected to respond. With gratitude? She gave him a half-hearted smile.

'You caught me at a bad moment – I've got some personal stuff going on. My wife is ill. But I spoke to Harry,' he said. 'Only good things to say about you.'

'Thanks.' So he'd felt the need to check up on her credentials. 'Anyway, I ambushed you, it's not surprising you didn't have much time for me. And I'm sorry about your wife – of course I wouldn't have bothered you if I'd realised.'

'So let's start fresh.'

'Thing is, I'm now working two cases – another body was discovered this morning – so I'm not sure I've got time now.'

He ignored her brush-off and pulled a stack of papers from the briefcase he was carrying. 'You left these behind.' They were the case notes she'd shown him earlier.

'It's fine – they're just copies.'

'I've taken a look at them. I thought I could share my thoughts with you.'

It sounded arrogant, but she had to remind herself that that had been the purpose of her visit to him.

Uninvited, he dropped into the empty chair opposite her desk. 'Right, tell me about this new case. Anything to make you think, given the timing, that the two are linked?'

Lexi filled him in on the discovery of the body in Chequer's Wood and the email they'd received alerting them to its presence. She pushed the photos of the body across the desk to him and he grimaced as he looked at them.

'It was a frenzied attack,' said Lexi, 'but then the killer had the wherewithal to move the body – because the murder definitely didn't happen in situ.'

'I agree,' said Harlow, studying the close-ups of the man's head and the ground immediately around it.

'I think it would be a good idea for the whole team to hear your thoughts. Do you mind if we go through to the incident room?'

'Sure.'

They went next door and Lexi called the team to order and introduced Harlow. Then she turned to him. 'So what do you make of it?'

Harlow looked around the room and took a deep breath. 'I would suggest the killer knew the victim. It's often the case when the face is obliterated in such a vicious fashion. Was there any staging?'

'I didn't see anything to suggest it,' said Lexi, 'but do take a look. It's nothing like the Carter murder site, but there doesn't seem to have been any attempt to bury the body or even hide it. This, and the fact that we received the email, tells us that the killer wanted it to be found – that means he's sending a message.'

Harlow studied the pictures. 'But if he wanted it found, why put it behind the tree? Why not leave it right on the path?'

'Buying time?' said Lexi. 'So he could put some distance between him and the body before sending the email, perhaps.'

'It's possible,' said Harlow, though he didn't sound

convinced. 'What about the suspects for the Carter abduction
that you mentioned in the notes – Yates and Madison. Could
either of them have sent the email? And more to the point,
could either of them be the man that abducted you and your
sisters? Am I right in thinking the girls' murders will have triggered some fresh memories for you?'

What the hell?

He must have guessed from her hurried departure from his
kitchen. But whatever prompted him, she wasn't going to
discuss her personal trauma in front of the team. Telling them
she thought the cases were linked was one thing, but reliving
her memories in front of them? No way.

For a couple of seconds Lexi didn't know what to say. She
could feel the eyes of the whole team upon her. She looked
towards Tom, but he had been rendered as speechless as
she had.

Finally, she found her voice. 'I don't know how reliable my
memories are.'

'I'm sorry,' said Harlow. 'I see I've touched a nerve, but you
told me yourself that you'd been to talk to one of the original
detectives on your case.'

This was news to the team, and there was a collective intake
of breath.

Lexi felt her face flushing.

'Surely you've got some insight into the man that took you
that would be useful to the team?'

Couldn't he let it drop? Lexi shifted her weight from one
foot to the other. 'I don't remember very much about what
happened at all.'

'So neither of these men seem remotely familiar to you?'

'No. Not at all. Madison is probably too young, and anyway,
he was in custody when the email was sent, so we've ruled him
out.'

'But what if he wrote it earlier and then scheduled it?' said Tom.

Lexi thought about it for a couple of seconds, but it didn't make sense. 'Why would he do that? He wouldn't have known he was going to be in custody at the time it was sent. But I'll ask the tech department to check whether that could have happened.'

Ed stepped forward. 'But it might be Yates – having to recover from a severe facial injury could fit very well with the narrative of a serial killer career that had to be put on hold for several years.'

'What do you mean?' said Tom. He looked interested and Lexi wanted to tell him to pipe down, but she knew she couldn't.

'Serial killing is a progression,' said Ed. He seemed to be moving into teaching mode. 'There are usually significant events and triggers that lead up to the first kill, and after that he'll be powerless not to kill again, and again, until he's caught. Each time, he refines his MO as he becomes more proficient at his art, but his signature – the thing that compels him to kill, the thing he does to the victim to trigger his own release – remains the same over time. We've seen this pattern a hundred times.'

'And "put on hold"?' said Tom.

'In the normal progression, the time between kills gets shorter each time as the killer becomes increasingly desperate to get his fix. But occasionally we see a gap in the murders – if the killer's in prison, or able to satisfy or dampen down his needs in some other way, as might happen if he gets into a stable relationship.'

Lexi had had enough of Harlow's lecturing. 'Thanks for your input, but we need to get on. Let's get back to work everybody.' She turned to Ed. 'Profiling is a useful tool but it doesn't secure conviction. We still need to find enough evidence to prove the case.'

'My pleasure,' said Ed.

'I'll see you out.' She led the way out of the incident room and he followed her.

Once they were alone on the staircase, Lexi couldn't hold it in any longer. 'How dare you bring up my past in front of my team?'

'I'm sorry, but it's entirely relevant to your current case. Surely you see that?'

'Yes, but it's my personal life, too,' said Lexi. 'I get to decide what I share.'

Ed Harlow stopped in front of her.

'What chance is there of solving this case if you hold back relevant information?'

Turning on his heel to take the remaining stairs two at a time, he left without saying goodbye or looking back.

Was he right? Was she hindering her own investigation because of her personal involvement? Instead of allowing the past to act as stumbling block, she needed to harness the experience to work out what had happened to Paige.

But how?

THIRTY-FOUR

Lexi stormed back to her office with a sour taste in her mouth.

What the hell just happened?

Ed Harlow was supposed to be an ally, but he'd just humiliated her in front of her whole team. Whatever his prowess as a profiler – which she had yet to see – he certainly wasn't blessed with people skills. She dropped into her chair and flipped up the lid of her laptop. She could solve this case without his input. After all, she'd studied profiling with the best in the world, and if she had one ounce of Harlow's arrogance, she would never have bothered to consult with someone else.

There were plenty of emails that needed her attention, but she was too riled to concentrate on them. Current mood: furious – and she didn't need that bleeding over into the rest of her work. She closed her eyes and took a few deep breaths, trying to calm herself. If Ed Harlow thought he had free rein to blunder about inside her case, with access to her most personal memories, he had another think coming.

Calm down.

Breathe.

Her mobile sounded. She glanced at the screen, prepared to just let it ring. But it was Mort.

'Don't say I never do anything for you,' he said, without bothering to greet her.

'I wouldn't. What have you got?' She took care to moderate her voice so he wouldn't guess her mood.

'The body from Chequer's Wood. When I undressed it, I discovered a tattoo on the left shoulder blade. A Thai Sak Yant tattoo.'

'Sacred script. And?'

'And it could be a match – in Josh Pendleton's file, it mentions a Sak Yant tattoo. On his left shoulder blade, from a holiday in Thailand. It's not certain yet. I need to get hold of a photo of Josh's tattoo to compare them. But I thought you'd want to know.'

'Brilliant, Mort – you're a star.' Looked like her suspicions about the body's identity would be confirmed.

'A pint'll do it.'

'Sure, when I'm next up your way.'

'Could be sooner than you think, Lexi – I'm about to start the autopsy, but I could wait a bit if you want to observe.'

'Count me in.'

She slammed shut her laptop and grabbed her bag.

'Tom?' she shouted as she passed the door of the incident room. 'We've got a tentative ID. Mort's about to do the PM.'

She heard his footsteps behind on the stairs as she ran down, and he caught her up in the car park.

'I'll drive,' she said. 'We'll get there quicker.'

She told him about the tattoo as she pulled out onto the ring road. 'I want to see it for myself. Call Ridhi and get her to check Pendleton's social media accounts for a picture we can use to match it.'

Of course, no matter how identical the tattoos, they'd have to wait for DNA analysis to make the final call on the ID, but a good match would be good enough for Lexi. It made sense to her that the body belonged to Pendleton, though she had yet to see why their man would have murdered Lucy's boyfriend.

Tom was quiet for the first half of the journey, sipping a coffee he'd picked up as Lexi had filled the tank on the outskirts of Canterbury. Eventually, he half turned towards her. Lexi was aware of it, but kept her eyes on the road.

'Big question,' he said.

'Shoot.'

'If our Chequer's Wood body is Josh Pendleton, does that take him off the suspect list for the murders of Eden and Lucy Carter?'

'I'd say definitely. If Mort gives us a time of death before when the girls were killed, then it will be safe to say he's not the perp. Even if he died later, him being a suspect doesn't make sense anymore. He's way too young to be the Triplet Killer.'

'In other words, he's off the hook?'

'Not much comfort to him, given the circumstances,' said Lexi with a wry smile.

Tom paused. 'But I'm still confused. We have to consider it might be the same killer, but the MO is quite different. And what about motive? Why would the man who took the girls kill Pendleton?'

They were good points. 'The email makes me certain it's the same killer – he used the salutation "Princess", and that was how my abductor addressed me, as well as how he *dressed* Lucy and Eden. You're right that it's a totally different MO, but this was a frenzied killing, maybe opportunistic rather than planned. Collateral damage possibly?'

'And how do we move forward from here?'

'You don't do small questions, do you?' said Lexi.

They lapsed back into silence for the rest of the journey, but that didn't mean Lexi wasn't thinking about the question. Where did they go from here? Pendleton's body turning up made her absolutely certain he wasn't the unsub, but she knew better than to look for evidence to fit the next potential theory. She would follow wherever the case led her next, relentlessly, until she'd tracked down the killer.

Mort was expecting them, and to that end he'd rolled the body onto its front so they could take a look at the tattoo before he got started. Ridhi had emailed several images of Josh's tattoo from his Facebook account, and Lexi held them up on her phone next to the shoulder. All three of them peered at the match for several seconds. The cadaver's skin was grey and waxy, mottled with purple patches of lividity, where the blood had pooled and become fixed in the hours after death. One of them slightly obscured the tattoo, but the remaining three quarters of the ink looked incredibly similar to the pictures.

'I'd call it a match,' said Lexi. 'You, Mort?'

'The script's the same and the positioning lines up, so, yes. I'd be very surprised if the DNA didn't check out.'

'I take it the height, hair colour and shoe size match too?' said Lexi.

Mort nodded.

'Got a time of death yet? This is critical. I need as exact an answer as you can possibly give me. Specifically, whether he died before or after Lucy and Eden Carter.'

'You don't ask much, do you?'

'And you never let me down. I won't forget you want payment in beer.'

Mort went to the countertop that ran along one wall of the mortuary, where he kept his notes.

'Taking into account the progression of decomposition, I would say he's been dead approximately a week.'

'Which would take us back to Friday, maybe. The last day he was seen alive.' Tom wrinkled his nose. 'Can you narrow it down further?'

'Not particularly,' said Mort. 'The body had reached

ambient temperature, which at the time he was found was approximately five degrees Celsius. Rigor had completely worn off. Given the cold weather and dearth of insects at this time of year, putrefaction wasn't that far advanced. In other words, dead approximately a week.'

Lexi could see Mort was going to get obstructive if they pressed him any further. Hopefully, he'd come back to her later with a more precise estimate.

'Cause of death?' she said.

'Obvious, isn't it?' said Tom.

Mort gave him a supercilious look and Lexi had to suppress a smirk.

'Because in your expert opinion that beating was administered pre- or post-mortem?'

'Umm...' Tom was quick to realise his mistake and his cheeks flushed.

'Go easy on him,' said Lexi, smiling at Mort.

He winked at her, out of Tom's line of sight. He always liked to make sure people appreciated just how skilled he was.

'Fine. Just take a closer look.' Mort pulled an arc lamp round to further illuminate the bloody mess that had been Josh Pendleton's face. Tom squirmed slightly as he stepped closer, and Lexi could literally taste the tang of iron as she breathed in. She might have seen a hundred murder victims during her time in America, but this was surely one of the most harrowing.

'The structures of the face – the bone, the cartilage, the teeth, the tissues – were all broken down by repeated blows with a blunt instrument. The amount of blood mixed with the tissue debris suggests that the man was alive when this happened, but not for long. It's impossible to say how many strikes were administered, but certainly the beating continued beyond the moment of death.'

'But that's how he died?' said Lexi.

'Yes, the beating can be logged as the cause of death.'

Tom stepped back, vindicated.

'However,' continued Mort, 'we'll need to wait for the results of the blood toxicology to see if there were any other contributing factors – for example, if he was drugged or drunk when it happened.'

'Will tox give us anything on the timing?' said Lexi.

'Not until I examine the stomach contents. If you can find out when he ate his last meal, I can assess how long after eating he died, which will give us a more accurate time of death.'

'Tom, can you get Colin to check back with his flatmates whether he actually ate any breakfast on Friday?'

'Will do.'

They left Mort to the business end of the post-mortem. It had been gruesome enough already. Tom was looking fairly green, and Lexi certainly felt relief when she was able to take a breath of fresh air outside.

The results from Mort's autopsy had implications for both cases. It looked certain to Lexi that Pendleton wasn't responsible for Lucy and Eden's deaths. And she could hardly imagine that his death was an unrelated coincidence.

But now they had a close-to-definite ID for the body, it was time to make the worst kind of house call. Ridhi relayed the information to her that Josh Pendleton's mother lived in Querns Road.

Lexi rang the doorbell of the 1950s red-brick semi with a heavy heart. It was answered by a woman with dark hair, wearing a baggy grey track suit.

'Josh doesn't live here anymore,' she said, trying to push the door shut when Lexi mentioned her son.

Lexi put out a hand to stop it closing. 'Mrs Pendleton, can I come in?'

'Why?' She was still putting pressure on the door, meaning that Lexi had to push back.

'I need to speak to you about Josh. I have some news.'

Mrs Pendleton let go of the door. Lexi practically fell over the threshold and into the hall. She straightened up, meeting the woman's frightened eyes with a steady gaze.

'Let's go and sit down.'

Mrs Pendleton led her down the hall and into an untidy living room that was dominated by a large screen TV. It was on but set to mute. Children's brightly coloured plastic toys were scattered across the floor and magazines lay strewn across the coffee table and sofa. Several empty coffee cups were in evidence, and a half-finished packet of biscuits leaked crumbs over a pile of newspapers.

Lexi picked her way through the field of toys to stand facing the sofa.

'Perhaps you'd like to sit down,' she said, but Mrs Pendleton had dropped into an armchair before she finished the sentence.

'What is it?' she said. ''As he been arrested?' She sighed, and Lexi saw that she was gripping the chair's armrests with white knuckles.

'Is your husband at home?'

She shook her head vehemently. 'Haven't seen that git in years. He's not around.'

Lexi wondered when a family liaison officer would arrive, but she couldn't put off the inevitable.

'I'm so sorry, Mrs Pendleton – I have to inform you that your son is dead. We found a body in Chequer's Wood early this morning, and we can say with reasonable certainty that it's Josh.'

Mrs Pendleton's hands went to her face and she slumped forward in the chair. She didn't cry or scream, but remained curled in on herself, absolutely still and silent.

Lexi waited, knowing a response would come. She looked around the room. An unopened bill on the TV stand told her that Mrs Pendleton's first name was Sara.

In the chair, Mrs Pendleton slumped to one side.

'Sara?' Lexi squatted down in front of her. 'Sara, remember to breathe.'

The woman took a huge gulp of air. She looked up. 'I'm dizzy.' She seemed confused. The shock of what Lexi had told her had hit her like a juggernaut. She attempted to sit up, but Lexi put a hand on her shoulder.

'Stay down, put your head between your legs and breathe slowly. I'll get you some water.'

She went to the kitchen and quickly returned.

'Sara, here's some water.' Sara Pendleton gingerly sat up and took the glass with shaking hands.

'What happened to him?' said Sara, after taking a long drink. 'Was it drugs? I told him so many times they was going to be the death of him.'

'I'm afraid he was attacked,' said Lexi.

That hardly began to describe what had happened to this poor woman's son.

THIRTY-FIVE

As soon as an FLO had arrived to look after Sara Pendleton, Lexi returned to the incident room. She needed to urgently redirect the team.

'Listen up, people,' she called to get the attention of the busy room. 'We are ninety-nine per cent certain that the body found in Chequer's Wood belongs to Josh Pendleton, pending DNA confirmation. The timing of his death takes him off the suspect list – my feeling is that he's a collateral victim, given the email pointing us towards the body.'

A wave of murmurs showed that most of the team agreed with her.

'The hunt for Josh Pendleton has been a costly distraction in terms of time and energy – and God knows what it's cost Paige Carter.' Lexi looked around the room and noticed that Maggie Dawson had slipped in and was standing by the door with her arms folded. *Damn!* She'd meant to call Maggie with an update when she'd got back from Chequer's Wood. 'That email was sent to me using the salutation "Princess", which is how the man who abducted me addressed me. For this reason, we have to consider that the two cases are linked and that the perpetrator is the same for both. I need you to factor that into everything you do now. We're looking for a clear thread that ties the two together.'

She finished assigning tasks to the team and went back to her office, all too aware of Maggie following her out of the room.

'Radio silence?' said Maggie, as soon as she'd closed the door behind her. 'I expected better from you.'

'I'm sorry, but it's been mayhem today.'

'And you're sure the body is Pendleton? Because before that, he was your primary suspect, right?'

'He was one of my suspects,' said Lexi. 'But he was never really a good fit for the killer's profile.'

'Share your current thoughts with me,' said Maggie, sitting down. This was her way – she would say her piece, but she wouldn't dwell on it. For her, it was all about moving the case forward.

'Late thirties to late forties, white male.' Lexi went through the list of known serial killer character traits she'd been building in her mind. 'From a broken family with an overbearing mother, probably abused as a child, nursing feelings of inadequacy. He feels unlistened to, unnoticed. The kill site at the Crown was very posed, and that takes composure to achieve, so I doubt this is his first killing.'

Maggie nodded, then she sighed. 'That all works with it being the same man as the one who abducted you. Who are you looking at?'

'Toby Yates still seems a possible fit. I think Mike Madison is likely out of the picture. And we're still following up on the alibis of some of the other customers of the Pole Star. I've got Greg Chambers working on tracing the email from the killer.'

'Supposedly from the killer.'

It wasn't like Maggie to second guess her like this. Lexi tried not to show her annoyance. 'I'm certain it was from him for two reasons – like I said in the meeting, he addressed me as "princess". The man who abducted me called me that several times, and it fits with the way the Carter girls were dressed up. Secondly, who else but the killer would have known where Josh Pendleton's body was dumped?'

'Okay.' Maggie stood, her expression serious. 'I'm taking some heat for this – from the brass, the press. It's headlining the *Courier*, and it's been featured in all the nationals, as I'm sure you know.'

Lexi didn't – she'd hardly had time to sit around checking the papers – but she nodded anyway.

'People want to know why we haven't found Paige Carter yet.'

'I get it. The team's doing everything we can. Everyone's working flat out.'

'Good. Overtime is fine, and let me know if you need more manpower.'

'Thanks.'

'Don't let me down.'

'I won't.' She meant it to sound upbeat, but that wasn't how it came out.

Maggie gave her a long look. 'I worry about you, Lexi. This case is taking it out of you.'

After she left, Lexi felt deflated. It was like she'd just had the 'I'm disappointed in you' speech from a parent. She was letting Maggie down. She was letting the team down. But most of all, she was letting Paige Carter down.

'Damn it!' Lexi swept a pile of papers from her desk onto the floor in frustration.

She knew Maggie's concern for her was protective, but it seemed to betray a lack of confidence in her. And who could blame her? Paige Carter was still missing and it seemed as if progress had stalled. The killer had successfully diverted them with the search for Josh Pendleton and was taunting her with nicknames from the past.

But giving in to her temper wasn't going to solve anything. As she scrabbled on the floor on her hands and knees to gather up the mess of folders and documents, her mobile rang. She jumped up, dropping the papers onto the chair opposite her own.

'Lexi Bennett speaking.'

'Don't say I never go the extra mile for you, DI Bennett.' She recognised Greg Chamber's voice, from the tech department.

'You've got something for me?'

'Certainly have.'

'So spit it out.'

'The anonymous email about the body in Chequer's Wood. Good news and bad news.'

'Good first.'

'I know where it was sent from. The Beaney.' The Beaney was Canterbury's combined library, museum and arts centre on the High Street.

'Brilliant – thanks, Greg. What's the bad news?'

'From the IP address, I can see it was composed on one of the library's public computers. So it could have been sent by, you know, anyone. Anyone at all.'

'Oh.' Not much help then. 'Was it written at the time it was sent or could it have been written earlier and scheduled for that time?'

'It was written at the time it was sent. If it was scheduled, I would have seen a "deferred" tag on it.'

'So surely we can find out who was logged on at the time it was sent?'

'I can't check that from here. You'll have to go down to the Beaney and ask if they keep records.'

'Okay. Thanks again.'

'You'll get a report for the file.'

Lexi hung up. She opened the case file on her computer and

reread the email that had tipped them off about Pendleton's whereabouts, adding this new information to her mental image of whoever had sent it. They'd used a public computer to protect their anonymity. But they'd still have needed to log in, and she guessed they'd need a library card to do that.

She pulled up the library's website. Users had to book to use the public PCs, so she clicked through to the booking page. She was right – a library card and pin number were required. Was Toby Yates a registered user? She grabbed her jacket from the back of her chair and headed for the door.

THIRTY-SIX

Lexi loved the Beaney, not least because it reminded her of Dr Who's TARDIS. From the outside, it appeared to be a small and ancient Tudor building, which had actually been constructed at the end of the nineteenth century. But once you went up the steps and through the baronial timber door at the front, you found yourself in a vast arts centre that housed a museum, a gallery and the bright, modern public library on its mezzanine level.

Her footsteps rang out on the mosaic floor of the entrance hall and, as always, she couldn't resist looking up at the penny farthing and Victorian tricycle suspended high from the ceiling of the foyer. A gaggle of primary school children eddied around her as she made her way up to the library, reminding her of school trips here to visit the museum and childhood Saturday mornings spent choosing books.

The public computers were in a small alcove off the upper level of the library. Lexi counted five, three of which were being used. She couldn't see a member of staff in the area, so she went back to the main library desk, where a couple of librarians were busy stacking books onto a small trolley.

'Excuse me, can I have a word?' She held out her ID as one of them, a man in a bright orange staff T-shirt, came across to her.

'Sure, how can I help?'

'I'm DI Bennett of Kent Police. Do you keep login records for your PCs?'

'Um... what are you looking for?'

'We received an anonymous tip-off which was sent from an IP address corresponding to one of your computers. I need to know who was logged on to your public computers at the time the email was sent.'

'I'm not sure if we have that information, or whether we'd be allowed to share it if we did.'

Lexi rolled her eyes. Data protection was making her job more and more difficult.

'When I get a warrant, you'll be able to share it. However, a girl's life might be at stake, so maybe you could just co-operate?'

The man looked uncertain, but he moved across to the PC on the library counter.

'Okay, okay, let me have a look.'

The other librarian, a sprightly-looking elderly woman, was all ears. 'Is it about that missing girl, the one whose sisters got killed?'

Lexi ignored the question.

The man logged in to the PC and flicked through a few pages. Then he shook his head. 'I can't find that information.'

The woman looked over his shoulder and then reached around him to press a few keys.

'Here it is, Rufus,' she said.

The man squinted at the screen. 'Oh yeah. Right, what date and time are you looking for?'

'First thing this morning.' Lexi called up the email on her phone and gave him the information.

After a bit of scrolling, he came up with a list of logins. Lexi counted three within the time frame she'd given them.

'So who do they correlate to?' she said.

'That might take a while to check up on,' said the male librarian. 'We have to do a search on each library membership number.'

'Well, go ahead. Do it,' said Lexi. 'I can wait.'

The woman started typing the first membership number into the system. The screen changed to show a set of membership details.

'Ah, I know her,' she said. 'That's Mrs Claire. She asked me for help getting onto the government website to check out her pension. I doubt she's your anonymous email sender.'

Lexi doubted it too. 'Try the next one.'

'Elizabeth Montgomery.'

'Do you know her?'

Both librarians shook their heads.

The woman scrolled through the details. 'It says here she's a student at Kent Uni.'

Another blank.

The woman read out the last number. 'That's a staff login,' she said. She glanced down at the staff ID card hanging on a lanyard around her neck. Then she held it up in front of her and peered at it more closely. 'Ah, that's my login.' She looked embarrassed.

'You? Did you write an email to the police tip-off address?'

She shook her head, looking genuinely confused. 'No. Honestly, I didn't.'

'What were you doing on one of the public computers?'

'We sometimes use them to get some work done if all the staff computers are busy.'

Lexi rubbed her face with the palms of her hands. She'd hit a dead end. No sign of Toby Yates. But then a thought came to her.

'What time did you log out?'

The two librarians studied the screen again.

'You didn't,' said the man. 'Look, automatic log out after 200 minutes.'

'I must have forgotten,' said the woman. 'I'm so sorry.' She was addressing the other librarian, rather than Lexi.

'Come on, Barbara. It's one of the first rules of using the computers. Always log out when you finish.'

'I know, I know. Brain like a sieve.' She was trying to make light of it.

'So what does that mean?' said Lexi. 'Could anyone have gone online on that computer after you finished?'

'Basically, yes,' the man said. 'And we'll have no record of who it could have been.'

'Do you remember what you did and how long you were on the computer for?' She looked at Barbara.

The woman thought for a moment or two. 'I wasn't on it long – someone came and asked for help finding a book. I think that's why I forgot to log out.'

'And then it would have remained logged on until the 200-minute cut-off point? And anyone in that time frame could have used it to send the email?'

'That's about it,' said the man, shrugging.

'One more thing,' said Lexi. 'Can you check if a Toby Yates had a library card?'

After some more searching and scrolling the woman looked up again. 'No. No one registered with that name.'

'But he could have come in here and used the PC you left online?'

'That's right,' said the man.

'Do you have CCTV coverage of the computer area?'

Both the librarians shook their heads.

Lexi had a photo of Yates in her bag. She pulled it out and showed it to the librarians. 'Do either of you recognise this man?

Did you see him here in the library at the time the computer was left logged on?'

Both of them shook their heads. 'Sorry we can't be of more help to you,' said the man.

Lexi put the photo away again and started down the stairs.

She had to think this through. She stopped on the staircase, completely lost in thought, and a man coming down behind her had to swerve so he didn't barrel straight into her. She didn't notice, because she'd thought of something. Toby Yates was being watched. The surveillance team would know if he'd visited the Beaney Centre within the time frame required.

She hurried back to the office.

THIRTY-SEVEN

I've always loved the Beaney Centre. I think everyone in Canterbury does. It's a repository for the town's history, while at the same time being thoroughly modern. If I sound like a tourist guide maybe it's because I view the Beaney as a sort of home-from-home. A place where it's always quiet and I can escape between the stacks of books, away from the incessant clamour inside my head.

I'm finding life pretty stressful right now.

When I feel like this, I spend some time browsing through the classics. I'm a big Dickens fan. Just stroking the spines makes me feel calmer. Someone's put a book by Dostoyevsky back in the wrong place – between Bleak House and Hard Times – so I move it. Order restored.

You might have thought that I would read true crime, for inspiration and for pleasure. But I don't particularly enjoy it. Breathless investigative journalists peppering the facts with their opinions, always full of self-regard at their marvellous powers of deduction. It's not for me.

Science, on the hand, can make for more useful reading.

I'm just walking round to the science section when I see Lexi. And she looks like she means business.

How very interesting.

I suppose she's here looking for me.

THIRTY-EIGHT

Lexi stared at the whiteboard, coffee in hand, waiting for Colin Flynn to return from wherever he'd drifted off to. Paige had been missing for almost a week. Still alive or long dead? The question sat like a cold stone in Lexi's bowels, a knot of anxiety that became heavier with each passing hour. She felt like she hadn't slept in days, she could barely eat. She was running on caffeine and fear, but maybe they had something at last.

She chewed on a hangnail impatiently. Colin came through the door into the incident room.

'Colin, can you get in touch with the teams watching Toby Yates? See if he visited the Beaney Centre anytime in the last two days.'

'Yes, boss.'

She went back to her office and tried to concentrate on clearing the pile up in her inbox. Most of them were press requests for comments or interviews, which she deleted automatically, but there were a few she needed to answer or forward to some other member of the team to be actioned.

After about ten minutes, Colin appeared in her doorway. She could tell from his body language that there was a problem

– he was standing with one shoulder leaning up against the outer edge of the door frame, as if to prevent himself from being sucked inside.

'Boss...' He paused.

'I'm listening.'

One hand fluttered, palm up. A gesture of apology.

Lexi raised her eyebrows and leaned forward to encourage him to speak.

'Thing is... there was a snafu yesterday afternoon.'

'A snafu?'

'Situation normal: all fucked up.'

Lexi remembered the expression. It was one her American colleagues had been fond of. 'And?'

'The afternoon handover between the surveillance teams... There was a gap because someone got the time wrong.'

'You didn't think to tell me this when it happened?'

'I didn't know until now. The teams didn't see the need to pass it on. After all, Yates hardly leaves the house.'

'But this time?'

'The team that took over assumed he was still at home – that's where he was when the earlier team left, about half an hour before they arrived. But then, when they'd been sitting there for an hour or so, he walked up the road and back to his house.'

'So he'd actually been out and unwatched for all of that time?'

'Yes, boss.'

Lexi bit down the string of expletives that came to mind, but that didn't mean she could talk to him. 'Get out!'

'It won't happen again,' stammered Colin, as he backed away from the door as fast as he could.

Yates could have been rattling around Canterbury or God knows where else with no eyes on him. He would have had plenty of time to go to the library and the fact that the two librarians didn't remember seeing him meant nothing.

She simmered for a minute, wondering what to do next, until her phone rang with a number she didn't recognise.

'DI Bennett.'

A coughing fit on the other end of the line told her it was Len Clayton. She waited for him to catch his breath.

'Lexi?'

'I'm here.'

'I need to talk to you.'

'Shoot.'

'Not over the phone.' She could hear a murmur of voices in the background. 'Somewhere private.'

'All right. I'll drive over. I've got a couple of calls to make first, but I'll be there soon. What's it about?' Privately, she had to wonder if this would be a good use of her time. If Len had something to tell her, why hadn't he shared it when she'd visited him?

'I've got something I want to show you. It probably won't help...'

'You never know.'

He started coughing again and hung up the phone. Lexi hoped he'd survive at least until she got there.

He didn't.

The calls took longer than she thought, and then she had to catch up with Ridhi, who had no new information from Josh Pendleton's flatmates – they couldn't remember whether he'd had breakfast or not before he'd disappeared. The ANPR had thrown up literally hundreds of vans that could be viewed as potentially suspicious and Toby Yates was still sitting tight after his unauthorised jaunt. She phoned Philippa Reid and asked her to find out from the Carters if any of the three girls had

library cards for the Beaney Centre, but even if they did, that
didn't necessarily mean anything. Most teenagers in Canterbury were members.

When she finally parked up outside the retirement home,
she had to pull in behind a bulky black transit van with the
words 'Private Ambulance' stencilled on the side. An undertak-
er's van. One of the residents must have passed away.

A body covered by a black sheet was being stretchered out
as she made her way in through the front door. She stood to one
side to let the undertakers pass.

Janet was standing in the hallway, pressing a ball of damp
tissue against her top lip. She looked tired, and a little shocked,
though it must have been a regular occurrence, given the
average age of her charges.

'I'm here to see Len Clayton,' said Lexi.

Janet looked at her blankly with red-rimmed eyes.

'DI Bennett,' she added, by way of a reminder.

Janet inexplicably burst into tears, and then Lexi realised.

'That was Len...?'

What had happened? She'd only spoken to him an hour and
a half ago. Reeling, Lexi stretched a hand out to grip the rail on
the wall. It was hard to comprehend.

The carer sniffed loudly and wiped her nose.

Regaining her balance, Lexi said, 'Can we talk somewhere?'

Janet led Lexi into the manager's office, where, thankfully,
she was able to find herself a fresh tissue.

'What happened?'

'He passed a little while after lunch. Simon found him in
the garden – he went out there to smoke. Thought he was
fooling us. Used to wheel himself all the way along the path
until he was out of sight. But, of course, we knew he was
smoking from the smell on his clothes when he came back.' She
grimaced. 'He wasn't supposed to smoke – the doctor told him it
would be the death of him.'

'What was wrong with him? Cancer?'

'Emphysema. We called the doctor. Simon hoped he'd be able to help, but I knew he was gone.'

'Is the doctor still here?'

'No, he left an hour ago.'

'Did Len say anything to you about why he called me? He said he had some information for me.'

Janet shook her head. 'I didn't know he'd called you. He didn't say anything about your visit last time. He wasn't one for confidences.'

Damn!

Lexi wondered what he'd remembered. 'Can I check his room, please?'

'Don't you need a warrant for that?' said Janet. She'd been watching too many crime dramas.

'Not once he's dead,' said Lexi.

Janet showed her to a small ground-floor bedroom, kitted out to facilitate a disabled resident. Lexi looked around. It was plain and impersonal – no photos anywhere, nothing much in the way of belongings. A pair of reading glasses on the bedside table. A drawer revealed some paperwork which she thumbed through, but none of it related to Len's working life. It was just bank statements, bills from the care home, letters about hospital appointments and test results. On a table by the window, she found a small sketchbook and a pencil. She thumbed through it – some landscapes, a boat pulled up on the sand, a bird perched on a branch. None of them were very good, but she supposed it helped a lonely man pass his time. The last picture he'd drawn was of three girls. She recognised them as herself, Amber and Rose. Not because of the likenesses, which were terrible, but because it had obviously been copied from a childhood photo she knew well. Another world that had evaporated into nothing but a memory.

Tears prickled her eyes and she stared out of the window for a minute so Janet wouldn't see that she was close to crying.

Janet was still hovering as Lexi finally turned to leave. Not caring what Janet made of it, she picked up Len's sketchbook and put it in her bag. Something to remember him by.

'Can you text me the doctor's phone number?' she said. Although Len had been ill, the timing felt off. It couldn't be a coincidence.

Janet nodded. 'It's in the office. I'll do it straight away.'

Lexi felt sad as she drove back to Canterbury. The Len Clayton she'd first known had purpose and drive, an aura of energy and determination to do his job. The man who had died in the home was a husk of that Len Clayton. Rudderless, waiting for death. His life reduced to sneaking cigarettes like a schoolboy, living in a room that practically denied his existence. It was depressing. Life dwindling away, then snuffed out.

A sharp stab of grief made her catch her breath. It surprised her. After all, she'd hardly known him. Theirs had been a relationship that was hard to define – fleeting but intense, at a time when she was hugely vulnerable and he'd been at the height of his professional confidence. And now? Time had made him vulnerable and had given her agency, but she'd still turned to him in her hour of need. She had no idea what he'd wanted to tell her. No way of knowing whether it could have helped the case or not, or even if it was something she hadn't known about what happened seventeen years ago.

Damn it, Len – if I'd got here sooner, would you still be alive?

THIRTY-NINE

Back in the office, Lexi slumped forward on her desk, resting her chin on her knuckles. She stared down at Len's drawing. The photo he'd copied had shown her and her sisters, arms clutched around each other's shoulders, laughing raucously. They'd been on holiday somewhere, south Wales, she thought. Innocent. Carefree. Before all the bad stuff had happened. And somehow, it had become the last image in Len's sketchbook. The last thing he'd worked on.

She flicked through the rest of the empty pages, noticing in passing that the page after the sisters drawing appeared to have been ripped out. Maybe he had sketched something else. Maybe it had gone wrong and he'd binned it.

She got up and stared out of the window at the crumbling city walls across the ring road. It was dark outside and people were hurrying along the pavement with their shoulders hunched against the wind. Was her nemesis really out there, somewhere in the deep black shadows? Loitering under one of the arched city gateways, or down one of the narrow medieval alleys, hiding in the darkness under the overhanging floors of an ancient building?

She knew he was.

And it was up to her to hunt him down. She couldn't let him kill another girl.

She turned abruptly and went back to her desk to review the progress – or lack of it – they'd made today. The timing of the email had confirmed that Madison wasn't the killer and Yates maybe was or maybe wasn't. The librarians had no way of knowing who'd been in the building during the crucial two hundred or so minutes when the logged-on computer had been left unattended. During this time, the anonymous email had been sent from an account that had, according to the tech report from Greg Chambers, been opened shortly before sending and deleted immediately afterwards.

In other words, it was a dead end.

Josh Pendleton's autopsy had given them scant information about his death or where he might have been killed. And although the team was carrying on with the grunt detective work of interviewing witnesses, checking ANPR records and analysing forensic evidence, they had yet to hit the big break they needed.

She needed to brainstorm with someone who could consider the case with fresh eyes. Not Tom – he was already in too deep. Not Maggie – she was acting as a buffer between them and the pressures coming from above and from the press, who were baying for blood without truly caring whose it was.

She called Ed Harlow. She was still angry, but she wanted to pick his brain. And he was the only person outside the team who knew the case almost as well as she did.

'I need to talk to you.'

'Yes, thanks, I'm fine. How are you?'

'Sorry.' She ran a hand through her unruly hair. 'It's the case. It's doing my head in, and I need a sounding board. Would you be up for an hour of brainstorming?'

'When?'

'Now or even sooner.'

'That bad, huh?' There was the sound of a car door slamming, and then his voice became louder and clearer as if he'd just got into his car. 'Listen, I owe you an apology for earlier. You were right, I was out of line.'

Lexi weighed up his words. 'Apology accepted. I'm not usually so sensitive, but this case has opened the door to some unpleasant emotional baggage.'

In the background, the car engine started. 'Of course – no surprise in that.'

'So, can we talk?'

'Absolutely. Have you had supper yet?'

Lexi glanced at her watch. It was nearly seven, and she hadn't eaten all day. 'No.'

'So let me buy it. I'm just heading back from Maidstone. I could be with you in forty-five minutes. Pick a pub.'

Lexi exhaled, giving it some thought. 'You'd probably know better than I do. I've been away the last four years – things change. But the Shakespeare was always pretty good.'

'It's still good. Bring your files and we'll talk through both your cases.'

Before leaving her office, Lexi made a quick call. Janet had texted her the doctor's number, but it went straight through to an answering service. Of course – he wouldn't be likely to pick up his phone this late in the day. She left a message asking him to call her back. She just wanted to check up on the details of Len's condition – was it really likely that he would just die so abruptly? The doctor must have concluded Len had died of natural causes or he wouldn't have signed the death certificate and allowed the body to be removed by the undertakers.

. . .

The Shakespeare was a short walk away in the centre of town, and so forty minutes later Lexi tucked the case files into her bag and left her office. There were still people working in the incident room, so she stuck her head in to let them know she was going out but she'd be back later.

What she hadn't expected was the phalanx of reporters doorstepping the front of the police station. As she appeared in the doorway, there a flurry of excited movement. Half a dozen microphones were shoved in her face and a barrage of flashes went off as news-hungry photographers caught their image for the next day's papers.

'DI Bennett, are you any closer to arresting anyone for the Princess Murders?'

'Lexi, Lexi, can we get a short interview about the case?'

'Is it true that you consider this case to be linked to your own abduction seventeen years ago?'

Jesus wept.

Apparently the press pack had made the link between the two cases.

'Paige Carter has been missing for six days now. What are you doing to find her?'

'Will you resign if Paige turns up dead?'

Lexi pressed her lips together tightly and pushed past them. There was no way she was going to comment. Half blinded by the flashes, she hurried down into the subway under the ring road. A couple of them followed her for a few metres, but quickly gave up when they realised they were going to get nothing.

Once she'd got away, Lexi meandered through the shopping centre and into the old part of the city, checking every now and again that no one was following her. The last thing she needed was a picture of her going into a pub, with the sort of story that was likely to accompany it.

Finally satisfied that she'd lost them, she pushed open the

door of the Shakespeare and felt relief as its wall of warmth enveloped her. Ed was already sitting at a quiet table at the back with a pint of Spitfire in front of him. On seeing her arrive, he stood up and asked what she wanted to drink.

'A glass of red, please.' She wasn't usually much of a drinker, but this evening she needed it.

'You look like you've been through the ringer,' said Ed, as he sat back down and placed the drink in front of her.

'Feels like it, too,' said Lexi, tasting her wine – a large glass of Merlot. Pub wines could be dodgy, but this was smooth, more than acceptable. She put the glass down. No more until the food arrived. It would be too easy to get tipsy on such an empty stomach.

Ed passed her a menu, then went back to the bar to order food. Finally, they were able to get down to business.

Lexi took the files out of her briefcase and put them on the table. She brought Ed up to speed with the events of the day – Len's sudden death, taking whatever information he had with him to the grave, her fruitless visit to the Beaney Centre and the mess up over the surveillance of Toby Yates.

'So Yates is looking most likely in your book?'

'This is where my problem lies. My other suspects have been ruled out and he's the last man standing, but does that mean he did it? So far, we've got no circumstantial evidence tying him to the murder scene. If he's our key suspect, it's by default.'

A waiter approached their table with laden plates – tall, stacked burgers that looked amazing. Lexi's mouth immediately started to water. Ed quickly closed the file so the waiter wouldn't catch a glimpse of the police mugshot of Toby Yates.

Lexi slipped the folders back into her bag, and they stopped talking for a few minutes to concentrate on the food. It was good – flavoursome burgers on brioche buns, perfectly crispy fries and generous servings of freshly made coleslaw. Lexi felt her strength returning almost immediately.

'Another glass of wine?' said Ed.

'Uh-uh.' Lexi swallowed her mouthful. 'Got to get back to the office afterwards.'

'Fair enough.' She noticed that he didn't order another beer for himself. Presumably he was driving. Every ten minutes or so, he would turn over his mobile, which was lying face down on the table next to his plate, and check for text messages. Usually, Lexi would find this incredibly rude, but was not above doing it herself when she was waiting on critical information, so she didn't say anything.

As they finished eating, they swapped a few stories about their experiences working with the Feds. 'Harry's a mensch,' said Ed, 'but it's his way or the highway.'

'I know what you mean.' Harry Garcia had ruled his team with a will of iron, perhaps justifiably because no one understood a killer's mind the way he did. And it meant he did what he thought was right for the case, not for his operatives. 'But he got away with it.'

'I often had to wonder if he's that dictatorial in his private life. The guy must be hell to live with when a case is going badly.'

Lexi knew exactly what Harry was like in his downtime, but it wasn't something she wanted to discuss with Ed Harlow. She steered the conversation back to the purely professional. 'I owe him a lot – he taught me everything, and he welcomed me onto the team despite knowing I'd eventually want to come back home.'

'Harry told me you were responsible for catching the Diamond River Killer in Virginia. I'd love to hear about that some time.'

Lexi tensed. 'When we've got more time.' It was an obvious deflection, but she wasn't keen to revisit one of the most harrowing cases she'd ever worked on. Or the way in which Harry had set her up to reel the killer in. He'd risked her life, and she wasn't sure she'd ever be able to forgive him. Or trust him again.

When the plates were cleared, they turned their attention back to the case.

'Here's what we know about Yates,' said Lexi. 'Let's see what matches our profile of the killer and what doesn't.'

Ed watched as she counted off the known facts on her fingers.

'He hasn't worked since the accident that disfigured his face. He lives on disability benefits, quite frugally, from what the surveillance team has reported. He shops at Aldi and doesn't go out much. Perhaps the Pole Star was his one indulgence. The girls there told us that he would come in once a week, sometimes less often, and nurse a single drink for as long as he could get away with it.'

'And they believed he had a thing for Eden?'

'Yes, she was the only girl he tipped. We believe he tried to speak to her outside the club once or twice, but apparently she would never have anything to do with the punters.'

'So he might have felt rejected?'

'Yes, definitely. He's never been married and since the accident, the odds are against it. He may feel resentful towards all women, not just Eden.'

'But she could well have come to symbolise that in his mind. By punishing Eden and her sisters, he could be sending a message to women everywhere. "Reject me at your peril."'

Lexi nodded.

'Coffee?' said Ed, checking his phone for the umpteenth time.

They ordered coffees and carried on the conversation.

'How does he stack up against the classic sexual predator

profile?' Ed stirred sugar into his coffee. 'Not a first kill, judging by the posing at the scene.'

'Not by a long shot.'

'So might he have been your...?' Ed realised he might be treading on dangerous ground here and let the question hang.

'My abductor? I'm pretty certain now that they're one and the same. But what I need to focus on is finding Paige. I think whoever's got her will be early forties and likely inexperienced with adult women.'

'Apart from a dominating mother?'

'We don't have anything concrete on his background yet,' said Lexi.

'I can guarantee he's an only child.'

For some reason his confidence on this point irritated her. 'I'm not sure of that – his obsession with triplets suggests some sort of sibling issue to me. We need to know more about him. I've asked Ridhi to dig around, talk to anyone she can find who knows Yates – but needless to say, he's something of a loner.' So much, so obvious. Sexual serial killers had certain traits in common.

'No sign of sexual assault, so it's all about the fear factor. He dominates through fear and manipulation – by having more than one victim, he can play them off against each other.'

The conversation was nearing the knuckle, but she maintained her composure. 'Controlling one by making threats against the other two. It's clever, and it's how he played my sisters and me against each other.' A shiver ran through her. 'This guy is about the mind games rather than physical gratification.'

'Definitely,' said Ed.

'In his daily life, he suffers a lack of control. People don't listen to him, and he's frustrated that no one realises how intelligent or brilliant he is.'

'Which feeds into his lack of confidence around others, especially women.'

'A feedback loop which is taking him on a downward spiral.' Lexi used her teaspoon to scoop up the remaining froth of her cappuccino.

'Another?' said Ed.

'Uh-uh. I have enough trouble sleeping as it is.'

'What's puzzling about this case is that the girls' murders indicate a highly organised, manipulative killer, while Pendleton's death seemed to be at the hands of a disorganised frenzied killer. But you're sure it's the same perp?'

Lexi considered the question for a moment. 'I believe so. I think he's highly organised, clever, manipulative – Josh Pendleton's murder was a smokescreen. The attack was frenzied – disorganised – while the dumping of the body was deliberate – organised. If it was a disorganised, frenzied killing, I would expect to have found the murder weapon nearby.' Lexi was thinking out loud. 'He killed Josh to divert us away from the main thrust of the case – and it worked.'

'There was no posing of the body in Chequer's Wood, unlike the girls on the crown. No staging, either.'

'Unless the obliteration of the face was deliberate staging – to make us think he's a crazed killer, when in fact he's not?'

'Interesting theory,' said Ed. 'But where does it leave you? What would it take to be able to arrest and charge Yates?'

'Something more than I've got at the moment. Because as compelling as the case against Yates might seem, the evidence just isn't there.'

The waiter drifted past their table. 'Last orders.'

Lexi was surprised. The last time she'd checked her watch it had been before nine. The time had flown by, and although they'd argued back and forth over the case, it had been a let-up from the grinding stress that had knotted her stomach most of the day.

It didn't surprise her when Ed insisted on paying, but it didn't sit comfortably with her either.

'We can split it,' she said.

'Please, don't worry,' he said. 'It's my apology for this morning. You can pay next time.'

'Next time' was another assumption. Was he always this high-handed? Lexi was keen to get back to her desk to write up some notes on the profile they'd discussed. Ed's car was parked in the opposite direction, so they said a slightly awkward goodnight and went their separate ways.

As Lexi walked back through the empty streets, she wondered if the press pack outside the police station had called it a night. She hoped so. She wasn't keen to have to run the same gauntlet on her way back in. Her route took her down Watling Street towards the Riding Gate in the city walls. She passed the Watling Street car park on her left, then the small park in the shadow of the walls. The street lighting in this part of the city was poor and she seemed to be the only person out and about.

She shivered and pulled her coat tighter, making sure that her bag hung across the front of her body, rather than swinging out behind her.

As she hurried down the ramp into the subway under the road, she heard heavy male footsteps ringing out on the concrete behind her. Catching her up. Turning the corner into the tunnel, she broke into a run. The footsteps were drowned out by the roar of the traffic above her, but she kept going at a sprint rather than her usual long-distance pace.

Emerging from the tunnel, she pelted up the ramp that brought her out onto Dover Street, just opposite the police station, and once she'd crossed the road, she felt safe. She stood, panting, on the steps in front of the main entrance, watching and waiting. Seconds later, a man emerged from the subway. He looked young, hands stuffed in the pockets of his bomber jacket, head down against the wind. He carried on down Dover

Street without so much as glancing across the road at the crazy woman who'd run through the subway.

He probably hadn't even noticed her.

Lexi turned to go into the building, her heart still pounding.

For heaven's sake, pull yourself together, woman.

FORTY

Ah, the Shakespeare – an excellent choice. And a glass of red. Always a favourite.

And back to work at a run. Such dedication to the job is heart-warming to see, Lexi.

But I leave Lexi and the man she's with to their pleasures. It crosses my mind that Paige hasn't had any water for nearly twenty-four hours. Letting her die of neglect isn't part of the plan. After all, she's my hook to haul Lexi in, and a dead worm on the hook isn't nearly as appetising as one that's live and wriggling.

Of course, once I have Lexi back with me, and then Amber, Paige will become redundant and it won't matter if she lives or dies. But I think she'll die. It'll make things less complicated in the long run... Tidier.

I think about ways to dispose of her as I drive through the moonlit countryside. The easiest would be to abandon her where she is, tied up, out of sight, where nobody will hear her scream. And where she probably won't be found until there's nothing left but a pile of bleached white bones.

Poor Paige.

FORTY-ONE

The incident room was empty and, still hyper from the surge of adrenalin in the subway, Lexi decided she wouldn't achieve anything sitting at her desk and staring into space. She was fizzing with energy and her mind was racing. There was no way she would get to sleep, so a run seemed like a much better idea. She hadn't exercised for a couple of days and she was missing the mental boost it gave her.

She texted Amber not to wait up for her, drove home quickly, changed into her sports kit and laced up her trainers. She needed to pound her frustration into the ground with a long, hard workout, and after that maybe she'd be able to escape the world for a few hours.

She'd avoided running to the Memorial Crown since discovering Eden and Lucy's bodies there, but the hill gave her the right amount of challenge, and now that Emily and her crime scene officers had left the site, Lexi decided to claim it back.

Still in fight-or-flight mode, she set off at a pace that was much too fast to keep up for the whole circuit, especially with the long slog up the hill. This time she'd had the good sense to wear a head torch – there was too much risk of tripping in the woods, where roots and stray brambles forced her to adjust her stride or take a flying leap to clear them.

It was freezing cold, but the night sky was clear, and away from Canterbury's lights she could even see some stars. Her breath exhaled in foggy clouds, and each inhalation felt like an icy stab at the back of her throat – another reason why she'd need to slow down a bit once she'd worked through her frustration. But it was only three months until her first competitive event of the season, an Ironman triathlon in Wales, and she was already behind in her training, so she was going to push herself as hard as she could.

She turned her thoughts to the case as she sprinted up the gentle incline of Wibberly Way at the foot of the Downs. Had the person who'd put the two girls in princess dresses and placed tiaras in their hair really smashed Josh Pendleton's face to a pulp with a mallet? She thought about how entitled Josh might have appeared to a man like Toby Yates, whose only interactions with women were paid for. From the photographs she'd seen, Josh had been good-looking – a long, narrow face with sensuous lips and wide-set dark eyes. Toby could easily be jealous of a man like that, and if Josh had stood in his way as he'd tried to abduct Lucy... It certainly wasn't beyond the realms of possibility.

She made a mental note to check whether the search warrant for Yates's house and car had come through yet – they would need to check the car for Josh Pendleton's DNA, and look for anything that could have been used as a murder weapon.

As she turned right off Wibberly Way onto the North Downs Way, the slope became steeper, forcing her to slow her pace. She needed to get into the gym and work on her leg muscles. The wind had picked up, and she was running into it which made things even tougher, but the flip side was that on the way down, she'd have it at her back and she'd fly. But for now the going was hard and she had to concentrate to keep pushing onwards at a pace she was happy with, while her quads and calf muscles burned and her knees felt the jolt of every step on the frozen ground.

Soon she could see the gap in the trees up ahead. She was nearly at the top, where she'd allow herself five minutes to get her breath back before starting down. Assuming there were no dead bodies there, she thought grimly, as she heaved herself over the stile and onto the grass.

Of course, there weren't. The only sign of the events of the previous few days were the bunches of flowers left by the girls' family and friends when they'd held their vigil. She dropped to a crouch and looked at them in the light of the head torch. They'd been buffeted by the wind and looked ragged, the flower heads drooping and turning brown, surrounded by a fluttering of detached petals.

She stood up and stretched her muscles. It was too cold to stay for long, and too sad. The Crown would now be forever linked with the murders. Blinking back tears, she made a vow to herself that she would come here for every training run from now on. She wouldn't forget Lucy and Eden, and she wouldn't rest until she'd found out who was responsible for their deaths.

She walked slowly back towards the stile that divided the pastureland from the woods. And what of Paige? Where was she on this cold, dark night? Was she still alive? Lexi had to take the fact that she hadn't been killed along with her sisters as a sign of hope – though what she might have endured between then and now didn't bear thinking about.

She hopped back over the stile and set off down the path at a brisk jog. Now her mind was crowded with questions about what she needed to do next to speed up the investigation. Maggie wanted an arrest, and most of the team viewed Toby Yates as an easy target – he came very close to fitting the profile. But somewhere in the back of Lexi's mind, there was still a niggling doubt. She just wasn't convinced that he was their man. From Ridhi's background check on him, they knew that he'd lived in Canterbury for over a decade. Serial killers follow a path and this one was quite far along it. If it was Toby Yates, where were his earlier kills?

But most compelling of all, for her personally, when she'd interviewed Yates there had been nothing familiar about him. She felt sure that if she was put in a room with the man who'd taken her and her sisters, she would know it – and she'd have a gut-wrenching physical reaction to it. Talking to Yates, she'd felt nothing.

But if it wasn't Yates, who was it?

She swore softly to herself as she ran. What had she missed? Was there something staring her right in the face?

It had started to drizzle by the time she arrived back in the village, icy pinpricks on her bare arms and legs, so she didn't let up her pace as she ran down the High Street in the direction of her cottage. It would be good to be back in the warm again, get a hot drink inside her. At least she should sleep well after this, once she drove to Amber's.

She dug her front door key out of her pocket. Stepping into the hall, she switched on the light. She was quickly enveloped in a comforting blanket of warm air. She kicked off her trainers, but then stood still and listened. Something seemed off. She sniffed. There was the faintest smell of vegetation on the air, of winter in a garden, rotting leaves...

Her stomach contracted. All thoughts of relaxation were left behind as she crept down the hall, muscles taut, ready for action. She slowly pressed down the lever of the kitchen door. Cold air rushed through the gap as she opened it and slid a hand round to the light switch.

'Is somebody here?'

No one answered. The house was quiet. The kitchen was empty, but on the far side of the room, the back door stood ajar.

'What the hell?'

She strode across and slammed it shut, locking it and then sliding the bolt across. She looked through the door's glass pane at the garden beyond. The wet trees and shrubs glistened in the light coming from the kitchen. Nothing moved. There was no sign that anyone had been there. She peered at the surface of the grass. No indents suggesting someone had recently walked across it.

Had she left the door unlocked? She couldn't believe she had. The things she saw at work every day probably made her more security conscious than most. But if she had left the door unlocked, could it have blown open on its own?

'No.' She shook her head, and a shiver ran down her spine. She listened again. Was there someone in the house?

Turning back to the kitchen, she scanned the room to see if anything was missing.

Nothing seemed to be.

But there was something on the kitchen table that hadn't been there before, she was sure of it. A book. As she moved closer, she realised it was a journal, a notebook with a blue linen cover, embossed with the words 'My Diary'. They'd been in shiny gold foil when it was new, she remembered. Now they were tarnished, and the cover was grubby and worn, stained with dirt and ink and grease spots.

But she'd recognise it anywhere.

It was Rose's diary, and she'd had it with her the day they'd been taken.

FORTY-TWO

I've been crouching in the shadows at the side of the cottage, but I can't control my curiosity any longer. The kitchen has a window just a few feet away from where I'm squatting. It's a massive risk, but when has that ever put me off?

I press my body hard against the wall by the window frame, then move my head sideways until I can see into the kitchen.

Lexi Bennett is standing, leaning against the edge of the table, staring down at the diary. Her face is in profile, so I stay where I am and watch. She's still in her running gear, damp with drizzle and sweat, and her upper body is swaying slightly. It's the only emotion she shows. Shock. She can't believe what she's seeing. But she doesn't snatch it up as I might have done, had I discovered such a long-lost treasure.

She stares at it for a long time, first biting her lip, then wiping a hand across her mouth.

As she studies it, I let my gaze wander to the muscles at the back of her thighs. Physically, she's very different to when I first encountered her. Now she's strong and athletic. A powerhouse. She came back from America transformed, and I've watched her *running and cycling and swimming like someone demented. As if she's chasing the devil, or the devil's on her tail.*

It's an obsession. We have that in common, the thing that pushes a person to go far beyond what others would do and still not be satisfied.

Lexi's motionless. She's thinking about what she should do.

It's a critical piece of evidence from the case involving her and her sisters. And she must suspect that it's somehow evidence in her current case. But it's also intensely personal to her. Rose's diary.

I've read it from cover to cover. Several times, in fact, over the years when I missed Rose. She was a sweet thing, but most of it's extremely banal. Teenage girl stuff. I honestly didn't know how silly they could be before I read it.

Lexi seems to wake from a trance and, like the good little policewoman she is, I see her getting out her phone and taking pictures before she touches it. When she's finished, she pulls on a pair of latex gloves from her bag. She's treating the diary as evidence rather than as a possession. I wouldn't have expected less from her.

But then I'm surprised. Rather than tucking it into an evidence bag, she picks the diary up and quickly flicks through it. Still clutching it, she leaves the kitchen, flicking off the light on the way out. I can just hear the thud of her feet on the stairs. Her bedroom light goes on, casting a rectangle of amber onto the front garden.

I guess she's going to read the diary before turning it in. I'd love to see her face when she finds out what's in it.

FORTY-THREE

Lexi flung herself down on her bed and stared at the tattered diary in her gloved hands. One of her calves twinged with cramp, but she ignored it. Her mind was racing and her thoughts were confused. She couldn't ever have imagined finding something so precious. It was like having a piece of Rose back. Reading it would be like having a conversation with her sister.

Someone had kept it all these years. Presumably their abductor... or could someone have found it and realised what it was? But why would they have hung on to it and then sneaked into her house at night to leave it on the kitchen table? The only thing that made sense was that it was a message – to her, from him.

And she knew what he was saying.

I'm back and I know where you live.

The man who had held her for those endless days – she'd lost count how many, though it had seemed like forever – was nothing but a dark shadow in her memory. She knew that her mind had obscured him for her own protection, but it frustrated her. She'd never seen his face but he was a constant presence, trapped in the deepest recesses of her brain, still holding Rose, still running after her and Amber. Pulling them down into darkness.

Now he was somewhere nearby, too close for comfort. She thought for a moment of the man that Amber had seen peering in at her window. Was that him too? Fear washed through her like a blast of icy water. She should be back at Amber's now, making sure she and Tasha were safe.

But not yet. She wanted to spend some time alone with Rose, before she had to seal the diary in an evidence bag and hand it over to Emily Jordan to check for fingerprints. Then it would become just a numbered item on a list, and she wouldn't have access to it again until the case was resolved. That might be never.

A rattle outside caught her attention. She launched herself towards the bedroom window which looked out over the front of the property. Was he still out there? The street lights bathed the road and front gardens in an amber glow. There was no one around, nothing moving. Lights shone in one or two windows, but most of the neighbouring houses were dark. She checked her watch – it was just gone midnight, though it felt even later. The evenings were long when it got dark between four and five o'clock.

She heard the noise again, then spotted a bin lid that was being blown along the pavement in fits and starts.

She went back to her bed, snatching up a cardigan from the chair by the window. She felt cold as her damp running kit dried. She propped up the pillow, pulled the bedspread up over her knees and started to read.

She'd never taken a sneaky look at Rose's diary while her sister was still alive, but the words that filled the pages sounded so familiar she could almost hear Rose's voice whispering in her ear. And she remembered some of the things that Rose had written about.

Yesterday we all turned sixteen and the bad thing was that mum made us have one shared party. No matter that I didn't want to party with Amber's stuck up friends or that I knew Lex would insist on one of her crappy playlists. But...

Lexi could just see her tossing her long blonde mane here.

Aaron came... ********

Lexi was pretty sure Rose had lost her virginity to Aaron that night. And then two weeks later, she'd seen him after school with his arm around another girl and her world had ended. Lexi flicked ahead until she found the day. The ink had bled across the page and the paper was wrinkled – probably by Rose's tears.

I'll claw her eyes out, I swear I will.

That hadn't happened.

Lexi carried on reading. Most of the entries made her smile fondly. One or two of them made her frown. Of course one's sisters were one's biggest critics, and there were moments where Rose was laser sharp at skewering both her and Amber. Usually for some minor infringement or slight – Amber borrowing clothes without permission, herself doing something embarrassing in front of Rose's friends. It all seemed very innocent compared with what the Carter triplets had been getting up to – a reflection of how things were changing. Today Rose wouldn't have a paper diary. It would be on her phone in the form of text messages to her friends.

Eventually, Lexi came to the day before the abduction. The last entry.

Hung out with Rory in the library after school today. What a dreamboat. He says he has a girlfriend, but I don't believe him. Otherwise, why would he be spending hours with me? Anyway, I think he's definitely interested... it's not like we got around to doing our homework at all. So I should be doing that now, but maybe I'll just do it in the morning – I can copy Amber's. Or pretend I forgot it at home.

Lexi wondered if she'd ever done the homework or not. She probably had, because if she hadn't, she might have been in detention when they were taken. Perhaps everything would have been different. But thoughts like that were torture, and Lexi had the sense not to fall down that particular rabbit hole.

She sniffed, and grabbed a tissue from the box on her bedside table. It would be easy to let the floodgates open. The empty pages in the diary should have been full of her sister's dreams and friendships and disappointments. She flicked through them, her eyes blurring with unshed tears.

Then she stopped and went back.

Black writing scrawled across one of the pages. Her sister's hand, but shaky and not entirely legible. Lexi's breath caught in her throat. Could these pages have been written after their abduction? They'd been held in different rooms, so Lexi had no idea whether Rose would have been able to or not, whether she'd had a pen or a pencil.

She looked down at what Rose had written. The handwriting was shaky, the ink smudged – maybe by tears? She guessed, heartbreakingly, it was from after Rose had been recaptured. Her heart clenched. What had her sister gone through? Fear was a fresh taste in her mouth. A burst of adrenalin made her feel the need to run and run and run...

She dragged her attention back to the page. It was a list. Had their abductor seen it? He must have done.

. . .

Things I miss

- *My Sisters*
- *My Mum and Dad*
- *Pookie – My Rabbit*
- *Captain Ahab – My Hamster*
- *The View from My Bedroom Window*
- *The Beach*
- *The library*
- *Chicken Nuggets*
- *KitKats*

Lexi read the list through twice. She felt perplexed. They'd never had a rabbit. They'd never had a hamster. And shortly before they were taken, Rose had announced she was becoming a vegetarian. None of it made any sense. And KitKats? Their captor gave them KitKats to eat. Lexi's stomach roiled at the memory.

What had happened to Rose after she and Amber had gone?

And then she heard movement outside.

FORTY-FOUR

Ouch!

From inside the house, I can hear the thump of her feet on the stairs. The kitchen light goes on.

I duck back into the shadows and squat down as she comes towards the window. She peers out into the darkness.

Really, Lexi, I must stop meeting you like this.

But I like to watch her, and it's a habit that's hard to break.

She turns away from the window and I need to decide. Should I stay or should I go? They say discretion is the better part of valour. I sneak away down the side of the house and then into the next-door garden where the hedge is low. From here I can make my way, unseen, through their shrubbery and climb over the back fence.

It was the right decision. As I make it to relative safety, I hear a key turn in a lock, and the creak of a door swinging open.

'Who's there?' It's Lexi's voice. 'I heard you. I know you're out here.'

To her credit, she doesn't sound nervous or afraid. She's angry.

I wait in the shelter of the hedge. Short, shallow, quiet breaths.

'Show yourself.' Her voice is on the move – she's walking down the garden. But she won't find anyone there.

I risk a peek over the hedge, but I'm too far away to see what she's up to. There's a flickering of light. She must have a torch.

In a blur of black and white, a cat rushes by on Lexi's side of the hedge. The torch goes off. The door slams shut. Lexi, having found a satisfactory explanation for the noise, has gone back inside. I hear the lock turning and bolts sliding home. She won't come out again tonight.

I creep away with one thought in my head.

When will we be together?

Lexi Bennett. My princess.

FORTY-FIVE

FRIDAY, 13 JANUARY

There was no chance of sleep now. Lexi's heart was racing. The sound in the garden had scared her and that damned cat had given her an even bigger fright. The subsequent flood of adrenalin meant she was wide awake and jumpy as hell. She looked at the half-empty wine bottle on the table. It was tempting, but she needed a clear head. Maybe a hot bath would calm her jangling nerves. She started to run one but let the water out before it was half full.

She needed to act. The fight-or-flight urge inside her wouldn't be sated until she'd... what? She had no idea. She threw on jeans and a leather jacket, picked up the diary and grabbed her car keys from the hook on the coat stand.

Outside, the street was quiet. Most of the lights in most of the houses were off, apart from a few upstairs. Lexi looked at her watch – it was well past midnight. She got into the Crossfire, hoping the roar of the engine wouldn't disturb her closest neighbours too much. She didn't have a plan, but she found herself steering through the village to come out of it heading north. Through Chilham and then Chartham, staying west of Canterbury, she wound her way through the countryside on empty roads – and suddenly realised where she was going. She had to slow down to stay at the speed limit as she drove through the village of Rough Common, but it meant she didn't miss the sharp left turn into Blean Woods.

Blean Woods was a nature reserve and, as she left the village behind her, there were no more lights. Just a narrow lane cutting through the trees, with a strip of only slightly less black sky above.

Seventeen years ago, she had run along this road, Amber practically dragging her as she constantly turned back in the hope of a miracle. She hadn't stopped crying as she ran, even though her lungs were bursting. They'd had to leave Rose behind and it was breaking her heart. They ran for just over a mile until they came to the village, but at the time it had seemed so much further.

This was the first time she'd been back.

She had been tempted before, but a strong sense of self-preservation usually kicked in within a few miles of the place. It would open a Pandora's box of memories that she kept tightly locked. The fleeting glimpses that had peppered her dreams for years were enough warning that this was a place left well alone.

So why was she here now, in the depths of night, without the benefit of daytime's bravery?

She realised that she'd slowed the car right down. Her subconscious didn't want her to be here. She fought the urge to turn around as anxiety blossomed into dread, moving from the pit of her stomach into her chest. It made her pause between breaths, as she peered through the windscreen at the next curve in the lane. Even though the car was doing all the work, it seemed to be harder and harder to move forward.

Finally, she rounded the bend. The trees gave way to a clearing, but what she saw before her didn't match the memory of what she'd seen over her shoulder as she ran for her life. The small cottage had been dilapidated then. Now it was a ruin.

The roof had fallen in, the windows were empty of glass and the front door hung from one hinge, half open, beckoning her to come and take a closer look.

She stopped the car. Right where she was, right in the middle of the road, about thirty feet from the tumbledown stone wall that separated the property from the forest. There was no gate in the wall – there never had been – just a gap, where the road ended and became a short, rutted driveway.

A bank of clouds drew back from the moon, and in the blue-grey light, for a moment Lexi saw the cottage as it had been, and fear gripped her so hard that she was her seventeen-year-old self again, running, forever running.

But the clouds returned and obliterated the memory. She was sitting in the Crossfire, her cheeks wet with tears, her hands gripping the steering wheel, the rest of her body set like stone. She took a deep breath, switched off the engine and drew the key out of the ignition. In the silence that followed, the trees seemed to come a step closer.

The click when she undid her seat belt echoed inside the car. Then a slight hiss as the belt retracted itself. Her every sense seemed heightened as she pulled the catch to open the door.

What was she doing here?

She moved slowly as if she was in a dream. The surface of the road crunched under her feet, then gave way to the squelch of mud as she passed through the gap in the wall. Trembling, she walked towards the door. Had it really been seventeen years? Sometimes it seemed as if it had all happened yesterday. At other times it felt like another lifetime.

A frayed strip of blue and white crime scene tape fluttered on the door handle. The police had gone over the property with a fine-toothed comb after the event, but they'd found nothing that helped them identify the man who'd spirited Rose away in the scant hour between Lexi and Amber's escape and the arrival of the first responders.

Lexi remembered that moment, sitting in the back of a police car with Amber and a woman detective, staring at the cottage as the response team streamed in. Craning her neck for a first glimpse of them bringing Rose out, and the man in hand-cuffs. But it didn't happen like that. They searched the cottage and then spread out through the woods. There was no sign of the man or the missing girl. And there never had been in the years since, despite one of the biggest investigations ever under-taken by Kent Police. Len Clayton had been there that evening, though she didn't meet him properly until the next day.

She reached forward and pushed the door inwards. It resisted her, creaking, then as she pushed harder it fell onto the floor with a loud thwump as the remaining hinge gave way. A cloud of dirt blew up around it, then settled slowly. Lexi peered into the dark interior, waiting for another break in the clouds to give her enough moonlight to see by. The space was smaller than she remembered. Of course it was. Everything had been exaggerated over time – the run had seemed further, the cottage had seemed bigger, the man had assumed the proportions of a monster.

There was a time when she'd believed that – that the man who'd snatched her and her sisters was a veritable monster. Evil incarnate. But now she knew better. She'd studied killers, hunted them down, caught them and interrogated them. They weren't monsters. They were pathetic men who shored up their inadequacies with games of pain and domination. There was a type, there was a pattern, and the more you learned about them, the more you were able to cut them down to size.

So why hadn't anyone managed to catch this particular beast? He'd failed, in as much as she and Amber had got away. But he'd kept Rose. He'd killed Rose – she had to accept that now. And whatever had compelled him to take them in the first place would have compelled him to act again.

The moonlight came and went, showing her broken furniture and empty beer cans. Of course people had been here in the intervening years. *The murder cottage.* She knew that was how locals referred to it, though nobody had died here. But it would have an irresistible draw on the imaginations of the village teenagers, which was another of the reasons she'd never come back here. She couldn't bear the thought of other people nosing around in the place where she'd last seen Rose alive.

'Rose, what happened to you? Where did he take you?' she whispered into the darkness, but no answer came. 'And what were you trying to tell me with your list?'

A gust of wind outside caused the bare branches of the trees to clatter against each other, but Lexi couldn't understand what they were saying.

She thought through the list in her mind. The objects, people, animals, places. What did it all mean? Two characters from books.

Go back to the books and you'll decipher the message.

Could that really be the answer?

FORTY-SIX

At that moment, the memories broke through the wall that Lexi had so painstakingly constructed. It was inevitable that they would at some point – there was only so long one could hold out against the past. She knew that coming to the cottage risked it happening, and she had to accept that now was the time to confront them. And by reliving what had happened to her and to Amber and Rose, she hoped to shine a light on what had befallen Paige Carter and her sisters.

She closed her eyes and saw the room as it had been when the man had first shoved her roughly through the door. Her hands had been tied behind her back and she'd stumbled – even then the lino had been peeling up from the floor. She remembered banging her hip on the corner of a table. The smart of pain seemed as real now as back then and she put a hand to the place, something she hadn't been able to do at the time.

She'd sworn at the man and shouted, and he'd struck her hard across the side of the head, making her world spin. He was wearing a mask – she'd learn later that it was a gimp mask, but at seventeen, she'd had no idea about things like that. She never saw his face. She could barely remember his voice.

She'd been the first to be taken.

She'd been walking home after hockey practice, carrying a stack of books, when a van had pulled up beside her. She thought nothing of it, she thought the van was just parking. It was a quiet residential street, with no one around in the middle of the day. The man had grabbed her from behind and smashed her head against the side of the van. Disorientated, she found herself being manhandled into the back. She dropped the books and, as the van door slammed shut, she remembered one of them lying face up in the gutter. The cover showed two pale hands holding a bright red apple.

For so long she hadn't been able to get that image out of her head. A picture she associated with pain and fear, then blind panic turning to anger as she realised what was happening. He'd brought her straight to the cottage, and when he opened the back of the van, now wearing the white rubber mask, the mix of terror and rage had made her reckless. She lunged at him and tried to rip off the mask, but he'd overpowered her. He used cable ties to secure her wrists, then left her locked in the stinking, filthy cottage, alone for hours.

Until he brought Rose.

Lexi could see straight away that the fight had already gone from her sister. Sobbing and shaking, she came meekly. The masked man had chains with him, and padlocks, as well as the cable ties. He pushed Rose to the ground, where she lay crying uncontrollably, and chained Lexi's leg to the leg of a cast iron stove that stood in the grate.

Lexi had called to Rose, told her to run, told her to save herself, but it was if her sister couldn't hear her. She was in shock, almost catatonic, and the man used her paralysis to his advantage.

Once Lexi was secure, he led Rose out of the room. Lexi heard the chains dragging behind him as they climbed the stairs. The floorboards above her head creaked, and she heard a sharp cry of pain. If the man was hurting Rose, she'd kill him. She'd yanked at her own chain and kicked at the stove. But although it was ancient and rusty, it didn't yield.

At some point in the night, he brought Amber to the cottage. She had a cut above one eye and her face was covered with blood. The man didn't care. He secured her to the post at the bottom of the stairs, then disappeared.

It was no relief to Lexi that her sisters were with her. It was worse, far worse, than if she'd been there alone. Her mind was spinning, speculating on his intentions. Was he going to rape them? Kill them? All three of them?

'Amber? Rose? Can you hear me? We need to escape before he comes back.'

That night, they could talk. It brought some comfort, but he heard them as he approached the cottage in the morning and after that he took steps to stop it. Gags and blindfolds. See no evil, speak no evil – but they could still hear it, and nothing was more terrifying than the sound of his foot on the step, his hand at the door.

He kept them there for days – Lexi had lost count of how many.

She heard him moving around, from room to room. She heard blows. She heard her sisters cry out behind their gags. She heard him masturbating.

Sometimes he took off her gag, holding a bottle of water to her mouth. She spoke once, and he rammed the plastic bottle hard against her teeth. She quickly learned to stay silent. He never brought them food, and Lexi felt herself getting weaker and weaker as the days passed.

And then she remembered the worst horror of all, the one that she'd buried so deep inside that she'd had no clue until now, this night spent in the ruins, that it had happened.

She had heard him speak.

He'd noticed the marks that showed she'd been rubbing the chain against the leg of the stove. She'd been trying to buckle the iron leg, but she'd had no success.

'Were you trying to escape, princess?' he'd asked. His voice was quiet and unremarkable. But just to hear it was terrifying.

She'd shaken her head, but of course he knew she was.

'Every transgression will be punished.'

But then, as she waited for the blow, he left the room. For now, she could breathe. She didn't know what might be coming.

The memory of what happened next hit Lexi like a sledge-hammer between the eyes.

A drawn-out scream of an intensity she'd never heard before came from upstairs. Followed by another which dissolved into wailing.

Rose!

What had he done to her? Was this the punishment of which he'd spoken? What had he done? Lexi remembered and wanted to die.

He had punished Rose for her escape attempt. Beneath the sound of Rose's howling, she felt the vibration of his feet on the stairs. Then she heard Amber scream. He came into the room and ripped away her blindfold. As her eyes grew accustomed to the light, he held out one of his hands, flat and open. There was something in his palm. Her vision came into focus and she saw what it was.

The top joint of a human finger, the cut end scarlet with fresh blood. The same size and shape as her own little finger.

She knew immediately what the bastard had done.

She'd never been so angry in her life. She threw herself at him with a furious power. The stove ripped out from the fire-place and crashed into one of his knees. He went down with a roar of pain. Her chain fell away from the stove leg – she was free. She kicked him as hard as she could in the ribs, then stamped on one of his arms. She needed him down long enough to release her sisters.

The newel post was easy enough to deal with. A forceful kick separated it from the top rail of the banister and Amber was able to lift the chain over the top of it. They both ran upstairs. Rose was chained to an iron radiator. They had it off the wall within seconds, causing a rush of stinking brown water to gush out of the twisted pipes, and released the chain round Rose's ankle.

Rose was weak, her clothes soaked with blood as she cradled her right hand. She was struggling to stand up, and even when Amber pulled her to her feet, she stood swaying and confused.

'She's in shock,' said Lexi. 'We'll have to help her.'

They stood one on each side and supported Rose, Lexi putting her arm around her sister's waist. Amber placed Rose's arms over each of their shoulders, but she slumped against them, unable to lift her feet to walk. They dragged her across the room, then had to file sideways down the narrow staircase. As they passed the room at the bottom of the stairs, Lexi glanced in. The man was just about on his feet, staggering slightly. Amber saw him too, and gasped.

'Come on,' said Lexi, the urgency making her sound sharp and angry.

But it was too hard to run while supporting Rose's weight. She and Amber were both weak as well – they'd had no food for days and barely enough water.

He came after them.

Lexi looked back over her shoulder, disentangling herself from Rose and Amber.

'Go ahead,' she hissed. She spun round, searching the ground for a weapon.

The man was lurching towards her, shouting angrily, his hands clawing the air.

Lexi spotted a rotten plank from a collapsed gate. She snatched it up and, using every final ounce of her energy, she smashed it against his approaching head. He staggered and fell, his howling cut short as the wind was knocked from his lungs.

She'd bought them an extra few minutes.

She turned back to see Amber and Rose, several metres up the lane, beyond the gap in the wall. But Rose was sprawled on the tarmac and Amber was squatting next to her.

'She fainted,' said Amber, looking up as Lexi approached them.

Lexi looked down at her sister. Her eyelids fluttered, showing only the whites of her eyes. She was out cold. They wouldn't be able to carry her, but they couldn't wait around for the man to recover.

'Quickly, hide her here in these ferns,' said Lexi quietly. 'If she's out of sight and we run on noisily, he'll come straight past her as he chases after us.'

'We can't leave her,' said Amber.

'There's no choice.'

'Then let me stay with her, while you run for help.'

'He'll see you if there are two of you.'

Amber didn't agree with the strategy, but Lexi knew it was their only hope. Together, they dragged Rose deep into a heavily covered area under the trees. She blinked and whimpered as they lowered her gently in among the ferns.

Lexi knelt by her side and put her forefinger briefly to her lips. 'Stay absolutely still and quiet, Rose-petal, so he can't find you. We'll go for help and we'll be back as fast as we can.'

Rose gave a nod of understanding.

Amber looked down at her, her face expressing all of the pain and fear she was most certainly feeling.

Lexi kissed her sister, then tugged on Amber's arm.

'Come on. We've got to go now. Can you run?'

Lexi had never run so fast in her life, Amber trailing behind her, the lane twisting through the forest in front.

She had no idea then that she'd just made the worst decision of her life.

They never saw Rose again.

FORTY-SEVEN

Lexi came to her senses with a jolt – it was like emerging from a dream. A nightmare of the most extreme intensity. Her cheeks were wet with tears and her chest tight. She hadn't noticed how cold she'd become, nor how long she'd spent squatting on the floor of the ruined cottage.

She looked around the room again, now painted with her memory of what had been. The battered stove still lay on its side, close to the hearth. The small kitchen table was still there, its surface littered with debris from the collapse of the roof above it. After what had happened, the police had taken the chains and all the other evidence of their captivity. She supposed they'd brushed for finger marks, but she could only ever remember seeing the man wearing gloves.

Seized by sudden dread, she had to get out.

She hurried back to the door, and once outside took great gulps of air. It was like coming to the surface again after nearly drowning.

She ran to the Crossfire as if he were chasing her all over again, and reversed at speed until the lane became wide enough to execute a three-point turn. She sped through the still-sleeping village without seeing another car and headed back towards Canterbury.

There was someone else who needed to see the diary.

Lexi could hear the clatter of breakfast and the chatter of the radio through the front door as she waited for Amber to answer. She hadn't slept and she was running on pure adrenalin. It was just getting light, and though she needed to get to the station, she had to show the diary to Amber before turning it over. She'd already broken the rules by keeping it to herself overnight instead of calling for a first responder to check the garden and a crime scene investigator to come and take custody of it immediately.

But it was too personal for that and, anyway, Rose's disappearance was now a cold case. Not that these excuses would hold much water if the diary was ever to be deemed evidence in a trial, but Amber had a right to see it before it disappeared into the bowels of the police station where the evidence room was located.

She rang the bell again – it must have gone unnoticed in the racket.

This time the door opened.

'Lexi?' Amber registered her appearance. 'You look terrible. Where were you? I thought you were going to stay here last night.'

Lexi grimaced. 'I'm so sorry. Something came up. I forgot.'

Amber looked wounded.

'It was unforgivable of me, but I've got something to show you.' She followed her sister through to the kitchen.

'I've got to get Tash to school. Can it wait?'

'It's important.'

Lexi was surprised to see Grant sitting at the breakfast table. He must have got back from his trip early. He stood up when Lexi came into the room.

'Grant, you remember Lexi?'

Grant was a tall man, square-jawed and solid in appearance – just the sort of man Lexi would have pictured Amber with. He was wearing baggy dad jeans and a blue and white striped shirt. Lexi had seen him once before, at her parents' funeral, but she'd never spoken to him. She'd missed Amber's wedding, and the births of her niece and nephew due to their estrangement. He could be forgiven for taking a dim view of her but he greeted her with a friendly smile.

'No need for introductions,' he said, 'you two are so alike.'

'Are you my aunt?' And there was Sam, her nephew – twelve years old and she'd never even met him. He reminded her of her tomboy self, when she'd had short hair as a kid.

'Yes, she is,' said Tasha, in the superior tones of a sister who'd already met her aunt.

'Hi Grant, hi Sam – it's great to meet you,' said Lexi. 'I thought you'd be away at school.'

Sam's grin reminded her of Rose so much it hurt. 'I get today off, as we've got to be in choir all weekend. Concert performance.'

On any other day, she would have fussed over her nephew and sat down with her brother-in-law over coffee, but now wasn't the time. She turned to Amber. 'It can't wait. It's something you really need to see.'

Her look must have conveyed its sensitive nature. Amber turned to her husband. 'Grant, do you think you can get Tash sorted for school?'

'Sure, no problem.'

She turned to Lexi. 'Come with me.'

Once they were in the living room and the door was shut, Lexi pulled on a pair of latex gloves and pulled the large brown envelope out of her bag. She fished inside it and produced the diary.

'Recognise this?' she said.

Amber's hand flew to her mouth. 'Oh my God, that's Rose's diary. Where did you get it?'

Lexi placed it on the coffee table between them and pulled another pair of latex gloves from her bag. She handed them to Amber. 'Put these on – it's evidence.'

Amber did as instructed and picked up the journal as Lexi told her what had happened. When she realised that Lexi was saying their abductor was the most likely person to have left it for her, she looked up, wide-eyed with horror.

'You think he's still out there? In Canterbury? The man in the garden?'

Lexi shrugged. 'Either he left it in my kitchen, or at some point he gave it to someone else and they left it. I'm inclined to believe the former.'

'But...' Amber fell silent as the ramifications dawned on her.

'It means that we are almost certainly looking at the same man for our case and for the Carter sisters.'

Amber looked back at the diary.

'I need you to be careful, Amber. Keep all your doors locked. Try not to be here on your own.'

'Grant's back and he was furious about what happened. He says he won't go away again until we've had all the locks changed and a whole new alarm system installed, with panic buttons.'

'Good – it's a wise move.' Lexi didn't want to alarm her sister, but she needed Amber to be safe.

Amber sank onto one of the sofas and thumbed through the pages, stopping to read entries here and there. She smiled at one or two of them, and it softened her features, making her look younger. Lexi would have loved to spend time poring over it with her, unearthing all sorts of childhood memories, but she couldn't. She desperately needed to be working the case.

'Look at the back of the diary. There's a weird entry that

must have been written after we'd got away. A list. None of it makes sense to me.'

Amber found the page and studied it for a minute.

'Pookie? Captain Ahab?' She shook her head. 'I don't get it.'

'Me neither.'

'Could she have been delirious when she wrote this?'

'Maybe. Or maybe she just didn't want to share with him whatever she did really miss. I suspect she was directed to write it. He was all about mind games.' Lexi held out a hand for the diary. 'Look, I've got to log this in. We'll get it back after, but that might be some time. I just wanted you to see it, and to see if you had any idea what that list might mean.'

Amber shook her head regretfully and handed it back.

'Let me know if anything comes to you,' said Lexi as she put the book back into the envelope.

As Lexi walked towards the door, Amber stopped her and took one of her hands. 'I'm glad you're back in my life, Lex. It's been too long.'

Lexi nodded, not sure how to respond.

'You know, it was bad enough losing one sister. Losing you, too...' Amber stopped, gauging Lexi's reaction.

'You're right,' said Lexi. 'Let's put the past behind us – for Rose's sake.' She wasn't entirely sure she'd be able to do that, but she would damn well try for the sake of Tasha and Sam. They and Amber were all the family she had.

'Will you come and have supper one evening this weekend? Spend some time with the kids?'

Lexi nodded. 'I'd like that. Maybe not this weekend, but as soon as the case lets up a bit...'

'Sure.' Amber sounded like she didn't believe her. Maybe because she realised there would always be a case demanding Lexi's attention. But she gave Lexi a quick hug by the front door.

'Stay in touch.'

'I promise,' said Lexi.

It was a promise she was making to herself as well as Amber.

FORTY-EIGHT

The incident room was already humming by the time Lexi got to the station. She fetched two double espressos from the coffee machine, desperately hoping they would contain enough caffeine to keep her going for the next few hours. She was dog-tired and despite being hungry, a feeling of deep inertia prevented her from doing anything about it.

She quickly photocopied the pages of the diary, sealed it in an evidence bag and filled out the case number, evidence number and the necessary chain of evidence information. Then she called Emily Jordan and arranged for it to be collected and fingerprinted. If there was anything on it, it might be their first bit of hard evidence.

She slung the envelope into the out tray on her desk, and wondered what to do next. Brain fog. She had to come up with her next move but she felt stumped.

Desperate to be doing something, she stared at the photo-copy she'd made of the last diary entry. *My sisters. My mum and dad. Pookie – my rabbit. Captain Ahab – my hamster. The view from my bedroom window. The beach. The library. Chicken nuggets. KitKats.* What did it mean? The first two items on the list – fair enough. But Pookie the rabbit. Why that particular book?

Pookie the rabbit.

It was a children's book about a small white rabbit with a pair of wings, old-fashioned and twee. She could remember studying the pictures in a dog-eared book when she could barely read. It had been on a visit to their grandparents' house. The book had belonged to their mother when she was a child and it was still on the shelf of her childhood bedroom.

But as far as she could remember, Rose hadn't even been interested in the book then. She was surprised that she'd remembered it several years later.

It had to be some kind of message, didn't it?

Pookie, the rabbit. Captain Ahab, the hamster. They sounded like family pets, but what if they were coded messages? A sharp stab of pain in her chest caught Lexi by surprise at the thought of her sister, desperately trying to compose a message that would mean nothing to the killer but everything to those who might find it, a flicker of hope burning in her breast that she, too, would be found before it was too late.

But she never had been found.

By the time Lexi and Amber had raised the alarm and help had arrived, she'd been spirited away. So, alone now with their abductor, she'd written this list of clues with a shaking hand.

And even now, when it was far too late for Rose, Lexi couldn't work out what they meant.

'Hey, what's all this?'

She looked up, realising she was crying.

Ed Harlow was standing in her office doorway. The last person she wanted to see. Digging around in her past for his own academic glory. It wouldn't surprise her if he was writing a book about the notorious Bennett abduction. *Decoding the Triplet Killer Case.* It would no doubt be a bestseller.

'Nothing,' said Lexi. She closed the case file and pushed it to one side as he came in, uninvited.

'Harry G told me you were as tough as an old boot, that you could handle working on the worst cases he could throw at you.' He sat down opposite her. 'But I think there's more to you than that. You really feel for each and every victim, don't you?'

'You indulge in armchair psychology on the side, I see.' She wished he would go away.

'You don't like me very much, do you?' he said. His tone was as casual as if he'd been asking whether she liked ice cream or not.

'I don't like being the subject of your scrutiny because of something which happened seventeen years ago. You don't know me, and you don't have any right to my memories.'

Harlow glanced away from her, breathing in and out before answering. 'Sorry. I hadn't thought of it like that.'

'How had you thought of it?'

'Look, like you, I want to catch these guys and put them away for the rest of their lives. Your way of doing it is by investigating and arresting them. My contribution is through understanding why they do it – so I can help identify likely suspects.'

Lexi didn't say anything.

'But of course, you know all that. You signed up for the programme and drank the Fed's Kool-Aid, just like I did. Only you've got something more than the rest of us. You've spent time with a subject *during* the commission of a crime. You know what it feels like to be the victim. You had what it took to get away. I think you, more than any of us, can see inside a killer's mind.' He stared at Lexi long and hard. 'You see, your memories are gold dust.'

'Maybe,' said Lexi.

'But I realise that exerts a heavy cost on you – using your personal experience to inform your work. I'm sorry if I seemed insensitive.'

'It's fine. You just caught me at a bad moment – and in fact, your input would probably be helpful.'

Ed's smile was full of relief. Lexi knew she could be prickly at times, but that was because she took her work seriously. They were in a high stakes game and a girl's life hung in the balance. Which was why she reluctantly decided to show him the diary entry.

She passed the photocopy across the desk.

Ed picked it up and scanned it with interest. 'What's this?'

'Last night, someone came into my house and left a diary on my kitchen table. It was Rose's diary – she had it with her when we were abducted. There was one last entry in it, written after we were taken, and after Amber and I had escaped. That's it.'

'How do you mean "came into the house"? Broke in?'

'No. I was out for a run, and I left the back door unlocked.'

'You won't do that again, will you?'

'No, clearly not.' Lexi felt like a chastised child. She certainly wasn't going to mention the fact that she wasn't entirely sure she'd left it unlocked – that would open a whole can of worms that she really didn't want to share with Ed Harlow.

'Things she misses...'

'Only they weren't. We didn't have a rabbit or a hamster. She was vegetarian. Also, I never saw her eat a KitKat – Haribos were her sugar fix.'

'So what do you make of it?'

'I think it's some kind of coded message, trying to give details about where she was being held.'

Ed studied it a big longer. 'Right. That makes sense. But it also means you're probably the best person to work out what she was saying. You and Amber – you knew her best.'

Lexi sighed. 'I could lose sleep wishing that we'd got hold of this in time... in time to save her. But the truth is, I have no idea what it means.'

'Item by item,' said Ed. 'The first two – parents and sisters – that much would be expected. I think they're cover for what was to follow.'

'I agree. So far, so easy. But the two pets? We never had any pets – my mother said it was hard enough looking after three girls without adding rodents into the mix.'

Ed smiled briefly. 'Captain Ahab. *Moby-Dick*. Do you know if your sister had read the book?'

'We all three knew it. My father had an audio version. He used to play it in the car when we went on long drives on holiday. We all hated it.'

'Could she be trying to tell us something about the man who took her? Ahab had a wooden leg.'

Lexi shook her head. 'No, the bastard wasn't one-legged – if he was, Amber and I would already know that, and it would be too obvious to include.'

'But what if she was told to write the list? Could it actually be a message from him, rather than her?' said Ed.

'I don't buy that interpretation,' said Lexi. 'Although I don't understand what she was driving at, that's her voice – she's thinking of things that could resonate with me or Amber. *Pookie the Rabbit* was a book in my grandmother's house. If the killer had dictated the list to her, he wouldn't have known about the book, or tried to hide the reference by making it sound like a pet.'

'Okay.' Ed nodded his head. 'She wrote the list. She was sending a message. What about the view from her bedroom window? What did she look out on?'

'Next door's garden – a small lawn, a few rose bushes and shrubs. A scrawny holly tree at the end. I promise you, I've racked my brains. There's no message there.'

'There is, Lexi. Without a doubt, there's a message. Maybe it'll come to you, maybe it won't – but it's arrived too late to save Rose.'

That was hardly the point.

'But what if it could save Paige?'

FORTY-NINE

When Ed left, Lexi didn't feel she was any further on. Progress was in short supply, and when she went into the incident room, the gloomy mood suggested to her that they'd all made up their minds that Paige was dead.

It was time to take control. 'Right, everyone. Grab a cuppa. Colin, go and buy some biscuits.' She thrust a fiver at him. 'Round table meeting in five minutes. I want updates on where everyone is.'

While she waited for the others to assemble, she phoned Emily Jordan.

'Got anything new for us?'

'We did get some prints off the camera pointing into the girls' changing room at the academy.'

'And a match?'

'Yup – Mike Madison. Only his.'

'That's great. He put the camera up, he's got the footage on his computer. Nice open and shut case against him, so at least we'll get to put that one to bed.'

'But you don't think he's the doer when it comes to the Carters?'

'No, I never really did. He doesn't fit the profile. Plus, he has an alibi for when the killer sent the email about Pendleton's body – he was in custody at the time. But no matter – what we've got on him means he'll never teach again.'

Tom brought her a cup of tea and sat down next to her at the meeting table in front of the whiteboard. Gradually the rest of the team joined them and Lexi dialled Maggie in on speakerphone so she could hear the updates as well.

'Okay, Colin, you've been running the surveillance on Toby Yates – anything?'

'Nothing we'd deem relevant. He's paid visits to a couple of other girly bars since the Pole Star is shut. Other than that, it's been the supermarket and home.'

'No trips to remote places where he could be holding Paige Carter?'

Colin shook his head. 'If he's got Paige and she's still alive, she must be hidden in his attic or garage.'

'Has the search warrant for his property been granted yet?'

'Not yet.'

'Chase it. Make it your top priority and then rip his house apart.'

'Be careful.' Maggie's voice interrupted from Lexi's mobile. 'If you're wrong about Yates, he could launch a case against us. There are more grounds to suspect Madison, as he's the one who was stalking Paige.'

'But the email timing puts him in the clear,' said Lexi. 'We can't afford to give up on Yates yet. Ridhi, what progress have you made?'

'I spoke to a woman at social services. She's sent me a copy of Yates's case file. He was taken into care at the age of seven. His teacher had raised the alarm that she thought he was being abused. His mother, an alcoholic, had a drug-addicted boyfriend. There was no case brought against either of them, but Toby was taken away. Then the usual chequered path of care homes and short spells with foster parents. He never got into any major trouble, but he didn't do well at school. Sounds like he was a difficult teen without being an out-and-out villain. There are details about the accident he had – some sort of chemical explosion in the plant where he worked. Sounds horrendous, burns all over his body as well as his face.'

'Thanks,' said Lexi. 'Tom?'

'We've now got a strong case against Mike Madison for accessing child pornography, and I'm prepping it to pass over to the CPS.'

'And you, Lexi?' said Maggie. She seemed to have taken over the meeting.

Lexi took a moment to gather her thoughts. 'Last night, someone entered my house and left a diary on my kitchen table. It had belonged to my sister, Rose, and she had it with her when we were abducted.' She paused to let the weight of her words sink in.

'My God, Lexi, are you okay?' It was Maggie, her voice taut with concern.

Lexi didn't like talking about Rose in front of the team – it was too personal – but it couldn't be avoided. 'Reading it was naturally very painful for me, but it quickly became clear that she'd written entries after we'd been abducted – a list of things she missed. I think if I can work out the meaning of her list, I might be able to discover where she was held after Amber and I got away.'

'But how would that help us on the current case?' said Colin.

'What if he's holding Paige at the same place?' said Lexi.

'Seems like a long shot, given that we don't even know for sure it's the same man.'

'Until you find something better, Colin, this is all we've got to go on.' Her temper flared.

'Where's the diary now?' said Tom.

'I've sent it to Emily Jordan. If Yates's prints are on it, then we've got him. Ridhi, can you follow that up? Colin, check in with the teams watching Yates last night – if they haven't reported any nocturnal activity, he could have given them the slip again. Everyone else, I'll circulate copies of the final diary entry – we need to work out its meaning and we're running out of time.'

Maggie cleared her throat. 'Thanks everyone, let's wrap this up. Lexi, can you call me from your office?'

It seemed a very abrupt end to the meeting, and Lexi made her way back to her office feeling like she'd been called in to see the head.

'I'm worried about you,' said Maggie, as soon as Lexi had redialled. Bluntness was Maggie's special skill.

'No need to be.'

'Ed Harlow called me just before the meeting. He's worried about you, too.'

'Why am I any of his business?'

'Oh, Lexi, I understand why you're being defensive, but people being worried isn't an attack on you.'

'Really? Because it seems that way to me.'

'Ed was wondering if this current case isn't a little much for you, given the links to the past.'

Lexi was ready to explode. 'How dare he? He's been trying to rootle around in my brain for memories, because he has a professional interest in what happened to me and my sisters. Honestly, Maggie, that's what this is all about. If it's okay with you, I'll get back to work.'

'Hold on. Tell me how you're going to move the case forward. What if this diary turns out to be a red herring?'

Lexi sighed. How was she going to make this sound good, when she felt like she was in a maze of dead ends, chasing wild geese? 'You know from the meeting we're still looking at Toby Yates. Yates's childhood means he fits the profile that Ed and I put together. We're waiting on forensics from both murder sites, and Tom's co-ordinating the follow-up on everything that came in after the appeal for information. If his prints are on the diary...'

'Yes, I'm aware of all that. I'm asking what you're going to be doing.'

'I'm going to arrange to have surveillance in the library at the Beaney Centre – the anonymous email which alerted us to Pendleton's body was sent from a public computer there, and I believe it was sent by the killer.'

'And that's the best you can do to find them? Stake out the library?'

It didn't sound hopeful. 'They used someone else's login on the computer, so we don't know who they are. But I'll also be working on Rose's final diary entry – it might lead us to where the unsub's keeping Paige.'

Maggie sighed. 'That's what Ed was worried about. You're too focused on the past. What Rose wrote all those years ago won't tell us the killer's current location. Don't make a priority of it, please, Lexi. Put your energies into finding Paige.'

Lexi was stunned. She didn't know what to say, so she just said, 'Yes.'

Ending the call, she sat at her desk, fists clenched on her thighs. Bloody Ed Harlow. He was all over her case and he had no business to be.

But there was still one lead to follow up.

She phoned Mort.

'It's highly irregular, you understand,' he said, when she'd explained what she wanted him to do.

'But you've got the clout?'

'Of course I have.' He sounded affronted. 'It's explaining it afterwards that might get tricky.'

'Come on, Mort. The doctor who attended wasn't expecting anything other than natural causes. But it seems to me...'

'Just tell me which funeral home he's at.'

Five minutes later he called her back.

'You're in luck. The funeral home doesn't have anything scheduled until late morning, and no one seems to have died unexpectedly in the night either. The body'll be here in half an hour.'

'Thanks, Mort. I owe you for this.'

'Damn right.'

The body in question was Len Clayton's.

FIFTY

It was mid-morning by the time Lexi parked outside the hospital. She hurried through the corridors to the morgue, practically colliding with Mort on her way in.

'You look rough,' he said. 'Case not behaving?'

'Do they ever?'

'Tell me why we need to do this.'

'Len was in charge of mine and my sisters' abduction case. I went to visit him the day before yesterday – I had some questions.'

Mort's eyebrows went up, but she didn't bother to explain.

'He gave me his old case files. Then, yesterday, he called and said he had something to show me, something pertaining to the case, I believe. By the time I got to Herne Bay he was dead. I think he was murdered.'

'According to the funeral director, the doctor at the nursing home certified death by natural causes,' said Mort. 'It's quite something to question his decision. Have you spoken to him?'

'Can't get hold of him. Look, I admit it's possible, maybe even likely, that it was natural causes, given the state he was in. But I need to be sure one way or the other.'

'Let's hope the nursing home doctor is right and that it's natural causes. If it's not, I'll have a whole raft of paperwork to do to get the first death certificate changed.'

'Like I said, I'll owe you.'

While she waited for Clayton's body to arrive, Lexi went to the toilet to freshen up. She could see what Mort meant – she looked like she'd slept under a hedge. She pulled a brush through greasy, tangled hair and pulled it up into a ponytail. Then she splashed her face with cold water, which did nothing for the dark circles under her eyes.

Caffeine. Another double dose. It helped somewhat, and she presented herself back at the morgue just as a pair of undertakers wheeled a plain wooden coffin in.

'Give us a call when you're done,' said the older of the two. 'Funeral's set for next Thursday, so we'll need him back before then.'

If Lexi's suspicion was right, they might need to hold on to the body for a little longer than that, but she didn't say anything. Mort could deal with that if he had to.

After donning gloves and a plastic apron, she helped Mort lift the body from the coffin onto one his stainless-steel dissecting tables. Len Clayton looked peaceful in death, if a little jaundiced. If the casket was going to be open at the funeral, the undertakers would want to use make-up. He was dressed in the clothes he'd died in – the same clothes he'd been wearing when Lexi had spoken to him. Cavalry twill trousers, none too clean, and a brushed cotton checked shirt. Brown lace-ups which could do with a polish. This time he was wearing a khaki gilet too.

Together, they undressed him, and Lexi folded his clothes and stacked them on one of the side benches.

'You really believe he could have been murdered?' said Mort, as he surveyed the body. 'He looks like he was a dead man walking as it was.'

Len Clayton had been a good man, and he'd been kind to Lexi in the aftermath of her world falling apart. She hated seeing him like this – a carcass on a table, the glare of the lab lights bleeding his already-pale body of any colour. But she needed to know.

She nodded at Mort. 'Len called me yesterday morning, literally a couple of hours before he passed away. He didn't sound like he was dying. He had a purpose for phoning – he wanted to see me. Since then, I have been given reason to believe that the man who abducted me and my sisters is back. The man who Len made it his life's work to catch.'

Mort looked bored, as if a simple yes or no would have sufficed. 'Fine. Let's see what we find.' He considered the naked body in front of him. 'No obvious wounds or trauma, so that rules out being shot, stabbed or beaten to death.'

'Too obvious. I'm looking for something more subtle that could have been overlooked.'

'Thankfully, they haven't embalmed him yet, so we should be able to do a tox screen – but the results will take a few days.' He picked up an ophthalmoscope and used a gloved finger to push back one of Clayton's eyelids. He shone the light into the eye, but almost immediately drew back. He crooked a finger at Lexi, who was standing near to Clayton's feet. 'Come and take a look.'

'What am I looking for?'

'See those red dots on the white of his eye? They're called petechiae. You know what causes them?'

Of course she did. 'So, I was right? He was asphyxiated?'

'Suffocated or strangled.' Mort placed both hands on Clayton's skull and gently twisted it from side to side, looking more closely at his neck. 'Possible faint bruising, but I'd say inconclusive.' He turned to his trolley of implements and swapped the ophthalmoscope for a vicious-looking hooked device that reminded Lexi of a pickaxe.

'What's that?'

'A laryngoscope. We'll take a look for damage on the inside.'

He lowered Clayton's jaw to open his mouth and slipped the blade of the laryngoscope into his throat. Lexi could see its light flickering inside Clayton's mouth.

'Yup, that confirms it,' said Mort, bent low over the body. 'Fragments of the hyoid bone. Some bruising and swelling at the site. Someone snapped Len's hyoid as they suffocated him.'

'But no external signs of strangulation?'

'He was old and he was ill. His bones were fragile. The killer wouldn't have needed to use much force to block his oxygen supply, or to have held it for very long. Just enough to give him a gentle shove into the afterlife.'

Lexi's heart sank. Though she'd suspected it, she'd desperately wished that it wouldn't turn out to be true. Guilt and regret made her feel nauseous. If only she hadn't gone to see him, he might still have been alive. She turned away from Mort, blinking back tears, and he pretended to be busy with the body to save her embarrassment. He could be brusque, but that didn't mean he was insensitive.

Lexi went over to the pile of clothes on the counter. They smelled fusty, a little bit sweaty.

'Got a bag, Mort?'

He went across to a steel cabinet and gave her an opaque plastic evidence bag.

'Thanks. I'll get these logged and then send them over to Emily for analysis.'

With any luck, whoever had done it might have shed a hair or flake of skin as they leaned over Clayton to strangle him.

But one question remained unanswered – what had he wanted to tell her that got him killed?

FIFTY-ONE

Back at the station, Lexi looked at the bag of clothes on the corner of her desk, waiting to be logged. First, she had to open a new file to investigate Len's death, and although she felt certain that his murder was connected to the abduction of the Carter girls, they would have to treat it as a separate investigation until they uncovered a concrete link. She'd better let Maggie and the team know what was happening.

With a sigh, she pulled Len's gilet out of the bag. He'd wanted to show her something but had never said what it was. She'd found nothing useful in his room, but it was possible he had whatever it was on him when he died, and that the killer hadn't taken it. She went through the pockets. Cigarettes and a lighter – Len's contraband. Some coins. A pair of reading glasses in a tapestry case. A piece of paper, folded into quarters, a bit creased.

This looked more interesting – it was the sort of heavy, textured paper found in sketch pads, and Lexi remembered the torn-out page stub in the sketch book she'd taken from Len's room. She unfolded it and flattened it out on the surface of her desk. The top edge was a jagged rip and it only took her a minute to match it to the narrow strip in the pad where the page was missing. Putting it aside, she studied the drawing. It was a pencil rendering of a tree, highly detailed, with a multitude of bare branches shaped and bent in one direction by the wind. He must have used a soft art pencil, as it had a slightly smudged quality, but Lexi could still see every blemish on the trunk, every tiny twig, even blades of grass between the gnarled roots. It was a work of art, much better than the other pictures he'd drawn. He must have spent hours on it.

But was this what he was going to show her?

If so, it suggested that this tree actually existed somewhere, and that it had some relevance to the case. She racked her brain but she couldn't think of a tree like this anywhere locally, or what the picture could mean.

Then she noticed writing on the back of the picture.

The dream tree

She called Tom into her office.

'Recognise this?' she said, as he planted himself unceremoniously in the chair opposite her desk. 'Found it in Len Clayton's pocket. He said he had something to show me.'

He took the picture and studied it. Then he shook his head. 'Nuh-uh. Plenty of trees like that along the top of the Downs, where the wind catches them.'

'What if it's a location he remembers from the case?'

'Well, he could have just told you where it is. But, look, it says it's a dream tree on the back, whatever that means. Not a real tree.'

'It must have been important for him to call me – he knew I was up to my eyes in the Carter murders. I was on my way to see him when he died. When he was murdered.' She explained what Mort had discovered about Len's body.

'So you don't even know for sure that this was what he wanted to show you?'

Lexi shook her head. 'We'll never know.'

Tom pulled a face. 'You have to admit it then – you might be barking up the wrong tree.' He ducked instinctively as Lexi reached for the stapler on her desk. She chucked it at him playfully and he caught it with one hand.

'That was really lame,' she said, laughing in spite of herself.

'I know – I'm sorry. I couldn't resist.'

Lexi looked at her watch – it felt like she'd worked a full day already, but it was only just gone eleven. She stood up. 'I'm going to the library. I need to check a couple of things.'

She was relieved when Tom didn't ask what, but went back to the incident room to add the details of Len's death to the whiteboard.

The Beaney Centre was quiet when she got there – a couple of pensioners browsing the shelves, a mum with a toddler in the children's area. Even the librarians seemed to be twiddling their thumbs. But she didn't need to bother them. She knew her way around the stacks well enough to find what she was looking for in a couple of minutes. *Moby-Dick* by Herman Melville.

It was an old hardback edition, and through the almost opaque protective cover Lexi could just make out a lively illustration of a small whaling boat in the shadow of a huge, rearing whale. She remembered the story well enough – the obsessive Captain Ahab of the *Pequod*, chasing down the giant sperm whale, Moby-Dick, which had bitten off his leg during a previous encounter, all told through the eyes of the grizzled old sailor Ishmael. But why had Rose named a fictitious pet hamster Captain Ahab?

She thumbed through the pages.

Certainly, Ahab was something of a monster, bent on

revenge and sporting a false leg made from the jawbone of a whale. She read Ishmael's description of him and then, in a flash, she understood – snaking out from Ahab's hairline, a vivid white scar ran down his face and neck, reminiscent of a lightning strike.

There was no doubt about it.

Rose was pointing a finger squarely at Toby Yates. She must have caught sight of him without the mask at some point. This was her way of telling Lexi that the man who'd taken them, the man who eventually went on to kill her, was scarred.

She slammed the book shut and replaced it on the shelf.

A shiver passed up her spine. To think that she'd been in the same room with, and had interviewed, the man who'd abducted them took her breath away. But now she knew who he was, she would show no mercy. Toby Yates was going to pay for what he'd done and it would start right now.

As she hurried out of the Beaney Centre, the librarian who'd helped her the previous day gave her a wave. But she didn't have time to stop. As soon as her phone showed a signal outside the building, she put through a call to the incident room.

'Arrest Toby Yates now. I think he's responsible for the murders of Lucy and Eden Carter, and I believe he's holding Paige Carter.'

FIFTY-TWO

What's she up to?

We're back at the Beaney Centre. I watch her going up the stairs to the library, but I don't follow her. I can't take too many risks – what if she recognises me? Instead, I slip into the exhibition room to the right of the main entrance where I can wait for her to reappear.

I don't have to wait very long. Barely fifteen minutes have passed before I hear the heels of her boots clicking down the stairs. Then she walks past me. Her cheeks are flushed with excitement – it's a good look for her – and she's staring intently at her mobile.

I follow her out through the main doors, and practically bump into her on the steps.

'Sorry.' I hurry past her.

She nods at me politely, but she's too taken up with a phone call.

'...Yates. Arrest him now...'

I desperately want to hear the rest of this conversation, but she keeps her voice low and urgent, and by the time I reach the bottom of the steps, I can't make out what she's saying.

Someone's going to be arrested. But for what?

I melt into the shadows of a tight alleyway between two medieval houses. I don't want to miss whatever's going to happen next. As soon as she puts the phone back in her pocket, she sets out at a brisk pace in the direction of the police station. I follow at a distance, lingering by shop windows, then catching up, then lingering again.

We're halfway through the Whitefriars Centre when she suddenly stops. I watch. She pulls out her phone and speaks, but this time I'm too far away to hear anything. She turns on her heels and returns in the direction from which she's just come.

I quickly turn and pretend to study the latest trainers on special offer as she passes within a couple of feet of me.

She seems to be heading back into the Beaney Centre.

Of course, I follow.

FIFTY-THREE

Oh, good God, how could she have been so stupid? If she hadn't been standing in the middle of Whitefriars, she would have slapped her face. She'd made the rookie mistake of making the facts fit her narrative, rather than her narrative fit the facts. She'd been so desperate to find a meaning in her sister's list that she'd invented one – and then she'd acted on it.

Thankfully, she'd quickly realised her error. But she should never have made it in the first place.

'Tom, cancel my last order. Don't, I repeat, don't arrest Toby Yates. I thought I had something concrete on him, but I don't.'

Of course she didn't. The scarring on Toby Yates's face had occurred long after Rose had written her list. The reference to Captain Ahab couldn't have been pointing towards him.

Idiot, idiot, idiot.

She strode back to the Beaney Centre, intent on taking another look at *Moby-Dick*. But as she climbed the stairs to the mezzanine level, she wondered what she was doing. What did she expect to find there? She was blundering around in the dark, wasting precious time.

This wasn't going to work.

She slumped down to sit on the top step, blinking back tears. She was exhausted and frustrated. Pushing so hard on the case meant she hadn't taken time to look after herself, and now it was affecting her ability to work. A sharp pain made her realise she was digging the nails of one hand into the palm of the other, furious with herself.

She looked down. The row of red crescents in her palm were doing nothing to help Paige. It was time to get a grip.

She went back outside and looked around. Opposite the library, there was a small coffee shop that wasn't too busy, so she went inside and ordered a mineral water – she'd had more than enough caffeine for one day. A night without sleep hadn't done her any favours and she was in real danger of messing things up.

The list is the key.

That thought was stuck in her head and she couldn't get past it. But if the list was the key, what and where was the lock?

There was only one other person who'd been trained to think about cases in the same way she did. She'd tried to keep him at arm's length, but she needed his help. She'd always thought of herself as a loner when it came to working a tough case, but this time it had got her nowhere. She had to accept that there were moments when two brains were better than one.

'Ed, are you busy? I need another brainstorm.'

'Sorry, Lexi. Now's not a good time.'

'Can you spare just ten minutes?'

Ed Harlow sighed at the other end of the line. 'Can you come to me? I'm at Maidstone Hospital.'

'Be with you in under an hour. I'll call when I arrive.'

When she rang fifty minutes later, Ed directed her to meet him at the entrance to the women's surgical ward. She hadn't thought to ask him what he was doing at the hospital, but now it dawned on her that maybe he wasn't here on his own account, or for a meeting with Mort.

She spotted him as soon as she emerged from the lift. His face looked grey and drawn, and his usually slicked back hair was unruly. When he saw her, he gave a curt nod and strode towards her.

'Lexi.'

'Ed – I'm sorry. I've pushed myself on you and I didn't think to ask if things were okay.'

'Like I said, it's not a good time.' He glanced back in the direction of the ward. 'My wife, Charlie, just had surgery to remove a tumour.'

Lexi felt awful. 'I'm so sorry. I assumed you were here for something work related. I can leave.' She remembered that he'd said something about his wife being ill the day she'd visited him at his house. Maybe it explained why he'd been checking his phone so often the previous evening in the pub. His wife must have already been in the hospital by then, but he'd said nothing about it.

He shook his head. 'No, don't leave. She's still in the recovery room. They've said it'll probably be half an hour or longer before I can see her. We might as well talk.'

'You're sure?'

He nodded, though his expression was grim.

'Let me buy you a coffee.'

There was a vending machine in an alcove opposite the lifts. The brown liquid it dispensed didn't taste much like coffee, and after one sip she dropped the cup into a bin.

'Come on,' said Ed. 'There's a family room over here that we can use.'

Seated opposite each other on hard plastic chairs, Ed sipped his drink in silence for a moment. Lexi wanted to give him time to gather his thoughts.

'The surgery went okay?' she said eventually.

'As expected,' said Ed. 'But we won't know the prognosis for some time.'

Lexi didn't want to pry, so she simply nodded.

'Anyway, what's your problem?'

'It's the list that my sister left. I needed it to be a message from her, and because of that I misinterpreted it and nearly had a Toby Yates arrested. Luckily, I realised my mistake before that happened.'

'You turned into a tyre squealer,' said Ed.

Lexi gave him a questioning look.

'One of our former colleagues in the Feds coined the term – the sort of agent who gets one tiny piece of evidence and races off to make the arrest.'

Lexi smiled. 'Almost. I was on my way.' Then she became serious again. 'I need help, Ed. I've got to get inside my sister's mind and work out what she actually meant, rather than what I want her to have meant. We might have had identical genes, but all three of us think – thought – in very different ways.'

'And how can I help?'

'By acting as the backboard. I bounce the thoughts and ideas off you and we see which ones end up through the hoop.'

'Okay – shoot.'

Lexi took a copy of Rose's list out of her pocket.

'So, what I've already done is work out that some of these items are genuine and some aren't. The rabbit and the hamster. We didn't have those pets. The chicken nuggets. She didn't eat them, nor KitKats. The man gave us KitKats – I've hated them ever since.'

'You think the fake items are the messages?' said Ed. 'Work out their relevance and all will be revealed?' His tone of voice revealed a heavy dose of irony.

'Exactly what I thought at first. But no. What if Rose was trying a double bluff? Those false listings were to make the man think she was giving coded information. He would focus on those and miss something in plain sight.'

Ed shook his head. 'If Rose let him believe she was sending a message, he'd make sure that no one ever saw the list.'

'Which is exactly what happened, until now – it's too late for Rose's message to save her.'

'But you still think it can tell you something?' Ed countered.

Lexi shrugged. They were going round in circles.

She took a red pen out of her bag. 'Look, I'm going to strike out the meaningless items.' She put a red line through the four she'd already mentioned. That left parents, sisters, the view from the bedroom window, the beach, the library.

'What's she telling us now?' said Lexi.

'What would she want you to know?'

'Her location. That she was still alive. The identity of the man, if she'd been able to work out who he was.'

'You think she might have known him?'

That was a tough question. 'I never had any idea who he was. Nor Amber. And when we were all three in captivity, Rose certainly didn't know him. But he was constantly masked, and barely spoke.'

'Okay, let's think about location.'

'Obviously, she wasn't at home. She wasn't in the library.' Lexi stared at the list, flat on the coffee table between them. 'She was near a beach? Do you think that's possible?'

'Anything's possible. But it would be a little obvious. As well as being so non-specific as to be useless. I mean, how many miles of coastline does Kent have?'

'This isn't getting us anywhere.'

'So we need to come at it from a different angle,' said Ed. He twisted the list round to make it the right way up for him.

Lexi stared at the words upside-down. It was a different angle all right, but it told her nothing.

Until it did.

'Ed, see the odd one out? It's been hiding in plain sight all along.'

FIFTY-FOUR

Before Ed could answer, a nurse appeared in the doorway of the family room.

'Mr Harlow, your wife's awake now, if you want to come with me.'

Ed glanced over at Lexi.

'Go, go,' she said. 'I've got what I need. Thank you so much.'

They both stood and she found herself in an awkward embrace. 'I owe you one, Ed. And I hope everything's okay with Charlie.'

He broke away and followed the nurse out of the room. Lexi tried to imagine the hell he was going through, having the person he loved most in the world ill with cancer. She'd never been married, never really loved someone enough to commit to them for the rest of her life, but that didn't stop her understanding the pain of loss. After all, she'd been as close to Rose as to anyone in the whole world. Far closer to Rose than she'd ever been to Amber.

She almost ran down to the car park and as soon as she was on the road heading back to Canterbury, she phoned the incident room.

'Ridhi, get in touch with the Beaney Centre. See if they can give you a list of everyone who worked there at the time when me and my sisters were abducted.'

'Yes – but why, boss?'

'I'll tell you when I get back. Just do it.'

When she explained it to Tom, she could see he was not entirely convinced.

'Look at the list,' she said, holding out her now crumpled and dog-eared copy. 'Don't you get it? There's an odd one out.'

He stared down at her. 'This is like one of those bloody IQ tests, isn't it? Find the odd one out. What comes next in the sequence? Where's the pattern? I hate those things.'

'The point is,' said Lexi, growing ever more frustrated with him, 'that "library" is the odd one out. All the rest are capitalised. The 'L' in library is lower case.'

'And that's a message?'

'I know how my sister's mind worked. She was the pernickety one. This was deliberate and the message is that the man who took us had something to do with the library.'

'Which library?'

'The Beaney Centre. That was the only library we ever went to when we were kids.'

Tom shrugged. 'But this is all ancient history, Lexi.'

'No. It's bloody not. Someone left Rose's diary in my cottage. The man who took us is the only man who would have that – and now another set of triplets has been abducted. It's crystal clear that we're looking at the same man.'

Tom nodded slowly. Finally, she was getting through to him.

'So what's the plan?'

'The obvious really,' said Lexi. 'Get in touch with the librarians who worked there and see if they remember anyone odd among their colleagues, or anyone who habitually hung around the library – and dig from there. Ridhi's chasing up a list right now.'

They both went into the incident room and Lexi briefed the team. 'Once we've got the list, we'll each take a name to track down and question if possible. Someone will remember something – then we'll have a lead.'

While they waited, most of the team grabbed the opportunity to get some lunch.

'Want anything from Greggs?' said Tom, appearing in Lexi's doorway.

She shook her head. 'Couldn't possibly eat now.'

She fidgeted at her desk, but she didn't have the concentration to answer any of the emails that had piled up over the last couple of days.

'Anything, Ridhi?'

'Not yet, boss.'

'You told them it was urgent?'

'Twice.'

Five minutes later she found herself dialling Ridhi's number again, but cut the call. It wasn't as if Ridhi would forget to let her know when the list arrived. She rearranged a stack of folders on her desk, her knee twitching against the side of the footwell. If this didn't give them a lead, she would have let the team down and, more importantly, she would have let Paige Carter down. She'd already let her sisters down, and she wasn't sure she could bear another failure. What was the point of everything she did, if she couldn't help the victims?

She had to succeed this time, for the sake of her own sanity. She was running on empty and was acutely aware that Maggie was starting to question whether she had the mental strength to take on cases like this. She had to show that she did.

Tom reappeared and tossed a greasy-looking paper bag onto

her desk. 'Got you a pasty,' he said. 'Eat while you can, whether you want to or not.'

Lexi's stomach roiled at the smell, but she pulled open the bag. A waft of steam warmed her face. 'You're right, Tom. Thanks.'

The first mouthful actually tasted remarkably good, reminding her that she hadn't eaten anything since the previous day. But before she could take a second bite, her phone rang.

It was Ridhi. 'It's here, boss – the list from the library.'

The pasty was left to cool on her desk as she scooted round to the incident room.

'How many names on it?' she said, as Ridhi stood up and went over to the printer.

'I'm doing copies for everyone,' said Ridhi. 'There are six librarians listed.' She picked up the first printout and handed it to Lexi. 'Apparently there would have been volunteers as well. They don't show up in the employment records, but the woman I spoke to was going to see if the file with the volunteer lists went back that far.'

Lexi scanned the list of names. She didn't recognise any of them – but that was hardly surprising. When she'd gone to the Beaney as a teenager, she'd spent her time trying to avoid the librarians as she dipped in and out of 'unsuitable texts' – from *Twilight* to anything by Stephen King.

'It gives us something to start on, anyway,' said Lexi. 'Ridhi, you and Colin take the first three on the list – John Marks, Sylvia Talbert and Jody Schwartz. Tom, you come with me – we'll take the other three.'

Each name on the list was supplied with an address, but no phone number. Tom scanned his copy. 'Christina Fox, Kenneth Cosbrook, Richard Drexler. And where they were living, what, seventeen years ago?'

It sounded like a moan, but Lexi was having none of it. 'Come on, get to it. Check the electoral register to see if they still live in the same place. Google them. For what it's worth, check police records – I know, they're librarians, not criminals, but they might have had DBS checks for working with children. You know the drill – anything that will give us an update on their whereabouts.'

Tom went towards his desk to sit down, but Lexi beckoned him.

'I'll drive, you research on your phone. It'll save time.'

As they hurried down the stairs, they worked out the most efficient route to the three addresses they had.

'Of course, it'll be all change if you find a more up-to-date location, but we'll start with these.'

The nearest was the address for Kenneth Cosbrook. He apparently lived in Fordwich, a small village to the northeast of the city, about fifteen minutes' drive from the police station. As Lexi negotiated the school run traffic around the ring road, Tom worked to verify if the address was still current.

'Not getting anything for Kenneth Cosbrook,' he said.

'You tried Ken or Kenny?'

'Yes.' He gave her a ferocious look.

He kept tapping away, but he'd had no luck by the time Lexi came into the village. He checked the map.

'Take a right. Go past the George and Dragon, then right again before you get to the church.'

A couple of minutes later, Lexi pulled up in front of a small Victorian terraced house, the front door of which opened directly onto the pavement. She stopped on the double yellow line.

Tom raised an eyebrow at her.

'Urgent police business,' she said. 'Don't tell me you haven't done the same?'

The front door Lexi knocked on was painted pale blue, and there were matching shutters on the windows to one side. The house was a narrow two-up two-down in a long row of identical properties.

Tom peered nosily through the window. 'Plenty of bookcases,' he said. 'Could be a librarian's place.'

A woman in jeans and a peasant blouse opened the door. She looked about twenty-five – too young to be the wife or partner of someone who'd been working in the library seventeen years ago.

'Excuse me,' said Lexi, flashing her ID, 'is this the home of Kenneth Cosbrook?'

The woman looked baffled for a moment, but then recognition dawned. 'Ah, he was the previous owner. He died a couple of years ago and the house came on the market. It was a good price, so we snapped it up.'

'Okay, thank you. Sorry to have bothered you.'

'It's not a problem with the house, is it?' She looked momentarily worried.

'No, nothing like that.'

They got back in the car. 'They're probably all dead,' said Tom. 'After all, it was a lifetime ago.'

Lexi ignored him. 'Who's next?'

Tom dug out the names. 'Christina Fox. Head towards Littlebourne.'

FIFTY-FIVE

Twenty minutes later, they reached the second address. Christina Fox was still as much of an enigma as Kenneth Cosbrook had been.

'What's with these people?' said Tom. 'Don't librarians have an online life like the rest of the world?'

'Guess not,' said Lexi. 'Noses always stuck in books.'

Tom shook his head in wonder. Something told Lexi he wasn't much of a reader.

The bungalow they were looking at had a neat front garden – all the shrubs had been pruned back for the winter, the beds were mulched and sweeping curves of snowdrops were just pushing their way up around the base of a small tree in the centre of the lawn. The deep eves along the front of the house were hung with a variety of wind chimes, sounding gently in the low breeze.

'Thank God it's not blowing a gale,' said Lexi, as they approached the front door.

Chimes rang inside as well when she pressed the bell. There was a consistency about Christina Fox.

The woman who answered the door was elderly but

sprightly, and Lexi immediately recognised her, despite her white hair and deeply lined features. She'd been the fearsome head librarian who'd told her and Rose off for talking and giggling on more than one occasion. She held out her ID, hoping the woman wouldn't remember her.

'I'm DI Bennett and this is DS Olsen. Are you Christina Fox?'

'I am. How can I help you?' She looked them up and down with interest.

'I understand that you were working at the library in the Beaney Centre in May 2006?'

She nodded. 'I was. I worked at the library for more than twenty years.'

'Can we come in? There are a few questions we need to ask you.'

'Of course.' She ushered them through her hall and into an expansive lounge to the right of the front door. 'Grab a seat. I'll put the kettle on.'

She disappeared. Lexi went to the bay window and looked out over the front garden from the other side. Tom prowled the room, studying photos on the mantelpiece and examining her bookshelves. Lexi could hear the clatter of teacups and the whistle of the kettle from somewhere nearby. It was time-consuming, but they needed maximum cooperation, and it was always better to humour a witness than rush them.

At last Christina returned with a laden tray. Tom took it from her and placed it on the coffee table at her instruction. Tea was poured and chocolate biscuits offered. Lexi thought long-ingly of the pasty she'd abandoned back at the station and took two.

'Now, Inspector, what was it you wanted to ask me about?'

It struck Lexi that this would be not only the highlight of her day, but would supply her with interesting gossip material for the rest of the week.

'Mrs Fox...'

'Miss, actually – but call me Christina.'

'Christina, if you can cast your mind back to 2006, can you remember any people, more specifically men, who used to hang around the library? Anyone who might have made other library users feel uncomfortable?' The sort of misfits that hung around in libraries would be an easy fit for the standard serial killer profile.

Christina Fox took a sip of tea. 'Give me a moment,' she said, with a slight frown of concentration.

Tom and Lexi waited in silence.

'There were always a few,' she said. 'Apart from the books, libraries represent a sanctuary to all sorts – the homeless, the unemployed, people who need a place to get away from what's happening at home. We always gave people the space they needed, but you can rest assured, we kept a close eye on them too.'

'Anyone you ever had to throw out or report to the police?'

She thought for a moment again. 'No, nothing like that. We once caught a man stealing books, but the police weren't particularly interested. And looking at girls is even less of a crime, apparently.'

Not if you were planning to abduct them. But Lexi kept her thoughts to herself. It didn't seem like Christina Fox could help them much.

'We've asked the library for a list of the volunteer staff who worked there at the time, but it seems unlikely that they still have records. Can you remember the names of any volunteers from around that time?'

Christina sucked air through her teeth and grimaced. 'It was such a long time ago... There was a girl called Liz.'

'Surname?'

She shook her head. 'Sorry, it escapes me. Another woman

called Rachel, but she didn't stay very long. And Rufus, of course.'

'Can you remember his second name?'

Christina grimaced. 'I'm no use to you at all, am I?'

But the name triggered something in Lexi's memory.

'Rufus?' She'd definitely heard the name somewhere recently. Then it came to her. The Beaney Centre. One of the two librarians she'd spoken to about the email. 'He's still working there.'

'Oh, I doubt it. He left a long time ago. Round about the time we're speaking of actually. I had to let him go – he'd been scatty for months, missing shifts, turning up late. I had words with him a few times, but he didn't get any better. I expect this is a different man.'

'Maybe he came back.' Cold dread lodged itself in the pit of Lexi's stomach. 'I wonder, would you come with us to the library and see if you recognise him?'

'I can do better than that,' said Christina. 'I've probably got a photo of him. We had a summer drinks do. There were some pictures taken and I'm sure he's in one or two of them.' She seemed a little excited. Perhaps she'd always fancied herself as an armchair detective.

She stood up and went across to the mid-century-style cabinet where her television sat and pulled open a drawer at the bottom. When she turned back, she was clutching two small photo albums. 'It should be in one of these, I think.'

Her chair creaked in protest as she dropped back into it. She started flipping through the pages quickly, as if she knew exactly what she was looking for. 'It was a weird summer, that one. The whole city was on edge with the disappearance of those girls. The Bennett sisters. Do you remember or were you both too young?' Then she peered over the rim of her glasses at Lexi and her mouth formed a perfect 'O'. 'Inspector *Bennett*? I thought you looked familiar when I opened the door. Your picture was in all the papers and I realised back then that I'd seen you a few times at the library. You and your sisters.' She fell silent and looked slightly embarrassed.

Lexi was used to it. There were a variety of reactions when people realised who she was, but this was the most common. Embarrassment, awkwardness. Followed by silence.

'It's fine, Christina. I don't expect people to recognise me at first sight after all these years. In fact, I'd rather they didn't.'

Christina nodded her understanding and went back to looking at the photos.

'Yes! That's it, that's the one.' She spun the album round so Lexi and Tom, next to each other on the sofa, leaning forward, could see the picture she meant. She jabbed at it with her forefinger. It showed a group of people clustered together round a table in what was obviously a pub garden. They all had drinks – pints for the men, cocktails or wine for the women. Lexi immediately spotted Christina at the centre of the group, back how she remembered her with dark hair and fewer wrinkles. Most of the drinkers were smiling, a few gurning or caught with a glass up to their face.

'That's him,' said Christina. 'Rufus Stokes, that was his full name. I can remember it, seeing his picture.'

Lexi shifted her gaze to where the finger pointed.

She gasped.

'What?' said Tom.

'That's him,' said Lexi, grabbing the photo album. 'It's the librarian I spoke to yesterday about the anonymous email.' She paused and looked from Tom to Christina and back again. 'He was there the summer we were abducted, and then left. Now he's back, and another set of triplets has been taken.'

'What are you saying?' said Tom.

'That hell would freeze over before I'd believe it was just a coincidence.'

FIFTY-SIX

Lexi and her trusty sidekick appear to be on a little driving tour. A day trip into the countryside, though they haven't got the weather for it. Steady rain and low skies don't show Kent off at its best. But at least she's not running or cycling, for once.

They're easy to tail in that ridiculous blue car of hers. I can drop back several vehicles and still get enough glimpses of it not to lose her. It wouldn't be so easy if she drove a silver car like nearly everyone else on the road.

I should be at work, but following Lexi gives me so much more pleasure.

I nearly miss it when she takes an unexpected right turn in Fordwich, but then I tuck in behind her and come to a stop when she parks outside a house in the heart of the village. I wonder who lives here.

They don't stay long or go inside. Then we're off again. But not back the way we came. Instead, she turns left at the main road and heads south out of the village with a sense of purpose. By which I mean she's breaking the speed limit at every opportunity. It's a quiet country road, with not much traffic on it, so I fall back quite a long way. I don't want her to spot me. And this means that I have to look down every side road we pass, in case she's turned off.

But there she is, slowing down as we come into Littlebourne.

It's one of those places that's popular with retired bankers – a small village green surrounded by gorgeous Georgian architecture, an ancient church, a pub and a post office. Smart houses at the centre, tacky bungalows on the margins.

The car winds through the village ahead of me and turns down a side road, then another. I stop at the junction and edge forward on foot. I can see where they've parked, just along a curve, and neither of them bother to look around as they get out of the Crossfire and walk up to a twee little bungalow.

She doesn't see me.

But I see her.

Knock, knock, knock on the door.

They wait. She's still. He fidgets. Stares in through the front window. Plain rude.

I sneak a little closer. I want to see who answers the door. What's she up to?

The door opens but the two of them block my view. I can see it's a woman. I can see a dress and a cardigan the colour of lemon curd.

The three of them talk for a moment.

Then the woman stands back and ushers them inside, briefly turning to look up and down the street as she closes the door.

And I recognise the bitch.

It's Chris Fox, my old boss.

Why the hell is Lexi talking to her?

FIFTY-SEVEN

There were days when Lexi wondered whether she really needed to drive a gas-guzzler with a 3.2 litre engine, but today wasn't one of them. Pedal to the floor, she roared up the A257, the most direct route back to Canterbury. Ed Harlow would probably accuse her of being a tyre squealer again if he were here, but as she drove, Lexi felt more and more convinced that the mild-mannered librarian she'd spoken to the previous day was the man they were looking for.

Gut feeling?

Intuition?

Or a certain recognition in her lizard brain that she knew him. The way a person moves is as unique as their fingerprints, their voice, the whorls of their ears. You don't forget these things. Deep within the subconscious, voices, faces, all the unique physical attributes that make a person an individual are catalogued. It's how we're able to recognise people we went to school with decades later, no matter how different they look.

Lexi knew this man. And she had nothing but ill feeling for him.

'Slow the hell down!' Tom was gripping the inside of the

door as Lexi took a corner without braking. 'We're in a forty-mile zone.'

She glanced down at the speedometer and applied a slight touch of the brakes. Tom was right. She wouldn't get to where she needed to be if she got pulled over for speeding. But she also knew this road wasn't often patrolled. She switched her foot back to the accelerator.

The Beaney was on the High Street, the entire length of which was pedestrianised. The closest she could bring the car was to drive as far up the nearest side street as she could.

'Tom, check on your phone – nearest access will be the end of Stour Street, right?'

Tom dug out his mobile. He seemed relieved that they'd now hit the traffic on the edge of town, which had forced Lexi to slow down. 'Yes, take Castle Street from Wincheap Roundabout, then you can cut through.'

Three minutes later, Lexi reached the end of the narrow, cobbled lane. She was blocked from emerging onto the High Street by three cast iron bollards, but she could see the Beaney Centre on the other side of the road as she got out of the car.

'Come on,' she said, jogging ahead of Tom, weaving between meandering shoppers, lengthening her stride to avoid puddles. She glanced at her watch as she ran up the steps to the main entrance. It was just after four, so the library would still be open.

Tom caught up with her, and together they hurried through the entrance foyer and up the stairs to the library on the mezzanine level. There was one librarian at the main desk, checking out a pile of books for an old woman leaning on a stick. It was the female librarian who'd been there the previous day, Barbara. She was telling the woman something about the book she was just checking out, the barcode scanner hovering while she dissected the plot.

Lexi stepped up to the desk and flashed her ID. 'Can I have a moment? It's important.'

Barbara looked sympathetically towards the old woman. 'Let me just...'

'No.' Lexi put a hand on top of the books the librarian was processing. 'I really need to speak to you now.'

'Are any of your colleagues around?' said Tom.

'No, I'm sorry. For the last hour there's always just one librarian on duty. It's usually pretty quiet.'

Lexi turned to the old woman. 'I'm sorry to butt in, but we really will be quick.' Looking at Barbara again, she said, 'Rufus Stokes – is he here?'

Looking more than a little put out, the librarian shook her head. 'No. He phoned earlier and requested to swap his shifts around this week. He'll be in tomorrow, instead of today. I'm covering today's—'

'Right. I need his home address.'

Now Barbara was truly affronted. Her back stiffened and her brow creased. 'I'm afraid I can't give out his home address – data protection forbids it.'

'Barbara, look...' Lexi held up her ID card. 'I'm the police. I need Rufus Stokes's address. Now.'

Barbara took a breath and muttered something that sounded like '...data protection... breaking rules...'

'I'm quite happy to arrest you for obstructing an investigation,' said Tom, placing a hand on Lexi's forearm to stop her from exploding. 'If you could just give us Rufus's address, we'll be on our way and you could get back to Mrs...'

'Cooper,' supplied the old woman, who had been following the exchange with a look of fascination.

'Mrs Cooper,' said Tom.

Lexi bit her lower lip. They really didn't have time.

But at last Barbara relented. 'Sorry, Mrs Cooper.' She turned the computer screen round until Lexi could see it. Then she tapped in a couple of words, scrolled, tapped some more. A list of volunteers popped up on the screen.

Barbara scrolled through it so quickly the screen was a blur to Lexi, but then came to a stop as Rufus Stokes's details came into view.

'Roper Road, wherever that is,' said Barbara.

Lexi tapped the address into her mobile, including Stokes's phone number. 'Thanks.'

Tom scurried after her as she left the library almost at a run.

'Wait up,' he called. 'Where are you going?'

'Where d'you think?'

'But what are you going to do?'

'Arrest the son of a bitch?'

He was level with her now as they both took the front steps two at a time.

'Grounds?'

'Killing my sister.'

Tom grabbed the top of her arm and stopped her. 'Don't blow this by rushing in too hard and too fast.'

She twisted to pull her arm free. 'Too fast? Do you know how long I've been waiting for this?'

She stormed away in the direction of the car. 'Up to you. You can come with me or you can go back to the station. But you won't find Paige Carter there.'

'Okay, okay, I'm coming. But we do it by the book, boss.'

'We do whatever we need to, to put this bastard behind bars.'

Roper Road lay approximately a mile north and a little to the west of the Beaney Centre, but with Canterbury's labyrinthine one-way system it meant driving at least twice that distance. The city's rush hour was in full swing.

Lexi swore and smacked her palms against the top of the

steering wheel as they sat stationary at a set of green traffic lights. By the time the car ahead of them was able to edge forward, the lights were red again.

'I swear, they left it to a six-year-old to programme these lights,' said Tom, equally as frustrated. 'No bloody traffic flow at all.'

Lexi didn't say anything. She was gaming in her mind what was going to happen next. If Rufus Stokes was home, they could take him down to the station and interview him under caution. If he wasn't...

She called the incident room. 'Ridhi, drop whatever you're doing. Apply for a search warrant for the address in Roper Road Tom is about to text you. Grounds – we have reason to believe the occupant of the property might be involved in the abduction of Paige Carter and the murders of her sisters. Call Maggie and ask her to expedite it. Also, see what you can find out about the house – ownership and so on.'

'Yes, boss.'

They turned into the street where Rufus Stokes lived and Lexi slowed down enough to see the numbers on the front doors. Running parallel to the so-called Crab and Winkle line from Canterbury to Whitstable, Roper Road was a mixture of commercial premises and run-down residential properties backing onto the railway track. The scruffy front gardens and plethora of wheelie bins strewn along the pavements on either side of the road spoke of bedsit land, and Lexi hoped Stokes was still at the same address.

They spotted the house and she drove a little way beyond it before they found a parking space. Switching off the engine, she turned to Tom.

'If he's co-operative, we'll ask him to come down to the station to answer questions. My experience with this type of perp is that they're not generally helpful, and they know the rules. Chances are he'll lawyer up, fast.'

'What if he won't even come down the station?'

'Then we'll put him under surveillance until the search warrant comes through – see if he tries to move anything off the property, get a fix on what vehicle he drives.'

It wasn't much, given Lexi's certainty that he was the man they were looking for, but she had to stick by the rules. If she blew it on a technicality, he could disappear without charge. Then other innocent lives would be in danger, and it would be her fault. Plus, she owed it to Rose to make sure she properly hooked Stokes.

The case against him had to be foolproof by the time it got to court.

'Ready?'

'Ready.'

The house they approached was tall and narrow, the end property in a terrace of six Victorian dwellings. It was built of red bricks, with an ugly, squared-off bay window on the ground floor. Lexi would hesitate to call the postage stamp of land in front a garden – it was gravelled over and the single potted shrub in its centre was dead.

'Look,' she said, pointing. At the bottom of the front bay window there was a small arch of brickwork at ground level and a lightwell. 'He's got a cellar.'

The significance of this wasn't missed by Tom, who quickly ducked down in front of it and peered in. 'Can't see a thing. I think the window's been obscured.'

Lexi's phone rang. It was Ridhi. 'The house has belonged to Rufus Stokes since 2017. Prior to that it was owned by Lydia Stokes, from 1993 until she died. My guess is that she was his mother, but I'll look into it.'

'Thanks, Ridhi.'

If he owned the house, he probably still lived there.

Lexi stepped up to the front door and pressed the bell. She didn't hear anything inside, so she rapped the knocker as well.

'Police! Open up, Mr Stokes.' She listened but there was nothing. 'We'd like a word with you.'

Tom stepped sideways to peer in through the front window. 'Doesn't look like anyone's home,' he said.

'No shit, Sherlock.'

There was an alleyway running down the side of the house. Lexi gave up waiting for the door to open and took the concrete pathway that led to the back. There was no gate, and just a low brick wall separating it from the driveway of the next-door house.

'Tom, there's a garage back here.'

Tom caught up with her.

'A garage and a cellar. Both come in handy for abductions and murder.'

'Right. And Paige Carter could be in either one of them, right now. I'm not waiting on that warrant.'

The driveway between the two houses opened out into a concrete expanse in front of two garages. The one on the neighbour's side had a newish electric door, painted dark green. On Stokes's side, the flip-up garage door was dented, and the faded red paint was flaking off. Lexi tried to twist the mottled chrome handle in the middle of the door, but it was locked.

'Hello? Anyone in there?' she called, putting her mouth close to one edge of the door.

No one responded.

'If he's keeping her in there, she'll be gagged,' said Tom. 'He wouldn't want the neighbours to hear her.'

'There's a crowbar in the boot of the Crossfire,' said Lexi. 'Can you?' She tossed the car keys to him.

Seconds later he was back and, using the crowbar, he made short work of the garage door. It groaned in protest as he raised it. Lexi bent forward to see inside. It was dark at first. Then, as the light flooded in, she felt both a sense of relief and disappointment.

Paige Carter wasn't there.

FIFTY-EIGHT

Although there was no sign of the missing girl, Rufus Stokes's garage was by no means empty. There were piles upon jumbled piles of books, and Lexi could see in an instant from the shiny plastic covers and the labels on the spines that they were all library books. They took up almost half the floor space, leaving no room for a car. Behind the piles, there were cardboard boxes, and an old chest of drawers. To one side of them, a couple of crates of empty bottles – Stokes seemed to have a taste for weak lager and cheap fizzy drinks. There were some folded dust sheets and tins of paint with dribbles of magnolia down the sides.

'Don't touch anything,' said Lexi as Tom stepped in beside her. 'Let's get Emily up here. He might have had the girls in here at some point, I want a full forensic examination.'

'On it,' said Tom. He backed out and got onto his phone.

Lexi stood in the middle of the small patch of empty concrete floor. She closed her eyes and breathed in. It smelled of books, paint, white spirit, stale beer, dust, motor oil, but it told her nothing.

Outside, the sun seemed blinding.

'Emily will be here in fifteen.' Tom gave Lexi a questioning look. 'Do you think this is it? Do you think we've got him?'

'It doesn't pay to speculate. Let forensics do their job – here and in the house. Then we'll see what we've got.'

'And what if we don't find anything?'

'Then we try harder. Call Colin. Stokes must have a vehicle. Let's find that, and put out an APB on him.'

'If nothing else, we can charge him with stealing library books.'

Tom's words snagged in Lexi's brain. She looked around at the books – there were romance novels, detective stories, textbooks, large-format books about art and photography, self-help manuals – clearly an eclectic reader. But what were they all doing here? Was he stealing them?

'Looks like he's got the whole library in here,' she said.

Tom was already walking back towards the house when her synapses flared. 'Shit – this is the whole library. The whole *mobile* library. Tom?' she called out and he turned around. 'He's driving around in a mobile library van.'

'Seriously? Wouldn't that stick out like a sore thumb?'

'What could be more normal than the library van winding from village to village on its rounds? He's emptied it to transport the girls.' She picked up the crowbar from the ground where Tom had dropped it. 'Come on, let's check out the house.'

She went to the door at the back of the property. It was flimsy – pinewood, with a glass inset in the top half, and a Yale lock. She was able to jemmy it open with the splayed end of the crowbar quite easily – it wasn't bolted on the inside. She put the tool down on the patio by the door and pulled on a pair of latex gloves.

'Got any shoe covers in the car?' said Tom.

'Good shout.'

A minute later, shoes covered to preserve what might be a crime scene, the two of them ventured into Stokes's kitchen. It was tidy enough and nothing immediately stood out to Lexi as evidence, but she knew Emily's team would check every surface for finger marks and pick up dust, fibres and hair for matches to anything found on the two bodies from the Crown or on Josh Pendleton.

They looked, but they didn't touch.

The living room at the front of the house was the same – everything looked normal. But this was what Lexi expected.

'I'm not seeing it, boss,' said Tom, practically echoing her thoughts.

'Experience tells us that men who kill for gratification are either chaotic or fastidious. Chaotic killers are often caught after the first or second kill.' Lexi came out of the living room and looked around for a door to the cellar. 'But their highly organised counterparts think things through, act hyper-ratio-nally and can kill repeatedly without getting caught. If Stokes is our man, he certainly falls into the second category.'

Under the turn of the stairs, there was a narrow wooden door secured with a padlock. Lexi's heart raced. For a split second she wondered if they would find Rose in the cellar, before she remembered it was Paige they were searching for. Rose was gone, but maybe they could save Paige.

Picking up on her sense of urgency, Tom shifted her out of the way roughly, then applied his boot to the lock. With a shriek of splitting wood, the door swung open and Lexi charged down the steep wooden staircase beyond. Behind her, Tom flicked on a light and the stairs were illuminated by the dull yellow glow of a low wattage bulb.

There was no door at the bottom and Lexi found herself in a low-ceilinged space. She looked around frantically, but the room was dark with fathomless pools of black shadows in the corners.

'Paige, are you here?'

The silence hissed in her ears, abruptly shattered by the

sound of Tom's boots on the stairs. He stood at her shoulder and shone his mobile's torch into the darkness beyond the pool of light at the bottom of the stairs.

There was no girl here. No dead body, thank God.

But there were items of interest. Lexi fiddled with her phone until she got the torch working and went across to the side wall, to which a large corkboard had been secured. Pinned to this was a phalanx of newspaper cuttings. Stories clipped from the Kent locals – *The Courier*, *The Messenger* and *The Gazette* – as well as from the nationals. They were all familiar to Lexi, because they all reported on one case.

The Triplet Killer.

She'd read all of them, more than once, as each and every one of them was included in Len's files.

'Don't touch anything,' she said.

'You couldn't make me.'

Looking around, on the wall opposite Lexi saw what she could only describe as a shrine – and it horrified her. A low workbench stood against the bare brick wall, and on it stood a row of photos in cheap plastic clip frames. Lexi passed the beam of her torch over them, one by one, and saw Amber, Rose, Eden, Lucy and, with a sickening jolt of recognition, herself. The pictures had been taken while each of them was in captivity, candid shots that none of them appeared to have been aware of.

She stared at the picture of herself. It had been taken in the cottage in Blean Woods. She was squatting on the floor and, from the position she was in, she remembered she'd been rocking backwards and forward on her haunches. She'd done it for hours, toppling over more than once as she became mesmerised by the movement. In the picture, she was covering her face with her hands and Stokes must have been standing in the doorway, watching her. It sent a shiver of revulsion – and fear – up her spine.

The photo of Rose didn't appear to have been taken at the

cottage. Lexi studied the background. It looked like it was taken here, in this room. It showed her lying on the floor, face down, and Lexi could only guess that she was unconscious. It must have been taken some time after she and Amber had escaped. So he'd brought her here? It was too painful to look at and, without realising it, Lexi let out a gasp.

'What is it?' said Tom.

She shook her head. A hard lump in her throat prevented her from speaking. She pointed her torch at the next picture of Rose. It had been taken in a different place, one she didn't recognise. The quality was poor, the image too dark and grainy to be of much use. Rose was sitting cross-legged, cradling her right hand in her lap. Her clothes were covered in dark smears. Blood from her severed finger. This had also been taken after Lexi and Amber had escaped. Rose appeared to be in shock – wide dark eyes like black holes in her ashen face, seemingly unaware that anyone else was in the room with her.

Tom put an arm around Lexi's shoulders and tried to twist her away.

'Don't look at them,' he said. 'Or at least wait until Emily sends copies to the office.'

Lexi broke away furiously. 'Don't you see? I have to look at them. One of these pictures will lead us to Paige.'

'Then let me photograph them.' Tom started taking pictures with his phone.

Lexi carried on studying the pictures. Here was one of the three of them, already bedecked in her princess gown and wearing the plastic tiara, looking anything but serene. She was on her knees, hands held out in front of her, imploring, a white blindfold across her eyes. Her mouth was open – begging? Crying? Screaming? They would never know. She was silent now.

Eden, pictured at the moment of death, on the Memorial Crown, with the blood at her throat fresh and red and shiny.

Lexi slammed the photo face down. No one should have to see this.

'There's no picture of Paige,' said Tom.

'Not yet – because she's still alive?' Could they interpret this as a glimmer of hope amid the depravity?

In front of the row of pictures stood a jam jar. It had no lid and the label had been cleaned off it. Lexi focused the beam of her torch on it and saw the glint of metal inside. She looked closer. A silver chain. It was a pendant with the letter 'E' on it. 'E' for Eden, presumably. There was a ring – gold, with a tiny opal. A button badge with the peace symbol on a yellow background. Lexi could remember pinning it to her school bag.

'These are his trophies.' She felt sickened. A collection of souvenirs that had belonged to his victims.

She turned the jar round to see what else was in it.

Amid the tangle of cheap jewellery there was something else. Something smooth and white. Lexi's legs gave way and she staggered, gripping the edge of the workbench. She struggled to speak, but she could hardly breathe. Disregarding crime scene protocol, she flipped the jar over so the contents spilled out.

She snatched it up in her fist, then opened her palm.

A small white bone.

There was no mistaking what it was.

The room spun and Tom guided her to a sitting position on the bottom step.

She was holding the tip of her sister's finger.

FIFTY-NINE

The tiny, polished knuckle bone had to be logged as evidence. Emily took it gently from Lexi's hand and placed it in a clear plastic evidence bag. She'd just arrived with a couple of CSIs, and she immediately initiated crime scene protocol. Tom and Lexi stood outside to allow them to get on with their work. Lexi had to admit to overturning the jam jar, but at least Tom had taken some pictures of it in situ before she'd done it.

Fresh air and a drink of water had been enough to revive her, while the shocking reminder of what Rufus Stokes had done to her sister had made her all the more determined to see him caught.

'Emily, the moment you or your team spot anything that could lead us to where he might be keeping Paige, let us know. We'll be right here until you've finished.'

She and Tom sat down on the low brick wall between Stokes's property and the shared drive. Lexi's foot drummed on the concrete path as she called the incident room.

'Colin, can you sort out a couple of uniforms to come and watch either end of Roper Road? I want to know if anyone approaches Stokes's house and then turns around or carries on by without stopping. Give them a photo of Stokes and tell them to alert me if they see anyone suspicious.'

'Consider it done.'

'And the vehicle issue...'

'Nothing registered in his name.'

'Not surprised. I think he's driving a mobile library van – that's what you're looking for. Pass it on to the traffic department and start checking the ANPR.'

Lexi disconnected and looked at Tom. 'Apparently Stokes doesn't own a car. But a library van would be ideal for abducting three people and moving them around.'

'Four, including Pendleton.'

It was almost dark when Emily Jordan came out of the house, pushing back the hood of her crime scene suit with a sigh of relief. Lexi and Tom stood up and went towards her.

'Please tell me you've got something for us,' said Lexi.

'I've sent you a string of images – photos we've taken of receipts in Stokes's rubbish.'

'For what?' said Tom.

'A petrol station out in the sticks between Bramling and Wingham.'

Lexi opened her phone and clicked through to Emily's message.

'Wingham?' she asked.

'About six miles out of town, east.' Tom peered over Lexi's shoulder at the screen as she scrolled through the receipts, all from the Casino Filling Station.

'Petrol, a couple of times, but quite often just snacks,' said Lexi. Mineral water. Sandwiches. *KitKats*. Her stomach lurched.

'Mean anything to you?' said Emily.

'Oh God, yes,' said Lexi. 'Tom, get back to the station and get a fix on the card that he used to pay for these – I want a full list of transactions so we can track where he's been, and tell them we need to be notified minute-by-minute of any new transactions.'

'What are you going to do?'

'Pay a visit to the Casino Filling Station.'

Tom was still asking questions but there was no time to waste. She ran across the road to where she'd parked the Crossfire. The satnav on her phone directed her to take the A257 through Littlebourne, and as soon as she'd cleared the city's rush hour congestion, she put the pedal to the floor. With a conspicuous police presence at his house, Stokes probably already knew the game was up and, if he had any sense, he'd be moving Paige. Or disposing of her. It was a grim thought and cold fear washed through Lexi's veins as she considered she might be too late to save the girl.

Bramling was a tiny hamlet, where the road swung sharply to the left. After taking the corner much too fast, Lexi gave the Crossfire full rein along a straight stretch, slamming her foot onto the brake as a Shell sign loomed into view. It was a small petrol station, just two pumps, with a used-car dealership next to it.

She pulled onto the garage forecourt, stopping with a screech, and ran into the tiny shop at the back.

'Whoa, where's the fire?' Behind the counter, a bulky man wearing sunglasses and a Bruce Springsteen T-shirt was sitting on a high stool, resting his back against the grey metal cigarette cabinet.

Lexi thrust her police ID across the counter, and he let the front legs of the stool swing down onto the floor with a crack.

'How can I help you, Inspector?' He took off his sunglasses so he could see her properly.

'I take it you've got security cameras?'

'Oh sure, sure we do.'

'And you keep the recordings?'

'They get stored on the computer,' he said.

That at least made a change. Most small businesses just paid lip service to security footage – either they didn't bother recording or it was wiped within a day or two.

'Good. I've got some dates and times I need to look at.'

The man stood up. 'In the office,' he said, jerking his thumb at a door behind the counter. 'Come through.'

Lexi followed him into a small, untidy room almost filled by a small desk which was hardly big enough for the PC that stood on it. There were shelves of ring binders on the wall behind the desk, and a calendar showing a woman in a string bikini on the wall in front of it.

'Nice view,' said Lexi, nodding at it.

'Sorry,' said the man, his face going red. 'It was a freebie from one of the tyre companies.' He hastily pulled it off the wall and put it face down on one of the shelves, making Lexi feel guilty for embarrassing him.

The man squeezed into the gap behind the desk and fired up the computer. It was an ancient-looking machine and Lexi could practically hear it creaking with the effort.

'Mind me asking what you're looking for?' he said while they waited.

'I've got receipts for transactions. I want to find out what vehicle the person was driving.'

'What've they done?'

'At the moment, we're just trying to rule them out of an ongoing investigation,' said Lexi. She wasn't going to give him any details.

This is the man who I think killed my sister. This is the man who murdered two girls on the Memorial Crown.

'Right. Hit me up with the first one.'

Lexi enlarged the first image on her phone. The receipt was for petrol and food, and was dated the day before at around seven in the evening.

'What's your name?'

'Pat. Pat Bradshaw.'

'Thanks, Pat. You're being really helpful.'

The man gave a nod. 'My dad was a cop.' He twisted the screen round so Lexi could see a grainy freeze-frame of the garage forecourt. The time stamp in the top corner was for fifteen minutes before the transaction had been logged. The low-resolution images jumped rather than providing continuous footage, and Lexi watched in silence as a number of cars stopped for petrol, with drivers dashing in and out of the shop to pay.

'Can you zoom in so we can get the registration numbers?'

Pat gave a bark of laughter. 'You seem to be mistaking this for some sort of high-tech surveillance. Sorry, this is it – the best you'll get.'

Lexi checked the timer on the image they were looking at – a dark-coloured estate with obscured windows. Two minutes before the till transaction as recorded on the receipt. But in the next frame the driver was striding across the forecourt. It was a woman. Lexi shook her head, disappointed.

'Keep going.'

As the woman drove off, another vehicle turned onto the forecourt.

A large white van.

And as it came under the lights of the canopy which sheltered the pumps, Lexi recognised the decals on its side.

The head of a white horse in a red circle. The white horse of Kent.

Huge red dots forming a trail. One of the dots was a ladybird.

Two words.

MOBILE LIBRARY.

She fist-pumped the air. She'd been right.

'That's it. We've got a fix on him.'

SIXTY

Together they stared at the image on the screen.

'You are joking, right?' said Pat.

Lexi pinned Stokes's photo to the desk with her index finger. 'No. This is the man we're looking for, and he's a librarian. Hence the van.'

Pat's expression registered disbelief, but it didn't matter to Lexi. She pulled out her phone. 'Tom, who's with you in the incident room?'

'Colin, Ridhi, a few other bods.'

'Right, get someone to check the ANPR. Stokes has definitely been driving around in one of the mobile library vans. Track down where it was on the day of the abductions, and any sightings of it you can find since.'

'Have you got the reg number?'

'No. You'll have to get that from the library. There are probably two or three of them, so find out which one he had the keys for.'

She turned back to Pat. 'Can you see when else he stopped here?'

'Sure, no worries.' Pat started fast forwarding through the

footage to find the dates on the other receipts. 'You know, I recognise him now. Comes in every two or three days. Sometimes for petrol, sometimes just for food and drink.'

'Does he always come and go from the same direction?'

'Yes, pretty sure he does – he drives in from the Bramling direction and carries on towards Wingham when he leaves. We can check on the footage anyway.'

Arriving from Bramling – that was coming this way from Canterbury. Then he would buy food and carry on along the road. If the food was for Paige, it meant he was holding her somewhere nearby, towards Wingham. Or through it and beyond.

She called Tom again. 'Please tell me there are some traffic cams in Wingham.'

She waited for a minute in silence before he came back with the answer.

'No, afraid not.'

She wasn't surprised but it still infuriated her. 'Damn! Can you get some cars out here. We need to start searching.'

'For what?'

'For Paige Carter. What d'you bloody think?'

'Yes, but what specifically? She's not going to be standing at the edge of the road, waving.'

Lexi sighed. 'Sorry. Let's organise a door-to-door in Wingham and surrounding villages. Ask people if they've seen anything suspicious, if they've noticed the library van coming and going at times when they wouldn't expect to see it. Check out all empty properties, farm buildings, barns, caravans. Chances are he's moved her already, but he's going to need to find another, less obvious vehicle. So get Colin or Ridhi to check for reports of car theft in the area.'

'Will do.'

'If anyone's gone home for the night, call them back in. This is time critical.'

She gave Pat a card. 'Call me immediately if he shows up here again.'

'You think he's got that missing girl?'

He'd clearly been listening to her conversation, and Lexi kicked herself for not leaving his office before calling Tom.

'It's possible. If you think of anything else at all about him, let me know. Even if you don't think it'll help. Sometimes things do.'

Pat nodded and tucked the card into the breast pocket of his shirt.

'Thank you,' said Lexi. She headed back out to the Crossfire.

What now? What now?

It would take time for Tom to organise a comprehensive search of the area, but she was here now, and there could be an innocent life at stake. Stokes must have realised they were onto him, with the forensic team taking his house apart. She might literally be in a race against him to reach Paige first.

And he knew the destination, while she didn't.

Still parked, she closed her eyes, trying to channel a location, but it was pointless. This wasn't a part of the county she was familiar with – rolling farmland with no doubt a hundred places you could hide a girl. And it was dark, making it less and less likely that she'd be able to spot the sort of empty and abandoned buildings Stokes might have chosen for his purposes.

But she wasn't going to be defeated.

Not this time.

She opened her eyes and threw the car into gear. Pulling out of the garage forecourt, she turned in the direction of Wingham. Now was not the time to drive fast. She had to keep looking round until she saw something that spoke to her.

A thought came to her, and she called the incident room.

'Ridhi, have you managed to dig up anything on Stokes's

early life – like where he was born and where he spent his childhood?'

'Boss, hi, give me a mo.'

Lexi waited, driving slowly as she came into the outskirts of Wingham. A car behind her impatiently sounded its horn, so she pulled over on the zigzag lines outside the village primary school.

'Right, I've got his birth certificate.' God, Ridhi was good – she would have to make sure her appreciation didn't go unspoken when she got back to the office. 'He was born at home, in Goodnestone. Does that help?'

'Do you have a full address for that?'

'Yup – Deerfield Cottage, the Street, Goodnestone.'

'Where the hell is that? No, wait, don't worry – I'll put it in the satnav.' She typed it into the app on her phone. The map zoomed in on a tiny hamlet surrounded by fields. Lexi expanded the area.

Bingo.

The tiny village lay about two miles south of where she was now. If Stokes had grown up there, that would be where he'd probably gravitate back to – and he'd probably know places he could safely keep Paige without fear of discovery.

'One more thing – can you see who owns that property now, if it's still owned by a member of the Stokes family?'

'Okay – I'll let you know what I find.'

Lexi disconnected and tapped the phone for directions. Once again she drove slowly, still on the lookout for likely hiding places. She was on a sleepy B-road and there were no other cars, so each time she passed a house or building she dropped to a crawl, checking it out. Most of the properties along this road, and they were few and far between, were either the swanky country houses of city money or rows of modest cottages built for farm workers before the industrial revolution. At this time of evening, most places had lights showing in the windows, and she didn't bother to stop and door knock them. Tom's team would sweep the area as soon as they arrived. She was more interested in places that looked empty, deserted or desolate.

She hadn't come across anything promising by the time she reached Goodnestone, so she decided to stop and take a quick look at the address Ridhi had given her for Stokes's mother. The unimaginatively named street formed the backbone of the tiny village, and she passed a pub and primary school before coming to a row of cottages that looked more promising. She pulled over and cut the engine, sitting for a few moments to take in her surroundings. It was a pretty hamlet, mostly built in Victorian Gothic style, which made Lexi guess it had been the pet project of a wealthy landowner. Now its appeal would be to London commuters – there was a sign for Adisham Station just a couple of miles away – or retirees looking for the quiet life in a Kent village.

But it had once been the home of a killer, and sitting alone in the dark interior of her car, Lexi experienced the same cold clutch of anxiety she'd felt in Stokes's cellar.

It was easy to spot Deerfield Cottage as she walked along the row of houses – there was a painted china nameplate to the left of the front door. It was a modest two-up two-down, with a neat front garden mostly given over to a rockery. The front room lights were on, giving Lexi full view of a knocked-through living room and kitchen. A woman was standing at the cooker, while a child did homework at a pine table. The furniture was modern, IKEA-style, and family friendly. She wouldn't need Ridhi's research to tell her that the Stokes had long since vacated the property.

But that didn't mean he wasn't in the area. People are drawn by the familiar, and childhood neighbourhoods exert a particular magnetism – especially to those whose troubled early years had left them struggling in adult life. She could count scores of cases she'd worked on in America in which serial killers had returned to where they'd grown up. Although she didn't know how long Stokes had lived in Goodnestone, the fact that he went to the nearby petrol station bore out the truth of this.

Determined to carry on the search, Lexi went back to the Crossfire and studied the map of the area on her phone. A network of narrow lanes spread out from the centre of the village like a spider's web, and she felt sure now that this was where Paige was being kept. She carried on driving along the Street and as she reached the far end of the village it became nothing more than a farm track. The moon had risen, painting the fields on either side in grey and silver. They were just ploughed earth at this time of year, the long furrows following the gentle contours of the land as they stretched into the distance.

There were no lights out here, no signs of human habitation, and the rural landscape that might appear benign by day took on a brooding malevolence. When the moon was blotted out by a cloud, it became otherworldly, as if she was plummeting down a deep ocean trench, all alone, as she followed the twin shafts of light cast by the Crossfire's headlamps. She shivered and turned up the heat in the car, glancing from side to side as she drove, looking for the black silhouettes of abandoned and empty buildings.

The sound of her mobile made her jump, and she pulled to an abrupt stop in the empty lane.

'Lexi? Where are you?' It was Tom.

She looked around, as if the view might tell her something, but it didn't. 'A few miles out of Goodnestone.'

'Which road?'

'No idea. I'm just driving round the lanes, looking.'

'Looking for what exactly?' Tom sounded worried.

'Anything. The pot of gold at the end of the rainbow. The lost kingdom.'

'You shouldn't be out there on your own.'

'No, I bloody shouldn't. You lot should be here too.'

'We're on our way.'

'So tell me when you're close and we can work out which areas I've covered and which still need to be searched.'

She hung up. Of course this was more than a one-man operation – or one-woman – but Stokes wasn't going to hang around waiting, so neither was she.

She carried on driving, following the sweep of the lane round a sloping curve and on up a steep incline. For a moment, the moon was on her side, lighting up the brow of the hill, where she saw, in sharp relief against the black sky, the silvered bones of a twisted, wind-sculpted tree.

It was the tree in Len Clayton's sketch.

SIXTY-ONE

The dream tree. Only it was real, and it was here. It was telling her something.

Lexi immediately switched off her headlights, then drove in first gear, ever so slowly, until she was within thirty metres of the tree. She cut the engine and waited. Nothing stirred. There was no sign of another vehicle, no chink of light anywhere to be seen. She switched off the Crossfire's interior light before opening the door, cursing to herself silently when it gave a low creak. Once out, she shut it gently, resting her body against it to muffle the sound of the door catch.

If she'd still been in the FBI, she would have reached for her gun. Though she fully accepted the UK's policy of unarmed police, there were moments when she'd have felt much more comfortable with a Glock in her hand. But it wasn't an option here and she'd have to go into whatever situation she found with just her wits as a weapon.

As she walked up the slope, her body primed itself for action. Adrenalin rinsed through her, raising her heartbeat, tightening every muscle fibre and putting her mind on full alert. She didn't know what to expect but she was ready for it.

The tree stood on the brow of the hill, its branches pointing somewhere beyond.

How had it come to the pages of Len's sketchbook? She didn't believe in prophetic dreams. Len had seen this tree, and remembered it, and linked it to the case, and now she would never know why.

As Lexi came to the highest point of the lane, there was a five-bar gate into the field in which the tree stood. Beyond the hedgerow bounding one edge of the field, there was a small wood which stretched down the far side of the slope. There was nothing in the field – it was just an acre of lumpen, churned up soil, waiting to be sown. But halfway along the hedgerow Lexi saw a stile, leading into a swathe of mature trees, their bare branches sounding a death rattle in the wind.

Lexi hurried down the side of the field. The ground was uneven and great clods of mud stuck to her boots, but intuition told her she was needed so she broke into a run. She threw herself over the stile, stumbling on stony ground on the other side. There was a path leading away, well-worn, presumably by dog walkers, meandering through the woods to God knows where.

She couldn't risk using the torch on her mobile – if Stokes was here, she needed the element of surprise. The moon dipped in and out of the clouds, momentarily showing her the path ahead, then plunging her back into darkness so she had to slow down for fear of falling. She went as fast as she dared, and the slope she was running down became gradually steeper, the path more twisty.

And she remembered running like this once before. With Amber. Her heart left behind with Rose, her legs pushing her forward to get help. This time she was the help, but she had no idea whether she'd arrive in time to save Paige.

Ahead, through the trees, she saw the dark outlines of buildings. Long, low sheds – as the path took her from side to side,

she could see that there were several of them in two wide rows.
She knew what it was. An abandoned battery chicken farm.
There was one similar near Wye, left to rot when the supermar-
kets switched to free-range eggs and barn-raised chickens.
These poultry gulags were silent and empty now, floors still
spattered with chicken shit, down floating in the dusty air.

The perfect place to keep a captive, or three. She stopped
running to send a text to Tom, using the what3words app on her
phone to give him the precise location.

As she got closer, the sheds loomed larger. She counted six
in all. There was no sign of any light, and no sound coming from
any of them. She slowed down – she didn't want her footsteps
to be audible, which meant treading softly and carefully. As she
reached the bottom of the slope, she saw that the battery farm
was enclosed by a high wire mesh fence.

She stopped while she was still in the cover of the trees.
The path swung round to one end of the rectangular area where
she could just make out a shadowy gate. It looked crooked,
suggesting it was broken. She held her breath, listening all the
time, but there was nothing to hear apart from the wind in the
branches above her.

Breaking cover, she skirted around the enclosure to the gate.
In front of it, there were tyre tracks coming from the other direction, and she could see the mud was churned up where the
vehicle had repeatedly turned round. The furrows were deep
enough to suggest something larger and heavier than a normal
car – the library van, perhaps?

As she'd thought, the gate wasn't functional and hung open,
the bottom of it jammed into the mud. It had clearly been like
that for some time. Whoever owned the place probably never
came here – there would be nothing worth stealing and it would
probably be left to rot and collapse in its own time.

The ground within the enclosure was overgrown. Long
coarse grass, brambles and shrubs crowded the narrow gaps

between the low wooden buildings, snagging on Lexi's trousers as soon as she went through the gateway. As she extricated herself, she looked around. She was facing two chicken sheds, end on, and beyond each of them two more stood in line. The area they covered was larger than she'd realised. Each shed was roughly twenty feet wide by fifty feet long. There were ventilation spaces at the tops of the wooden slatted walls, plus a couple of small, glazed windows along each of the sides. A couple of the sheds were already starting to decay – one was missing part of its roof, while another had a slumped-in corner where a timber post must have collapsed.

There was a rough beaten track leading from the gate, which split into two paths, one towards each of the first two sheds. She wondered which branch to pick, still listening for any sound that would give her a clue. But it had to be a snap decision. She looked at the ground where the path divided, directing her gaze along each in turn. She didn't know what she was looking for. The ground was muddy but flat with no distinct footprints to guide her way. The vegetation was encroaching on both forks in equal measure.

But on the right-hand path, a few metres away, something glimmered pale in the moonlight. Something flapping in the grass, pale on one side, dark on the other.

Lexi went to it and bent down, and as she saw what it was, a cold fist of fear grasped her heart.

A discarded KitKat wrapper.

During the ten days that Stokes had held her hostage, he'd only given her food once. A couple of fingers of KitKat. A starburst sugar rush that had left her hungry for more – and afterwards, she could never again look at a KitKat wrapper, let alone eat one. She felt sick and scared and weak. She wanted to run again, as fast as she could, to get away from this place.

She was unsteady on her feet, but she gritted her teeth and straightened up. In front of her, the end of the chicken shed was a blank wooden wall, and the path stretched away along one side of it. The door must be at the other end. She crept along the side of the building. When she reached the first of two small windows, she ducked down. She didn't want to cast a shadow across whatever light it allowed inside. She waited again, catching her breath, listening. Then she pressed her face against the wall by the window frame, inching sideways until she could just see inside.

It was entirely dark and she could distinguish nothing. She didn't want to risk using her torch at this point, so she carried on along the side until she reached the corner. A quick look round it showed her a heavy metal door on a steel runner that would slide open along the wall, rather than swinging in or out. It didn't appear to be locked, so she pressed her weight against the edge of it to see if it would move.

Without warning, her phone rang. She checked the screen as she silenced it – a call from an unknown number. Her cover was blown. There was nothing she could do to reverse that, so she pushed against the door. There was a loud screech of metal against metal. It moved a few inches and she peered inside. Her nostrils were assaulted by the smell of mould and decay, with an acrid edge of chicken shit that caused bile to rise in her throat. She flicked on her phone torch and shone it around the interior.

Empty.

A hole in the roof gave access to a shaft of moonlight, creating a silver dollar on the concrete floor. A few planks and steel struts littered the place, and there were marks on the plasterboard walls that showed where tier upon tier of cages had been attached. For a second, the squawking of a thousand chickens rang in Lexi's ears, but it was just the silence making itself heard. Never had she seen such a forlorn place – where living things had existed in agony, only to be slaughtered when they'd outlived their usefulness.

And had the three Carter sisters been kept in these sheds,

like three trapped birds, waiting for the flashing blade of Stokes's knife?

Quickly, she made her way out and around to the front of the next shed in the row. This time, she kept her torch on. She'd made enough noise to wake the dead and if anyone was here, they'd have seen the flicker of light. A freshly broken bramble shoot told her that someone had been here recently.

She rounded the end of the second shed. It had the same type of sliding door, but this one sported a large silver padlock. It was shiny and certainly didn't date back to when the battery farm had been in operation.

Damn!

She hadn't thought to bring the crowbar from the car. So stupid. She could have used it to get this door open, and as a handy weapon if she'd needed one. Running all the way up the hill to fetch it didn't seem like a good plan. She had a sense that her time was limited – she needed to get this door open now. Then she remembered the debris on the floor of the first shed. Surely there would be something there that she could use to smash the hasp that the padlock held in place.

She ran back along the length of second shed and into the first one. The beam of her torch quickly picked out a sturdy-looking steel reinforcement bar. It was slightly bent, but that was a plus – she could put one end through the metal loop on which the padlock hung and use leverage to bust it open.

She ran back, and as she slid the bar through the metal loop, she called out a warning.

'Paige, are you in there? I'm a police officer and I'm here to get you out.'

There was no answer.

What if she was too late? What if all she found inside was Paige's body? Or if Stokes had beaten her to it and spirited her away, just like Rose?

Raising her knee to put one boot firmly against the metal

door, she used her full body weight to pull down on the steel bar. Nothing happened. She took another breath and gritted her teeth, pulling again, straining every sinew. Something had to give. Her arm muscles were burning and she felt like her back might break but, with a shrill screech, one of the screws attaching the hasp to the door finally gave way. Another followed a second later and then the whole lock broke away. Lexi flew backwards and landed in a clump of spiny gorse. It felt like a hundred needles were being driven into her back and she cried out.

Taking a deep breath, she scrabbled out and ran back to the door. The padlock had fallen to the ground and using what strength she had left, she was able to slide the metal panel along its runners.

She grabbed her torch from her pocket and stepped inside.

She was immediately hit by the smell. The stench of human excrement overlaid the mustiness she'd smelled in the first shed. Her eyes chased the beam of light as she swept it across the concrete floor and wooden walls. There were a couple of over-turned hen cages and piles of broken wooden racks. Dead leaves had blown in through an empty window. Litter. And the one thing she hadn't wanted to see.

In the far corner, pushed into the darkest shadows, there was a body.

A human body.

A girl.

SIXTY-TWO

I know something's up as soon as I walk into the shop at the Casino Filling Station. The guy who works there, usually half asleep or glued to his mobile, is suddenly self-conscious and awkward. His hand trembles as he rings up my items.

So, you've been here, have you, Lexi Bennett?

That's my guess.

Perhaps our little game of cat and mouse is coming to a close. But who's the cat and who's the mouse?

It's been fun to watch as you've blundered around town. And that touching reunion with your sister? I wouldn't have missed that for the world.

But now, Lexi Bennett, I'm coming to get you. I've waited long enough.

I drive round the long way, so I can approach chicken shit alley from the opposite direction to Lexi. I dumped the library van, and I'm using Barbara's car instead. I pinched her car keys from her bag while she was among the stacks. She didn't even see me sneaking into the library.

Of course, she will have realised by now. But I don't suppose she'll guess it was me.

I park Barb's car across a farm gate, about a mile south of the battery farm, on a little lane that's actually a dead end. It means that Lexi's backup won't be tearing past, and won't spot the car. It means trekking across a couple of fields, but she has to find the place from scratch. With any luck, we'll both arrive there at the same time.

When I reach the woods adjacent to the farm, I select a good lookout spot and wait to see Lexi approaching through the trees on the other side.

This is falling in line with my plan beautifully. I knew she wouldn't be able to resist if I dangled Paige in front of her. Once I have Lexi in my grasp, I'll be ready to move on to the next phase. She ruined my plans once before, but I won't let it happen again. This time, she'll get everything she deserves and more.

I hear her scurrying down the slope, almost out of control by the time she reaches the bottom. She looks around and listens for a moment. I hardly dare breathe. I press one finger against the point of my knife. Anticipation is a delicious thing.

When she goes into the first shed, she turns on her torch. But she won't find anything in there. She comes out, and as she makes her way to the second shed, I creep down from my hiding place. I crouch in the ferns and watch her assessing the padlock.

Maybe she needs my help. She only has to ask.

But it turns out that she's quite resourceful on her own. And surprisingly strong. It must be all that training she does.

I pull on my white rubber mask, and take a deep breath.

It's time for our reunion.

SIXTY-THREE

Lexi ran forward and crouched down by the body – Paige. She placed two fingers on the girl's neck, feeling for a pulse. Nothing. She moved her fingers slightly, searching for the place. Yes... no... It was so faint, she couldn't be sure she wasn't imagining it.

The girl was lying on her side, curled in the foetal position. Lexi gently rolled her onto her back and looked for any wounds. There was nothing that stood out immediately, no blood, and no signs of stabs or cuts, though one of her hands was amateurly wrapped in a strip of torn fabric.

In the harsh glare of the torch, Paige's face looked grey and drawn. Her lips were flaky and chapped, and Lexi immediately recognised the signs of severe dehydration. Paige blinked at the light and tried to raise an arm to cover her eyes, but she was too weak.

Lexi pulled off her jacket and tucked it under Paige's head. If only she'd thought to at least bring some water. She pulled out her phone but there was no signal. Hardly surprising – they were in the lee of a steep hill, in a remote rural area.

'It's going to be okay, Paige.' Her words didn't prompt a

reaction. Hunger, dehydration and shock all exacted a heavy price, from the brain as well as the body.

Lexi considered her options. Tom and the rest of the team should be somewhere close by now. If she could get to a place with a signal, she could guide them here. But where? The top of the hill? She glanced down at Paige, who stared back at her wide-eyed.

She couldn't leave the girl.

She'd done that once before, and she had yet to forgive herself.

If she went anywhere, Paige would come too. That meant she would have to carry her. A fireman's lift, up the hill through the woods in the dark. Where a serial killer might be lurking. God, she missed her Glock.

'Lucy?' Her voice was a dry croak.

Lexi looked down.

'Eden? Where are they?'

She doesn't know they're dead?

'Don't worry about Lucy and Eden. We've got to get you out of here.'

'We can't leave them.'

'We won't.' It was heartbreaking, but as Paige seemed to be becoming more lucid, Lexi needed to take her way from danger. 'Do you think you can stand up, if I help you?'

Paige shook her head, but she tried all the same.

As Lexi put one arm around Paige's back and started to haul her up, she heard a sound outside. The snap of a branch underfoot. With a cry, Paige slid down and slumped back onto the floor.

Lexi ran to the entrance of the shed. 'Who's there?'

Behind her, Paige whimpered like a trapped animal.

She stared out into the dark wood. She thought she saw a flash of movement in the deep shadows of the closest shed.

'Who's there?' she said again.

But she knew perfectly well who it was. She bent down to pick up the steel bar from where she'd dropped it after busting open the lock.

'Princess...'

It was just a whisper in the dark, but Lexi recognised the voice from meeting Rufus Stokes in the library. And she knew that when she'd heard his voice that day, her lizard brain had recognised it and hidden it from her. Protecting her like it always had. But now she was stronger – she didn't need protecting anymore. If anything she needed access to her memories. They helped her understand. They gave her the strength to know she could survive whatever was about to happen next.

'Princess...'

'You've got that wrong,' said Lexi, her voice sounding strong and fierce. 'I'm not your princess.'

There was a rustling in the ferns to her left. A dark figure appeared.

'Of course you are. You always have been.' His voice was sharper.

As he stepped towards her, the moon came out and she saw him properly. He was wearing the white latex mask that had haunted Lexi's dreams. She gasped and Rufus Stokes laughed.

'You know, it's good to see you. Really good.'

'You don't need the mask. I know who you are, Rufus.'

'I know. But I thought it might bring back some fond memories.'

Memories she didn't want. Lexi hated this man from the depths of her heart – he had blighted her life and stolen her beloved Rose.

She gripped the steel bar tighter with both hands. He was standing in front of her. He was smaller than her memory had painted him. In her dreams, he was a monster. But here and now, he was just pathetic. At least, she had to tell herself that. She had to hold her nerve.

She could take a swing at him, but he would deflect it. She couldn't be certain she would overcome him, and she had to think of Paige, lying in the barn behind her. She needed to choose her moment with care.

'Why us, Rufus? Why triplets?'

'Who better to play off against each other? I've taken siblings a few times over the years, but twins and triplets are even closer. I like to watch what they will do for each other – the sibling dynamic between them, given they're all wired the same.'

'Tell me about the other triplets you've taken.'

'Do you think I'm stupid?'

'Tell us or not – we'll find the evidence, and you'll go down for them all.'

Stokes laughed. 'It's just a research project. All in the name of science.'

Lexi felt sickened, but she needed to keep him talking.

'Can't you do that without killing?'

'It's complicated.'

'Tell me.'

Stokes raised a hand to the mouth of his mask. Tiny metal teeth glinted in the moonlight – it was a zip, and he swept it shut.

Damn!

He took a step towards her. Lexi had no choice. She drew the steel bar back and without pausing swung it forward with all her might. But Stokes was expecting it. He raised his right arm to deflect it. Lexi heard the crack of metal against bone and Stokes grunted with pain, but the steel jerked back in her wrist with a force that almost overbalanced her.

Lexi gasped, but managed to sidestep him as the bar flew

from her hand. She stumbled backwards into the shed, turning in the darkness to look for Paige.

'Get up, Paige, get up.'

With a sob, Paige scuttled across the floor to the furthest corner, but she couldn't manage to get to her feet.

'Come on, we've got to get out.'

Stokes was blocking their only escape route and now he had the steel bar in his hands.

Lexi knew she should have waited for backup, but she had no time for regrets.

Stokes was stronger, and he had a weapon. She remembered what he'd done to Josh Pendleton. She was as scared as she'd ever been in her life. But she wasn't going to show it.

'If I agree to be your princess, will you let Paige go?'

Stokes unzipped the mask and laughed. 'Go? Where would she go? She wouldn't get as far as the gate.'

'You and I could go. We could get away and leave her here for my team to find.'

'Do they know where you are?'

'They've got a tracker on my phone.' Untrue.

'No signal down here, so that won't help them.'

'They'll be here any moment.'

Stokes considered this. 'I doubt it.' But he couldn't know, and Lexi saw a slight twitch in his neck, betraying the desire to look around, to see if Lexi's men were creeping up on him from behind.

'Please, you've got me. You don't need Paige as well.'

'You see what one triplet will do for another – and you're not even part of the same set.'

'I'll do anything if it will save Paige's life.'

'I doubt it.'

They were at an impasse. Lexi knew she would have to force the situation – but how could she ensure the outcome would be in Paige's favour?

Base instinct took over. Reason hadn't worked, and the anger that had been ever-present, every waking hour, for seventeen years, roared up within her. She took a dive, leading with her head, aiming at just below his centre of gravity to knock him onto his back. If he went down and was winded, she could get the bar back and incapacitate him enough to give her and Paige a chance of escape.

But she hadn't counted on his lightning-fast reflexes. As her head smashed into his stomach, he brought the steel bar crashing down on her back. They fell together in a tangle of limbs. She was on top of him, but he had the bar across the back of her neck. He was crushing her against his chest.

She couldn't scream.

She couldn't breathe.

She knew she wouldn't survive.

SIXTY-FOUR

'Rose! Rose! You have to run!'

There was a weight on her back.

Movement was impossible.

'Rose! Rose! You have to run!'

She tried to run, but the brambles snaked out across the path and wrapped themselves around her ankles. Branches entwined her upper body. She was trapped, motionless, even though her legs never stopped moving. Cold water closed over her head as she swam for her life. But something was sucking her under. And far away, above the surface, her two sisters beckoned to her and called her name.

No, wait... she wasn't Rose. She was Lexi.

She opened her eyes, but it made no difference. Was she blind? She put a hand to her face to feel for a blindfold, but there wasn't one.

How long had she been out? Where was she?

Peering around in the darkness, she cast her mind back for her last memory. But it was the acrid smell of human waste that jolted her back into the present. The battery chicken farm. Paige. Rufus Stokes...

Where were they?

She staggered to her feet, experiencing a series of dagger-like pains down her spine as she did. The back of her neck, where Stokes had applied pressure with the bar, was on fire. She winced, then gritted her teeth with determination, limping across to the doorway. It was open. Thankfully Stokes hadn't locked her in.

Outside it was still dark, though relatively lighter thanks to the moon. Light enough for her to see the outline of a small car just beyond the enclosure's broken gate. A man... Stokes... was heaving something into the hatchback's open boot.

Paige. Was she still alive?

Ignoring the clamour of fear inside her chest, Lexi moved slowly towards them, testing the ground softly with each foot so as not to make a noise.

Stokes was whistling to himself and muttering as he crammed the girl's inert body into the small space, bending her legs up to put her in the foetal position so he could close the lid.

'Stay back, princess,' he said, without even bothering to look round.

So much for moving silently.

'Let her go. Take me instead.'

Now Stokes turned to look at her. He was no longer wearing the mask and in the moonlight his face looked grey and tired.

He shook his head. 'You misunderstand what I'm doing. It's not either or. I've got you both. I'm just going to dispose of this tiresome little creature and then we can get on.'

The menace in his words sent a shiver down Lexi's spine.

'Get on with what?'

'First of all, I'll go to fetch Amber.'

Cold dread washed through her and turned her legs to water. She slumped against the shed door frame, shaking her head. 'No... no... leave her out of it.'

'Not a chance.' His response was whip fast. He knew he had the upper hand. 'You spoiled everything, Lexi. I'd hardly got started with the three of you. And now you're trying to spoil things again.'

He turned back to the car and slammed down the boot. 'Besides, I have new plans for you and your sister.'

Hold your nerve.

'We're going to find out which one of you is stronger. Which one of you will last longer. I'm going to enjoy myself.' He stepped towards her.

Lexi shivered.

'Don't be scared now, princess.'

But there were plenty of reasons to be scared. She was injured. Paige was unconscious, in the boot of Stokes's car. Stokes, the man who'd killed her sister. The man who'd killed Paige's sisters. The man who'd killed Josh Pendleton. These were all reasons enough to be very scared indeed.

She felt for her phone. It was missing – he must have taken it when she was unconscious. Another reason to be frightened. She couldn't call for help even if she was able to get a signal. She would just have to hope and pray her earlier message to Tom had got through.

Reasons to stay brave. She wasn't incapacitated. She wasn't tied up.

She was smarter than him.

And that was it. Her brain was her only weapon.

'What can I offer you to let Paige go?'

Stokes was silent for a moment before speaking. 'There is something I'd like.'

'What?'

'I left something precious in my house. Which means now your filthy swarm must have it.'

'What are you talking about, Rufus? We took a lot from your house.' Lexi thought of the boxes of human detritus

Emily Jordan had removed, all to be sifted through and checked over.

'There was one thing that was particularly precious. Only you can replace it.'

'I don't know that I have it.'

'Don't worry, you do. Or at least an exact replica of it.'

'What is it?'

'We'll come to that.'

He pulled something from his pocket. There was a glint of metal in the moonlight. Lexi began to get a very bad feeling. Had the message to Tom got through? Even if it had, help wasn't going to arrive soon enough. She wondered where they would discover her dead body, and started to panic.

No. Get a grip.

She knew Rufus Stokes. She knew how his mind worked – after all, he'd been rattling around inside her head for the past seventeen years. And now she knew what he wanted. He wanted to taunt her, and to play her off against her sister. He wouldn't be able to do that if she was dead.

He took a step towards her. 'If you scream in the forest and no one hears you, did you really scream?'

'You'll hear me.'

'Yes, but I don't count.'

'If I agree to what you want, you'll let Paige go?'

'Of course.'

'How can I trust you?'

He smiled. She saw the gleam of his teeth. 'You can't. But what choice have you got?'

Her mind was working in warp speed, gaming her options and the likely outcomes. Playing for time would bring the team nearer.

Lexi stood her ground even as he came closer to her. 'I want to know what happened to Rose.'

He paused, smiling, and the moon brightened as the clouds

scudded away. For the first time she took proper note of what Rufus Stokes, the man who'd wreaked so much havoc in her and Amber's lives, looked like – a slight man with a pale, handsome face. Unkempt, sand-coloured hair. Glasses. Wrinkled clothing. But nothing to suggest the darkness that lurked within. In her mind, he'd been a monster. In real life, he looked mundane.

'Of course you want to know about your sister. And I'm the only person in the world who can tell you.'

'Then go ahead.'

'When you've paid your dues.' She could see now what he was holding. A pair of poultry shears. Banal in a kitchen drawer but, here, laced with so much threat her blood ran cold. He wanted to use them on her, the way he presumably had on Rose.

She thought of the small white bone she'd found in his cellar. A bone that he could replace by taking one from her.

Her head spun.

She would do anything to save Paige Carter. She would do anything to recover Rose's body. But more importantly, she'd do anything to bring Rufus Stokes to justice.

She held out her left hand and stepped over the threshold to hell.

SIXTY-FIVE

I love the weight of the shears in my hand.

There's a sheen of sweat on her forehead, a tremor in her voice when she speaks.

Are you afraid, princess?

You should be.

I meant what I said about fetching your sister.

I meant what I said about seeing which of you will survive longer.

Let the games begin.

SIXTY-SIX

'Take what you need.'

Her hand was shaking, but she pictured Rose. Then she was able to hold it steady.

Stokes grabbed her by the wrist and pulled her close to him. He put his other arm around her back, pressing her up against his chest. She could feel one of the handles of the poultry shears jutting against her spine. Her mouth went dry.

'You never had to run from me,' he whispered in her ear. 'I wasn't going to hurt you.'

She struggled to pull herself back. 'You hurt me when you hurt Rose.'

He was stronger than her and she was caught.

'Behave nicely, and I'll make it up to you. I'll let you win against Amber.'

In his warped mind, he thought he could pit her against her own sister, and it made Lexi feel sick. She had to put an end to this, but she didn't know how. He held all the cards. He had her phone, he had the car keys for both her car and the car he'd come in. She let her eyes skim the ground for anything she could use as a weapon.

He followed her gaze. 'You know there's no one coming for you.'

Stalemate. But if they were playing a game of chess, each of them needed to think several moves ahead. None of Lexi's options seemed good.

'What happened to you when you were a kid?' His grip on her tightened and she could see the tension her question caused in the cords of his neck.

He looked down at her blankly. 'Nothing.'

Lexi nodded her head. 'Something happened to make you this way. Someone treated you badly, didn't they?'

'Spare me the pop psychology. No one made me this way but me.'

'"This way"?'

He smiled at her. Self-effacing. Calm. 'This is what I am – a man who kills women for pleasure.'

Lucy. Eden. Josh Pendleton, too. And Rose. But she and Amber and Paige were still alive. He wasn't very good at it. She didn't believe what he said about being a self-made killer. Someone had damaged Rufus Stokes terribly, maybe when he was too young to remember, or maybe his memory had taken the trauma and buried it away – just as her own memory had buried the trauma he'd wrought on her seventeen years before. She wondered who was to blame.

'It was your family, wasn't it, Rufus?'

'Leave them out of it.'

'Were you an only child? Longing for a brother or a sister to play with? Is that it? Were you jealous of people like me and my sisters, and the Carter sisters? All for one and one for all. You had no one, did you?' As she spoke, Stokes's breathing seemed to quicken. She was getting to him.

'I had sisters. Hated them.'

'Why? What did they do to you?'

His brow lowered in anger. 'They hurt me, but they're dead now. Dead and gone.'

'Did you kill them?'

'You want to know what happened to them? Or to our darling Rose? Your choice.'

Lexi couldn't reply. *Our darling.* It sickened her, that he could be so proprietorial about her sister. She bit down on the inside of her lower lip until she tasted blood.

He pushed her from him, seemingly confident that she was too invested to run away.

She glared at him, because he was right.

'Don't frown at me.'

His sudden snap of anger shocked her, and reminded her that she was dealing with a man who wasn't rational and whose plans more than likely included her demise. Fear slowly uncoiled in her belly. She couldn't afford to let it overwhelm her. She had to stay sharp.

'Rose was distraught when you left, you know? After you and Amber deserted her, I was all she had. I was her only friend in the world.'

The thought of what Rose must have gone through after they left her was unbearable.

'Where did you take her?'

Stokes raised a finger theatrically to his chin. 'Where did I take her? Where did I take her?' He pursed his lips and glanced away. 'I know this part of the county like the back of my hand. There are lots of abandoned places that could be useful to a man like me. Let's just say I took her somewhere safe.' A fleeting look of sadness crossed his face. 'I tried to make her happy. Really, I did. But she wasn't you, Lexi, and it was you that I wanted. Rose never forgave me for what I did to her.' He brandished the poultry shears in the air, snapping them together a couple of times.

'Would you expect her to?'

'It was such a trivial thing.' He sounded annoyed. 'And you were to blame. It could have been avoided if you'd obeyed my rules.'

Anger trumped fear, burning through her like napalm.

'She refused to eat and she refused to wash. I brought delicious things to tempt her, but she spat at me, and snarled like an animal. That's what happened to Rose. She turned into an animal. A stinking, filthy animal.' Spittle flew from his mouth and landed on Lexi's cheek.

'Don't you dare talk about her that way.'

'She was a stinking animal, so I put her out of her misery.'

Her rage became an inferno. How dare he speak of Rose in that way? Without a coherent plan, Lexi raised a hand to strike him, driven only by the need to avenge Rose's suffering. But he was just as fast and caught her by the wrist.

'Now I'll take what's mine,' he hissed.

Ice-cold fear liquified inside her.

But he'd leaned forward and his balance was compromised. Lexi swung her right leg out to the side and brought it back with all the force she could muster against his left calf. He was holding her right arm, so when she pulled it down, the two moves combined to overbalance him. He sprawled on his front in the mud, letting go of Lexi's arm with a grunt. She saw the shears fly out of his hand. She kicked them as hard as she could into a patch of brambles where they couldn't be retrieved in a hurry.

He was down, and she had to ensure he stayed down until she and Paige could get away. It wasn't something she normally would have done, but she kicked him as hard as she could in the side of the head. Then kicked him again for good measure.

'That's from Rose. And from Amber, and Eden, and Lucy, and Paige, and most of all from me.'

His face slumped into the mud and Lexi reflected how differently the whole thing would have played out if she'd had a gun. She saw the steel bar lying on the ground nearby. She could pick it up. She could make good use of it.

She could kill him. And it was nothing more than he deserved.

She stood stock-still, holding her breath, as he lay motionless at her mercy. She clenched her fists, as tightly as – even tighter than – the knot in her stomach.

She was better than that. Retribution had to come through the law. It was everything she stood for. She took a deep breath and tore her gaze from the steel bar. Then she bent over him and searched his pockets until she found her phone and the car keys.

She ran back to the car and threw open the boot.

'Paige, can you hear me?'

The girl's closed eyes were dark and sunken, but on hearing her name, the lids fluttered slightly.

'Stay with me. Help's coming.'

But Stokes was already stirring in the dirt. She needed to secure him, or he'd either come after them or get away. She couldn't let that happen. There had to be something in the car she could use. Leaning over Paige, she gently felt around her, looking for a rope, but there was nothing. She went round and opened one of the rear passenger doors, lighting up the front compartment.

Please, please…

There was a black canvas bag on the back seat. She pulled it closer, upturning the bag to tip out its contents. A balled-up T-shirt, socks and underwear, a washbag… looked like Stokes was planning a trip. A torch. A leather pouch, vaguely moulded in the shape of a pair of shears. A pouch of tobacco. A ball gag. And finally, what she needed. Cable ties.

She pulled three from the bundle and ran back to where Stokes was gasping for breath on the ground. There was a trickle of blood at his temple where she'd kicked him and he appeared confused. Quickly, before he realised what was happening, she slipped a cable tie onto each wrist, pulling them tight enough so he wouldn't be able to wriggle out of them.

They were less than five feet from the metal gate post on which the broken gate hung. Taking a deep breath, Lexi shoved her arms under his armpits and dug her heels back into the mud to drag him closer. It took a couple of attempts, and her feet skidded from under her a couple of times. But she persevered. Time was running out – Paige was in desperate need of medical attention.

As soon as they were near enough, she took the third cable tie and used it to tie him to the gate post. He seethed with anger, and attempted to bite her arm. She pulled it out of the way just in time. Standing up, she grabbed the post with both hands and shook it to see if it was stable. It held fast against all the pressure she could muster. Good – it would hold him for long enough.

She ran back to the car. There was no time to move Paige onto the back seat, so she yanked out the rear shelf. At least that would give her some air. She jumped into the driver's seat and started the engine, and turned the car. Up ahead, the head-lamps showed a dirt track winding further down the hill and disappearing into the trees. It must have been the way Stokes had come.

She drove as fast as she dared on the rutted, muddy lane. Reaching the bottom of the hill, she forded a pool of standing water and started to climb again. Paige groaned in the back as she slammed against the door of the boot.

'Sorry, sorry,' said Lexi, still accelerating.

After a mile or so winding uphill, the lane reached a junction with a tarmac road. Left, uphill. Right, downhill. Lexi turned left, drove a few metres and stopped the car at the brow of a long ridge.

She got out her phone and prayed.

A signal appeared on the screen and she pressed the speed dial.

'Tom? I've got Paige. She's alive. Come and get us.'

SIXTY-SEVEN

Lexi ran around the car and opened the back. She sat on the lip of the boot and took Paige's hand, and when she saw that Paige's little finger was missing from the top knuckle, she finally gave in to the tide of emotions coursing through her. She'd done it. Although injured, Paige Carter was alive, and while it would never expunge the guilt and grief she felt about her sister, it was moments like this that made sense of what she'd chosen to do with her life.

She squeezed the cold, bloody hand within hers and gently rubbed it to try and bring back some warmth. Paige's lips opened slightly as she let out a shallow sob.

There had to be some water in the car. Setting Paige's hand gently down, Lexi jumped up to check. Nothing in the glove compartment or the door pockets in the front. The cupholders in the front console were empty, and there was nothing in the grip bag on the back seat. But when she felt under the passenger seat with her hand, there was a plastic bottle. She drew it out – it was a dusty, buckled Coke bottle, but there were a couple of inches of brown liquid at the bottom. It would be better than nothing.

She took it back to Paige and helped her up into a semi sitting position. She held the bottle to Paige's dry lips and, though the girl winced as she tasted the flat, stale liquid, she drank it greedily.

She phoned Tom again. She'd already texted him the map co-ordinates that her phone had given her, along with a request for paramedics and an ambulance.

'How long?'

'Nearly there,' said Tom. 'Three minutes.'

'Please tell me you've got some water.'

'I have.'

Before they finished speaking, she saw the flashing blue lights coming along the road at the bottom of the ridge. A minute later, Tom was climbing out of an unmarked police car and walking towards her.

'You're crying,' he said incredulously.

'Thank you – I'm well aware of it.' Lexi wiped her eyes with her shirt cuff as she made way for a young motorbike paramedic to bend over Paige.

Tom put an arm around her shoulder and guided her to one side. A uniformed PC came up with a large flashlight and held it so the paramedic could see.

'You did good,' said Tom. 'But you should have waited for us. What if he'd hurt you? Or worse?'

Lexi glanced up the road. There was a phalanx of police cars driving up towards the lane.

'There was nothing he could do to hurt me more than what he's already done.'

'Come on, Lexi. What would you have done if he'd attacked you?'

'He did attack me. I prevailed.' She was suddenly exhausted.

. . .

An ambulance arrived to take Paige to hospital. Emily Jordan and her team turned up to process the scene. Once Lexi had had a few minutes to recover herself, she and Tom drove down to the chicken farm.

By the time they got there, Rufus Stokes was sitting in the back of a police car, secured in regulation police handcuffs instead of cable ties. There was still a smudge of blood on the side of his head and Lexi could see the beginnings of a bruise colouring his swollen cheekbone. She felt no remorse.

Stokes scowled at her through the car window.

'You did that to him?' said Tom. He sounded impressed.

'He deserves far worse, but I'll leave it for the courts to punish him,' said Lexi, her tone grim.

'Princess...'

Lexi turned her back on him. The fear had gone, and now she felt only contempt.

Leaving the uniformed officers to take Stokes back to Canterbury, they checked the other four sheds. There was clear evidence that Eden and Lucy had been held in separate sheds, which would also need processing.

'I wonder if he held anyone else here,' said Tom.

'It's entirely possible.' Lexi looked around the last shed. 'We'll need to cross reference any forensics Emily discovers with current and historic cases of missing girls. Come on, let's go – I want to see if Paige is up to talking to us.'

The paramedic had said that he thought exposure and dehydration were the main issues, though he cautioned them that she would need to be more thoroughly checked over when she got to the hospital.

As Tom drove them back to town in the Crossfire, Lexi called the Carters' home phone number. Philippa Reid, the FLO, answered the phone.

'I've got good news,' said Lexi. 'Can you put me on speakerphone?'

Nothing could ever beat the feeling of telling worried parents that their missing child had been found alive and was now safe. There was the sound of whispering and the shuffle of chairs being pulled closer.

'Mr and Mrs Carter, can you hear me? It's DI Bennett.'

'Yes, loud and clear,' said Andrew Carter. He sounded upbeat and Lexi guessed that Philippa's face must have told them it was good news.

'We've found Paige alive and she's on her way to be checked over at the Kent and Canterbury Hospital.'

Joanne Carter gasped, then seemed to laugh and cry at the same time.

'Is she all right? Is she hurt?' There was still a tinge of fear in Andrew Carter's voice.

'As far as we know, she has no major injuries. She has damage to one of her fingers, she's lost some blood, and she appears to be suffering from exposure and dehydration. Philippa will bring you to the hospital and the doctors will be able to tell you more. You should also know that we have the man who did this in custody.'

'Thank you, thank you so much.' Joanne Carter was undoubtedly crying now, but Lexi felt unashamedly good about being the cause of it.

'We'll see you at the hospital in a bit.'

She disconnected.

'Not crying again, are you, boss?' Tom could hardly keep the laughter out of his voice. 'Not what I expected from a tough nut like you.'

'Bugger off, Olsen! And drive a bit faster, can't you?'

Lexi had packed away all her emotions by the time they reached the Kent and Canterbury. Paige Carter was being assessed in a curtained bay in A&E and they immediately came across her parents and Philippa Reid, pacing the corridor and getting in the staff's way. But nobody was going to ask them to move – the rumour had spread quickly that the missing Carter triplet had been brought in and there was a buzz of hopeful excitement in the air.

Joanne Carter flung her arms around Lexi's neck.

'Thank you, thank you, thank you,' she gushed. 'She'll be allowed home soon, won't she?'

Lexi extricated herself from the crushing bear hug, but she didn't mind. This was what made her job worth doing.

'That's for the doctors to decide, not me,' she said.

Andrew Carter stepped forward to shake her hand. He looked like a different man – the relief that his daughter was alive had taken years off him in an instant. It would never make up for the loss of Eden and Lucy, but it was still a better outcome than they would have believed possible just half an hour before.

Lexi sank gratefully onto a hard plastic chair in the corridor. Tom brought her a cup of water and some biscuits. Her hands were shaking as she took the cup – she was beyond exhausted. She dozed, but kept waking fitfully, expecting to find herself still in one of the battery farm sheds in the woods.

'You all right, boss?'

She opened her eyes to see Ridhi standing in front of her, her face clouded with worry.

She smiled. 'I'm fine. Tired but fine.'

'You should go home.'

'Not quite yet. I need to know that Paige is okay.'

It was well after midnight by the time the doctor treating Paige came out to talk to them. She made the Carters sit down. Philippa sat next to Joanne Carter, holding her hand, ready to offer whatever support might be needed.

'I'm Dr Elstead,' she said.

Andrew Carter nodded impatiently. 'How is she?'

'Given the circumstances, she's doing remarkably well. She came in suffering badly with hypothermia and dehydration, but we've got her on a drip, and she'll be good to go in a few hours. She's awake if you want to see her.'

Lexi wouldn't have thought Joanne Carter could have moved as fast as she did when she heard that, and the Carters disappeared behind the curtain to be with their daughter. Lexi looked up at the doctor.

'Were there any signs of injury or assault? Her hand?'

'She's missing the distal phalange of her right little finger. The blood loss didn't help with her overall condition, but we've cleaned it up and put her on a strong course of antibiotics.'

'Sexual assault?' said Lexi.

Dr Elstead shook her head. 'Thankfully not.'

'Is she talking?'

'She's awake, but she's barely said a word.'

'Would it be all right if I had a word with her?'

Elstead rubbed her eyes with her hands and sighed. 'Could it possibly wait until the morning? She's been to hell and back.'

Don't I know it?

'I wouldn't ask if it wasn't important. I went through a similar experience when I was her age. I think I can offer her some reassurance.'

Elstead's expression softened, and she shifted sideways a little to block the way into the bay. 'Not too much, though. She'll find talking about what's happened incredibly distressing.'

'I understand.' Tonight would only be the start – they would need to talk to Paige multiple times to cover everything she knew about what Stokes had done to her and her sisters. But for now, she would need comfort and support.

'Okay, but keep it short. She's very weak.'

'Thank you, Doctor.'

Elstead stepped aside and Lexi went into the treatment bay.

Paige Carter still looked more dead than alive, but at least she was awake. A cannula was attached to the back of her left hand, its tube snaking up to a saline drip beside the bed. Her hair was still tangled and matted, and she looked frail in the voluminous mint-green hospital gown. Her right hand was heavily bandaged and lay limp across the sheet. None of this, however, could dim the glow of sheer happiness on her parents' faces as they crowded on either side of her bed.

Lexi stepped into her line of sight.

'Paige, my name is DI Bennett. Do you remember me helping you earlier?'

Paige gave a barely perceptible nod.

'DI Bennett is the one who rescued you,' said Andrew Carter. 'She saved your life.'

'Thank you.' Paige's voice was a rough whisper.

'No thanks needed,' said Lexi. 'I know you've been through an awful lot, and over the next few days we'll need to ask you about it. But I just wanted to check in with you tonight to tell you how brave you've been. I understand what its's been like, but you're safe now and it will never happen again.'

Paige looked up at her with wide, tired eyes.

'We've caught the man who did it, and he'll be going to prison.'

Tears coursed down Paige's cheeks and she clutched her mother's hand.

'I'm so sorry this happened to you, Paige – but I'll make sure he pays for it. Believe me, Mr and Mrs Carter, if I have anything to do with it, he'll never be a free man again.'

On my sister's life.

SIXTY-EIGHT

SATURDAY, 14 JANUARY

Lexi gritted her teeth against the pain – it felt as if her spine was a river of molten lava. The hospital had sent her home with a week's supply of tramadol, but she'd flushed the pills down the toilet. There was no way she was going to succumb to the sweet release of opioids again, even for such a short period. She'd seen their effects over and over during her time in Virginia, and then experienced them herself after the events at Diamond River. There was no way she was going back down that road.

Paracetamol hardly took the edge off, but it would have to do.

She'd taken a shower and gone to bed, but she was too tanked up on adrenalin to sleep. Two hours of tossing and turning later, fuelled by black coffee and drugs, she was back behind her desk. It wasn't even light outside.

There was a knock on the door and Maggie came in, awkwardly bearing a large bunch of white lilies, the flower heads still tightly closed. She plonked them down on the desk before even saying hello.

'You realise I'm still alive?' said Lexi, examining the bouquet. 'These look like you were expecting a funeral.'

'I knew I'd find you here. Sleep is for wimps, eh?'

'I tried.' She almost smiled. 'But someone's waiting for me down in the cells – and I've been waiting for this for seventeen years.'

Maggie's eyebrows came together in an apologetic frown. 'That's why I'm here. I can't let you do that, Lexi. You understand why.'

Disappointed but hardly surprised, Lexi bit back the sharp reply that sprang to mind and kept her tone neutral. 'It's my right to interview him.' She could barely bring herself to say his name.

Maggie shook her head. 'You're hardly a disinterested party, are you? You have a right to hear what he says. And whoever interviews him will talk to you first and take advice, but putting you in an interview room would almost certainly be challenged by his defence lawyers when it comes to trial.'

'If it comes to trial. How can he plead anything but guilty?' It was a rhetorical question. 'So who is going to interview him?'

'I thought Tom could do it.'

'Come off it, Maggie!' Lexi slapped the heel of her hand against the desk. 'He's great, but he doesn't have the experience to take on a man like Stokes.'

'Who does?'

'Here, in Canterbury, I do. Four years in Quantico, remember. Only I have the experience dealing with this sort of shit.' She knew she sounded arrogant, but her expertise was hard-earned, and for one reason only. To bring down the man in the cells.

Maggie rubbed her eyes with her thumb and forefinger, pinching the bridge of her nose as she considered Lexi's words.

'I know how to press his buttons.'

Maggie sighed. She was going to relent. 'Okay, here's the deal. I'll conduct the interview, with Ed Harlow on hand for guidance. You can observe by camera from the next room.'

'But...'

'No buts. That's the way it's going to be.'

'Promise me one thing, then.'

Maggie frowned. She wasn't used to being spoken to like this by her subordinates.

'I need to know what happened to Rose.'

'I'll ask him, but you know I can't make any promises.'

The room next to the interview room was freezing, making Lexi wonder if it was a budget issue or a maintenance issue that kept most of the radiators in the station stone cold. She shivered and pulled her jacket closer round her shoulders.

There was a laptop on the table in front of her. On its screen, she could see Maggie and Ed waiting for the custody sergeant to bring Stokes up from his cell.

Tom came into the room and sat down next to her. 'We've got enough on him to bang him up for years,' he said. 'We don't need a confession.'

Ed looked up at the camera and saluted them from the other room.

'Don't mind me,' he said. 'I'm simply here to observe.' His chair had been placed in a supposedly neutral position, a couple of feet away from the interview table where Maggie and Rufus Stokes would face each other. Naturally, Ed had dropped whatever he was doing when Maggie had called him and asked him to sit in on the Stokes interview. This would be gold to a man who studied serial killers for a living. Lexi tried not to be cynical about his motives – she'd decided that she liked Ed – but she had a hard time fully trusting anyone who showed too much of an interest in her past. However, hopefully he'd know how to get Stokes to open up about what he'd done to her sister.

There was a knock on the door, and Ed sat down in his assigned position.

'Come in,' said Maggie.

The door opened and Stokes was led into the room. His hands were cuffed behind his back, and the custody sergeant spent a couple of minutes uncuffing them, bringing them round to his front and re-cuffing them, before directing him to sit down in the chair opposite Maggie.

Stokes looked across at Ed Harlow with interest. Lexi wondered if he knew who Ed was.

Maggie switched on the tape recorder, logged the time and the date, and listed the people in the room. 'Maggie Dawson, Ed Harlow, Rufus Stokes.'

Maggie kicked off the questioning by asking whether he required a lawyer. Stokes shook his head, until she reminded him that he needed to speak his answers for the recording.

'Mr Stokes, can you tell us what you were doing on Friday 6th January this year?'

Stokes leaned forward in his chair, his elbows on the table. The observation camera through which Lexi and Tom were watching was angled to face him, so they could watch his reactions to Maggie's questions. Somehow, he seemed to know. He stared directly up at the camera, right at Lexi, and even through the screen, she felt his eyes boring into her, burrowing into her mind. It was all she could do not to push her chair back in response.

He didn't speak.

'Mr Stokes, please answer the question.'

'I think you know what I was doing that day.' His eyes were still on the camera.

'Are you admitting that on Friday 6th January, you abducted Paige Carter, Lucy Carter and Eden Carter, and also Josh Pendleton, who you later bludgeoned to death?'

He leaned further forward still.

'Yes.' It was barely more than a whisper.

That was it. That was the confession. Lexi's blood pounded

in her ears. Not that they needed it, with the weight of evidence they already had against him. But did this mean he was going to explain his actions? Did this mean she might get a step closer to finding where Rose's body was?

'Can you say that again, a bit louder,' said Maggie. The recorder was sensitive, and it would need to be unequivocally clear when the jury came to listen to it.

'Yes, I took the girls and I took the boy, too.'

'Jesus,' murmured Tom under his breath, and although they couldn't see him, they heard Ed's sharp intake of breath somewhere to one side of Maggie.

Stokes grinned, satisfied with the effect his words had had on his small audience.

'Can you tell us the exact sequence of events in more detail?' Maggie sounded so calm and in control, but Lexi felt sure that the nervous tension inside her would be going through the roof.

'No. Not you. Where's Lexi? She's the only one I'll talk to.'

Lexi pushed her chair back, but Tom placed a hand over hers on the table. 'Wait,' he whispered. She paused as they listened for Maggie's answer.

'I'm afraid not, Mr Stokes. DI Bennett isn't available.'

Stokes shrugged. 'Then neither am I.'

'For God's sake,' hissed Lexi, pulling her hand away from Tom's. 'He wants to talk, and he wants to talk to me. I'm not going to miss this opportunity.'

She left the side room and went straight into the interview room without knocking.

Maggie sprung to her feet. 'Lexi, no. This isn't right.' She pushed Lexi out of the room, closing the door behind them both.

Lexi leaned back against the opposite wall, panting from the sudden burst of adrenalin.

Maggie glared at her. 'How dare you?'

'It's the only way he'll talk.'

'We don't need him to.'

'It'll make conviction easier. And he might tell me things we'll never know otherwise.'

'Rose? Is that what this is about?'

'Let me do it, Maggie. You won't regret it.'

Maggie's expression softened. 'It's not my regrets that I'm worried about.' But she stepped away from the door.

Lexi took her chance and went inside.

'Princess,' said Stokes, with a smile.

'Ed, could you give us a minute, please?'

Ed stood up, barely able to hide his disappointment as he went across to the door. But Lexi didn't care – he'd be able to watch and listen next door with Tom and Maggie. When the door closed and they were alone, Lexi sat down opposite Stokes and leaned forward with her elbows on the table. Their faces were only inches apart and Lexi could feel the warmth of his breath. A coil of anger tightened inside her, but she wasn't afraid of him anymore. Seventeen years of abject terror had evaporated. She had bettered him, for a second time now, and all she saw in front of her was a librarian with bitten nails and unkempt hair.

'Princess,' he said again.

She wasn't wasting time with that. 'Tell me about Josh Pendleton. Why did he have to die?'

Stokes pursed his lips momentarily. 'Collateral damage. He got in the way of my plan and I wasn't going to derail it just for him.'

'How do you mean he got in the way?'

'I wanted Lucy. He was there, at the wrong place at the wrong time. They were walking in the direction of the Carters' house. If they'd gone inside, I would have lost my chance to take Lucy and the whole plan would have been aborted. It had happened before, but this time I ran out of patience. I knocked them both out and shoved them into the van.'

'The library van?'

'The very one.'

'Where is it now?' It would be a goldmine of forensics.

'I dumped it in a cul de sac off Broad Oak Road. It stank of blood inside.'

Lexi knew Tom would take note and immediately send out a retrieval party. 'Whose blood?'

'The boy's.'

'You killed him in the van?'

'I did. And I kept him in there for a few days before dumping him in the woods. To give you and your team an added distraction. Then I hid him, just enough, so he'd eventually be found.' He smiled again. 'It worked, didn't it?'

She wasn't going to rise to the bait.

She took a deep breath and decided to come in from another angle. 'Mr Stokes, can you tell me what you were doing on the afternoon of Thursday 12th January?'

Stokes's eyes widened with interest. 'I was at work.'

'You know we can check that.'

'You don't say. But why that afternoon? What happened?'

It was when Len Clayton had been murdered, but Lexi wasn't going to tell him that. She felt sure that his alibi wouldn't stand up to scrutiny, and she made a mental note to put Colin onto it as soon as she finished the interview.

'Something else. So, you admit you were responsible for the murders of Lucy and Eden Carter?'

Stokes pushed his chair away, and leaned back, lifting one ankle onto the other knee as if he was relaxing in front of the television. 'It's a shame you're recording this,' he said.

'Why?' said Lexi, fighting to keep her tone even and light.

'You've got to understand, Lexi, there are certain things I can't tell you if it's being recorded.'

'Why not?'

'Things you'd definitely want to hear, believe me.'

In her jacket pocket, Lexi fingered her phone, wondering if she could set it to record without Stokes noticing. The ping of a notification gave her the perfect excuse to get it out and study the screen.

'Excuse me,' she said, turning away from the table. Then she clicked into Voice Memos and pressed the red button to record.

'I don't have time to mess around,' she said, facing Stokes again. 'If you have something you want to say to me, say it now. This will be your only chance.' She reached across to the tape recorder on the table and flipped the switch off. Stokes appeared to have forgotten about the camera at the top corner of the wall that was relaying the interview to the next room. Fine.

'You killed Eden first, didn't you?'

He nodded. 'She was so whiny. I had to shut her up. She wouldn't play the game. That's why Paige got punished, why I took her finger. Because of Eden.'

Lexi bit down on her bottom lip to stifle her anger.

'You took her up to the Crown and killed her. Then you went back for Lucy.'

'I nearly killed Paige and kept Lucy, but I changed my mind at the last minute.'

'Why?'

'None of your business.'

Lexi couldn't help but think of what it must have been like for Lucy – taken up to the Crown, where she must have seen her sister lying dead, the blood from her throat still glistening on the chalk.

'And the dresses and tiaras? The roses? Were they just for my benefit?'

Stokes leaned forward, resting his chin on his hands. He gazed at Lexi in a way that made her stomach turn. 'Yes, all for you. I wanted to let you know that I was back, and that we had unfinished business.'

'What was that?'

Stokes's face creased into a sly smile.

'There's something else you want to know, isn't there?'

'Tell me, Rufus – what is it?' Lexi's voice was friendly, wheedling, soft, though there was nothing she wanted to do more than rip his heart from his chest.

'Rose's last words, before I...'

'Before you what?'

'You know what I did to her.'

'No, I don't. What did you do?' It felt like a knife was being twisted in Lexi's heart, but the fires of her rage gave her the courage to continue. The prize was too great to miss.

'Listen, this is what she said, just before I killed her...'

Rose's last words. According to him. She changed her mind. This wasn't a prize she wanted. She pushed her chair back violently and strode towards the door.

'Goodbye, Rufus,' she said.

Stokes stared at her, confused. 'But wait... you haven't heard what she said.'

Lexi pulled open the door and practically threw herself out of the room. She didn't want to hear Rose's last words coming out of Stokes's mouth. She'd never know if he was telling the truth or not. The whole idea of it disgusted her.

She leaned against the wall, her heart pounding, blood roaring in her ears.

Tom stepped out into the hall from the next-door room, looking almost as confused as Stokes. He was followed by Maggie and Ed.

Lexi pulled her phone from her pocket and held up the screen for them to see.

'We got him, Tom. It's on here – he's confessed to killing

Josh, Lucy and Eden. And Rose. He's going down, for a very long stretch.'

'Not sure that's admissible, Lex,' said Tom.

Lexi shrugged. 'We can leave that for the lawyers. But there'll be plenty more. Emily's going over his house and the library van he used will confirm all that he said about Josh. There's plenty of evidence now to put him away for all three murders. And I believe Paige will testify.' She shook the phone. 'But this is enough for me.' And before she realised it, she was crying. Big gasping sobs, wet cheeks, snotty nose, relief washing through her.

Finally, she could be free of him.

Tom waved to the custody sergeant at the end of the corridor. 'Take him back to the cells. We'll start the interview again later.'

That was fine with Lexi. She had the confession she needed. She straightened her back and gained control of herself again.

'Tom, can you put Colin onto checking that alibi with the Beaney Centre? I don't believe he was working on Thursday afternoon.'

'Begs the question though, doesn't it?' said Tom. 'If it wasn't him who killed Len Clayton, who the hell did?'

Ed took her by the arm.

'That's a question for another day,' he said. 'Come on, you need a drink. I'm taking you to the pub.'

Lexi looked at her watch. 'It's only just eleven, Ed.'

'Yeah, and?' His smile was a challenge.

'All right. But just the one. I'll need to get back here and coach Tom for the interview later.'

'Fine, just the one, then.'

But it was a double, and it did her the world of good.

SIXTY-NINE

If the colour hadn't quite returned to Paige Carter's cheeks, she was at least looking significantly better than she had done the night before. Philippa Reid told Lexi that she'd slept for twelve hours straight and woken up mid-afternoon with a voracious hunger. It was good to hear. The physical healing was starting, even if the mental recovery would take much longer.

Her parents were by her bedside when Philippa led her into Paige's room, still thrilled by their daughter's return. Lexi supposed that the happiness of having Paige back would, for a time, eclipse the grief of losing Lucy and Eden. But she knew that would come back. All three of them would continue to suffer in untold ways for the rest of their lives. And it would be worse for Paige than it had been for her – Paige had lost both of her sisters. At least she now had Amber back.

'Do you mind if I come in?' she said from the doorway.

'DI Bennett,' said Joanne. She smiled and shook her head. 'I can't thank you enough. I won't ever be able to thank you enough for bringing her back to us.'

She opened her arms wide, and Lexi allowed herself to be enveloped in a hug.

'Let the poor woman go,' said Andrew Carter, as the embrace became prolonged.

Lexi extricated herself and looked at Paige. 'How are you feeling this morning?'

'Tired,' said Paige. She didn't seem to want to expand on that.

'Would you be able to answer a couple of questions for me?'

Paige's eyes swept from one parent to the other and Lexi immediately understood. There were things she wouldn't want to talk about in front of them.

Lexi turned to the Carters. 'Why don't you two go and grab a coffee and some fresh air while I talk to Paige.'

Joanne shook her head. 'Oh, I couldn't leave her, not now.'

But Andrew Carter seemed to understand. 'Come on, love,' he said. 'We'll be back in a little while.' He took Joanne's arm and steered her out of the room.

'Thanks,' said Lexi as they disappeared. Philippa took a chair on the other side of the bed. As the family liaison officer on the case, she would act as a witness to anything Paige said, and make sure Lexi didn't overstep the mark with any questions.

Paige sank back onto the pillows. 'It's not that I'm not happy to see them, or that I don't love them,' she said. Her voice was small and nervous.

'I know that,' said Lexi. She sat down in the chair next to the bed. 'But you can't tell them how awful it was, can you?'

'They're so happy,' said Paige. 'But I can't stop thinking about Luce and Edie.' Her hands fluttered to her chest, the right one swathed in heavy bandages.

'How's your finger?' said Lexi.

Paige shook her head. 'It's nothing compared to what he did to them.' Huge tears spilt down her cheeks.

Lexi took Paige's left hand in both of hers. 'I know.'

'It happened to you, didn't it? Philippa told me – the same man... he... Your sister died, too.'

'She did,' said Lexi. 'And it was the same man.'

She felt so much for Paige. At least she'd had Amber to cling to for the first few days after they escaped. Until the guilt of what she'd done became too much for her to bear and she'd withdrawn from her sister, from her family. She decided she would do as much as she could to support Paige Carter over the coming months. She squeezed Paige's hand. Now wasn't the time to ask her about what had happened. The whole story would have to be prised out of her, slowly and gently, by people with the appropriate training to guide her through it.

'Did you know him?' said Paige.

Lexi shook her head. 'No, not at all. The man worked in the library and saw us there. I think it was the same for you and your sisters.'

She nodded, sniffing loudly. 'Yes. Later I think I sort of recognised him from there.'

'Did he leave you alone together at all?'

'Not for long. Just for a bit at first, but then he came back and separated us and tied us up away from each other.'

'Just one question, and then I'll leave you be. Do you know why he took your "P" necklace and put it on Lucy?' It was the one part of the posing of the crime that Lexi hadn't been able to work out.

'He didn't. I gave it to her, to comfort her. I told her we'd all get out okay and she could give it back to me when we got home. I think it made her feel better.'

Of all the things that Paige told her, on that day and on many subsequent days, that was the one that made Lexi cry the most.

. . .

It had been a long day. She looked around Amber's living room, taking in the framed photos of Tasha and Sam on the mantelpiece, the Chinese vase of luscious yellow roses on a small mahogany table in the bay window, the plumped up blue velvet cushions on the sofa opposite the one she was sitting on.

Their lives were so different now. With Rose, they'd seemed an invincible trio, but when they lost her, the path seemed to have forked and she and Amber had chosen different directions. Lexi didn't think she could ever live like this – an ordered family life in which everything had its place, and everyone lived up to expectations. Maybe it was all a shiny veneer, covering old wounds. What had happened to them couldn't have left Amber unscathed. But Lexi supposed she'd found solace in creating her own nuclear family.

They both had their own coping mechanisms. Their lives had been torn asunder and Amber had chosen to stitch hers back together as tightly as she could, as quickly as she could. It had worked for her. Lexi had picked at the scabs. She hadn't been able to let the wound heal – but now perhaps things would be different. Stokes was vanquished, both in real life and in her dreams. Maybe she could allow herself to start to heal.

The door opened and Amber came in bearing a tray with a bottle of Sauvignon Blanc, and a bowl of plump green olives. She'd insisted that Lexi should stay and rest until her back felt better, and she seemed determined to feed her up with wholesome – and less-wholesome – mountains of food.

'Here,' she said, putting the tray down on the glass-topped coffee table that sat between the two sofas. 'Finally, you get an evening to relax. That was one hell of a first week. But at least tomorrow's Sunday. Please don't tell me you're working.'

'I will be. Stokes is still being interviewed, and we'll probably charge him tomorrow – not only with Eden and Lucy Carter's murders, but also for Josh Pendleton's.'

'Seriously?' said Amber. 'What about Rose's? You said that he admitted killing her to you.'

'We've always known that he killed her, haven't we?' said Lexi. 'But what he said to me won't be admissible in court. Not unless we can come up with some physical evidence as well, and that's unlikely given the time involved and we don't know where he did it.'

Amber looked crestfallen.

'Listen, he'll still be going to prison for life, and that's what matters.'

Amber dropped heavily onto the sofa. 'Honestly, I never thought we'd see the day...'

'I was determined we would.'

'Tell me what he told you.'

Amber had been bustling around like a mother hen since Lexi had got back from seeing Paige at the hospital, and Lexi sensed she had been avoiding talking about everything that had happened. But now she seemed ready.

Lexi wasn't entirely sure she should share what Stokes had told her. How could she tell her sister about the way Stokes had treated Rose? Or how casually he'd admitted to having killed her to 'put her out of her misery'? She didn't want to sully Amber's mind with these details, but on the other hand didn't her sister have the right to know?

Amber poured the wine and offered Lexi the olives.

Lexi shook her head. 'Nothing more than I already said. Just a simple statement that he'd done it. No details.' She took a sip of her wine. 'I need to start running again. I'm supposed to be in training.'

'Don't be ridiculous. You can't run at the moment, not with all that bruising. What if you fell?'

'I'm not in the habit of falling.'

'You've been through a lot, and they told you to rest, didn't they?'

'It's not something I do.'

Amber skewered her with a knowing look. 'You haven't changed a bit.'

'You have,' said Lexi. She waved a hand at the room. 'So grown-up. So responsible.'

'We're halfway through our thirties. Probably the time for it.'

She had a point.

Lexi took an olive and chewed it thoughtfully. Amber sipped her wine.

'Lex? Tell me what happened.' She gave her sister a searching look.

Lexi stood up and went over to the window. The garden still looked mid-winter bleak, the trees bare and the grass muddied. There were a few snowdrops under one of the trees at the far end, but it wasn't enough to lift the winter palette of grey and brown.

'I can't talk about it yet, and it's not stuff you'd want to hear.' She paused, taking in the disappointment on Amber's face. 'Let's talk about Rose. Let's honour her memory.'

There was a photo of their sister on the mantelpiece, and Lexi picked it up and studied it. Rose had been beautiful, her features more delicate than Lexi's, her expression warmer than Amber's.

'I miss her,' said Amber. 'Still. So much.'

'Me too.' Lexi returned the photo to its spot. 'She always brought out the best in all of us, didn't she?'

Amber nodded, and brushed her eyes with her hand. 'I'm glad you're back, Lexi. I'm glad we found each other again. We're going to be okay, aren't we?'

Lexi smiled at her. 'We're triplets.'

'I wondered if what happened relegated us to twins?'

'No, always triplets. Triple trouble.'

Amber smiled through her tears at their ancient rallying cry. 'Triple trouble.'

Lexi pictured Rose in her mind and for the first time in a long time it wasn't an image of her lying wounded and abandoned in Blean Woods. She saw Rose as the happy, carefree girl she'd been before all this had happened, beckoning to her sisters to come out into the garden, running in the sunshine, laughing and joking. Sneaking into the kitchen to steal biscuits behind their mother's back. Curled up on her bed, bent over her diary.

Thank you, Rose.

The diary that had finally given Lexi the clue that had enabled her to find Paige.

She glanced across at Amber. She would never let Rufus Stokes come between them again.

A small person appeared at the door. 'Mum, why are you crying?'

'I'm not crying, Sam. I just got something in my eye.'

Lexi turned and grinned at her nephew, so Amber couldn't see her face. 'She's crying,' she mouthed. 'She'd forgotten what a terrible sister I could be.'

Sam ran across to them and jumped on the sofa, tucking himself under Lexi's arm. Tasha followed him into the room, eager to show Lexi the book she was reading. Lexi loved them already.

And she knew Rose would have loved them, too.

A LETTER FROM ALISON

Thank you so much for reading *The Girls on Chalk Hill*. In these busy days, reading time is a scarce commodity and I'm hugely grateful that you chose to spend some of your precious hours with Lexi and her team. I hope you found it as enjoyable and rewarding to read as I found it to write.

If you're interested in hearing more about the Lexi Bennett series, please sign up using the link below for details of forthcoming releases. Your email address will never be shared and you can unsubscribe at any time.

www.bookouture.com/alison-belsham

You'll know from reading *The Girls on Chalk Hill* that Lexi Bennett has had a traumatic personal history, but this is what makes her the person she is today. With Lexi, I wanted to create a character who has total empathy with the victims of the crimes she investigates, and a fiercely burning desire to see the criminals caught and justice dispensed. As a writer, you get to spend innumerable hours in the company of your characters, and I adore and admire Lexi for her intelligence, her bravery and her humanity. I can't wait to write more stories with her and to challenge her with ever more diabolical crimes and criminals.

I hope you feel the same way about reading them.

And I have one small favour to ask of you. If you enjoyed meeting Lexi and loved *The Girls on Chalk Hill*, I'd be hugely grateful if you could write a review. I'm intrigued to know what you think of her, and it would help new readers to discover one of my books for the first time. Feedback from readers is truly what makes the hard work of writing a book worthwhile – so I'd love to hear from you via Facebook, Twitter, Goodreads or my website.

Until next time,

Alison xx

facebook.com/AlisonBelshamWriter

twitter.com/AlisonBelsham

instagram.com/alisonbelsham

ACKNOWLEDGEMENTS

In starting a new series with a new editor, one always faces the question – how is this going to work? Thankfully, from my very first meeting with Ruth Tross, before Lexi was even a spark of an idea, I felt that we were very much on the same page with what we wanted to achieve with the series. And as this first Lexi Bennett book comes to fruition, I'm hugely grateful to Ruth for all her input in devising the story, her stellar editing and her huge contribution to the book's evolution. She's Team Lexi all the way and I'm thoroughly looking forward to working with her on the next title and beyond!

Thanks are also due to the rest of the wonderful Bookouture team – in particular to Richard King, Head of Rights, for championing my move to Bookouture, to Sarah Gunton in production, Mandy Kullar in managing editorial, Melanie Price in marketing and the wonderful PR team, Kim Nash, Noelle Holten, Sarah Hardy and Jess Readett. Thanks also to copyeditor Dushi Horti and proofreader Shirley Khan.

I'm enduringly grateful to my fantastic agent Jenny Brown, steadfastly in my corner, and always full of enthusiasm and support – meetings with her are a tonic and I wouldn't be where I am today without her professional input. Thank you, Jenny.

And finally thanks to Mark, happy to act as my excellent chauffeur on several research trips to Kent, and enthusiastic sampler of seafood in Whitstable, craft beer in Margate and wine on our visit to Barnsole Vineyard. It's clear that further research trips to other vineyards will be in order moving forward!